A
Season
of
Sinister
Dreams

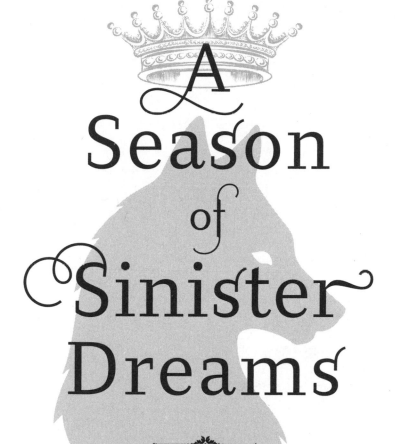

A Season of Sinister Dreams

TRACY BANGHART

LB

LITTLE, BROWN AND COMPANY
New York Boston

Little, Brown and Company
Hachette Book Group
1290 Avenue of the Americas, New York, NY 10104
Visit us at LBYR.com

First Edition: June 2021

Little, Brown and Company is a division of Hachette Book Group, Inc. The Little, Brown name and logo are trademarks of Hachette Book Group, Inc.

The publisher is not responsible for websites (or their content) that are not owned by the publisher.

Library of Congress Cataloging-in-Publication Data
Names: Banghart, Tracy E., author.
Title: A season of sinister dreams / Tracy Banghart.
Description: First edition. | New York : Little, Brown and Company, 2021. | Audience: Ages 14+. | Summary: "Annalise must wield her magical powers of persuasion carefully in order to become the queen of Tyne. Nonmagical Evra discovers she's a Clearsee who receives mysterious visions of the past and future. Told in alternating points of view, the young women must decide whom to trust"—Provided by publisher.
Identifiers: LCCN 2020052573 | ISBN 9780316460408 (hardcover) | ISBN 9780316460422 (ebook) | ISBN 9780316460439 (ebook other)
Subjects: CYAC: Fantasy. | Magic—Fiction. | Kings, queens, rulers, etc.—Fiction. | Visions—Fiction.
Classification: LCC PZ7.B223 Se 2021 | DDC [Fic]—dc23
LC record available at https://lccn.loc.gov/2020052573

ISBNs: 978-0-316-46040-8 (hardcover), 978-0-316-46042-2 (ebook)

Printed in the United States of America

LSC-C

PRINTING 1, 2021

For Mom and Dad
And for Scrabble, who is and always
will be a very good boy

CHAPTER ONE

ANNALISE

I should not be able to do what I can do.

Every day I try to tame it, ignore it. But it bubbles up inside, always there, humming in my fingertips, my chest, my throat, building up friction. Building. Building.

Thirsting for a spark.

My magic is a wild thing, a wave, a way to stay alive.

Tonight, I twirl in a gown with a skirt like a big golden bell, and I smile and allow my hand to be squeezed too tightly and pressed against moist lips. Every ball is a swirl of color and sound, too glittering, too made up. But I dance anyway, at every one. Because each clasped hand, each brush of bare skin, each kiss is a conduit. A thread in my web. A way to control.

I must weave my schemes as beautifully, as invisibly, as a poisonous spider.

My dance partner spins me out a few feet from the throne just as the music ends. Normally I would smile as I filed away the courtier's name and face, mentally take note of how he could be of use to me one day. But I'm distracted. King Alder has been joined on the royal dais by a man I've never seen before. He's tall, with a pointed beard to match the pointed look in his eyes.

King Alder's advisors fill the shadows behind the throne. None of them look particularly happy to be here. The four men and one woman are stiff and frowning. Even the king's grandson, Prince Kendrik, off to the side and slightly more relaxed, glances toward the arched doorway longingly.

King Alder pushes to his feet, his back hunched. The thick blue brocade of his jacket hangs from his painfully thin frame. He stretches a hand toward the stranger. "Count Orlaith, of Maadenwelk, may I present Lady Annalise."

From Maadenwelk, the kingdom to our south. No wonder I didn't recognize him. He bows more deeply than my rank as the king's grandniece deserves. A sycophant, then.

I curtsy again and raise my hand to be kissed. The tips of the count's gloved fingers tighten on mine as he bends over my hand. My magic-tinged suggestions rise to meet him: *Her chin is too sharp, her hair too dull. Her eyes not bright enough.* It only takes a moment of contact, and most men are easily influenced. But his lips never quite brush my skin, and he remains unpersuaded. A pity.

King Alder sinks back onto the velvet cushion of his twisted golden throne. Behind him, Advisor Halliday shifts closer. I can't see the advisor's hand, but I know he's snaked it through the gaps in the gold to touch King Alder's neck. Every day, he and the finest healers in the kingdom sink their magic deep into the king's bones.

But they cannot stop time.

"Is she acceptable?" King Alder asks, gesturing to me with a single palsied hand. He does this every ball. Parades me before countless magic workers turned noblemen and courtiers, discusses me as if I cannot hear. I know the gallantry, the compliments these questions elicit are for *him*, not me. Usually, I am eager to use the introductions and dances for my own designs. But I have no use for foreigners with no sway in this kingdom.

I smooth my hands down my golden skirt. Its round shape is meant to soften my sharp angles. My chin *is* too pointed and my hair *is* too dull, my shoulders bony and my elbows like knives. But I am grateful for my deficiencies. They are my protection from the machinations of these men.

Count Orlaith's eyes narrow. He's twenty years my senior, at least, and stands as if his spine were a spear.

"She is very beautiful, Your Majesty."

Liar.

"Then we have an agreement?" King Alder asks.

A shiver of unease slides up my spine. *Agreement* is a strange word for *dance*.

King Alder doesn't look at me. He hasn't, once, in this entire exchange. Prince Kendrik shifts his weight. Beside him, the king's advisors stare stony-faced.

Count Orlaith bows to the king. "We do, Your Majesty."

King Alder nods, his rheumy gaze fixed on the count. "Lady Annalise, your betrothed."

Betrothed.

Shock races through me. I make a strange sound. "Excuse me?"

"Count Orlaith has accepted your hand in marriage," King Alder explains. He sinks further into his chair, his shoulders rounding. "You will leave for Maadenwelk in the morning."

The morning. Maadenwelk. No. *No.* My heart beats hard and fast, a hammer drumming against my ribs. I cannot leave Tyne. This is my home. *This* kingdom, this court, is where my purpose lies.

A sudden rage licks along my bones, charging them like lightning rods. My skin starts to shiver. Thunder rumbles above the Great Hall, loud enough to be heard over the musicians' efforts.

Count Orlaith reaches for my hand. "A dance, my lady, to celebrate our joyous union. You will love Maadenwelk. The air is warm and soft as gossamer, the ground littered with flowers. A kingdom truly worthy of a lady such as yourself."

His voice has a slithery quality, lies lined in silk. His smile has too many teeth, like a wolf.

Again, I note his gloves. The long velvet sleeves of his jacket, the high neck. Dancing won't help me get out of this.

I curtsy once again, hands deep in the bell of my golden gown, out of his reach. "Excuse me, Count. I am not feeling well. I fear I must retire early."

"Annalise." The name is a warning on King Alder's lips.

At last, he looks me in the eye. My hatred runs deep as a river, fathomless and dark. It fills me, always, rushing *rushing rushing*. I never let it lap into my smile where he can see it. I never disobey his orders.

But I cannot stay. If I do, the power that is building beneath my skin, that is electrifying my bones and breath, will find an outlet. There is so much, and I am a poor vessel. It will find its way out.

"My lady." Count Orlaith's gloved finger brushes my arm. Even through the cloth, a tiny current of energy finds him. He draws back. The smallest bite of static. I can tell he thinks little of it.

He doesn't know that was *me*. That I could have killed him if I'd let myself go. I glance at his hooded eyes a second too long before I flee. Maybe I *want* to kill him.

I certainly don't want to marry him.

The corridors beyond the Great Hall teem with servants. I round a corner to find two courtiers locked in an embrace. I lift my heavy golden skirt and run.

At last, I arrive at my chamber. A fire roars in the hearth. Sybil, my maid, is gone, likely bolting her supper before her evening duties. I don't ring the bell for her.

With a snap of my fingers, the candle on the small table by the window erupts into flame, singeing the curtain. I grab for the pitcher on my washstand and put out the small fire, a frantic tremble igniting under my skin. *Careful careful.* I light the rest of the candles by hand.

Thunder shakes the small glass windows in their leading. It's late afternoon, but you'd never know it with the mass of dark clouds curling above the castle. I need to calm down.

I stand before the fire, stare into its depths, and breathe.

How can I stop this betrothal? How can I stop the king? How can I stop the magic pulsing within me, desperate for release?

I will not leave Tyne. I'll die before I leave the land that cradles my mother's restless bones.

Someone knocks. Before I can respond, Prince Kendrik opens my door. "Lady Annalise, you must come back to the Great Hall."

He looks nothing like his grandfather. Gangly, still growing, soft around the eyes. A little awkward in his fine velvet coat. If Count Orlaith is a wolf, Kendrik is a puppy.

"I can't, Your Highness. I need—I need a moment." The magic is pushing, stretching, aching. I am too distracted, too upset.

"I'm sorry, cousin. I know this news is a shock." Kendrik closes the door and steps closer.

"Surely you can talk to your grandfather on my behalf." I didn't spend all these years weaving my web—ingratiating myself to the prince, gaining his trust, getting close to King Alder—to be shuttled away before dawn.

I am not a political marriage, or a foreign boon. I am a weapon, I am vengeance.

I am meant for the king.

"Please, Kendrik. I can't leave," I plead.

"I wish Grandfather would listen to me." His frown has a

twist of anguish to it. "But I do believe he's doing what is best for Tyne. Count Orlaith is a powerful man."

I roll my eyes heavenward. "Of course he is. You are all powerful men, and my life is in your hands. But what if I don't *want* to live in Maadenwelk? What if I don't *want* to marry a stranger?"

Kendrik bows his head. "It's not fair," he says softly. "And I will miss you. No one understands...listens to me the way you do. You're the only family I have aside from Grandfather. But we all have our roles to play. Our duties. It's what makes our kingdom strong."

"Our kingdom isn't strong," I growl, no longer careful with my words. The magic is too consuming, too distracting. I am too desperate. "The king has drawn all of the strongest magic workers to the city, and what happens to the farmers and tradesmen, the mothers screaming their babies into life on dirt floors? Where's the magic to help and heal them? The king only uses his power for himself. The sacrifices he demands do *not* strengthen Tyne." I step back, toward the fire. My hands clasp at my stomach, trying to hold it all in. The anger and the magic weave together and grow, like vines. But there aren't enough empty spaces inside me. I'm full. I'm bursting.

Kendrik needs to leave. *Now.* He has no idea the danger he's in.

"You know the reason he does that," Kendrik says, his voice tight with pain.

"That doesn't make it right," I snap back. I'm giving too

much away, saying too clearly how I really feel. I've no patience, no strength left for subterfuge. The king's pain—Kendrik's pain—does not take precedence over the rest of us. Their grief does not absolve them from causing mine. "It's been *ten years*, Kendrik, and still he orders them here."

"Please come back to the ball," he says. "Count Orlaith expects to dance with you. Come, cousin. I'll escort you. We'll—we'll get through this together."

"Leave me alone." The words grind from my chest. "Please. I will not dance with that wolf. I will not leave with him in the morning. I *can't*, Kendrik."

He can tell I'm deadly serious. But he doesn't truly know, he doesn't understand.

"I'm sorry. Please, Annalise—"

"No, no…" I try to remember that he is the puppy, not the wolf. This is not his doing.

But he doesn't listen, damn him. Instead, he grabs my hands.

A bolt of yellow light arcs between us, the power leaving me in a clap of thunder. *I want to hold back but I don't I love the force of it the strength. I am not myself I am will and the wave and the light and the wild.*

I am safe.

Kendrik flies across the room and slams into the wall. The light consumes him, its jaws opening wide.

The storm rages outside and within.

I let it all out.

I let go.

CHAPTER TWO

❖

EVRA

I shouldn't be here. I shouldn't be doing this. I should have stayed home.

My body begins to go quiet. My steps slow.

I balk.

"Oh no you don't. Keep moving." Tamsin pulls me forward by the arm. "Don't you lose your nerve now."

"But what if it's a trick?" I've argued this point to her before.

"Ronan fancies you, Evra, I know it." Tamsin strolls me down the middle of the street, ignoring the grumblings from behind us. We're blocking Bastian and his cart of bread deliveries.

"We should move out of the way," I murmur, veering toward the edge of the road. *We should turn around and forget this whole thing.*

She doesn't let go of me as she slows us down even more. "After what Bastian said about you last week, he can wait."

My cheeks flush. "That's exactly why meeting Ronan is a

mistake. I don't know what I was thinking agreeing to this. Tam, I don't need—" I break off, but the thought continues in my mind. *I don't need another reminder that I've become an object of suspicion and scorn.*

Tamsin flicks a derisive glance back at Bastian before answering. "Ronan looks at you like you're the sweetest berry on the vine. He's *always* staring. And anyway—" She steers me out of the road and onto the curving track to the churchyard. Behind us, I hear a relieved grunt. "He knows what Hagan and I'll do to him if he's cruel to you. Evra, he wants to *court* you." She makes such a revolting kiss face, I have to laugh. But I'm not as convinced as she is.

It would be easier not to get my hopes up if Tamsin weren't my friend.

She pauses before Windhaven's tiny chapel and turns me to face her. I wince under her gaze, but she smiles. "You look perfect. Well, almost." She places the tip of one slender finger against my chin and closes her eyes. A sudden prickle edges into pain beneath my skin.

I yelp, bringing my hand up to rub the sore place. "What was that for?"

"You had a bruise, no doubt from your dagger lessons with Hagan. Now it's fixed!" She squeezes my shoulders encouragingly.

The bruise is actually from a log kicking up when I was chopping wood for Old Marnie this morning. Normally the activity is good for settling my mind—but I suppose, for once, I was too distracted even for that.

"Stay with me, Tam," I plead.

"Can't." She smirks and shrugs. "I've got things to do. Besides, I don't think Ronan would appreciate a chaperone."

My mouth goes a little dry.

She glances back down the road as a faint whistled trill reaches us. "Come see me tomorrow morning. Tell me everything." And, with a wink, she abandons me.

Sighing, I enter the cold quiet of the church. Squares of red and blue light fall from the chapel's single stained-glass window to pattern the floor. Along the wall, a bank of candles flickers.

I pick a spot near the altar and plant my feet, my hands on the throwing knives at my waist. My knife belt looks a little strange cinched around the ivory dress I borrowed from Tamsin, but I couldn't bear to leave it at home. And my usual clothing—hand-me-down trousers and soft, baggy shirts from my brothers—didn't seem appropriate for a courting session.

The wooden benches that line the aisle are empty. Father Camden is always gone this time of day, administering what comfort he can to his flock. In his absence, the magic of his prayers keeps the candles burning, the floor free of dust, and the altar hangings unattractive to mice.

I wish there were a spell to tell me what to expect, but magic doesn't work that way in Tyne. Here it's a small, useful sort of thing—a way to cool water or calm a horse, a prayer to keep a crop thriving. It is a wish: a wish the people give to the land.

A wish I can't make.

Most people in Tyne come to their magic by fourteen, some as late as sixteen. I'm seventeen now, with nary a whisper. And Windhaven has begun to notice. *Which is why it was foolish to come here*, I remind myself.

A thud echoes through the chapel. I whirl, a knife fitted to my hand.

Ronan's silhouette fills the doorway, and then, with a creaking of hinges, the door closes behind him. Slowly, I lower my arm.

For years, I've admired his sleek dark hair and sparkling eyes, his little tricks and pleasantries. But always from a distance. Aside from an occasional glance my way, he's never paid me any attention before. Until yesterday, when he sidled up beside me and asked me to meet him.

The dim light of the chapel hides his expression.

"Well, I'm here. You wanted to meet?" My voice is too loud, too belligerent, and it wobbles a bit at the end. For some reason I can't bring myself to sheathe my knife. The cold metal steadies my hand.

Ronan murmurs a few words. Suddenly, a butterfly flutters up from the darkness near him, shimmering and golden, and lights a path toward me. When it alights on my shoulder, I can't mask my delight. The illusion is beautiful, the filigree finer than any hand could make.

"You've the look of a fairy when you smile," Ronan says, his rough-quiet voice echoing in the small chapel.

I laugh a little. "Perhaps. If fairies were not dainty, nor fair, nor beautiful."

He approaches, his lanky frame barely eclipsing mine. As he nears, the butterfly bursts into a patina of sparkles that disappear as they fall.

"Evra, you *are* beautiful."

No. I'm too tall, too strong. Too farm girl. And my hair is too wild.

But Ronan doesn't stop until he stands close enough that I can feel his heat. He says it again, very softly, "You are so beautiful."

This can't be real. My heart jumps wildly. Was Tam right about the way he looks at me?

The scents of woodsmoke and fresh-cut timber fill the small space between us. He leans closer, so slowly, until his lips lightly touch mine. I hold my breath. Ronan is *kissing me.* My first kiss.

I have absolutely no idea what I'm supposed to do. I am frozen. A shocked, nerve-shackled statue.

This doesn't seem to bother Ronan. He moves his mouth softly over mine, teasing the corners, gently nipping at my bottom lip. His hands slip up my arms. Belatedly, I try to follow his lead, my body swaying closer. I want to put my hands on his shoulders, or maybe touch his hair, but I'm still holding one of my throwing knives. And I'm scared. Scared that if I move too quickly or too much, this moment will end.

Or maybe I'll wake up.

Ronan works his arms around me and draws me closer, pinning my hands against my stomach. His tongue slips along my lower lip, seeking entrance. It's suddenly a little too much, too fast. I draw back. Ronan follows, pressing even closer for an instant before he realizes I'm trying to put space between us.

"Evra," he whispers. "You're so sweet."

He leans in again, but I need to catch my breath. I press my empty hand against his chest. He subsides, but he's still so close. I move to sheathe my blade, but he brings his hands up to cup mine, knife and all. So warm—they burn against my cold fingers.

"Can you really feel nothing?" he murmurs.

I don't know what he means. I feel *everything*, from the callus on the edge of his thumb to the pulse in my own fingertips to the memory of his lips against mine. Before I can respond, another golden butterfly blossoms in my palms.

"It tickles," I say as the tiny butterfly's wings flutter against my skin.

"Will you do something for me?" Ronan raises his gaze from his creation to look at me.

In the dimness of the chapel, the butterfly throws golden threads of light across his face, like fairy netting. His eyes remain shadowed.

"What do you want me to do?" I want to kiss him again.

His fingers tighten a tiny bit. "Make this trifle disappear. Such a tiny thing. Surely you can do such a simple trick as that? For me?"

At first, I don't understand. "What do you mean?"

"Use your magic. Make it disappear." There's more challenge than sweetness in his voice now.

The chill in my fingers spreads, ice pouring up my wrists, my arms, straight to my heart.

Tamsin was wrong after all.

I crush my palms together, knife flat between them, extinguishing the butterfly's light. "No. I won't play that game."

Ronan's hands fall away. "So it's true. You really have nothing, feel no hint of magic."

"Why should it matter?" I shoot back, flushing. "There's little enough these days. Perhaps that will be the way of things for everyone soon."

Anyone with any *real* magic moves to Ironwald, the king's city, at King Alder's command, and even they cannot do all he asks. *No one* can turn iron into gold or topple kingdoms or reverse death. Magic here is *small*. My breath hitches. Though it could have been enough to save my father.

"No magic, yes, that's the fear," Ronan says, interrupting my thoughts. "That's why you scare us all so much."

No one's ever said it to my face before. I've felt the discomfort, but *fear*? Now I wish I could erase the memory of his lips, his warm breath against my skin.

"So why are *you* here?" I snap. Tears burn the back of my throat. My grip tightens on my throwing knife, still liberated from my belt. "I thought—you *kissed* me, Ronan. You don't seem afraid."

He lets out a little laugh. "Maybe afraid isn't the right word. But my family thirsts for magic, just like everyone else. I can't attach myself to someone so...bereft." He smooths back a bit of hair that's come free of my braid. "But I've seen you watching me. I thought we could have a bit of fun."

"A—a bit of fun?" A crushing weight presses the air from my lungs.

He takes my question as one in need of an unspoken answer, putting his mouth on my neck and pressing his body heavily against mine.

I yank myself out of his grasp and slash his throat.

Not deeply, not enough to elicit more than a few drops of blood and a squeal of pain, but he stumbles back. While he's unbalanced, I shove him. He clatters to the floor, rage bubbling into his handsome face, turning it ugly.

I stand over him; from this vantage, with my height and my strength, he looks pathetic and small. "I may not have magic, but I have perfect aim. Do not insult me again."

When he doesn't reply or try to stand, I wipe the blood from the tip of my blade and sheathe it with its sisters. Then I leave, my chin high. By God's grace, I don't hear what he yells as the door slams shut behind me. That he'll never know that I weep as I flee is the greater mercy.

I pause when I reach the last line of trees before my family's homestead. I've avoided the road up from town, preferring to make my own way through the forest so no one will see me or ask what's wrong. My cheeks burn with frozen trails of tears, and my eyes are surely an angry red from rubbing them.

With trembling fingers, I try to tame my hair, the memory of Ronan's lips and hands lingering, his words leaving a dirty residue.

The earth beneath my feet feels unstable, like sliding sand instead of the hard-packed ground I can see with my own eyes. A strange buzz sounds in my ears, and a distant rumble of thunder. Thunder? At this time of year? My heart is still beating too fast, but I'm no longer entirely sure it's Ronan's doing. Maybe I need to eat something. Maybe I need to sit down.

Hagan is walking up from the road as I enter the clearing. I freeze; I don't want him to see me like this. Mama knows where I've been, but my brother doesn't, and I don't want to have to tell him. It's too humiliating.

He swings his dagger in a thoughtful arc. Sunlight sparks white across the blade, and then a thin reflection of cobalt sky. When he notices me, he tilts his head. "Back so soon?"

"Where were *you*?" I ask, a deflection.

"In town," he says, his cheeks flushing with cold. "Ready for our fighting lesson?"

I can only shake my head.

Hagan studies me more closely. "Are you well?"

"Yes," I croak, but he doesn't look like he believes me.

"What happened?" he asks. "Tam said you were meeting Ronan."

Curse Tamsin.

I can't tell him what Ronan did, not yet. He'll want to talk retaliation, while I am still drowning in shame. "That—that was fine. He—wanted, ah." Sputtering, I grasp at a rumor I heard a few days ago. "He said something about the king. It unsettled me."

"About King Alder ordering Farin to the castle? I heard." Hagan pounds his empty fist against his thigh. "She was our best healer. We *needed* her."

I think of Father, gone these eight years. Gone because of King Alder. Bitterness coats the back of my tongue, for once a welcome distraction. "We've needed all of them. Ten years since the Sickness and still the king pulls the best magic workers to his side. It's not right."

Hagan's dark blue eyes go hard as sapphires. "The storm-seers say it will be a bitter season. It'll take all of us to protect Windhaven from the worst of it. We need Farin *here*."

Not all of us. Not me. I'm no help at all.

I have tried so hard to convince myself—convince the village—that this isn't true. So much wood chopping and message running and helping to farm other people's fields. So many times I've smiled and swallowed the betrayal of an odd look from someone who used to cheerfully ask after my mother. But it's clear now that Ronan, perhaps all of Windhaven, sees only my void, not the space I fill.

Mama emerges from the kitchen, using the large woven basket in her arms to push the door open. The scent of roasted potatoes follows her into the yard. "Evra, there you are."

Mama is shorter than the rest of the family, with faded blond hair she wears in a braid down her back. I share her heavy-lidded gray eyes and narrow nose, but that's where our resemblance ends. She is dainty and pink and nonthreatening, while I am long-boned and strong, with freckles and ruddy cheeks. My thick black hair came from Father; my stubbornly well-defined jaw is mine alone.

Just the sight of her brings tears to my eyes. After Hagan and Deward are asleep tonight, I'll creep down the ladder to her room and climb into her bed. I'll tell her my sorrows, the hurt that lies heavy on my heart, and she'll sing me a lullaby as she did when I was a child. She won't ask me to be strong or expect me to plan my revenge. She'll hold me and let me cry.

"Hi, Mama," I say with a wobbly smile.

In the space of a breath, she's met my eyes and read the hope and disappointment there. She knows, just from looking at me, how the meeting went. I won't have to explain. The tightness in my chest eases. She shifts her basket to one hip and runs her other arm around my back. "My dear," she says. "It's almost suppertime. Come help me with the potatoes."

Hagan sweeps his dagger in an arc. "Good. I'm starving."

I move to help Mama with the basket, but once again my

eyes catch on his blade catching the sun. A tingle starts in my fingers and my legs tremble, suddenly heavy. Strange.

"Tomorrow we'll practice, Evra. I think—"

Another sweep, another jolt of light. I can't seem to move, to look away. I open my mouth, I start to say something, I'm not sure what, when the knife flares red in his hands, becomes flames that reach blood-black fingers to engulf me. I can't hear him anymore nor see him. All I see is fire.

I try to scream, but a blast of heat fills my mouth, burning the moisture from my throat.

I am mute.

I am deaf.

But I am not blind.

The fire becomes a wall of red glass and before it, on a massive throne, sits King Alder. He wears a crown of twisted gold, his white hair flowing in crisp waves to his shoulders.

His wrinkled skin begins to peel away from his cheeks in papery strips and his eyes roll back in his head until he is all skull. All white, lifeless bone.

On a matching throne beside the king sits a giant yellow wolf, its mouth open, its sharp teeth framing a panting pink tongue. Its eyes glow like two candle flames, and the red wall behind the dais cracks, pouring blood.

"Evra!"

With a sickening lurch, my legs return to me, tingling and painful. They give way, the cold ground rising to slam against my knees and palms.

"Evra!"

I curl in on myself, breath rattling.

My eyes are closed.

When did I close my eyes?

I blink the darkness away.

CHAPTER THREE

ANNALISE

My knees buckle, but the frame of my gown keeps me from falling to the floor. A sob wrenches itself from my throat.

"Kendrik?"

I stare at the heap of velvet against the wall. No movement.

No. Oh no.

What have I done?

The magic has left me scorched and spent, my mind frizzled at the edges. While the power flowed through me, I felt safe. Now I am anything but. I want to sink onto my bed and sleep for days. But I can't.

I have to fix this.

I pace my bedroom. Twilight creeps toward the stone turrets, the sky now calm and clear of storm clouds. But the last streaks of daylight won't find their way to this dark corner of the castle. I can't keep my gaze from falling on Kendrik's still form, again and again.

So still.

Damn him. Why couldn't he just leave? I didn't want to hurt him, I wasn't angry at *him*.

A wave of panic threatens to pull me under. He was so kind, *so concerned*, and I...I...

I pick at the lacing of my dress; suddenly, its weight is too much to bear. When I made it to the court, I was dazzled by the gowns, the silk sliding against my skin. But now the heavy fabric is a restraint. I can't call Sybil to help. Instead, the faintest whisper of magic is enough to loosen the stays. I remove layer after layer of petticoat and slip out of corset and frame. I stand in my shift next to the carnage and let my weary lungs expand.

A hint of movement catches at the corner of my eye. The flicker of a candle?

My mind flits and worries. I've created a new problem for myself, I've done the one thing I said I wouldn't do. But I cannot let myself surrender now. Grief has a scale to it. Layers, like a gown. And sometimes, even in agony, you must get things done.

I pull on a simple black robe, tightening it to hide every bit of my white shift. I grab Kendrik's ring from where it's fallen—it was always too loose—and, with a deep breath, slip into the corridor.

Only minutes have passed since the prince opened my chamber door. The ball still spins the sounds of revelry up and along the empty halls. I hurry down the passageway, grateful

Kendrik's chamber is not so far from mine. I make it to his door without being seen.

Now for the difficulty. Is his manservant within, or has he joined the other servants in the kitchen until Kendrik calls for him? I know nothing of men's customs or requirements. I chance a quiet knock. No answer.

Quickly, silently, I enter Kendrik's chamber.

A fire burns in the hearth, but there are more shadows lurking in his room than in mine. Tapestries of men charging into battle atop screaming horses hang on the cold stone walls. Kendrik's bed is draped in bloodred damask, with a carved wooden headboard depicting a deer hunt. The decor was probably King Alder's idea. He was always trying to tease out Kendrik's more brutal instincts.

I hurry to the desk, made of more heavy carved wood. With a snap of my fingers, a candle ignites.

Parchment. Ink and quill.

> *Dear Grandfather,*
> *I cannot do this. My heart and wishes lie elsewhere.*
> *I'm sorry.*
> *~Kendrik*

My magic sinks into the letters to make them look as if written by his own hand. This, near the last of my power, feels as if it's sucking me dry. I place Kendrik's signet ring beside

the note. Perhaps the king will not believe his grandson abnegated. Perhaps I should give a better reason.

But I have time only for simplicity. The simpler the lie, the
harder it is to expose.

Now, for Count Orlaith. What am I to do about him? I
drum my fingers silently against Kendrik's desk, thinking.
Thinking.

I cannot go to Maadenwelk in the morning. Not after
everything I've done to gain power in Tyne.

Closing my eyes, I examine the faint pulse of electricity
along my spine. How much magic lingers? For my full power
to return, I need a night of sleep, a good meal, and time. But
I have none of these things. I coax the whisper down my arms
to my fingers, where it tingles under my skin. It sips power
from other places, from the strength of my legs, the very beat
of my heart. My body begins to feel sluggish as the magic
grows.

Is it enough?

It will have to be.

If I can get my hands on Count Orlaith, touch my sparking
fingers to his skin, I should be able to persuade him to leave
without me. But I'll have to do it somewhere private; I can't
risk an interruption.

My stomach sinks. *Somewhere private.*

I shoulder this as I have other distasteful tasks: with a
steadying breath and a promise.

I won't fail you again, Mama.

I slink down hallways like a shadow. The sleeping chambers for visitors are in another wing of the castle, far from the family rooms. It will be difficult to remain unseen, but I can't waste any magic on hiding myself from notice. I'll need all I have left, and if it's not enough...I shudder at the ruse I'll have to maintain, thinking of Count Orlaith's sharp beard and shrewd eyes, his breadth and musculature, his strength.

I know what hands like his can do. How easily they can span a throat, how tightly they can squeeze. How a man's weight can press you down.

I lean against the rough stone wall and close my eyes. I invite the memories in.

Once, they helped me do what I needed to do. For Mama, and for myself.

They will help me now. My breath stops, blocked by phantom hands around my throat.

My mind clears. Anger walks with me, constant and unfailing.

I can do what must be done. Sometimes, survival demands sacrifice.

"Lady Annalise, are you well?"

My eyes snap open, and I cough as air rushes into my lungs. Panic seizes me. "Advisor Burke."

I curtsy awkwardly in my flimsy dressing gown. I want my crinoline and whale-bone armor back.

Burke, the youngest of the king's advisors, bows, his thick

brown hair falling forward to hide his eyes. He wears crimson robes and a tight frown. He's new to the retinue; his uncle, Advisor Veron, convinced King Alder to appoint him last year.

"What are you doing?" he asks bluntly.

"I—" There's nothing for it but to own the lie. I hide my anger beneath a voice sweet with regret. "I know I shouldn't have left the ball. I wanted to apologize to Count Orlaith."

"In your dressing gown?" Burke's frown deepens.

"I displeased the king. I thought this would make it right." I give a calculated shrug to say I know my place, and my duty. I don't let him see how livid it makes me, that *this*—subjugating myself—is my place. My *duty*.

Burke shakes his head and says something under his breath as he turns around.

"Pardon me?" It almost sounded like he said *a bad catch.*

Without looking at me, he mutters, "Count Orlaith is unworthy of you. I argued against the match."

"You did?" It never occurred to me that this was a decision the king discussed with his advisors. Or that one might argue against him. "Why?"

He glances back at me. In the dim light of the hall, I can't read his expression. "After Prince Kendrik, you are next in line to the throne. Orlaith is only a count, and a foreign one at that."

Next in line to the throne? I am just a cousin, and a rather distant one. I only thought to get close to Prince Kendrik, to the king, to influence...

I never thought to study lines of succession...family ties...

And now . . . Prince Kendrik lies dead in my chamber.

My knees wobble. Suddenly, the hallway is too warm, my thin shift as heavy as a winter cloak.

I am the heir.

My head pounds against the words, the new knowledge unfurling.

The heir.

This changes everything.

"Thank—thank you, Advisor Burke. For trying," I add, after a beat. My head is swimming. Spinning. At some point, Kendrik's manservant will return to his chamber and see the note. Someone will inform the king. He'll investigate. And then he'll send for me.

I say good night to Burke, and after he disappears down the hall, I hurry back to my own room. The king cannot marry me off to a foreign-born count now. And I must conserve my magic, should anyone need a reminder of my role and importance in this kingdom.

Besides, there's one more thing I have to do, though I'll have to wait until the castle sleeps.

I pause outside my chamber door, mind whirling with guilt and joy. I truly did not mean to harm the prince. But all I want, everything I've worked for—no, *more*, more than I ever dreamed—is now within my reach.

When I open my door, a strange sound greets me. In the flickering light cast by the fire, something moves.

I swallow back a scream.

CHAPTER FOUR

EVRA

I look up to find Hagan standing over me. Mama hovers behind him, her mouth pinched with worry. "Are you all right?" she asks, reaching for me.

"I..." I don't know how to answer her.

"Did you have a fit? You just collapsed," Hagan adds, his eyes wide. Together they help me sit up.

I swallow. The taste of blood and cinders fills my mouth. "I don't know what happened. I felt...I felt as if I went somewhere else for a moment. Like a dream." I struggle to my feet, the world still shimmering slightly, as if our worn, wood-planked house is the dream. Hagan puts an arm around my waist when my knees threaten to give.

"Somewhere else?" Mama murmurs. She and Hagan share a look I don't understand.

Hagan carefully leads me inside. With a thud, I drop to the bench that runs the length of the kitchen wall. Heat from the hearth fire envelops me, but my fingers still burn with cold. I tuck my hands under my arms to warm them.

The coppery, charred taste in my mouth won't fade. "Mama, could I have some water please?"

She grabs a mug and ladles some from the pot over the fire, muttering a few words into the steam. When she hands the water to me, it's cool and sweet.

"Thank you." My hands tighten around the cup. Images from the dream swirl in my mind. A waking dream? I was awake, wasn't I?

"That was so strange. I wonder—I hope I'm not taking ill." I try not to let my mind linger on the memory of the king's face, but I can't shake the sense of some evil lurking.

"The only one with no magic... but there is so little these days," Mama mumbles.

I stare hard at her, my thoughts snapping back to the moment when Ronan asked me to destroy his butterfly illusion. "What does this have to do with magic?"

A hissing spit from the hearth grabs Mama's attention. With a pained look, she hurries to the fire to stir the potatoes. Automatically, I move to stand up, to help her, but Hagan pushes me back down.

"Your dream," he says. "Do you remember what you saw?"

I shudder as I tell him. The king's face, the wolf... "And then the glass wall behind the throne cracked and ran with blood." My breath hitches in my throat.

I take another sip of water. My head is starting to swim. I'm so tired, out of nowhere. Parched. As if I've been working in the sun on the hottest day of summer. As if all the liquid that holds me together has been sucked away.

"Mama," I whisper as the world tilts. "I—"

"The spirits, Mama." Hagan wraps his arm around my shoulder. "Evra, don't faint."

I want to say that of course I won't faint—I've never fainted in my life—but the shadows in the corners of the kitchen are growing, reaching for me, and I'm leaning heavily against his side. I can't seem to move, to push myself back up.

"Here." Mama pours a biting drink into my mouth. I sputter weakly as I swallow. "That's it, a little more," she says, as another wave of liquid burns down my throat.

The fire spreads through my belly, and I choke and heave. Am I dying?

But the heat doesn't kill me; it flows through the dry places, fills the chinks in my muscles and skin and bones. It clears my head, which I am certain isn't the usual purpose for such a drink. After a moment more, the black clouds at the edge of my vision recede and my breath flows more or less normally from my lungs. I straighten up in my seat.

"Better?" Hagan asks, his arm still around me.

I nod. My mouth burns a little.

The furrows in Mama's forehead smooth. I take the small bottle from her and swallow more of the drink. "Spirits?" I ask, and my voice sounds strange and not my own.

She nods. "The ones I use for cooking. Tomorrow you

and Hagan can go down to the village for some firecane. The stronger the spirits, the more quickly they will bring you back to yourself next time."

"Next time?" My stomach leaps to my scalded throat. "Why would it happen again? Do you—do you think I'm sick?"

Ten years ago, when the Sickness ravaged Tyne, it caused chest pains and weakness, hallucinations and, for many, death. My mind whirls, trying to remember those days, trying to remember which effects came first.

Mama brushes a wisp of my hair off my face. "No, Evra, you're not sick." But she still looks sad. "Do you remember the stories you heard as a child, about our family and their visions?"

A sizzle of shock courses through me. Surely she's not saying...

"Those are just legends," I whisper.

She shakes her head. "They are much more than that."

Shadows cling to the low beams of the ceiling and for a moment they look like black grinning skulls, and they laugh at me.

I can scarcely breathe. "You can't mean I'm a Clearsee."

Hagan shifts at my side. "Father thought it would be Deward, when the Sickness came. Clearsees awaken when the kingdom is at its worst, its most dangerous, and those were dark times."

"Are you saying now is *worse*?" I twist to glare at my brother. "Why did no one tell me? How could you keep this a secret from me?"

Hagan stares down at the worn wood of the table.

"It was never meant to be a secret," Mama says gently. "Your father waited until the boys were ten to speak to them of such things. It was his family that bore this legacy. There wasn't time, my dear—" Her voice cracks. "You were nine when he passed. There was so much he would have told you, would have taught you, if he'd had the chance."

The room falls silent, pulled down by the weight and sorrow of memory. I drop my head into my hands. There have been so many moments when I've felt lost without Father here.

"*You* could have told me," I whisper.

"The Clearsee magic has never chosen a girl. I thought— I thought it was a conversation we could have in the future, when you had your own children to pass the knowledge to."

"You have magic now, Evra," Hagan says softly, almost eagerly, as if he means this to be a comfort.

And, for a moment, it is. *I have magic.* I focus my attention on the cup of water before me. I curl my hands around it and very carefully draw it closer. Under my breath, I ask it to boil.

No steam rises from the cup.

Mama's hands cover mine. "I'm sorry, Evra. It's not that kind of magic."

My eyes snap to hers. Every day for the past three years, I've prayed to be like everyone else. To feel the whisper, to have the power in my blood. Magic isn't just one wish, it is many, made over and over throughout the day. The grease that moves each person smoothly forward.

Without it, I am a shrieking, clumsy wheel.

"Your vision showed the king in danger," Hagan says, interrupting the dark spiral of my thoughts.

"Yes. And may the danger find him quickly," I mutter.

"It is a Clearsee's job to *protect* the king," he reminds me, "no matter what he's done. You will be expected to help him."

Mama smooths her hair back, straightens her shoulders, and turns to pull three shallow wooden bowls from the hooks above the washing basin. Because she's shaking, they rattle like bones. "Hagan, dear," she says, "the potatoes are done. Could you carry the pan over for me?"

I sag without Hagan's steadying weight beside me. He takes up a rag to protect his hands and carefully lifts the heavy iron pan from the fire to the table.

Mama ladles the crisp roasted potatoes into our bowls and pours a thin stream of milky soup on top. Flecks of green and red herbs from her garden float in the liquid, and fragrant steam wafts up. I bring a spoonful to my lips and force it down my throat. Hagan sits down again, across from me this time, and begins to eat, his slurping the only sound in the room.

"I can't," I whisper. "I can't help him." I won't leave my home to save a king who leaves his kingdom broken and weak. I won't.

Eight years ago, Father scratched himself with a bit of rusted metal. One small, jagged wound. When it swelled and reddened, when he felt the fever coming, Mama and Deward tried to help him. Others in the village tried too. But it was a persistent infection, unbothered by untrained magic. Our only healer had been forced to Ironwald during the Sickness. We were still rebuilding. The villages around us were too. No one had enough magic to help.

Father died in the late afternoon, just before the last dregs of sun leached from the sky. He sighed with a jerky shudder and was still. The endless night that followed follows me still.

I cannot be Clearsee to this king.

A tear dribbles down Mama's cheek and into her soup.

"Are we *sure*?" Hagan asks, a little desperately. "Perhaps it was a spot of fever. Evra, are you sure you're not ill?"

I want to say I am. I want to laugh this off. *What a silly little dizzy spell.* Or I could blame this on Ronan, say his crude proposal had caused some kind of episode. But I can't forget how *real* it all felt, how clearly I saw the king's skin flay from his bones.

I cannot deny that something is shifting within me. This new realization, this new magic, burrows beneath my skin and fits itself to me, as if it has always been there, waiting. Part of who I am. If Ronan and Bastian and the rest of the village were afraid of me when they thought I had no magic, that's nothing to how they'll feel now. I'm the black dog bringing death, the white-footed mare, the harbinger of new horrors to come.

Because in every tale I was told as a child, in every story I thought was nothing more than a myth, Clearsees were prophets of doom.

The door blows open and Deward sweeps into the room on a gust of biting wind. He shakes out his shaggy dark hair, which is dotted with white. "Snow's come. The weather shifted so fast it looked like the end of the world as I was walking up from Molly's."

"Have you eaten?" Mama asks automatically.

Deward shakes his head again and slips off his sheepskin coat, hanging it on a hook by the fire. Before Mama has time to stand, he grabs a bowl. "Molly and her mother promised to take a bit of chicken to Old Marnie. Her knee is aching something awful with the cold weather come so early this year. I didn't want to trouble them to feed me as well."

He scoots onto the bench next to Hagan and helps himself to the remaining potatoes and soup. It takes a few moments for him to register the silence surrounding him. He looks up at our drawn, tearful faces and narrows his eyes. "What's happened?"

For a moment, no one replies. The crisp scent of pine and snow clings to Deward; I want to fling myself into my oldest brother's arms, breathe deeply, and forget this whole afternoon.

Instead, I finish my soup as Mama explains my vision.

Deward's face sinks into thoughtful lines. "But what does it mean? The king's face peeling away, and a wolf?"

"I don't know." I start to tell him more, about the silence and sense of dislocation, the blood, but thinking about it makes me dizzy. I take a deep breath and try to hold my hands steady.

"Well, I suppose the king will," Deward says. When he frowns, he looks so much like Father. "We'll leave tomorrow."

"We will?" My stomach drops. "For—for where?"

But I know the answer. Which is why he, rightly, takes my questions as objections.

"We must tell the king, Evra, and as soon as possible. If word were to spread, and the king to find out a Clearsee existed and hadn't come forward..."

His men would find me and force *me to come. Just as they're forcing Farin. Just as they've forced all the best magic workers in the kingdom.*

Hagan runs a hand through his short blond hair. "I'll go with Evra. Mama needs you here, Deward. Molly too."

Mama stands up and gathers the bowls. Her small frame curls in on itself. This time, I feel strong enough to rise, strong enough to help. I take the dishes from her hands.

"The storm should blow through by morning," she says softly. "If you leave by midday, you'll put some distance behind you before nightfall."

I want to argue that there is the farm work, the wood chopping and message running. There's my dagger training with Hagan. And I have plans to see Tam tomorrow. But there isn't a point. It will not be the first time the king's will has forced a life to change.

Hagan and I spend the evening packing. I climb up and down the ladder from his room to mine, comforted by the quiet sounds of Mama and Deward talking in the sitting room. Mama is darning my favorite pair of socks so I can take them with me.

There are four rooms on the first floor of the house—the kitchen, a sitting room, Deward and Hagan's bedroom, and Mama's too—all surrounding the giant central hearth that opens into each one. My loft would be the largest room, but the roof is sharply peaked and allows space to stand only in the center, around the stone chimney. We use the cramped spaces under the eaves for storage.

As I weave through each room, collecting the things I'll need for our travel, I find myself lingering, my hand brushing across Mama's favorite book of fairy tales, catching against the thick woolen weave of Deward's jacket. I steal one of his old shirts and stuff it into my bag, as if all of my clothes—my brothers' hand-me-downs—aren't already reminders. I wish I could stuff *him* in with our supplies. I wish I didn't have to go.

It is late, moonlight bright, when I climb into Mama's bed and curl against her. Her arms wrap me in their warmth and her breath feathers my forehead as I whisper my fears and worries into the soft hollow of her throat. Her heart beats strong in my ear.

For the span of this one last night, my world remains the same.

CHAPTER FIVE

ANNALISE

I've let the wild out.

I didn't mean to, not like this.

Sheets to protect my hands and face. My thickest, sturdiest ribbons for chains. It lunges for me, again and again.

It. Prince Kendrik. The thing he has become.

My chamber smells of sweat and rot and animal fear.

The hours pass slowly. I can only gasp and pray.

"Leave me alone, I am not well!" I shout through the door when Sybil comes to help me into bed. I'm sobbing now, and stretched thin—my magic sucks at my muscles and breath and bones, its last gasp masking the creature's snarls and inhuman shrieks.

Oh God, what have I done?

Somehow, hours later, I make it down through the castle's abandoned back corridors, fighting the beast for every step. My magic creates an unnatural silence, our battle raging as a vicious pantomime. The guards at the small rear gate don't stop me—maybe I've put them to sleep, or perhaps they can't see me for the storm raging overhead. I can barely see my own feet, already slick with mud.

I can't tell where my will ends and the magic begins. My mind is a swirl of chaotic desperation. I've lost my tether to the ground beneath my feet, the logic and ambition that guide my days. All I can do is move forward, staggering into the darkness.

Into this horrid dream.

Maybe I should kill the beast, but I can't. I don't have the strength. Not the magic, nor the will. Not now.

I don't know what to do.

One night, and my world has irrevocably changed.

CHAPTER SIX

EVRA

Weeping River Lake has frozen flat and milky white, like a huge, blind eye. A figure stands at its banks, recognizable even after all these years. He turns at the sound of my boots crunching through the snow. He wears his favorite hat, a worn mess of floppy leather that looks as well-loved and comfortable as he does. His blue eyes glow, almost like candle flames, and deep shadows form half-moons beneath them.

"Father?" My voice is that of a child, lost and looking for comfort.

"It is a bitter season," he says in a voice that is harder, colder than I remember. "Bitter as blood."

"Father, what is happening? How does the Clearsee magic work? What do I do?" I can hear the yearning, the fear in my own voice. I have missed him so much.

"I miss you too, my girl." The strange glow in his eyes fades. For one moment, there is nothing but my father and his gentleness standing there. "You are strong enough for this, but you must *be* strong. You must pay attention."

A cloud moves across the icy blue sky, throwing his face into shadow. Behind him, I hear someone else cry out. I look— there, across the lake, curled into a ball in the snow. Do they need help? I take a step, and the world rends itself from end to end. The lake shivers apart, darkness falls, and the ground itself bucks beneath my feet.

"Evra, remember, blood cannot lie." Father's voice cracks like a sheet of glass, like ice breaking. I can't see him anymore in the swirl of snow and lightning and shadow. Sobs catch in my throat. I have grieved for him, I have raged for him. This moment, this dream is not enough.

The stranger across the lake screams again.

I wake, mouth open and throat burning, as if the screams were mine. But Mama shifts and sighs against me, still asleep. I fumble for the candle beside the bed; my shaking hands make it difficult to ignite. Again, I wish for the magic to create a spark. I whisper the words, snap my fingers. *Please, magic, please.* But Mama is right. The Clearsee magic doesn't seem to work that way. After several tries with the flint, a small flickering light throws jerky shadows across the bed.

"Evra?" Mama murmurs, her eyes still closed.

"Sleep, Mama," I whisper back. I leave the room, taking the light with me, and hunch down on the bench in the kitchen. I draw my arms tight to hold myself together, and stare into the candle flame. *Breathe. Just breathe.* Shallow gasps are all I manage at first. A few sips of Mama's cooking spirits help ease the parched feeling in my chest. My fingers tingle with cold, even though the banked fire breathes a little warmth into the room.

Father spoke to me. Was it a dream, born of my longing for his presence, born of the knowledge that he holds the Clearsee legacy in his blood? Or was it something more? It had felt real, like the king's hall had felt real. But if it was a vision, what warning had it given? What use can I make of it?

I don't have the answers I seek, only more questions. More fears. Seeing Father was a comfort, and yet the dream has left me with the creeping dread of a nightmare.

Blood cannot lie.

Am I callous and cruel for wishing he'd given me more?

There's no use trying to go back to sleep, so I stumble up the ladder to my dark room in the eaves. I don a pair of Hagan's old leather trousers and the woolen shirt I stole from Deward. I'll go see Tamsin. I did promise, and she won't mind that it's so early.

Carefully, I climb down into my brothers' room. Deward snorts. I freeze, but he doesn't move when I sneak by him and out into the sitting room. He'll be waking soon at any rate; the gray glow of dawn is just touching the window. Hagan's bed is empty; he's likely already out in the barn preparing for our journey.

I can hear Mama stirring as I pad silently to the kitchen. I don't know why I'm being so secretive—it wouldn't surprise anyone that I wish to talk to Tam—but I find myself slinking to the door anyway. I am not ready to face Mama, Hagan, and Deward, with Father's sad eyes and sparse words still lingering in my mind. In truth, I'm not ready to face any part of this day. Not yet. I need the fresh air and the quiet and the walk to calm me first. I slip my cloak from its hook and step wide to avoid the creaky board just before the kitchen door.

Outside the air is brittle, so dry and cold it feels as if it might break as I move through it, might shatter like glass. Our horses, Gobber and Daisy, whicker when they hear me in the yard, so I run before Hagan can investigate, sliding on the slippery, shallow layer of snow.

Soon I'm halfway down the hill that leads to Windhaven, and my cloak is dusted with white from the times I've fallen. Beside the path, Weeping River skitters down tiny rock falls and around small bends. The sound of the river, usually comforting, is menacing today, a cackling as the water tears away at the ice encroaching its banks.

It sounds like the skull-shaped shadows that laughed at me last night. Every pocket of darkness I pass is a threat. Why do I feel this way? Why do I keep looking at the sky, waiting for it to break apart?

I pick up my pace. The stream veers away, into the forest that surrounds Windhaven and the lake. The road curves east, toward the brightening glow of sunrise. I take a circuitous route, breaking from the path into deeper hillocks of snow. I have no interest in meeting anyone from the village. Bastian can save his grumbling insults.

I reach Tamsin's house just as the sun crests the hill and throws blades of light across the windows. As Windhaven's steward, Tam's father lives in the nicest house in the village. It is two full stories, with two chimneys and delicate rosebushes that climb up the gray stone on either side of the heavy oak door. Now, the vines are bare and thorny, speckled with white.

I grab two fistfuls of snow, packing them into a single, solid ball. My hands burn; I forgot my gloves—and my throwing knives. The realization sends a bolt of ice down my spine.

I position myself below one of the second-story windows and heave the snowball. It explodes with a quiet *plop*, splattering against the glass. I throw another. In a moment, the wavering glow of candlelight tinges the snow on the window yellow.

It's a few minutes more before the back door opens.

Tam slips outside, yanking her quiver and bow onto her arm and her gloves onto her hands. Instead of a cloak, the jacket she wears is soft sheepskin, with the wool sewn inward, an extra protection against the cold. Her hair is hidden beneath her fox hat, made from her first kill; its fluffy red plume streams behind her as she yanks me away from the house.

There's no question that Tamsin is the most beautiful girl in Windhaven. Her parents doted on her as a child when they saw her flawless skin, thick flaxen hair, and large dark eyes; it wasn't until she, like me, grew to outmatch most of the village men in height and developed a rebellious streak unmatched by *anyone* that they tried to discipline her. And failed, miserably.

This morning, her face is open and eager. She pulls me down the path toward the lake. "It's so early, does that mean good news? I could barely sleep last night for wondering. That, and Mother was talking of marrying me off to Gillis again. Gillis! Not only is he balding and *old*, but he couldn't tell which end of an arrow is which if I *shot* him! If Mother thinks I'll even *consider*—" She clears her throat, visibly reining herself in. "At any rate, tell me you have good news!"

I stare at her dumbly. Good news? My whole world is cracking and tumbling around me.

She pulls at my arm again. "Come on, Evra. What did Ronan say?"

Of course. With everything else, I had forgotten about Ronan. I try to answer, but the words freeze in my mouth. I don't want to talk about him. I want to talk about my vision, my dream, my terror at facing the king. But how do I begin?

She notices my silence and stops so suddenly I almost stumble. She studies my face and whatever she sees makes her mouth fall into a frown. "Oh no. I was sure he fancied you. I'm sorry, Evra. Don't worry, we'll teach him to—"

"Tam, it's not that," I say. "I mean, it *is*, but—"

"So it went well?" she asks, obviously confused.

"Oh no, it was terrible. I hope he spends the winter with the rashes."

Tam lets out a snort of laughter. We've reached the lake; it looks nothing like my dream. The banks are frozen and white with snow, but the center is still black and silver, the wind picking up sparks of light as it ruffles the water's surface.

"Truly, Ronan is the least of my concerns. Last night, I . . . I had a vision." The word drops between us like a stone. She can't see the ripples, but I can. They are already changing, shaping everything.

"A vision? What on earth do you mean?" Her eyes are such a dark brown they often look black in low light; this morning, the brilliant winter sun hits them in such a way that they show a clear mahogany.

What if she doesn't know the stories?

What if she does?

"Mama thinks . . . she thinks I'm a Clearsee. I saw the king die, right before my eyes. . . . I had a dream where my father spoke to me. I leave for Ironwald today. I have to seek an audience. . . ." The words burst forth in a rush. They make no sense, even to me.

Tam's eyes widen. "A Clearsee? Ironwald?"

I pull my damp cloak closer; the rising sun does little to cut the chill. My feet are two great blocks of ice stuffed into my boots. I suddenly wish I hadn't said anything. It was bad enough when I had no magic. Now . . . now I am the mad prophet, and I will serve a king everyone loathes. Tam will turn her back on me, just as the rest of Windhaven has.

But Tamsin doesn't give me time to sit with my regret. She throws her arms around me and says, "Well, then. I'm going with you."

"What?" I pull away.

She smiles gently. "I know you're terrified. I can see it in your face, feel it all the way down your body. So much tension." She squeezes my arms, and she's right. They're so tight, the pressure of her hands makes them ache. "I know how to navigate the court, and I have dresses you can borrow. We've always talked about going together, haven't we?"

I've never been to the capital, even for the yearly feast King Alder holds to celebrate Prince Kendrik's birthday. We live close enough—it is only two days' ride—but the feast is during threshing time. Once, years ago, Tam and I concocted a scheme to hide me in her family's carriage, but Deward caught me sneaking out and lectured me for days.

I've always wanted to go. But as an observer. An invisible party guest, there to collect new sights and smells and tastes, sparkling treasures to turn over in my mind during dark winter evenings. I wanted to go for the stories, like Tam does, for the pampered courtiers and clever troubadours. Not for the king, never for him.

And what if he thinks *I* am the danger?

"But, Tam—"

"But nothing. You need your best friend. When our lives change in huge and scary ways, we're there for each other. Remember?" The words are light, but the look in her eyes isn't. I know she's thinking of when we met, when she was the one scared and wishing she could run.

Tam moved here shortly after my father died. People were still afraid of newcomers, still scarred by the Sickness and the ways it changed our world. Windhaven met their new steward and his family with suspicion and distrust. But I could see in Tam the same loneliness, the same dislocation and pain I was feeling. She was grieving her old life, as I was grieving mine. We became friends long before the rest of the town warmed up to her family. Now, they're the highest society Windhaven can boast.

When my magic didn't materialize, Tam did what I had done for her. *I won't let someone else's ignorance ruin our friendship*, she told me, when the odd looks I got started to include her too. And she has never wavered.

I hug her again. "You don't have to come. Your parents—"

"My parents will be thrilled. They'll fill their tiny brains with fantasies of me marrying a nobleman and birthing ten magic-stuffed squallers. It's what they've always wanted anyway, me a courtier in the castle." She looks so deeply offended at the thought, I can't help but laugh. It comes out a little too loud, a little hysterical, but somehow suddenly it's easier to breathe.

"Then let's hurry," I say. "Our goal is to leave by midday."

"And which of your gallant brothers has offered to escort you?" she asks.

"Both," I answer. "Hagan won."

"Of course he did." She smiles lightly.

Before I have time to turn away, she touches a spot on my cheek, igniting a spark of pain. Not again.

"I didn't have a bruise there!" I say, exasperated.

"It was a blemish. You've got to look your best for court."

I roll my eyes. "You're the one husband shopping, remember? No one will care what the mad Clearsee looks like."

She cups my face in her hands, her expression suddenly serious. "You are not mad, and you never will be. You are stronger than any magic. The stories are just stories. I know *you*."

Her words, so like what Father said in my dream, worry rather than comfort me. With a last nervous look at the restless lake, I thread my arm through Tam's and turn to go.

CHAPTER SEVEN

ANNALISE

*T*he summons comes at first light.

I stare into the mirror at the bruise-colored shadows under my eyes, at the sallow cast of my skin. My cheekbones are hollowed out, my lips pale and thin. There's a deep scratch along my neck and a smudge of coal-dark dirt on my forehead.

Behind me, in the hearth, the shredded ribbons, torn sheets, and dirty clothes of last night are making the fire roar.

"Lady Annalise?" Sybil calls from the other side of the door, her voice laced with worry.

I don't let her in.

Slowly, I clean myself up. My shoulders ache, my head pounds, my gut twists every time I think of what I did. The prince—he was a puppy, not a wolf. He didn't deserve this.

I dress myself in a deep purple gown with a tall, white lace collar that hides my throat. I wipe my face clean. My hands... well.

When the room and I are presentable, I ring for Sybil and ask her to pack my things for Maadenwelk. I apologize and say I was overcome with grief. She pauses before the hearth, her face draining of color. I notice a scrap of bloody fabric still burning and ask her to put more wood on the fire.

When I arrive in the king's receiving room, he has already taken his place on the throne. His advisors, including Burke, stand behind him. Count Orlaith isn't here.

It's smoky from all of the candles. Smoky and too warm. The lace at my throat itches.

I curtsy, my gaze on the floor. "You wished to see me, Your Majesty?"

"Have you packed?" he asks.

A shudder runs through me, a gasping little jolt of magic sparking under my skin. Was Burke wrong? Is the king still going to send me away?

Somehow, I manage to nod. "My maid is gathering my things now." And then, because it's what I would say if I didn't know about the prince, because it's what I feel in my soul, I add desperately, "Please, Your Majesty, please let me stay in Tyne."

King Alder studies me closely. His chest rises and falls as if each breath is an individual, exhausting labor. He usually ignores me or stares over my shoulder, but he is giving me his full attention now. It's disconcerting. My instinct to cower before him hasn't faded in the years I've been at court. But I find the strength to meet his eyes. I harness the faint wisp of magic in my blood and send it toward the web of invisible fibers I've spun him up in, to remind and reinforce, to strengthen the strands I've already set in place. I don't need physical contact for this; once the first connection has been made, it gets easier.

"My niece Althea's child," he murmurs. "Raised away from the court, until she died in the Sickness. And so we sent for you."

The next in line for the throne.

"Yes, Your Majesty."

"It seems I will be granting your wish," he says, and his body sags. All of his finery—the extravagant velvet, the fur-lined cowl—cannot hide his weariness. His age.

The whole kingdom knows he was ready to pass the crown to his son ten years ago, and would have, until tragedy stole that dream.

Stole a lot of dreams.

And now you've made him think his grandson abandoned him, my conscience reminds me. Even so, hope blooms in my chest. "My wish, Your Majesty?"

Say it, say it.

With a sigh that reaches deep, he bows his head. "You will not be going to Maadenwelk. Prince Kendrik has renounced his place in this family, and this kingdom. He once told me he didn't want to rule, but I was foolish enough to believe his sense of duty would prevail. You, Lady Annalise, are my near-est kin. As such, you are now heir to the throne."

I stumble back a step. My shock is real, at least in small

part. I had no idea Kendrik had told King Alder of his reluctance. I thought that was something he'd shared in secret with me. This bit of true surprise helps me sell the portion that's feigned.

"What—what about Count Orlaith?" I glance toward the door, half-expecting him to enter, and my gaze lands on Burke. The corner of his mouth lifts into his beard. A smile, or a grimace? At least he's not frowning savagely like his uncle Veron, who looks like he'd happily feed me to the palace dogs.

"The count has left Ironwald," the king says. "He is not pleased. Nor am I. That would have been a good alliance, and you are entirely unprepared to be queen. You've no knowledge of the crown or the people I rule. You've nothing but the blood in your veins—" In a flash, he reaches out and grabs my wrist, turning it soft side up. His nails dig into my skin. "And blood so often spills."

I resist the urge to tear my arm away. Instead, I lean into the pain, let it remind me of my purpose.

He's wrong about me. I know far more about the people of Tyne than he does.

"Perhaps the prince will change his mind," I say humbly.

The king releases my wrist one finger at a time. The effort of these movements takes its toll—a phlegm-filled cough racks his thin body. When he catches his breath, he says, "That is my hope, but I must be ready either way."

I incline my head. "Yes, Your Majesty. I will do all I can for Tyne, and pray the prince returns."

"Burke has volunteered to prepare you for your new role as heir," he says. "I've sent messengers to my stewards. We will have a feast in a fortnight's time to announce the change in succession."

"Yes, Your Majesty," I say again. His disappointment is an almost tangible thing. But while I might feel sorry for Kendrik, and horrified by what I've done to him, I've no sympathy for King Alder. His age and ill health, a grandchild's abandonment... it is but a fraction of what he deserves.

"Go," he says now. "Tell your maid to stop packing. You'll need new gowns. Training in diplomacy and the traditions of the royal family. You have two weeks to learn how to behave as a future queen."

Another nod, another curtsy, and I am free.

I sweep down the corridor. My life is about to change. Again. Only this time, I'll have the power to change the world too.

It's so much more than I let myself hope for.

"Lady Annalise!"

I turn to find Burke striding toward me, his robes billowing.

I'm so tired of curtsying I could scream. And yet, stiffly, I comply with the customs expected of me. When I am queen, I will curtsy to no one.

"We must begin your preparations, Your Highness," Burke says, with the smallest pause before my new title.

I laugh a little before I can help it. I'm exhausted down to my bones; my vision is sparking around the edges. I'm not in any state for *preparations*. "I'm very sorry, Advisor, but we will have to delay. I couldn't sleep last night for grief, and this morning's events have shaken me. I need rest. Please understand."

I make to continue on my way, but Burke draws my arm through his. Firmly. "Of course, Your Highness. But first I would like to discuss one small matter with you."

He turns me around and leads me to a narrow stair at the end of the hall. We climb down carefully into darkness.

My stomach tightens, churning on its own emptiness. "Where are we going, Advisor?"

He's taller than I am and heavy through the shoulders. I don't like how closely he holds my arm, right up against his side. Not that there is much room to escape on this narrow, twisting stair.

"We're going outside," he replied. "It's a beautiful morning."

But it's not. By the time we reach the courtyard, with its small, spring-spelled garden, clouds have rolled across the sky, heavy and thick with electricity. Burke glances up, frowning at the unexpected squall. Still, he walks me to the center of the courtyard, to the stone fountain and its spelled splash of unfreezing water. The fresh air slices through my gown, but the shiver that runs through me has more to do with the magic sparking to life under my skin.

I pull my arm from his grasp and turn on him. "What are we doing out here?"

He meets my gaze. His eyes are as dark brown as his beard. In the strange combination of dawn and stormlight, they almost look black.

"Last night, we had a conversation," he begins. I fight to steady my nerves. "You were upset about leaving Tyne. You were upset about Count Orlaith. And somehow, this morning, you're not leaving Tyne and Count Orlaith is no longer a problem for you."

I wait, but he doesn't say more. "Is that a question?"

Inside, my heart is a trip hammer, and around us, the wind is picking up.

"I wondered," Burke says, "if perhaps you went to Prince Kendrik's room instead of the count's last night."

I stare at him, my mouth opening slightly. "To do *what*, Advisor?"

Does Burke know I didn't go to Count Orlaith's chamber? Did he somehow see me with the beast, when the night had turned to velvet and the castle was quiet and dark?

Without actively thinking about it, I assess every point of exposed skin, the distance between us, the strength of the lightning coursing through me. He shifts his weight and his robes ripple. They hide his hands, his wrists, his legs, much of his neck. His cheeks are a little ruddy, which is odd—aside from General Driscoll, the king's advisors do not have occasion to spend much time in the sun. Regardless, his face is close enough to touch.

"Do you know where Prince Kendrik went?" He steps a breath closer. "Do you know why he left?"

Yes. And yes.

"I don't know anything," I say, and somehow my voice

sounds calm. The magic is helping me hold this moment together, but I'm far from certain Burke will believe me. My hands twitch to remove my gloves, to be ready to convince him. But I've little in reserve without sleep and food. So I keep talking. "Am I sorry to stay in Tyne? No. But I had nothing to do with Prince Kendrik's decision. He came to speak to me when I left the ball. He told me I had to respect his grandfather's wishes. He was the reason I chose to—to speak with Count Orlaith. The prince seemed...himself. He seemed fine." I drop my gaze to the ground. A few raindrops chill the back of my neck, but I'm steady. For now.

What if I'd listened to Kendrik? What if I'd been able to control myself last night? What if I'd gone back to the ball and danced with the count?

Kendrik would be here. And I would be gone.

"Something happened." Burke's words are a slap.

"What do you mean?" I hook a finger along the edge of my glove. I'll have to move quickly.

Burke turns away. Paces. "It must have," he continues. "After he spoke with you, he must have seen something, or thought something...*something* that led him to make this choice."

The pulsing fire beneath my skin subsides. My hands drop, unclench. "Perhaps he struggled with the decision for a long time. The tipping point needn't have been much."

"He was never interested in speaking about his role in this kingdom." Burke runs his hand through his hair. "But he'd accepted his duty. He *knew* it was his duty."

"Duties can be weighty things. Sometimes heavy enough to drown you."

Burke looks up. For a long moment, neither of us speaks. Inexplicably, my cheeks warm.

Very softly, he says, "Were you drowning?"

"Last night?" He already knows my answer is, "Yes."

"And now?"

A glimmer of sun breaks through the clouds. The storm has passed.

"I don't know." It's the truth. "How heavy are these duties?"

He shrugs a little. "As queen, you'll hold lives in your hands. There is no duty more weighty than that."

He doesn't know I've held lives in my hands before.

And that somehow, I always seem to crush them.

CHAPTER EIGHT

EVRA

Mama is just leaving the barn with a basket of eggs when Tam and I hike into the farmyard, Tam's traveling trunk slung between us. Relief brightens Mama's features. "Ah. I had hoped that's where you were."

"I went to say goodbye, but she is insisting on coming," I say.

Mama smiles. "Of course she is."

With a thud, Tam and I drop the chest. My own belongings take up far less room—most of my clothes are sturdy hand-me-downs from my brothers, not exactly useful in the castle, where women are expected to wear gowns and jewels and other such frippery. Tam packed a few extra dresses for me to borrow.

My stomach clenches. Court is a foreign language, a foreign country, a wholly different world. Even with Tamsin as interpreter, I'll surely embarrass myself.

"Is Hagan ready?" I take Mama's basket for her and follow her inside, Tam behind me.

Mama cracks a few of the eggs into a skillet over the fire, where they sizzle and spit. "He went to get the firecane. He should be back soon. You'll make it a fair distance before nightfall." She glances at Tamsin. "It's kind of you to go with them. You spoke to your parents, of course?"

"Of course," Tam says solemnly.

Mama knows we have a tendency to not always "remember" to inform Tam's parents of our exploits.

"Good." Mama nods. "You'll take Gobber to Ironwald. Why don't you girls get the cart packed up? I've got bread baking for you to take, and a meal cooking to eat before you leave. Oh and, Evra, Tansy needs you."

Mama is fighting to make this moment feel normal. Her voice is telling me I am her daughter, late for my chores, that this journey will be ordinary, in some ways at least. I kiss her forehead on my way back outside, and for an instant she holds tight to my arms, as if she's holding me together, or propping herself up. As I leave, she makes a sniffing sound, and I'm scared she's shooing us out so she can cry.

Daisy whinnies when I push open the heavy wooden door to the barn. The thick, warm scents of horseflesh and hen droppings embrace me. Stalls run along the left wall; to the right is Mama's henhouse. We have ten hens and a proud black rooster who sits in the rafters, watching us. Just when you've forgotten he's there, he'll crow, and the sound will echo loudly enough to rattle your teeth.

"Evra, is that you?" Deward calls from the back of the barn.

"Yes. And Tam. She's coming with me." I run a hand down Daisy's velvet nose and let my fingers ruffle Gobber's golden forelock. They're big, sturdy plow horses, fuzzy and awkward now in their winter coats. They wink at me with their giant, soft brown eyes. Daisy whinnies again. "Hush, you ninny," I say, continuing down the straw-strewn aisle.

"Your parents didn't object?" Deward asks, glancing up at us. He works on a bridle, his nimble fingers twisting the leather to fix a weak spot.

Tamsin shrugs. It's not as if they could have stopped her. Deward knows this, but he takes his role as the eldest so seriously it often spills over to Tam too. It was he who taught her how to shoot a bow. And, when that proved too difficult for me without magic, showed me how to throw knives.

My hair has come free and the dark strands hang like shadows at the corners of my eyes. I quickly loosen and retie my braid before grabbing the stool and pail beneath the work table. "I'll take care of Tansy."

"Your mother said we should help pack Gobber's cart. I brought a small trunk. What else do we need?" Tam and Deward get to work, as I let myself into Tansy's stall.

She moos a little desperately when I lift the latch. "Sorry, Tansy, sorry," I whisper, my voice pitched low and soothing. "I'm here now."

I set the stool next to her hindquarters and place the pail beneath her. She heaves an impatient sigh. "Hush, my sweet, my baby," I murmur, almost sing, as my fingers latch onto her teats. Tansy likes lullabies when she's milked; "My Lady Lost" and "The Bumblebee" are her favorites. I sing to her softly now, in time to the rhythmic ding of milk hitting the pail.

> *My lady, my love*
> *Where do you hide?*
> *Shall I find you in the garden*
> *Lost among the roses sweet?*
> *My lady, my love*
> *Where do you abide?*
> *Shall I find you in the meadow...*

There is a voice singing with me, soft at first and then growing louder, until it drowns out the hiss of milk in the pail.

Until it drowns out everything.

A little girl in a threadbare dress lies on her tummy in the grass, plucking wildflowers. Sitting beside her, her mother sings as she brushes the girl's chestnut hair.

> *Lost among the grasses green?*
> *My love, my lady*
> *Where have you gone?*
> *My lady lost, my lady lost*

"Where is the lady, Mama?" the little girl says. "Do you think she's scared?"

"It's just a song, goose. Just a song." She hums the tune softly.

"I don't ever want to lose you, Mama. *I* would be scared."

The woman's fingers tremble as she smooths her daughter's hair. "You won't lose me. I'm your mama. I'm not going anywhere."

"But Papa went away. Is *he* lost?" The little girl rolls to her side so she can look up at her mother.

The woman traces a finger down the girl's forehead and off the slope of her nose. "Your father isn't lost. He's just ... away. Working. He's finding us more food to eat. He will be back, little goose."

The girl's gaze drifts upward from her mother's face. Catches on mine. She stares straight into my eyes and opens her mouth to speak.

I jerk forward, heaving, and my head slams against Tansy's warm side. She moves and I tumble to the ground, the pail crashing over, milk spilling across the straw.

My hands and knees sink into the mud, and I breathe as if I've run for miles, my lungs burning. With every gasp my skin becomes a desert, my tongue as dry as sand.

"Mama," I whisper.

This time I welcome the bottle shoved into my hands, the fire that fills the empty spaces as it burns down my throat. Deward helps me sit up, pulls me until I am leaning against the wall of Tansy's stall. He crouches beside me, holding the vessel to my lips as I gulp more of the spirits.

Tansy whuffles worriedly at my hair, but Deward pushes her away. She chews her cud, watching us.

"What did you see, Evra?" Deward asks, when my breathing has slowed and my hands aren't shaking quite so violently. I still feel so unbalanced. So sick and stretched thin. Will it always be like this?

"I—I don't know. It wasn't so much like a dream this time," I say shakily. "More like a memory? But I don't know whose. All I saw was a little girl. A little girl with her mother." I almost run my hand across my hair but stop when I notice my fingers are coated with mud. "What do you think it means?"

"I don't know." Deward glares intently at his hands, as if trying to recall a memory of his own. "All last night I tried to think, tried to remember everything Father taught me about the Clearsee magic. I know he said it would be harder at first, but that it's possible to learn control. He said the spirits would help, and the visions would become clearer with practice. He talked about Clearsees seeing the future, the past... receiving riddles they had to solve." He takes a deep breath and shakes his head, frustrated with himself. "Telling you it's a riddle does you no good in solving it." He stands up, his hands clenched at his sides. "I'm sorry, Evra. I think his knowledge was more about surviving the magic than interpreting it. Maybe he knew more.... I wish I did."

I stand up too and hug him around the belly. "Thank you for trying. What *I* care most about is survival, anyway." *I'm sure the king will feel differently*, I think to myself. *But perhaps the visions will make sense to him. Surely he has the context I lack.*

Deward nudges a muddy chunk of straw with his boot. "You've wanted magic so much, Evra. You've worked so hard. Are you pleased you've been given this gift?"

This magic is not the flower-floating, dish-washing kind I yearned for. This magic rides me as if *it* is the master. I have no power over when the visions come or how they will weaken me.

"Gift?" I meet Deward's eyes. "This magic feels more like a curse."

CHAPTER NINE

———— ❖ ————

ANNALISE

*A*s soon as Burke is finished speaking to me, I return to my room and fall into bed, unbothered by the sunlight pouring across my pillow. At last, *at last* I sleep.

I wake with the memory of my mother's voice in my ear.

Where have you gone?

My lady lost, my lady lost

Two lines of a lullaby she sang to me as a child. Just those two lines, and the soft, warm timbre of her voice. A dream clings to the edges of my mind, but I can't seem to grasp it. *I want it back I want her back.*

Without her, I am lost, as lost as the lady.

"Lady Annalise, it is time to rise," Sybil speaks softly above me.

With an inner sigh, I open my eyes. The light has changed. Dimmed. The day is almost gone.

"King Alder has requested your presence at a meeting with his advisors," Sybil says. "It begins shortly."

My back creaks as I slowly sit up and pull the covers away.

Sybil makes a small noise of dismay. "Your legs, my lady."

I look down to find my bare legs covered in scratches, some deep and crusted with dried blood. I yank the blanket back over them. I'd forgotten....I was so tired, so dry of magic I didn't tend them. I didn't think—

"I'll—I'll call a healer," Sybil says, backing away.

Her golden hair, braided and curled into buns behind her ears, catches the morning light. As she turns, the sunshine also illuminates her ivory cheeks and the wash of fear in her pale blue eyes. She has only been my maid for a few months, since I suggested to Prince Kendrik that the king's grandniece should really be housed in the family wing of the castle. I chose her as my maid because she is quiet, polite, unobtrusive, and pliable.

"Please don't," I say, my gentle tone masking my panic. I hold my hand out to her. For a split second, before she schools her expression, she stares at it as if it were a snake.

Her hand trembles in mine as I draw her to the edge of the bed and urge her to sit beside me. She perches like a frightened bird, ready to fly away.

"I know I'm strange," I begin, still linked with her, hand to hand. "I see the fear in your eyes. You don't know how to explain me to yourself—especially now, these past few days."

"Your Highness, you owe me no explanations." She bows

her head, her calloused fingers tensing in mine. I think she wants to pull away.

I put my other hand over hers. Gently. The touch of a friend.

"I've been leaving my room at all hours. I've been coming back dirty and disheveled. I've sent you away when I should have needed your help. I've eaten little. I know you notice all of these things."

"It is not my place to wonder."

"But you do. You're human, Sybil. Of course you wonder. You're a good girl, so you do it in your own mind. You don't spread gossip or talk to the other servants about me."

At this, she looks at me. "I would *never*."

I pat her hand. "I know."

Slowly, the magic slides from my hands to hers, like a poison but sweet. Slowly, she relaxes.

Soon, she trusts. There are webs there already, webs I've threaded through her mind and heart. She has trusted me before, and now she will again. I strengthen our bond, her regard for me, her loyalty. I, too, relax.

"I know your value, Sybil. I know you're the best handmaiden in the entire castle."

She blushes and looks at her feet again. Her body drifts a little closer to mine. She no longer looks like she wants to flee.

Should I go a little further? I hate to, but I need her support, her eyes and ears, now more than ever. "I know you will do anything for me," I say, squeezing her hands.

She nods, a small, dreamy smile touching the corner of her mouth. "Yes, Your Highness. Of course I will."

"You'll tell me any rumors you hear."

"Yes."

"You'll keep our discussions—and my activities—to yourself. You'll not speak of unexplained scrapes, or anything else. I know you can be discreet, can't you, Sybil?"

"Oh yes, Your Highness."

I shift, still holding her hands, until I am kneeling at her feet. "I will be queen of Tyne one day. And a queen needs those she can trust, true *friends* to help her keep her kingdom safe. I need you to help keep me safe too. Can you do that?"

Sybil meets my gaze, her eyes glinting with a whisper of gold. The magic sinks until only pale blue remains. "Yes, my lady," she replies. "I can do that."

A sudden swell of emotion fills my chest, pressing against my lungs. A little breathlessly, I add, "You should know, Sybil, that everything I do—*everything*—is for the good of this kingdom. I promise to be worthy of your faith."

I know it isn't faith that makes her nod, looking a little dazed. But I choose to believe there's a little bit there, buried deep. When I am queen—the prospect is still so new it sets my heart racing—none of this will be necessary. I will give the people what they need, I will treat them with respect, and they will love me for it.

With a final, friendly squeeze, I release Sybil's hands.

I stand up, brushing a hint of moisture from the corner of

my eye, not quite a tear, and turn toward the weak streak of sunlight that runs across the floor.

"It's time I get ready," I say. "The king is waiting."

Sybil helps me change out of my rumpled dress into something heavy with brocade. Fit for the woman who will be queen.

Tyne hasn't been ruled by a woman in a century. King Alder and his advisors don't look pleased at the prospect. They barely acknowledge me as I enter the circular, tapestried study. It's smaller than the king's receiving room and less adorned. This is where they meet to discuss affairs of state, and it looks it. The table is piled with books and maps, all lit by low-hanging lamps filled with bright, magic-made fire. Unlike in the Great Hall and receiving rooms, here the king's guard waits outside.

Advisor Burke shows me to the seat at King Alder's right hand. His own place is at the far end of the table, as befits the youngest member of the council.

The rustle of my dress sounds loud in the face of their pointed silence.

The king's countenance is more animated this afternoon—I can feel the echo of magic on him. But even with the strongest magic workers at his disposal, time is time. He is buying himself comfort only. No one can give him more days, not even me.

I would happily give him fewer if I could.

"General Driscoll, your report," King Alder begins, inclining his head toward the only other woman in the room.

General Driscoll is probably in her forties, with coiled black hair pulled into tight braids and harsh lines across her forehead. She doesn't wear the burgundy robes of the other advisors, instead dressing in uniform. Years ago, King Alder demanded the woman's presence in Ironwald because her magic made her particularly skilled at logic games. He parlayed that into military strategy, using her preternaturally clever tactical assessments to strengthen Tyne's borders and subdue dissent within.

She has always frightened me. Of all the king's advisors and sycophants, she seems the most likely to find me out. *Her* mind, unlike those of the men around her, is very difficult to influence.

"Your Majesty," she says now. "I've sent out two units to search for Prince Kendrik. I'll inform you at once when I have news."

The king nods and gestures for her to continue. It's hard to decipher his feelings about Kendrik's "abnegation," whether he's angry, heartbroken, or suspicious.

General Driscoll continues, "Thieves have been preying on travelers just beyond the city. Two bodies were found this morning. Throats slashed, their belongings gone. The Laughing Feather Inn has petitioned repeatedly for protection. I can send men to guard it and other inns in the area, try to catch the criminals, and dissuade others from following suit."

King Alder rubs his forehead with a trembling hand. "Send four men, no more. There are always thieves."

My stomach clenches. Only four men? What will they be able to do?

General Driscoll's mouth tightens and she looks like she wants to argue, but the king continues, "What about the rumors of rebels hiding in the Winterlands? What of that?"

General Driscoll clears her throat. "I'm still waiting on confirmation. There's some disagreement about whether they're rebels intending to threaten you, or merely families wanting to avoid sending their magic workers to the city."

King Alder's lips thin. "Either way they're a threat."

"I will have more information within days," General Driscoll replies.

Rebels in the Winterlands. This is the first I've heard of such a possibility. I know some have tried to flee Tyne altogether, though General Driscoll's border patrols make that difficult for those who are being sought by the king. But hiding within the kingdom? Banding together? A little thrill races through me.

"Inform me as soon as your scouts return," King Alder orders. He shifts his gaze to Advisor Niall. Veron and Niall are the oldest in the room, next to him. Both hide their expressions behind heavy beards, Niall's stark white and Veron's black peppered with iron gray. "Niall, what about the magic worker in Spire Falls? Will she come willingly?"

Niall glances at his fists, clasped together on the table. "She is reluctant to leave her village, Your Majesty. She has a large family, far more than could accompany her to Ironwald." He glances up, the wrinkles around his eyes deepening. "Shall we offer more?"

King Alder stares at him. "Offer more? Ridiculous. Tell her if she doesn't come willingly, she'll get nothing at all. This isn't a negotiation."

Niall bows his head. He doesn't argue, doesn't disagree. The rest of the advisors are silent. Veron shifts his glare from me to the table.

"Spire Falls needs its strongest magic workers." My voice is so soft and raspy I hardly recognize it. Burke and Advisor Halliday at the far end of the table don't hear me.

But the king does.

"What did you say?" He turns to me, for the first time acknowledging my presence. If looking at a bug under his boot could be considered acknowledgment.

My blood burns, fiery as the magic coursing through me. Part of me wants to back down, apologize, keep my mouth shut. But isn't this the moment I've been waiting for? To speak up and wield the power I've been building? Up until now, being silent was smart. It was watching, waiting. Learning. Sending out my threads of suggestion, weaving my webs. But a queen can't be silent. If I want the king's advisors to take me seriously, if I want the kingdom to see me as the real, true, and legitimate heir, I have to begin now. I have to speak *now*.

I raise my chin even as my hands, hidden in my lap, tremble.

"Spire Falls is a poor village far from the trade routes to Maadenwelk and Greenbriar. It has little farmland and harsh winters. The woman you wish to remove from her home is reluctant because she knows it will endanger her community. No amount you offer will be enough, and force will only make her want to run."

King Alder's face drains of color, followed closely by a flush of red. "Are you *questioning* me?"

Advisor Burke stands up. "Your Majesty, I think what Lady Annalise was trying to say—"

I stand up too and raise a hand. Burke falls silent. I don't want him to twist my words into something palatable to the king. I've held so much in, I've seethed in silence for so long. I didn't come to the castle to simper at sweaty courtiers. I didn't come to be married off to a man from another kingdom.

I came for this. I came for my mother, and I came for Tyne.

"I'm not questioning you, Your Majesty," I say. "I'm offering insight from my time outside the castle. You pay the best magic workers of the kingdom to live here, though your money is a sore substitute for the forced separation from their families. And it's not *your* money, really. It's the taxes you raise year after year on an already-suffering people. They suffer without the magic workers who could keep their homes safe and their crops thriving. And they suffer in poverty. It's no wonder they resort to thieving. It is a dangerous cycle you have created, Your Majesty."

King Alder stares at me with death in his eyes. Not his, mine.

I've gone too far. He'll throw me out of the room. He'll

find another distant cousin, one who'll lie meek under his thumb.

But I will not go without a fight. Wisps of magic snake up my arms, providing me the illusion of stature, an air of intimidation. After years of studying him, biding my time, I've made the gamble that showing the strength of a ruler will impress him. I cannot back down now. So I push even further. I let a little of my anger show. "Your advisors do not serve you well, if they do nothing but sit in silence. I know I am not the heir you wished for, and perhaps you'll depose me or kill me for my honesty, but I will not lie to you, Your Majesty."

I will not let you destroy Tyne.

King Alder's face is a powder keg with a lit fuse. He will explode, he will rant and rave, he will threaten to have my head on a pike. But I've shown him that I am more than an empty vessel. I am more than a body to be shipped to Maadenwelk.

And his advisors know it too. The silence around the table is different now.

Even so, the goal is not to *actually* get myself killed. I lean toward the king and gently cover his hand with mine. Softly, soothingly, I add, "I know why magic is so important to you, Your Majesty. I am not saying you give up. Only that you don't burden your people *so* grievously. There are many who have leapt and will leap at the chance to serve you here in the castle. Take them. Leave the others be." My anger is snuffed from my voice like a candle's flame, and no one can see the smoke. I use my magic to do the same to King Alder. So many threads to strengthen, so many tendrils of thought to twist to my own use.

He laughs, suddenly, and Advisor Halliday jumps.

"You're just like your mother was," King Alder says, patting my hand in a doddering way. But his expression is calculating. "Quiet and then *snap*."

I bow my head. "She would have told me to hold my tongue, Your Majesty. I miss her guidance."

A sharp pain pierces my chest. *I breathe it in invite it in hold it in hold it close.*

I miss you, Mama.

With a whisper of heavy brocade, I sit back down in my chair.

"The woman in Spire Falls," the king says thoughtfully. "Offer her more, as you suggested, Niall. But *if* she refuses, do not force her. Lady Annalise is right—there are others who will not turn their noses up at our gold."

It's a larger concession than I expected. A bubble of joy expands in my chest.

I have likely saved the woman's life.

King Alder moves on with other business. The feast in a fortnight's time, the search for the prince. His advisors say no word to me, and I don't break into their conversation again. But my ebullient mood persists. I've only changed one woman's life; I shouldn't let it go to my head. But it feels so good to have helped, especially in the face of my mistake with Prince Kendrik. There's a hint of vindication in this moment, and it's making me heady with relief.

Advisor Burke gestures to me to wait as the others file out of the room.

"What is next on the agenda?" I ask, practically bouncing on my toes. "Dress fittings? Practicing my signature for royal decrees?" I hope it's table manners. I'm famished.

Burke glances toward the doorway. When he's satisfied we're truly alone, he says, "That was a pretty line, about not lying to the king. But if your aim is to build trust, you'd be better served by earning the respect of the council. We're the ones actually leading the country."

His stern tone does little to chasten me. I clasp my hands together and rest them against my voluminous skirt. "And you were all appointed by the king, were you not?"

When he nods slowly, I raise an eyebrow. "Why should I worry about earning your respect when I can appoint my own advisors?"

Instead of responding in anger, the corner of his mouth quirks. "Well, you don't have to worry about earning *mine*. You articulated, very clearly, my concerns about the king's priorities. But he is old, and ill, and there's no need to antagonize him. The rest of us know how to give him what he needs and protect Tyne at the same time."

"Do you?" I cock my head to the side and think of all that's happened—all I've seen—in the past few years. "I believe you're giving him what he *wants*. I've seen very little protection of Tyne."

He takes a step closer, and suddenly the air between us holds a different sort of charge. "What do *you* want? I've been trying to work it out."

Burke doesn't speak or act the way I expect him to. He, like most men, uses his presence, his body, to communicate, but he lacks Count Orlaith's wolfish lies and Prince Kendrik's gawky earnestness. I examine his face, my fingers ready to touch him, my magic ready to influence, and search for the trap. It's usually in the eyes, and by extension the hands, so easily used as weapons.

He meets my gaze, and I'm not prepared for the admiration I find there.

Heat climbs up my throat. I clear it awkwardly. What has he asked me? I've forgotten. I'm certain I'm misreading this moment, but I'm flustered nonetheless.

"Lady Annalise?"

"I—" And suddenly I remember what he asked. *What do you want?*

I harden my expression. "Advisor, what *I* want is to make Tyne safer. I didn't grow up in Ironwald—I grew up in a village just like Spire Falls. I know what a hardship the king's obsession is."

"He lost his son and daughter-in-law. He almost lost his grandson. Surely his desire to have the best magic workers here to protect the royal family isn't hard to understand."

"But his job isn't *only* to protect himself."

Everyone wants me to be sympathetic. To understand.

I do.

The king suffered a loss. And then he used his power to make everyone else lose too.

"What did Prince Kendrik think?" I ask.

Burke runs a hand through his hair. "The prince…I don't know what the prince thought. He didn't speak of his parents, and I wasn't here to know him before. You know"—he looks away for a moment, his jaw clenching—"I didn't grow up in Ironwald either. It was my uncle's idea to bring me here. I was reluctant too."

"You are eager enough now," I counter.

He chuckles softly under his breath. "I am eager to mitigate the damage. But I have little power. The king doesn't listen to many, and certainly not to me."

It's a strange echo of what Prince Kendrik said, about wishing his grandfather would listen to him.

"How much did they offer you to come here? To change your whole life?"

He looks away. "They didn't offer, they commanded."

An icy finger draws a line down my spine.

The soldiers who came for my mother didn't offer either.

CHAPTER TEN

EVRA

*M*ama lays out a deerskin on the cart's bench and sets another over the rail for us to cover our legs with. Tam hops up as I turn to give Deward a hug. Now that the moment is here, it's moving too quickly. I grasp at threads—it's been hours since my last vision, maybe they've stopped, maybe I don't have to do this.

I don't want to do this.

"You'll have to sing to Tansy," I say. "She'll worry at first. She doesn't like change, and—"

"She'll be well, Evra," Deward says gently. "Don't fret about us. And try not to worry about yourself either. There could be good in this, you know. Some Clearsee stories have happy endings."

"*I* can't think of any," I sniffle into his shirt. His arms tighten around me, and for a moment I let his calm, his safety, seep into me. Deward's the reason the sidelong glances and frowns never truly bothered me—I never doubted that he would defend me, love me, to his last breath. If I told him about Ronan, he'd probably say I should have cut deeper.

"I'll miss you," I say.

"And I, you, baby sister."

Reluctantly, I pull away. Hagan is drawing out of Mama's arms—her admonitions to be careful follow him as we switch places. Mama squeezes me tightly and too briefly, setting me back, hands still on my shoulders, so she can look me in the eye. Her expression is sharp as steel. "You have the power, Evra. This is *your* magic. The king is in *your* debt. You must remember that. You are not a magic worker forced to the castle. You are going of your own free will. You can ask for things, you can negotiate. Make him let you come home to see me." Her voice cracks, and her face too, and I see beneath the hard words to the raw misery underneath. She pulls me close again. Her head comes up to my shoulder, my frame solid and sturdy compared to hers. I use it to hold us both up.

Too soon, Hagan and I are climbing up beside Tam, Hagan is taking the reins, and Gobber is trotting away from Mama and Deward, away from our small house, away from all I've ever known. As we clatter down the narrow, rutted road, I force myself to keep gazing forward. If I turn around, I'll break, I'll cry.

I won't go.

Tamsin puts her arm around my shoulders. I'm wedged

between her and Hagan on the narrow bench, piled with deer-skin and encased in my heavy woolen cloak, and yet sneaking fingers of cold still nip at my cheeks and nose.

My heart pounds in time with Gobber's hooves, my head full of questions and fears.

I've never been farther south than Hutchins, the next village. We conduct most of our trade to the east. The land goes flat and sandy beyond Weeping River Lake; the farms of Windhaven provide much of the grain and corn for that region. To the south and west, between Windhaven and Ironwald, the soil is richer, and there are many small farm holdings dotted among thick swaths of forest.

The road we follow is lined with tall silver birches. We see few other travelers: the public carriage, black and hulking; a rickety cart pulled by the slowest, oldest horse I've ever seen; a courier dressed in king's red, whose eyes constantly scan the path and woods as his horse races past.

Head turned sideways, I gaze past Tamsin's profile, into the gaps between the trees. The play of sun and shadow gives the illusion that the dark is running—that it is a living thing, pacing us. I shiver, hand drifting to my knives.

"When I was little, during the Sickness," Tamsin says, "Mother told me a Clearsee was awakened when the kingdom was in danger of succumbing to the darkness. She said as long as the Clearsee magic slept, there was still light in the world. It made those days when everyone was sick and dying, when the king started forcing all the best magic workers to Ironwald, seem a little less terrifying." She pauses. When I glance at her, there's a deep furrow between her brows. "Is it really worse now than it was back then? How can that be?"

My fingers claw into the tops of my thighs. "I think the Clearsee is—I think *I* am supposed to stop the *next* darkness from coming."

"So it's not worse now...it just *will* be? *Could* be, if you don't tell the king what you see?" Hagan asks. "That's a lot of pressure." He snaps the reins along Gobber's back, hunching forward a little. I think we'd all like to outrun this truth. This responsibility.

"But I don't know what the threat is. What I've seen... none of it makes any sense." The cold bites at my cheeks, and the shadows run with us.

"You've had two visions and a dream," Tam says. "You saw the king dying, a wolf, and a little girl. Anything else?"

Father saying *blood cannot lie.* And: "Someone screaming, I heard someone screaming." I'd almost forgotten. I don't know why I can't bear to mention Father.

"Is it a riddle? Do all the pieces add up to one truth, one threat to King Alder and Tyne?" Hagan asks.

I shrug. The jerky ride is giving me a headache. But the pounding in my head—*is* it the cart, or another vision coming on? I touch the bottle of firecane strapped to my hip. I have always trusted my body—without magic to rely on, my muscles and breath and blood are all I have. I don't want to question each new sensation.

"You said a wolf was sitting on the throne," Tamsin muses. "That seems pretty clear. You know, 'a wolf at the gates.' The question is what the wolf represents. What the actual threat *is*."

"Maybe King Alder will know," I say with a grimace.

"I've always thought *he* was the greatest threat to Tyne," Hagan says, echoing my own thoughts.

I'm a farm girl—I count failure and success in ears of corn, buckets of milk, sheaves of wheat. I've no idea what forces might menace the king.

The conversation stumbles. For a time, the only sounds are the thud of Gobber's hooves and the rustle of wind among the dead leaves. At some point, Hagan gets tired of the uncomfortable bumping and spells the cart for a smoother ride. I brace myself for another vision, for that sickening lurch as reality falls away, but it never comes.

When the sun sinks below the trees, Hagan breaks from the road and leads us down a rutted cart path into the forest. "It's not so cold tonight. We should make camp and sleep outside," he says, the first words anyone has spoken in hours. "I think we'll be safer if we stay away from the inns. Too many stories of thieves."

"Too many women for you to guard properly, you mean?" Tam asks with a little smirk. "You know we can protect ourselves."

I try a grin, but my mouth is chilled and stiff, just like my legs.

"I think we'll be safer," Hagan says simply.

"We don't want anyone asking questions about why we're traveling," I say by way of agreement. We could lie, of course, but keeping to ourselves seems the easiest option. It's not as if people will be happy to hear a Clearsee has awakened.

Hagan stops at a small clearing with a scrub border. Branches interlock above us, revealing slivers of the darkening sky. There's a charred hollow in the center of the clearing; the space has been used as a campsite before.

We climb down from the cart on creaking legs. Tamsin groans as she presses her hands into her hips and stretches backward, chin to the sky. Hagan unhitches Gobber and turns him loose near the tree line with a small pile of hay. A few quiet words of magic keep him from wandering off.

"I'll find water." I grab a couple of empty leather flagons from the cart. Over the wind, I can hear the quiet gurgle of a stream.

Tamsin reaches for her bow and quiver of arrows. "I'll find dinner."

"I'll start a fire," Hagan answers.

Flagons in hand, I pick my way through the line of scrub. The land is quite flat here, with a shallow slope down to the stream. I find a private spot to relieve myself and then continue down to the water, which runs fresh and cold. I look for fish, but the fading light isn't bright enough to illuminate anything beneath the surface. For a moment I sit on my haunches, listening to the meaningless babble of the water. The journey has been smooth so far, the weather chill but clear. Two nights, and we'll be there. The stream shimmies over the rocks, gig-gles along, whispers *pay attention.*

I stand up jerkily, and the water sounds like water again. Hugging the damp flagons to my chest, I hurry back to our camp.

Hagan has the fire burning merrily when I break the line of trees. A few minutes later, Tam returns with a skinned rabbit and a grin. We trade off—Tam to magic the water pure and clean, and I to spit the rabbit. Soon we're stretched out around the fire as the rabbit cooks, its fat sizzling and spitting. This feels so like one of our hunting trips that tears come to my eyes.

"Did you have any more visions today?" Hagan asks as he sets another branch on the fire, sending sparks up into the darkness. Night has come, stealthy and swift as one of Tam's arrows.

"No. I wonder if maybe I do have a touch of fever. How silly if we're making this journey for nothing." But the voice of the water lingers in my ears, the screams of the figure at the far side of the lake, the king's face peeling to the bone. I know how empty my words are.

Tam stares into the fire. "Do you have to wait for the visions? Can you call them up?"

"I don't know." I rub my hands over my face.

Hagan bumps my shoulder with his. "I think you can. Father said a Clearsee can learn to control the visions. And you've always been a quick study."

I push him back. "This isn't a dagger lesson. It's—it's in my mind. And it's not a comfortable experience." I suppress a shudder.

My eyes catch on the dance of red flame and white smoke, veiling and revealing the black and glowing orange of the burning wood. What if King Alder expects me to have visions on command? What if he tries to force me? "Maybe I should try. You know...see if I even can."

"We're here," Tamsin says quietly.

"Give me the firecane," Hagan murmurs. "I'll be ready."

I can feel them share a look over my head as I comply, and I want to be annoyed, but I take a deep breath instead. The fire draws my eye, like the rhythmic motion of Hagan's knife yesterday. I start to lose focus. Like the water, the crackle of flames almost sounds like a voice, almost sounds like Father...

Stare into the fire and let your mind wander. The visions will come when you are able to lose yourself. Breathe...

Losing myself is the last thing I want to do. But perhaps it's better to let the visions in when I choose than to wait for them to claim me.

Inhale. Exhale.

Slowly, with a sustained, concerted effort, I relax. The voice changes.

The crackling of the fire becomes breathless laughter, and a hiss of rabbit fat turns low and menacing, almost like a growl—

The fire winks out, like a star obscured by sudden, invisible clouds. And the black is, for one tortured moment, endless. Infinite. Then the king's hall flashes into being around me, empty and vast, lit by torches and a blazing fire in the massive hearth.

At the end of the long room, on the royal dais, the great golden wolf paces. A woman in a beautiful gown stands before the throne, facing me. She wears the king's crown, with its twisted gold, and her face is pale as a corpse's. Every time she moves to sit, the wolf growls and snaps at her.

The woman heaves a deep breath, her crimson dress rippling, and lowers herself onto the throne in a rustle of silk and petticoats, her expression determined.

The wolf roars.

She grips the golden arms of the chair so tightly her hands look like talons. When the creature leaps, she screams.

With a bellow of thunder, the room splits apart, lightning blasting through the ceiling to pierce the floor in a shuddering explosion of stone and flame. Wrenching against some invisible force, I throw myself to the ground—

And land in darkness, curled on my side. The cacophony of destruction is replaced with my own heaving breath and the quiet crackle of the cook fire. Sharp edges of dead leaves press into my cheek. A whining gust of wind blows through the trees, sending a burst of ash into my face.

Hagan helps me sit up and guides the small blue bottle of firecane to my lips. My throat burns. The dry places fill almost immediately.

"Well, that worked," I say, my voice shaking only a little.

"How do you feel?" Tam asks. She's clinging to my wrist and squeezing so tightly my fingers are going numb.

"Rattled." I try to calm my breathing. There's a faint rumble in my ears, as if the building is still crumbling around me.

"You screamed a little," Hagan says in a strangled way. "But it's good—it's good, right? You were able to call up a vision."

I swallow a little more of the firecane to clear my throat. "I saw a woman wearing the king's crown, sitting on his throne. The golden wolf attacked her. Then the castle fell to ruin all around me."

"So the king is soon to be replaced?" Tamsin suggests hopefully.

"By a strange woman who is then attacked by a wolf?" My eyes burn at the smoke from the fire. Weariness seeps into my bones. Perhaps that's what Father was speaking of: bloodlines breaking. But: "The castle falls, Tam. I don't think the vision is showing good news. I've seen nothing of use."

"You don't know *what* you've seen." Hagan pulls the spit with the rabbit from the fire. "Until we get to the castle, until you speak to the king."

My stomach twists, thinking of the shuddering ground and the great blocks of stone that fell, ready to crush me. The slow, rhythmic hammering has started again at the back of my skull. "I wish I *knew* helping King Alder will help Tyne. What if saving him from whatever this threat is just makes it worse for the rest of us? I don't want to make things worse."

Hagan hands the stick with crispy, cooked rabbit to me, so I can eat the first bites.

"In all the stories," he says, "the Clearsee serves the kingdom, not just the king."

"It's okay to be terrified," Tam says softly. "I am. But isn't it better to know, so we can stop the darkness, whatever it is?"

I shiver. Staring into the void beyond the fire, I see again the wolf growling, the king's castle crumbling to dust.

"What if I can't?" I whisper into the dark.

CHAPTER ELEVEN

ANNALISE

I can't escape Burke's words.

They didn't ask. They commanded.

After a fitful night, plagued by memories that have become nightmares, I move through the motions of the day. By afternoon, I'm shaking with exhaustion. Another restless nap, and when I wake, I pace my chamber, waiting.

Finally, the castle quiets. I dress in dark clothes and slip to the kitchens. The chef and her staff work nearly all hours, but there is a small window after the evening dishes are cleaned and the meat is brined and before the bread is kneaded and left to rise, and it is in this window I sneak inside. I shove a haunch of venison into a burlap bag and steal away. Out the back gate, out to the abandoned spring house. Out to the invisible barrier that keeps all living things from crossing. In the distance, in the darkness, the prince-turned-creature growls.

I heave the sack into the clearing before the small, ramshackle cottage without crossing the barrier. The growl becomes a snarl. It's too dark for me to see clearly, but the moonlight catches in his eyes and makes them glint and snap. I stand for a long time listening to the prince's desperate frenzy of hunger. I send my magic seeking, searching out weaknesses in my containment spell. As I strengthen it, I try to strengthen my own resolve.

I stare up at the moon, cold and white and eternal. "Mama, I miss you," I whisper, just to hear her on my lips. She was a healer. She'd be appalled at what I've done to the prince, to the people in the castle. "But they killed you, Mama," I whisper to the moon. "You deserve justice."

You mean revenge, I can almost hear her answer. "That too," I agree. "You deserve revenge as well." *As so many of us do.*

"It is so hard without you," I tell her in the stars.

"I miss you every day," I say, pulling the darkness close.

"Without you, I would not be here." Would I be with her?

You know what you have to do. She speaks out of my memories. The words were spoken in our kitchen, with bread dough resting on the table and my hands in hers, floury and warm. I do know.

I have to change Prince Kendrik back.

For Mama and her memory. For myself, so I can be more than King Alder, who doesn't see the worth of one life.

But I don't know how to undo magic of this magnitude. I don't know if the attempt will kill him. I pray if it doesn't, I'll have enough power left to convince him to abnegate for real. The suggestion will be easier if the inclination is already there. I need Kendrik gone, but if I let him live like this, we will both be monsters.

I plant my feet as close to the invisible barrier as I can. Kendrik is still busy with his meal, hunched and panting. I let my magic spark. The wild comes willingly, springing along my arms, pooling in my fingers. I close my eyes, envision the prince as he was. It would be easier if I could touch him, but I know the beast won't let me near. I reach my arms out, point my gold-veined fingers.

I *will* Prince Kendrik to be as he was. *I sink into the fire the light let the wild do its will.*

With a wind rush and a smell like scorched earth, the magic leaves me. A knife of lightning splits the night in two.

Kendrik howls.

I fall down hard. My head tips back, mouth open, breath a useless wisp. My eyes are useless too, shocked white and staring.

Silence falls before my eyes adjust. I strain to hear a voice, a shout, a sign that Prince Kendrik has returned to himself. But it never comes. When I can see again, it is clear my magic has done nothing, *nothing*, but cause the prince pain. He lies on his side, panting and whimpering. I don't know if he can move. *I have injured him have I killed him?*

I turn and run.

Tears stream down my cheeks, burning like fire.

I tried. *Mama, I did.* Didn't I? Did I want to fail? Why wasn't my will enough? Would it make a difference if I had touched him? The questions follow me, consume me. And the one I can't escape, that I am not quite ready to accept:

Is my only answer really his death?

How often can I sneak out at night to leave slabs of meat? It won't be long until someone catches me or notices a thief plaguing the castle. And my magical boundary won't hold forever; it's only been two nights and it's already begun to weaken, needing reinforcement.

This can't go on. It's no life for Kendrik, and it's too much for me. I will need my strength for the battles to come. Burke may be pleased with me, but the other advisors will need convincing. The kingdom will need convincing.

And the king has weeks left, at most. I can feel the light, the life beyond pulling at him. This is a different kind of magic, one with echoes. Once you've been close to it, you can recognize its shape in others. Like a stone thrown into a quiet lake, death has ripples, arcing ever outward.

I see ripples everywhere.

By the time I reach the gate, I have answered my own questions, and what I must do has become as clear as it is agonizing. If Kendrik lives through whatever I did to him tonight, I will have to kill him. I will have to fully own my horrible mistake.

Oh, Mama. You would know how to save him.

I sneak through the castle on silenced feet, listening to the echoes, the ripples, the promises Death sings. Planning. Praying.

Begging forgiveness in whispers no one will ever hear.

CHAPTER TWELVE

EVRA

𝒜 violent red bleeds across the sky. I am standing in a field of grass, green and fresh as summer. Before me on the ground, a man lies curled on his side. The memory of a scream fades in echoes I'm not quite sure are real.

This is a dream. This must be a dream. And yet I'm compelled to kneel beside the man—he shifts slowly, coming up to sit with his arms heavy over his knees and his back bent, as if his body aches. But he is young, my age maybe. His golden hair hides his eyes but not the pallor of his face, the grimace that twists his lips.

"Are you well?" I ask, before thinking to wonder if I have a voice in this place.

He makes a noise, not quite a groan but certainly not a word, in response. His clothes, deep purple velvet and fine gray wool, hang in tatters. He is a stranger to me, long-boned and a little gawky, handsome if his amber eyes weren't ringed in purple shadows and his mouth weren't tight with pain.

The red of the sky is draining away, like a sunset or a sheet of blood. It's difficult to tell if night or day is coming. The stranger's face falls into shadow.

I wait for him to give me a riddle or a word of warning, like Father did. Perhaps he'll speak more of lies and blood.

"Who are you?" I ask at last, when he says nothing.

He picks at a rent in the knee of his trousers. "I've been trying to remember."

A jolt of doubt runs through me. What kind of vision is this? What insight can he give me if he doesn't even know his own name? Could this be some kind of test?

"What are you doing here?" I ask, even though I am the interloper, appearing in a place I've never seen before.

"I—I don't know. I don't know what's happening to me." His voice is rough and quiet, and he looks up, pleading. "Do *you* know?"

I study him, the open fear in his face. I don't think he's trying to trick me. But that doesn't mean all is as it seems. The air isn't normal air here; it holds a hint of shimmer around his edges.

The silence stretches. The ground stays solid beneath my feet. How long will this dream last? Why are there no castles crumbling or wolves howling? It is so quiet.

Perhaps I haven't found the right questions or answers yet.

I sit down beside him in the grass. "I'm Evra."

He stares at his scuffed leather boots. "I was about to say I don't feel like myself, but how can I know, when I don't know who I am? How can it all be gone? Name, memories, why I'm here...I don't know anything."

"I don't know *why*, but I think I know *how*," I offer. "I am...well, I am a Clearsee." The word still tastes strange in my mouth.

"A Clearsee has visions of the future and can speak to the past," he says suddenly, and my blood freezes.

"How do you know that?"

He shrugs, looking uneasy. "I don't know. The words were there. Beginning and ending in themselves. I don't even really understand what I said."

"Are you from the future," I ask, "or the past?"

"I don't—"

"—know. Right." I shake my head a little. Panic is unspooling from the base of my spine and threading itself around my belly, tightening inch by inch. I force myself to remain seated, casually twisting a piece of grass between two fingers. This vision is lasting much longer than the others, and I don't know how to make it end. And what if I *can't*? What if I'm stuck in this dream state with this stranger forever?

"What else have you seen?" He leans back, his hunched body loosening, limbs unfurling. If he stood up, he'd be tall. His feet and hands look like he hasn't quite grown into them yet.

"Mostly things to do with the king," I say. I wonder if he's here to help me make sense of my visions. Maybe... "Are you the ghost of another Clearsee?"

His big hands dig into the ground on either side of his hips. "I suppose I could be. I must be *something*. There must be *some* reason I'm here. Right?"

A Clearsee can speak to the past....

The past. Ghosts. Like my father. Like this man. I have so many questions, am in such need of guidance. But how can a Clearsee with no memories help me? Perhaps I will be here, trapped in this dream, until I figure it out.

I wish it was my father, here with me. I could be at peace trapped with him.

"What should I call you?" I ask, tamping down the grief. It is an old pain, worn soft around the edges, but still there every day.

He rolls his head back slowly, stretching. Thinking. "Call me Nothing. I have no memories, no knowledge, no name. I am nothing. No one." The gaze he gives the sky is bleak. He is lost, so obviously, entirely lost.

My heart clenches. He knows enough to understand what he doesn't have, just as I do. Did. My lack of magic made me useless. Ronan made me feel like nothing.

"I'll call you Foundling," I say firmly, "for I have found you. And you are *not* nothing."

He turns to look at me, his hands loosening their grip on the green grass and black dirt beneath him. He opens his mouth, and the world goes fuzzy. Whatever he says, I can no longer hear him. My body is rushing backward, out of this place that feels so real, into a darkness that feels like sleep.

But something else, something new, creeps in.

Low, menacing laughter. A flash of narrowed eyes. The choking scent of burnt onions.

I fly into a crouch on top of my bedroll, knife in hand. Freezing sweat slicks the back of my neck, and my heart pounds so hard I can feel my pulse in my temples. Quickly, I take two big gulps of firecane. That last moment before I woke up, there was a threat, something—

No one is here.

My eyes sweep our campsite for danger. The moon's glow and the dying fire are enough to reveal the two humps of Tamsin and Hagan on the ground, and Gobber's peaceful, tail-flicking slumber. Tonight, our last night before we meet the king, we are camped at the edge of a fallow field, the forest at our backs.

All is quiet.

But the scent of burnt onion breath still lingers in my nose. My hand clenches the hilt of my throwing knife. It isn't the man in the field. He gave no hint of danger. This is someone else....

I creep to Hagan's side. Bending close to his ear, I put my hand over his mouth at the same moment I whisper his name. His body jerks beneath me, then freezes, his blue eyes blinking. As soon as I'm sure he knows it's me, I remove my hand.

"What's wrong?" he breathes.

"I don't know. Something," I whisper back, driven more by instinct than conviction. My mind is a whirl. I want to stop and think about the dream, about the stranger who spoke to me. But there isn't time. My heart hammers *danger*, my magic-sense says *pay attention*.

Hagan starts to sit up, then stills. I hear it too.

The crunch of leaves.

Gobber lifts his head and I pray he won't make a sound. I would ask him to keep silent if I could. I flick my eyes from Hagan to the horse. He understands. His lips move and Gobber stays quiet.

The footsteps are louder now, quick and syncopated. At least two people.

I reach out and grip Tamsin's arm. She wakes and moves to stand up, eyebrows raised in question, but I shake my head, finger against my lips. Hagan touches his ear and Tam sits still, listening.

The footsteps halt and then resume, slower. The newcomers, whoever they are, don't speak; there's no sound save the faint whisper of leaves and the momentary, mournful hoot of an owl.

In silence, we stand up, hands on our weapons, and spread out across the clearing.

The footsteps turn furtive, creeping.

The sound thunders in my ears as my eyes strain for signs of movement. A chill breeze electrifies the skin at the back of my neck, each sensation clearer, more intense than the last. My hand remains steady on the knives at my belt, but the rest of me feels raw. Exposed.

Moonlight streaks the tall, black trees around us with silver, flattening the landscape. Without warning, a branch cracks as it falls into the ashes of the fire, sending up a small explosion of sparks. I jump. Gobber whinnies, broken from the silencing spell.

A Hagan-shaped darkness leaps for the horse. A man and woman burst into the clearing on a wave of bitter onion. I swallow a gag.

Dead leaves and sticks pop and rustle as Hagan grapples with the man. The woman lunges toward our packs, but Tamsin lets loose an arrow, grazing her side. She howls in pain.

"Back away," Tamsin growls, toweringly tall and steeled of spine, another arrow fitted to her bow. "Your throat's my next target."

Quiet as a shadow, I slip behind a tree. The thieves haven't seen me yet. A throwing knife in each hand, I watch the fighting, waiting for my chance, pulse hammering in my ears.

The woman eyes Tam narrowly; she doesn't drop her dagger.

Hagan's breathing is loud but steady as he twists and parries, driving his opponent ever farther from Gobber, who snorts and shifts nervously.

I hold my breath.

Suddenly, Hagan groans. Tam's eyes dart in his direction, fear blossoming, and the female thief barrels into her, knocking her on her back.

Then she laughs—the low, malicious sound I heard in my

dreams. She's got Tam pinned on the ground, her bow useless. Hagan is on his knees, panting. The man wrenches Hagan's dagger from his hand. Hagan's lips move, probably trying a spell, but nothing happens. The immense magic needed to change a man's will has been lost to our land for generations. Even the attempt makes Hagan's face go gray.

Both bandits are swathed in worn cloaks, the tattered edges hanging like torn spiderwebs. Their shaggy, unkempt hair masks their features, but I can see the dull gleam of teeth as they share a nasty, satisfied smile.

These criminals will feel no qualms about killing us.

Before either has time to move, my knife flashes silver and buries itself in the shoulder of the woman. She roars in pain, and then shrieks a full octave higher when Tam knees her in the stomach. Hagan ducks away from the blade at his throat, hands reaching for the thief's wrist.

The man's mouth is still open in surprise when I let the second knife fly. With a muffled thump it lodges in the back of his hand. He drops his weapon and cradles his hand to his chest, wailing. Hagan snags the knife and silences him with a sharp blow to the head with its hilt. The man crumples and falls, nothing but an unmoving shadow on the ground.

Another crack echoes in the clearing and I spin, a third knife in my hand, to see the female thief falling face-first at Tam's feet. Tamsin stands over her, her bow brandished like a club.

"Hurry." She heaves the woman onto her back and yanks

my knife from her shoulder. Even in the dark, I can see a faint movement as the woman's chest rises and falls.

It isn't until Tam and Hagan return my knives and I clean off the blood with some leaves that I realize my hands are shaking.

Moonlight illuminates the path as Gobber pulls us through the night. The hood of my cloak falls back, and even though the wind bites at my cheeks and numbs my ears, I don't want to let go of Hagan's and Tam's arms to fix it. The cart jerks beneath my aching legs.

"How did you know?" Hagan asks, his breath warming my ear for an instant before the wind flings it away.

"It was the Clearsee magic. I think." My teeth chatter as I gulp the frigid air.

The realization dawns as slowly as the brightening streaks of light along the horizon. I had a vision...*and I averted the danger.* Those thieves would have killed us in our sleep. But the Clearsee magic warned me in time.

Maybe—maybe this magic *isn't* just about helping the king. Maybe it will help me protect those I love as well. For the first time in days, I smile into the wind.

The dream, the stranger come back to me. My Foundling, the former Clearsee. Maybe I'll see him again. Maybe next time, now that I've proven myself, he'll have the answers I seek.

See? I will say, smiling confidently. *Neither of us is nothing.*

In the distance, a wolf howls.

CHAPTER THIRTEEN

ANNALISE

$\mathcal{I}$pick at the poached eggs and fresh warm bread on my plate. Around me, the female courtiers of the castle gossip and argue in polite undertones while servants refill goblets and plates of pastries. The ladies' breakfast room is warm and close, with a roaring fire in the hearth and heavy tapestries on the walls, and yet a cold draft has found my feet. I work my toes in my pointed boots, flexing and releasing, to keep them warm. Usually I am busy listening, influencing, using this time to solidify my place and learn more about the politics of the castle. But I can't stop thinking about Prince Kendrik. My magic, so much stronger than it should be, has never failed me before. It has never not been enough to satisfy my will. Until last night. Until I left the prince whimpering, still inhuman, and ran away.

Was it my magic that was too weak? Or was it me?

A servant pauses by my elbow and says quietly, "Advisor Burke wishes to see you."

I stand up too quickly, grateful for a reprieve from my thoughts, and hurry to the hall. Burke is pacing, his robe swirling about his legs. His hair is a bit more disheveled than usual, and there's a distraction, a desperation to his expression that puts me immediately on edge.

"What's happened?" I ask. And, to protect myself, I add, "Has the prince come home?"

Burke runs his hand through his hair. "No, it's not the prince. General Driscoll's scouts have returned. She's about to brief the king on the rebels. We must go."

I fall into step beside him, my stomach flipping. "So there *are* rebels? She's sure?"

"I believe they're refugees more than rebels, personally," he says, without looking at me. "But yes. There is an encampment in the Winterlands. I fear what the king will do when he hears."

"You don't think those people should be punished?" I ask. Somehow, I can't imagine his uncle, Advisor Veron, sharing his concern.

"I do not." He looks so worried. Without thought, I reach out and touch his hand.

The gesture startles him so much he pauses mid-stride. I move to draw away, but his fingers have tangled in mine. I panic. Send a thread of suggestion, just a little something to make my touch not unwelcome, something to reduce the awkwardness of this moment. I pull away, gently, and bow my head.

"I apologize, Advisor. I merely sought to show my agreement. I too believe the people hiding in the Winterlands should not be harmed."

He looks at me for a long moment. "Even if the king lets them be, they'll freeze or starve by spring," he says softly. "The people of Tyne should not be so desperate."

It's disconcerting, hearing my own feelings expressed by someone else. I thought I was the only one in the castle who cared. Did I somehow put that thought in his mind? No... no, I don't think so. Belatedly, I realize I've been staring into his eyes, dark brown and ringed by thick black lashes, for too long. I duck my head and continue down the hall.

We arrive at the king's study just as King Alder is helped into his chair by Advisor Halliday. He doesn't wait for the rest of us to sit before asking General Driscoll for her report.

"Your Majesty, it is as we feared," she says, her words dragging. "A group has settled in the wilds to our north, between Graceridge and the Winterland Pass. My scouts say they number maybe forty or fifty people. Children, families... they've been trading game for other necessities in Graceridge."

Slowly, as she speaks, King Alder's eyes go cold. "Forty or *fifty* people? How many are skilled magic workers?"

"I don't know, Your Majesty. We believe there are at least three whom you've already sent for, ones who had fled before your emissaries arrived at their homes. There may be others. There was... a barrier of some kind. Only strong magic could have built it. It prevented my scouts from entering the camp." General Driscoll speaks dispassionately, as a soldier, but there's a tightness to her features that suggests a deeper emotion roiling underneath. It's impossible to tell what that emotion is—distaste, discomfort, distress?—but I note the subtle repetitive way she rubs her fingertips together at her sides, almost a nervous tic. She hasn't sat down. She stands at the edge of the table, her spine stiff.

"Did your scouts try to access the camp by force?" King Alder asks, his voice strong in anger.

A thread of ice knits itself to my spine.

General Driscoll says, "They tried several times at several points. They said it appeared weaker when they split up and attempted to cross the barrier at different places in tandem, but they were never able to breach it completely."

I think of the invisible cage I made for Prince Kendrik. How I left him, still and sparking from my magic. Did he die? Will carrion birds overtake the barrier to feast on his corpse? Or does it reach impossibly high, beyond even where birds can fly? My stomach twists at the knowledge that I do not know.

"Can weapons pierce the barrier?" Advisor Veron asks. His quill scratches against a piece of parchment as he makes a record of the meeting.

"One of my scouts said his arrow bounced back harmlessly."

"Unacceptable." The king curls his hands into fists on the table. "I will not allow such treason. The camp must be routed."

Burke clears his throat. "But, Your Majesty, respectfully,

the families are not a threat. It could hardly be considered treason to withdraw into isolation."

"Are they paying taxes?" King Alder growls.

General Driscoll shakes her head. "They would not let my scouts approach. Their apparent leader, a man named Liam, said they had claimed the land and would defend it if necessary."

I can't seem to take a full breath. Burke's chin sags, his mouth disappearing into his beard. Claiming land...that *is* treason. And it doesn't matter that it's the king's fault. It *should*—it should matter that he's driven these families to settle in an unforgiving wilderness. But it won't. Because he's the one who'll decide their punishment.

"King Alder," I say, trying to keep my heart from squeaking out with my voice. "They may not be willing to speak to scouts, but perhaps they'll be more inclined to discuss their grievances and terms with the heir. I can go. I can negotiate with them."

"No," says King Alder, the word as deadly as a viper strike. "There will be no negotiating." He raises his gaze to General Driscoll, and it doesn't matter that he's old and doddering, or that he's shaking with age. Or maybe with rage. The command in his voice is unmistakable. "Kill them all," he says. "And anyone in Graceridge who trades with them."

"But there are children," I reply, power sparking under my skin. I want to touch him, tell him to take it back. To change his mind. But it would be too obvious now, here, in front of everyone. "You can't mean—"

"I do. Every last traitor will be put to death." He turns to stare me straight in the eye. "You will not rule this kingdom for long if you do not quash rebellions. Show your strength, or drown."

It's too late. I'm already deep below the surface and out of air. It's not my lack of strength but *his* lack of mercy that holds me down.

Die, you old man, you remorseless monster.

If we were alone, I'd touch him now and end all of this for good.

CHAPTER FOURTEEN

EVRA

The forest drops away to a flat, dead-yellow sea of farmland. At a great distance, Ironwald's walls are visible, gray and stagnant as a bank of clouds along the horizon. By the time Gobber clatters onto the cobblestones before the main city gate, twilight has arrived. Fresh torches release oily smoke and a bloodred flicker to light our way.

Two guards stand at either side of a vast archway carved out of the stone wall. Though the entry is wide enough for two carriages to pass through abreast, the walls are so thick the opening feels tunnel-like, and when Hagan disembarks to speak to the guards, their voices and the noise of Gobber's hooves echo strangely.

Tamsin slips her arm through mine when she feels me shiver. It's damp here between these walls, and the smoke of the torches clings at the back of my throat. I swallow a cough and try not to think of small, dark, suffocating places.

"My thanks to you," Hagan says as he climbs back onto the cart bench, moving slower than usual. Our fight with the thieves and today's urgent pace have left us all weary; even Gobber's head droops.

One of the guards trots into the tunnel toward the city. The other raps twice against a door carved into the stone archway, summoning another pair of guards to stand at attention. Then he nods to us. "Follow me."

As soon as we are free of the heavy wall, sounds and smells heave over me in a giant, frantic wave. The screaming laughter of children. The stamp and snort of horses. The sharp competing scents of waste and woodsmoke. It's suppertime; few people straggle on the streets, but voices eddy around corners and slip through empty alleys nonetheless. Squat houses rub shoulders, yawning over the narrow road. Everything is gray: gray stone, gray cobbles, gray sky.

I search for the riches King Alder's magic workers have no doubt wrought among the people of his city. Here, so close to all that skill and power. But these homes are scuffed and broken, just like those in Windhaven. That woman there, her face is as gaunt as Old Marnie's. Several men sit crumpled against the stone walls, their clothes a filthy mess of rags.

A sudden, lengthy yowl drowns out the clank of dishes and rumble of voices, and two squalling cats tumble and leap from roof to roof. Gobber snorts nervously, the whites of his eyes flashing in the gloom.

"Shh, shh. Hush, you great pony," I whisper.

Hagan also plays at a calm he doesn't feel—he sits too still and stares straight at Gobber's withers, as if afraid to turn his head. Tamsin's hands clench in her lap. My heart races faster and faster the closer we get to the king.

Will he deign to see us? What if he doesn't believe me?

Tam's stories are little to go on. She has always spoken of the ridiculous clothes, the gossip, and the courtiers who try to flirt with her. She prefers the awkward boys, their joints loose as marionettes when they dance, to the paunchy, red-faced widowers. Worst are the handsome men made insufferable by their vanity—and white face powder, which clogs her throat when they bend to whisper in her ear. Because of Tamsin's beauty, the fact that she's merely a steward's daughter and not a true member of the court is often overlooked when it comes to her matrimonial prospects.

But she has said very little about the king over the years. Perhaps because he was old, even when she was a child at her first feast day, and therefore of little interest.

I wonder if he will be taciturn and frightening... or frail, as he seemed in my vision.

As we move through the city, the houses grow in stature, the architecture finer and, in some places, hidden by ivy. It's a comfort to see something living and green among the cold stone. Along one doorway, I even catch a glimpse of red: small, bright holly berries. There are no men in rags here, and the streets are clean. Perhaps this is even where the magic workers live.

As twilight darkens into night, candles glow warm and

golden through warped-glass windowpanes, throwing wavering rectangles of light across the road. Above us appears the first faint twinkling of stars.

Deward and Mama are probably sitting down to eat. I can see them so clearly, their faces warm with the heat of the kitchen fire after the chill outside. Their voices soft—I hope not too worried—as they wonder how we are faring. In the barn, the hens will be roosting, clucking to themselves, and Tansy will sigh, her thick, velvet lips slack as she dreams. Has Mama had trouble milking her? Tansy can be ornery when I'm not there to sing her favorite songs.

I think about the thieves that accosted us in the night. They won't be the only ones roaming the countryside. As the weather turns frostbitten and harsh, those with nothing will get more desperate. And villages like Windhaven have lost more than our best menders to the king. We've lost the harm warders who used to travel from village to village setting up protective spells, the blacksmiths with preternatural skill who forged the sharpest weapons, and the stormseers, who could warn us of dangerous weather. I try to tell myself Mama and Deward will be safe, that they can protect themselves, that Deward's rudimentary wards will be enough. I wish I could use the Clearsee magic to protect my family, and forget about the king.

The thicker, more solid darkness of the castle rises before us. I straighten, though the muscles in my back ache, and strive to put Mama, Deward, and home from my mind. I need my wits about me now that we're finally here.

The guard leads us past a final row of houses to a wide well-tended lawn, beyond which the castle's moat and outer wall curve. Iron bowls of orange flame light the way to the castle gate. The magic fire's uniform color and smooth undulations throw unnatural shadows along the frost-tipped grass. The castle's carved edifice climbs beyond the flame into darkness.

"Evra," Hagan whispers, his voice colored by the same awe that swells in my chest.

If the castle was built to intimidate strangers at its gates, the long-dead architects were skilled indeed.

Gobber's hooves clop hollowly against the wooden bridge that spans the moat. When we reach the castle wall, two men in leather tunics appear, flanked by half a dozen soldiers. One of the soldiers approaches our guard and whispers something in his ear. I hold my breath.

At last, the guard turns to us. "King Alder is waiting."

My heart gives a great thud. The guard gestures to the two men in leather. "They will tend to your horse. If you'll come with me?" He pitches it as a question, but it's obviously a command. We disembark on sore and shaking legs. I try not to stare at the grim faces of the soldiers waiting behind the guard.

The grooms grab Gobber's bridle and lead him away. I envy the lucky beast, with a warm stable and grain and rest before him. For me, the real trial is about to begin.

"Weapons?" The guard reaches out a hand.

Without a word, Hagan hands him his dagger. Tam points to the cart, where bow and quiver lie. My stomach sinks. I hesitate for a moment, hand resting against the cool comfort of my throwing knives, before removing the thick leather belt.

"Will we get them back?" In this vast and unfamiliar place, I feel the lack of my weapons like the lack of an arm.

The guard doesn't answer my question. I search for some sign of condescension or distaste, but his eyes remain blank. No curiosity. Not even distrust. He gives away nothing.

"This way." His light armor clanks when he moves; I hadn't noticed over the sound of hooves.

We follow him through the castle gate, the silent soldiers falling into step around us. The inner ward is large and yet oddly claustrophobic, surrounded by looming gray stone. Birds chatter and swoop above us, their black bodies caught in the flickering light of torches. Their moving shadows make me dizzy.

The feeling of enclosure is much worse when the guard ducks into a doorway, leading us down a narrow, damp passageway, lit at long intervals by the strangely constant magic fire. Hagan walks ahead of me, Tam and the soldiers behind. I can't shake the sense that I am a prisoner being marched to my death.

Hagan stops short and I bump into him with a muffled *whoomph*. A heavy door screams on its hinges. Now we are climbing endless spirals of shallow stairs, on and on into the darkness. I can hear the huff of Tam breathing, the clank of the soldiers' weapons behind me. I feel the chill of the curved wall against my trembling fingers. My foot catches on a stair and I stumble, banging my knee against stone. Hagan turns and reaches down to help me up.

And still, we climb.

When I was seven, shortly before the Sickness came, Hagan dared me to lower myself into the village well on the bucket used to retrieve water. He'd gotten it into his head that sprites lived down there, on the surface of the water and in the crannies of the well's stone walls. He said it had to be me who checked if he was right—he was too big. But I was too.

The rope had broken with my weight, and the bucket had spilled me into the black depths. I'd plunged into the icy water, clawing desperately at the rough walls, finding no purchase. It had taken nearly an hour for Hagan to run screaming for Father and for the villagers to find a rope long and sturdy enough to haul me out.

In that hour, I saw no sprites. I saw nothing but the suffocating darkness. Felt the walls squeezing tighter, squeezing all the air from my lungs as I waited for my arms and legs to give out. As I waited to drown.

Hagan had been mad with fear, so frantic at the thought of me coming to harm that he was ill for days afterward. Father's silent disappointment hadn't helped. I couldn't be angry. But I never forgot the snakelike constriction of those walls. The terror.

Here, now, the dank air presses against me in just the same

way, like a physical thing, so thick and heavy I can barely breathe. The sound of my wheezing becomes loud, heaving itself against the close, solid walls. Going nowhere.

My nails scrape against rough stone.

My steps falter.

I can't—

Above, another scream of iron.

Candlelight stretches a comforting glow toward my face.

I push upward, stumbling in my desperation. I can't seem to breathe, and black spots are dancing across my vision, threatening to swallow the brightness radiating from above.

Suddenly we are all free of the dark, endless stairs. I'm so relieved I bend over my knees and draw gasps of air into my lungs, ignoring all else. Tamsin reaches for my hand. She squeezes it tightly, she holds me together.

"Evra," Hagan says at last, low in his throat, as he touches my shoulder.

The air in this room is warm, a little smoky, and edged with the sharp, clean scent of beeswax. I take one last, deep breath, eyes closed.

I have survived seventeen years with no magic. And every one of Tamsin's schemes and Hagan's stupid dares, even that horrible day in the well.

I straighten, shoulders back. I can survive an audience with the king.

CHAPTER FIFTEEN

ANNALISE

$\mathcal{B}$urke stands with his chest puffed out, his right hand held up and his fingers curled, as if holding an invisible chalice. He says in a sonorous voice, "As heir to the throne of Tyne, I will bring honor to the people, up—"

"The ones who haven't been murdered," I mumble under my breath, but he hears me anyway.

"Lady Annalise," he warns. We've been practicing since supper finished in the Great Hall. Servants still bustle around the room, clearing the long oak tables and sweeping up the floor.

In answer, I hold up my own invisible cup. "As heir to the throne of Tyne," I say loudly, as I have several times already, "I will bring honor to the people, upholding this great nation's laws and values. I will serve the king in his wisdom until such time as it is necessary for me to fulfill the duties of queen. I accept this responsibility with great humility." I curtsy deeply toward the empty throne.

"And then you drink from the chalice," Burke instructs. Again. "King Alder will talk about Prince Kendrik some, I'm certain, but the focus will be on you, Your Highness."

"And then I'll be expected to dance with all the important men," I say, sighing inwardly. Once the ceremony is over, it's just another ball. Another swirl of silk and sweaty palms.

"No," Burke says shortly. "You will not dance. This is a precarious time, with the prince abandoning the throne. Wolves will circle, looking for weakness. There will be no talk of courtship, nothing of that nature, until your position is more secure."

His answer surprises me. As the heir, marriage to a man of relatively little consequence like Count Orlaith was out of the question. But I assumed King Alder would at least attempt to shackle me to someone else. Perhaps someone he saw as more fit to rule the country.

Excitement washes through me. This was a battle I expected to have to fight.

"So . . . no dancing." I almost can't believe it.

Burke's beard twitches. "Are you disappointed?"

"Definitely not," I reply, smiling a little.

For an instant, our eyes meet. I think, suddenly, of rich melted chocolate, a river of it, warm and smooth. His eyes are the same color, hold the same warmth. And, maybe, a hunger. Burke turns away abruptly. "Do you need to practice again?"

I clasp my hands over my elbows. Draw myself back inside.

"No." I knew my part of the ceremony an hour ago. "I want to talk about the Winterlands."

He glances at the servants again, and then nods to the stone archway leading to the corridor. We head for the more private spot.

"I spoke to General Driscoll," he says. "She's concerned as well, but she's had a direct order."

"Does it matter that the heir would give a different one?" I ask quietly. "Isn't there anything we can do?"

"As I said, it is a precarious moment." The dark circles under his eyes speak as loudly as his words. "She said it will take time to get the troops and provisions mobilized. That we have perhaps a fortnight to convince the king to change his mind."

I could do it in seconds, but not without raising suspicion.

"What can I do as heir? Will I have any recourse once the ceremony is complete?"

We've spent the last two days working on my manners and the ceremony itself, but we haven't talked about what I'll actually *do* as heir. Will I have the power to issue my own orders?

"Not so long as the king lives." Burke still isn't looking at me, glaring instead toward the last few servants putting the Great Hall to rights. The faint scents of roasted duck and woodsmoke find us in the doorway. Within the two massive hearths at either end of the room, the fires are burning low, letting the early winter chill creep inside. Gooseflesh rises along my bare arms. My gown, a pale green that's supposed to bring out my eyes, leaves too much of my skin exposed to the draft. A shiver seizes me.

"So my job will be standing at the king's shoulder looking miserable, like Prince Kendrik." The last comes out before I have a chance to reflect on how disrespectful it sounds. So I add hastily, "I hope he is safe. I hope he's at peace with his decision." I can't bring myself to lie and say I hope he changes his mind and comes back. I'm the only one who knows he can't.

Burke lightly kicks the stone archway. "Publicly, you'll do what the prince did, although hopefully with less misery. Privately, we'll continue our lessons. The other advisors and I will prepare you as well as we can for what happens when... after..." His voice trails off. He doesn't need to say it.

When the king dies.

It was so simple, in the end. I still can't quite believe I will become queen.

Loud footsteps ring on stone. Advisor Veron is striding toward us, his face set in hard lines. "Burke, I need to speak with you."

My heart trips and sputters. There's an urgency to the older man's movements, his voice. Something has happened. And I think I know what it is.

They've found him. It. The prince. Or, the fleeting voice whispers, *the king has died.*

Veron doesn't spare a glance at me, all of his attention focused on his nephew. When he reaches us, he bends to whisper something in Burke's ear.

My magic leaps inside of me, bursting full and electric to the surface of my skin. What do I have to do to stop this? To stop them? My stomach twists. My blood pounds *danger danger danger*. The wild is rising.

When Burke glances at me, a deep furrow has appeared between his brows.

A touch. That's all I need. I don't want to hurt him, but I can't let him learn the truth about me.

"Excuse me, Your Highness," he says, as I step toward him. "I'm needed in the receiving room. We'll continue your training later."

Before I can reach out, before I can breathe, Burke and Veron have left, and I stand alone, magic writhing uselessly in my veins.

I lift my skirts and hurry in the opposite direction, toward my bedchamber. I pass a few maids and servants in the halls, and the whispers follow me. *Something has happened, something is happening*, they seem to say. Rumors travel quickly in the castle.

I ring for Sybil as soon as I reach my room. I pace. I listen to the rising thunder overhead. I brush my fingers along my arms, feeling the magic spark to my call. How do I use this? What do I do?

At last, Sybil arrives. I close the door behind her and turn, my eyes burning.

"What has happened?" I ask. "I know something has."

A monster has been found, I expect her to say. Or, *They know what you did*.

Sybil scratches the edge of her jaw. "The king has a visitor, Your Highness."

"A visitor?" Not a monster?

Sybil nods. "Claiming to be a Clearsee."

The blood drains from my face.

A Clearsee.

I wrap my hand around Sybil's wrist and try not to squeeze too hard. "The king is seeing this man in the receiving room?"

Sybil nods, her eyes wide. I bind her to me more, just a little magic, just a little thought *but it's hard to control it's hard not to let the wave break over me.*

She sucks in a ragged breath when I release her.

A Clearsee in the castle.

What might this man have seen? What can he expose about me?

As a crack of thunder rattles the windowpanes, I flee my chamber and make for the receiving room.

I have to know. I can't fight what I don't know.

CHAPTER SIXTEEN

EVRA

I open my eyes to a large chamber, its stone walls lined with dark wood paneling and golden-threaded tapestries. Thick ivory rugs muffle the sound of Hagan's shifting feet, and the room shines with the glow of many candles. It is more beautiful than any room I have ever seen, even in Tamsin's house.

King Alder presides from an ornately carved wooden throne in the center of the room. He so closely resembles my vision—wrinkled skin and long, curling white hair—that I freeze, waiting for the horror of his face to peel, the room to run with blood. But his face stays quiet, his head cocked slightly, and no yellow wolf appears. Instead, other horrors lurk in his eyes, in the careless, powerful set of his mouth. This man has left his own country defenseless. He left my father defenseless.

His advisors stand at attention behind him, all wearing burgundy robes, thick beards, and stern looks except one: a woman in military garb. Her look is worse than stern. It is suspicious.

The soldiers who followed me up the stairs take their places behind me. My neck prickles, knowing they are cutting off any means of escape.

"Your Majesty," Hagan says, "I am Hagan Orenson, of Windhaven. This is my sister, Evra, and Tamsin Bellweather, the daughter of Windhaven's steward." He bows, and on my other side Tam curtsies deeply. I quickly dip into my own curtsy, which involves some wobbling and a slight listing to the right.

"I'll help you with that later," Tam murmurs under her breath. There is little occasion for a farmer's daughter to curtsy in Windhaven. As I straighten, my hands brush my dusty, travel-worn trousers. How does Tamsin feel in her own hunting gear, when she is used to wearing gowns to formal events? Is she embarrassed? Should I be?

I run a nervous hand through my tangled hair. Beside me, Hagan completes his bow. His eyes are bright. Somehow, he manages to exude the same relaxed energy with which he began this journey. He smiles, and only I can see the hatred curling in the tight corners of his lips.

"So." King Alder leans forward, his golden robes shimmering in the candlelight, and stares at Hagan. "You're a Clearsee." He has the phlegm-filled voice of an old man, but his eyes miss nothing.

I clear my throat and take half a step forward. "I am, Your Majesty."

His incredulous laughter creaks like rusty hinges. "You? But you're a girl."

I can only shrug.

The humor drops from his face. "Come closer, dear. Let me see you," he says, like an old woman in a fairy tale.

With a quick sidelong glance at my brother, I step forward. My hands grasp at my waist. I miss my knives. Is the guard who took them still here? They all look the same.

"Why, you're little more than a child," King Alder says. No one has called me a child in years, not since I grew taller and stronger than most of the boys in the village and learned to defend myself. King Alder nods at me in a kindly, doddering manner. Is he trying to put me at ease? This is not what I expected. And it's not working. His eyes are too calculating. "Where did you say your home is?"

"Windhaven, Your Majesty," I reply.

He raises a brow. "Interesting. I was not aware the Clearsee family had settled so far from the city." He gives me a considering look. I wish I'd had the chance to at least wash the dirt from my face. "Well, then. Evra, is it? Now that we've completed our introductions, if you would be so kind—"

The door behind him flies open, thudding against the wall. A young woman enters, the skirts of her pale green gown swishing madly. Her brown hair is pulled up into an elaborate coiled braid sparkling with jewels, a style that accentuates the sharpness of her features. Her eyes narrow when they find mine, and for a moment I am trapped within her piercing gaze. She looks familiar in a way I can't seem to place.

"Is it true?" she asks. "Has a Clearsee come to the castle?"

One of the advisors hastens to her side, whispering in her ear. She turns and murmurs back, angrily enough that I can hear. "I am the heir. I should *know* about these—"

"Enough." The king doesn't raise his voice, but the woman falls silent nonetheless. He doesn't look at her, doesn't address her at all. Instead, he smiles at me.

A shiver slides down my spine.

"Evra, this is Lady Annalise, my niece's daughter. She is— well, she is our new heir to the throne. The prince has, sadly, abnegated, and left the castle to pursue God knows what." The speech starts lightly, but King Alder has sunk into a quiet rage by the end. He is obviously boiling at his grandson's betrayal.

My own mind stutters to a halt. The prince has abnegated? Why have I not heard of this? Why did the Clearsee magic not *warn* me? "Your Majesty, I am so sorry, I—"

He holds up a hand. "If you are indeed a Clearsee, your insights could be very valuable. What have you seen?"

Lady Annalise steps closer to the king's throne. "But how do we know—"

He turns to her at last with eyes like burning coals. "We do *not* know. That's why I am asking questions. Silence, girl. You are not queen yet."

Lady Annalise takes a step back, her cheeks flushing. The

mix of panic and determination in her eyes frightens me. She twists her hands into her skirt as if holding her own legs back. From what, I don't know. Fleeing? Attacking me? The air around her practically sparks with tension. Her reaction is so strange that for a moment, I can't remember what I'm meant to be doing.

"Evra?" The king looks at me oddly. "Please proceed."

"Your Majesty." A fine tremor runs along my fingertips. My heart is beating too fast. Everyone is staring at me, waiting. I feel as I did in my last year of school, when the teacher would make each of us stand before the class in the tiny, cold schoolhouse and practice the small spells and magic she taught. "Just *try*, Evra," she would say impatiently. "It's so *simple*. You're too old to have *nothing*. You're just not trying hard enough!" The little ones would watch me, eyes wide, worried for themselves. What if *their* magic didn't come? The older girls tittered, most behind their hands, but the really nasty ones openly. Tamsin never laughed, of course. But it was Ronan who—

The Clearsee magic swells within me, shattering the memories. It sends me no visions, merely presses itself up into my chest and outward toward the king with an urgency that sets my teeth on edge but calms my trembling hands.

Yes, yes, all right. I remember. I breathe deeply, pushing back against the alien force.

The words come, halting at first. "A few days ago, I had a vision.... I saw you, Your Majesty—" I swallow, my voice cracking. "You were on your throne and there was a great yellow wolf with glowing eyes beside you...and then...well, you died." The king's encouraging smile stills, frozen upon his face. My gaze drifts to Lady Annalise and suddenly I know her. *I know her.* "And another vision, of...of Lady Annalise. I didn't know who she was then, but now I can see it....I recognize her. She was trying to sit on the throne, but the wolf wouldn't let her. It was there, snarling at her. And then...and then the castle crumbled to dust."

There's a sudden, soft intake of breath; Lady Annalise's eyes are wide and her face deathly pale. For a moment, the air tightens and I brace myself for—something.

King Alder steeples his fingers and leans forward. "What do these visions mean? Have you seen my grandson?"

"I'm sorry, Your Majesty. I have not seen the prince." I don't dare shrug. "And I'm not sure what the visions mean. I thought...I hoped they would make sense to you."

"If you were to guess?"

"I—" If I guess and am wrong, will he have me killed? Perhaps merely tortured, so I can still tell him of future visions. He has been known to use similar methods on other magic workers. I must choose my words carefully. "I have no way to be sure, Your Majesty. But it seems that this wolf is a threat to you and your family in some way? Perhaps there is some danger to your throne?" Though how a wolf can threaten a kingdom, I have no idea. Oh, why couldn't I have seen something *useful*?

For a long time, the king says nothing. Beside him, Lady Annalise has turned away from me to glance back at one of the king's advisors, the youngest one, with a thick dark beard and careful eyes.

Hagan and Tamsin stand so still and silent I may as well be flanked by statues. I want to reach out, feel the reassuring warmth of their hands closing over mine, but I'm afraid to draw attention to them. Whatever my fate, whatever the king decides...it will be *my* fate. I won't let them suffer for this curse.

Lady Annalise moves closer to King Alder and says quietly, "A wolf, Your Majesty. It could be a Grim."

He twists to look at her, his head moving sharply. "Grims are black. She said the wolf was yellow."

"A Grim?" I've never heard the word as an *it*. As a thing.

King Alder moves one shoulder in an approximation of a shrug. "A black dog that represents death. Clearsees used to see them often before battles or when their leaders were ill. But the dog is always black." He cuts his gaze to Lady Annalise.

I bow my head. Embarrassed. "I thought—" I glance at Tam. "I thought perhaps it was a wolf at your gate, as it were. Some kind of threat. I'm sorry. I know very little about this. The visions are very confusing."

The king waves a frail hand. "There are books in the royal library you may read."

I resist the urge to wring my hands. "Thank you, Your Majesty."

A tightness creeps into his features, and he asks again, with that same quiet, simmering anger, "You are sure you've seen nothing of the prince?"

I think of the figure across Weeping River Lake, who screamed in pain. And of my Foundling, the former Clearsee, likely long dead and a ghost, same as my father.

I shake my head miserably. "I'm sorry, Your Majesty. Not yet."

"Well, then." King Alder clears his throat, and I can feel his dismissal coming on a wave of wary disappointment. "You and your companions must be exhausted. How rude of me to question you without first offering food and a place to rest."

I glance at Hagan, whose brows rise in surprise.

"I must speak with my advisors about these... developments. Please. Refresh yourselves. Sleep after your long journey. In a week and a half's time, we will host a ball to announce Lady Annalise's new role as the heir to the throne of Tyne. You will be my honored guests for this affair." He pauses, his breath rasping.

"Thank you, Your Majesty," I reply. This time I bow; a curtsy really doesn't work in trousers.

"And, Evra, dear." His weariness does little to steal the sharpness from his eyes. "Please inform one of my advisors at once when you have another vision."

"Yes, Your Majesty." My stomach sinks at the thought. I've done my duty, I've told the king. But it doesn't end here, as much as I wish it did.

The female advisor in uniform beckons us to the door through which Lady Annalise entered. I say a small prayer of thanks that I won't have to descend the dark cave of a stair-well we used to reach this room. As I pass her, Lady Annalise brushes my hand.

The instant she touches me, the air fills with flame.

Oh no, not here, please not here—

The room falls away.

I blink against the featureless night.

Before me, a star appears. No. The tiny pinprick grows, wobbling, into the uncertain flicker of a candle flame.

With each breath I take, its gleam brightens. Soon, I'm sit-ting in a small, wavering circle of light. Terror clogs my throat, tasting of ash and blood.

Across from me, at the edge of the darkness, my Foundling appears. He stands this time, and he is tall, as I suspected. He has the awkward proportions of someone still growing into himself: nose a little too large, cheeks still rounded, the faint-est hint of blond stubble along his chin. He wears another set of tattered finery, this time in deep blues.

He stares at me. "It's you. You've come back."

"Do you have a message for me?" I ask anxiously. Surely now he will explain.

"A message? No. Should I?" Even the golden warmth of the candle can't brighten his expression. Sadness pulls at his face with an odd gravity, transforming his eyes into endless, dark pools and his lips into a downward crescent.

Behind him, in the darkness, something growls.

Behind *me*, the faint hiss of a bow string tightening.

"Are we safe?" I ask, fear washing over me.

He reaches out his hands, palms up. An entreaty, too far away to touch. "I don't know," he says. "I don't know. Won't you save me?"

Me save *him*?

The candle flame jumps violently, casting wild flashes of light into the darkness. The growl becomes a roar.

I reach for a throwing knife, but my belt is gone. How will I—

Someone screams.

CHAPTER SEVENTEEN

---◆---

ANNALISE

The girl—Evra—falls into her brother's arms. I stagger backward, my hands dropping uselessly to my sides. My magic bites and howls within me, like a dog snapping at the bars of a cage. For some reason, inexplicably, it could not touch her. I can feel it seething, wanting, wild.

Did she resist me consciously? Why did she swoon? Did she have a vision right here, when I touched her? Panic washes through me.

What did she see?

The Clearsee blinks, her eyes clearing. She closes her mouth and looks around. General Driscoll has taken a step toward her, and the soldiers along the far wall have drawn their weapons. King Alder watches the girl closely with his rheumy eyes. But no one speaks. The silence drives a wedge through my chest, threatening to split me open.

"Are you well?" I ask, because the not knowing is chok-ing me.

I wait for her to tell the king who I am, what I've done.

She doesn't. Instead, the girl pulls a flask from her hip and takes a long drink. Her brother puts an arm around her, hold-ing her up, and the considerate, familial gesture carves a small hole in my chest. She lowers the bottle. "More. I need more spirits. Please, is there..." Her voice fades.

Again, no one moves or speaks. So I grab a decanter off the table underneath the window and pour some amber liquid into a goblet. I offer it to her, and she takes it without hesitation. I study her face as she sips. Where is the suspicion? The hatred? The righteous anger?

Could it be the Clearsee magic hasn't yet shown her the truth?

"My sincere thanks, Your Highness," Evra says softly. The girl's voice is the only soft thing about her. Her dark hair curls wildly around her face, barely contained by a single braid down her back. Her jaw is sharp and wide, her nose a blade. Even her body is more hard muscle than soft curve, and she is tall. Taller than I am, nearly taller than her brother, who stands beside her with worry in his eyes.

The spirits seem to steady her. She pulls away from her brother's protective embrace and straightens her spine.

King Alder responds to her shift in posture, leaning back in the throne and raising his untidy white brows. At last, he speaks. "Was that—episode—another vision?"

Evra nods, gripping the goblet with both hands. "It was, Your Majesty."

"And what did you see?" he asks.

I try to calm the pounding of my heart. She's not pointing at me and screaming out my sins. Not yet, anyway.

But the wolf the wolf.

The king doesn't know what her visions mean, but I do.

"Little of use this time." She rubs a hand over her eyes and shakes her head. She looks about to cry. "The last Clearsee was there, and I heard a growl, the hiss of an arrow..."

I watch King Alder closely. He's impatient. Annoyed. Weary, as ever. But he smiles gently at this girl and says, "You've overtaxed yourself, dear. Please, rest from your journey. We will speak more tomorrow. General Driscoll, their rooms." He flicks his wrist in dismissal.

I step out of the way, hands buried in my skirt so I don't touch Evra again. The door closes with a thud behind her and her companions. Immediately, the mask of concern drops from King Alder's face.

Evra's lack of useful information is not a comfort to me. She is new to her magic—it will work differently, better, when she learns to control it. It was the same when I came to my power. She is likely frightened, frustrated. She feels out of control. I felt all of those things, and more.

Grief. Guilt. Rage.

But I can use this moment, use the doubt I see in King Alder's eyes.

"Your Majesty," I say, sending the gentlest of suggestions his way. "Can we trust this woman? She has said nothing of use, and there's never been a female Clearsee before. We all know the wolves are circling. That is not magical insight." I cut my gaze to Burke—didn't he warn of wolves?

King Alder begins to speak, but a hacking cough nearly bends him double. When he can catch his breath, he turns to Advisor Halliday. "Have you your full strength?"

When Halliday shakes his head, King Alder says, "Then send the others to my chamber. All of them."

Burke and Veron help King Alder rise. He turns carefully to me. "Lady, you of all people...should hope this girl proves... to be a real Clearsee. It's *your* future...she's here to protect." Long pauses punctuate his words.

I watch him leave the room, stooped and shaking, flanked by men younger and stronger than he is. My own breath clings painfully in my throat.

He is right. My only hope, my only chance, is to ensure the Clearsee's loyalty.

But without my magic to influence her, what can I do?

CHAPTER EIGHTEEN

EVRA

 "You can breathe now," Tamsin says quietly, eyeing the uniformed woman accompanying us. "The king believes you."

Does he? Or is he reserving judgment, waiting for me to be useful or proven a liar?

"I hope they feed us soon," Hagan mutters. Tam digs an elbow into his ribs. He catches her arm and pulls her into his side for a moment; with them it's hard to tell if they're about to embrace or start a brawl.

Our guide leads us to a small sitting room with a single tiny window, too high to reveal more than a faint hint of moonlight. A small fire burns in the grate. The woman lights a candle in an ornate sconce and heads to the door. "Wait here."

As soon as we're alone, a great sigh gusts out of me. I bend forward and drop my head into my hands. "Oh, this is too much. These visions have so little purpose! What good—"

"Shhh." Tamsin pinches my arm to cut me off. She cuts her gaze to the door, which hangs ajar by a few inches. "One thing I know," she says softly, "is that the castle walls have ears. This is not the time to speak freely."

I hadn't even considered eavesdroppers. I give her a quick, fierce hug. "Thank you for being here."

"As if I would miss an adventure with the two of you," she murmurs with a smile.

Hagan prowls the room, inspecting the brass sconces and the fine wooden furniture. I'm about to tell him not to touch anything when the advisor strides back into the room, followed by a gaunt woman in a gray dress.

"Bretta will show you to your rooms." The advisor bows and retreats into the hall.

"Come now," Bretta says, looking at us as if she's smelled something bad. Perhaps that's just the shape of her face, curled up and wrinkled like a withered peach.

"Will there be food?" Hagan asks as we follow her into the hallway.

She sniffs. "Of course."

My stomach tightens, not with fear this time but hunger. I fall into step beside Hagan, Tam behind us, as we follow the bobbing path of the servant down a long, torch-lit corridor. Narrow slits have been carved into the stone, letting in ribbons of cold, fresh air that smell of woodsmoke and snow. Relief at not having to negotiate the black, curving tower stairs again makes me giddy. "I'll cry for joy if it's duck."

"At least it won't be slop in the dungeons," Hagan whispers conspiratorially.

"Don't tempt them," Tamsin says, giving Hagan a not so gentle push.

We follow the woman up shallow flights of stairs and down others, along empty halls, and around blind corners until we are so deep within the castle there's no hope of finding our way out. Maybe she *is* leading us to the dungeons.

But no, of course not. She stops halfway down a long hall with slits for windows on one side and a line of heavy oaken doors along the other. Narrow crimson rugs line the floor. The wind has turned cold, and I try not to shiver. "Sir, your room," she says, her voice rasping. Hagan puffs up a little at being called *sir*.

But he doesn't open the door. We exchange glances. Even as guests, separating feels dangerous.

The servant's small, dark eyes miss nothing. "The young ladies will be just there and there," she says, pointing to the next two doors along the corridor.

The torch beside us flickers with my expelled breath. Hagan nods. "Thank you." He turns the knob. "Let's clean up. Then we'll meet in your room, Evra, to discuss our, uh, plans." He glances again at Bretta.

The old woman says, "I'll have the food brought to the Clearsee's room, sir," and departs before we can thank her.

At my expression, Tam says, "You're the guest of a king, Evra. For now, we have nothing to fear." It's the *for now* that unsettles me. With a little sigh, she pushes into her room. Hagan disappears into his, and I am entirely alone. The oily flames of the torch on the wall warm my cheeks, while the breeze from outside slowly freezes my back. My lungs burn as I inhale a confusion of acrid smoke and biting wind, but I stand still for a moment anyway, soaking in the quiet. It is a relief after the long journey and audience with the king.

The impatient rumble of my stomach gets me moving.

As soon as I shut the door behind me, the chilly draft from the hallway dies, replaced by heat from a big, natural fire raging in a wide stone hearth. Before it, a copper tub gleams golden red. Pale pink and yellow petals float on the gently steaming water, filling the air with the summer scent of roses. I take an automatic step closer and inhale more deeply. *Ahh* ... I haven't even touched the water yet, and already my shoulder muscles are loosening, my fingers tingling at the prospect of washing the dirt from my hair. At home, we take our baths in a tall tin barrel that loses heat almost as soon as Mama spells the water, and there never seems to be enough time to properly relax with Deward and Hagan stomping around outside the kitchen waiting their turns. But *this* bath, oh, the water smells so sweet, and the heat—

Someone lets out a small gasp.

I whirl.

At the edge of the large bed, which is piled high with rose damask blankets and feather pillows, a girl cowers behind one of its tall mahogany posts. Despite her neat white apron and dove-gray dress, she looks too young for service. Her flaxen hair curls around her wide-eyed face in an imitation of a chick's fluffy newborn feathers.

Here, finally, I find the reaction I have been expecting ever since my Clearsee magic manifested. The girl looks utterly terrified.

"What is your name?" I stand still, worried if I move she'll bolt.

She swallows visibly. "Gianda, my lady."

"And you're afraid of me." I can't bite back the small sigh that escapes. "Have you heard I'm a harbinger of doom or some such?"

She clears her throat. "They...they've been saying in the kitchens..." She pauses, swallows again. Tamsin was right. Word travels fast.

"What have they been saying?" I want to tell her I'm the last person she needs to be afraid of, that I'm so tired she could flick a finger in my direction and I'd fall over. I want to beg her to relax so I can peel off my muddy, sweat-stained clothes and slip into the hot bath. But I should know what they're saying about me. Why she looks so afraid.

Gianda whispers, "They say you can kill with your mind. You speak to ghosts and they do your bidding."

How do people think of such things? Kill with my mind, speak to ghosts... My father's face, and my Foundling, flash against my inner eye. Well, perhaps in a way Gianda's second assertion is true, though I certainly don't command ghosts to do my bidding. I offer Gianda a reassuring smile. "But surely you're too clever to believe that nonsense? Such things aren't possible."

Her clawed fingers relax slightly against the post.

I remove my cloak and start yanking at my leather vest and thick woolen shirt. "I assure you, I'm harmless. But even if I *were* able to do those things, you would be the last person I'd want to harm. After all, you're here to help me get cleaned up, aren't you? And I'm desperate for a bath." I hop on one foot while tugging on my other boot, and sneak a glance at her from the corner of my eye. My comical act has its intended effect; she releases the post and her eyes aren't quite so wide. Another ineffectual tug and she hurries to help me out of my clothes.

Before long I am sinking into the slippery, flowered heat of the bathwater, each and every muscle sighing.

I lean my head back until most of my hair is submerged and dig my fingers into my scalp, massaging until it tingles. My half-open eyes gaze languidly around the room. Unlike the king's receiving room, these walls are not paneled with wood but lined with fabric: deep purple damask. The rich color might have felt confining in a smaller room, but in such a large space, and with such a high ceiling, it adds warmth. Thick drapes hang in front of the windows, keeping out the draft. Several heavy pieces of furniture lurk along the walls; beyond these, the bed, and the fireplace, there is little else.

Gianda clears her throat. I tip my head to find her holding a block of soap in my direction. "Do you want me to wash your hair?" she asks timidly.

I smile. "I'm not used to having help in the bath." *Or anytime.* Mama still brushes and plaits my hair sometimes, when the winter months are long and we have little to do in the dark evenings but sit in front of the fire. But it is usually me braiding Mama's hair, or darning socks, or carving simple wooden bowls to sell at the spring markets. Still, I don't want to be rude. "Maybe you could help me brush it when I'm done? It's not very long and shouldn't take much time. If you don't mind?"

She looks confused—she must be as little used to serving someone like me as I am to being served. "Why, of course, miss."

I might have stayed in the warm, soothing water all night, the firelight playing against my face, but my stomach chooses this moment to remind me of its presence. I scrub away the last of the travel grime and give my hair a final rinse. By the time I'm finished, Gianda has fetched a warm dressing gown. She helps me dry off and wraps me in the soft fabric, much like Mama used to do when I was small.

Gianda directs me to sit in a chair by the fire and quickly brushes and braids my hair. A soft knock jerks me from my stupor. The maid opens the door to admit several footmen carrying trays laden with food. Hagan and Tamsin follow them in, their faces clean and hair damp. Tam is wearing a fine dressing gown as well, with rabbit fur slippers, and Hagan's changed into clean trousers and a soft flannel shirt.

One of the servants spells the copper bath, probably to lighten it, before they heave it to their shoulders and depart. Gianda curtsies to me, her cheeks pink, and follows them, but not before pointing out a cord hanging from the wall near the bed. "Pull this to ring for me," she says. And then she's gone.

Hagan crowds around the oaken table, where the food trays are steaming. "Stew," he says happily. "And fresh warm bread."

The scents of rosemary and rich wine waft toward me.

No one speaks as we savor our meal. After two days of charred rabbit, smoky turnips, and hard bread, each bite disappears in a joyful sigh.

There's even dessert—an apple tart, crusted in cinnamon, that rivals Mama's.

"Well," Hagan says at last, leaning back in his chair. He belches, then smiles sheepishly.

I laugh. For the past few minutes, I've been able to forget why I'm here. The warmth of the room, the bath, the delicious food—it's all felt like a dream. But the truth is waiting; our purpose is waiting.

"Do you think he believes me?" I ask softly, staring into the whorls of the fire.

"I do," Tamsin replies. "But King Alder has a reputation for volatility. He'll wait to see if you have more information for him. Tomorrow we should find the library, the books he spoke of. The more we know about the Clearsee magic, the more leverage you'll have."

I remember King Alder's face, the calculation. The hungry curiosity.

"He's going to make me stay here," I say. "He won't take the chance that I'm not telling the truth." I'm too tired, too numb, to do more than say the words. The grief will find me soon enough.

Hagan blusters, "We don't know that."

But we do. It's what he always does. When magic workers are brought to the castle, they don't come back. Sometimes their families join them in the city, sometimes they're never heard from again.

When I said goodbye to Mama and Deward, I pretended it was for a few days. I wouldn't have been able to leave otherwise. I know Mama told me to demand trips home to see my family, but it's clear that the king is not one to negotiate. Still, perhaps...in time...

"We're not leaving you here by yourself," Tamsin says. "My parents will be here in a little over a week anyway, for Lady Annalise's ceremony."

"Thank you." I can't imagine them leaving and me being alone here. I can't think of how much I miss Mama and Deward.

I find myself thinking of the prince instead.

"How strange that Prince Kendrik abnegated," I say. "I wonder why?"

Hagan's lips thin. "We've all been holding on to the hope that Prince Kendrik will be different from his grandfather.

Perhaps he is... but in the wrong way. You know, in the running from his responsibilities way."

"I danced with the prince at his last birthday celebration," Tamsin says thoughtfully. "He was miserable. I think the king made him dance, because I don't remember him ever doing so before. He usually stands behind the throne and broods until he manages to sneak out hours before the ball is over. I am not surprised that he *wished* to abnegate, but I *am* surprised he actually *did*."

"I wonder where he went. It doesn't seem like King Alder knows. Why would he leave the castle altogether?" It's worrying that the king is asking *me* for information.

"Out of shame?" Hagan posits. "Would you want to face King Alder with such news? I bet he's hiding out until the dust settles and Lady Annalise has been named heir. He probably doesn't want to give anyone the chance to change his mind."

Maybe it's the Clearsee magic guiding me, I'm not certain, but suddenly my Foundling comes to mind. His sad ignorance, his golden eyes. The tattered velvet of his clothes.

"Tam, what does the prince look like?"

She sits back in her chair, her hair glowing in the firelight, her legs crossed delicately at the ankle. It's strange how quickly she can shift from hunter to courtier, from my best friend to this elegant stranger. Even in my lovely borrowed dressing gown, I feel crudely built and unsuited to the finery surrounding me. I'm a rough-hewn ax in a fine silver sword's place.

"Prince Kendrik isn't as handsome or as princely as you'd

expect," Tamsin begins, and even her voice has changed, the words round and refined as they leave her mouth. "He's gangly and awkward, a truly terrible dancer. But polite and quite sweet when he bothers speaking. One time he told me a little joke about a frog and a feather....I can't remember how it went."

"But what does his face look like?" I ask, with more urgency. "Does he have light brown hair, a little shaggy, and amber-colored eyes?" I close my own eyes and try to picture the man in my dreams. "Ears that stick out a little and hands that are too big...he looks a touch forlorn, sad but kind around the eyes. I imagine he'd have a loneliness to him, even in a crowd...." My voice fades.

I open my eyes when the silence stretches longer than feels natural, when Tamsin doesn't answer.

She's staring at me, her tanned cheeks a shade lighter than usual, her dark eyes wide. "Why'd you ask if you already know?"

An invisible vise closes on my throat.

My Foundling...he's the prince.

Does that mean Prince Kendrik is dead?

CHAPTER NINETEEN

ANNALISE

As I pace my bedchamber, I yank the pins from my hair. If I can't influence the Clearsee's mind, I'll have to find another way to keep her quiet. I can't live in fear that at any moment she could see what I did to Kendrik.

I pause by the window and stare out of the warped glass. The sun set hours ago, but magic light still illuminates the courtyard. It's an easy trick—most gardeners can refresh the torchlight themselves. The magic workers in King Alder's chamber have a harder job.

He is weakening. Everyone can see it. I can feel it, every time I touch his mind.

I press my palms together, feel the power sparking there. I can convince the king the Clearsee is a fraud. He'll send her home.

No. If she's a fraud, he will have her arrested. Put into prison for lying to him.

I want the thought to bring relief, but my stomach twists. Evra is just a girl, probably four or five years younger than I am. Anyone can see she's been sheltered, protected by her family. Loved. She is scared, and lost, but she is no criminal. She is nothing, except a threat to me.

Once, I was loved and protected too.

Frustration tears at me. I was so close, I'm *still* so close. But she could ruin everything...and I don't know if I can stop her.

I don't know if I can bring myself to hurt her.

I wrench the last hairpin free, and my hair uncoils down my back. There is one thing I can—must—do. I didn't want to hurt the prince, but I did. And now I must again.

There are too many people looking for him. Too many questions. I can't have *two* loose ends for the Clearsee to find. I must not weaken my resolve again.

I ring for Sybil. She'll help me undress. I'll need a weapon. I rifle through the drawer of my vanity, pull out a small, sharp hunting knife wrapped in leather. The only thing I have left of my father. I've kept it, all these years. Once, I thought I'd use it on myself.

Can I get close enough to use it on Kendrik before he rips my throat out?

I speak to the magic, tease it out. The possibilities. The ways the magic can make me strong. I'm so deep in thought that the crisp rap of a knock catches me off guard. I jump, and the knife clatters to the floor.

"Sybil—" I say as the heavy wooden door opens, but it's not Sybil standing there.

"Advisor Burke." My voice falters. I wasn't expecting him, not so late. Not tonight. For an instant, I wonder if he somehow read my intent. If he's here to stop me.

Shadows crowd beneath Burke's eyes. He's tired. Worn down. He steps into my chamber slowly, likes he knows he shouldn't be here but can't help himself. He doesn't look anywhere but at me.

"What's happened?" I ask. Because something surely did. Otherwise he'd hold on to his hard veneer. He'd ask me to join him in the hall.

Before he replies, he closes the door, trapping us in the room together.

"King Alder has taken to his bed," he says. "He has less time than we'd hoped."

My breath freezes in my throat. "The ceremony. It's still more than a week away...." I trail off. We're standing too close, and now all the air has been sucked away. I turn around and head for my vanity, half intending to put my hair back into some semblance of decorum. I must do something. I don't want Burke to read the lack of grief on my face.

"He has signed the decree making you heir. It won't have the same gravity in the eyes of the people, but I'm afraid the ceremony is too much for him. We're—we're still deciding how to make the announcement." His voice doesn't sound right. There's something he's not telling me.

I turn to face him. "Everyone is expecting a ball, and an announcement. We can't sneak around as if this is some sort of *plot*. There will be resistance."

He stands still, but I can *feel* the way his body aches to move, to pace, to fill up the space of my room. "It's not that plot I'm worried about."

My mind stills. *That plot*. Does that mean there's another? "The advisors?"

Burke can't hold back anymore. He walks fully into the room, stopping to stare at the fire crackling in the hearth. He rocks on his heels. "They know you won't keep them after the king is gone. And now, with his condition declining so rapidly, they see an...opportunity. If they can cast your claim as illegitimate or suspect in any way...they can 'hold' the throne for the prince, and rule in his stead."

Panicked magic is pounding along the back of my skull, sharp and hot as lightning. What he's saying, what the advisors are planning, makes perfect sense. They *should* question my legitimacy. But this is so very, very bad.

"Why are you telling me this?" I ask, heart racing. "Why would you warn me?"

He turns to me and again I'm reminded how much younger he is than Veron and Niall and Halliday. General Driscoll too. Still, she would never look this stricken. Burke's dark eyes burn into mine.

"You are the legitimate heir. We can't ignore the laws and

the king's decrees to suit ourselves. It doesn't matter what anyone thinks of you. Plotting against you is treason."

It is the right answer, it is the truth, and yet there's a small sinking in my stomach, a tiny flare of disappointment I don't understand.

"What do *you* think of me?" The question slides out of my mouth before I can stop it.

He turns back to contemplate the fire. Part of me wants to run my hands along his arms and let my magic solidify his inexplicable loyalty. Part of me just wants to run my hands along his arms.

I shake away the thought.

"You care about Tyne," he says thoughtfully, at last. "My uncle Veron, Halliday, and Niall, they care about their own power. They have amassed wealth for themselves, influence and deference that in turn affect the advice and information they give King Alder. They don't acknowledge that the people are hurting. Even General Driscoll, who plays at being concerned for the refugees in the Winterlands, keeps amassing her forces. She plans to begin the journey within days. I believe she will follow orders and lead a massacre. And yet here you are, showing you have principles, showing you care desperately about saving those people, enough to go yourself and try to negotiate. You stood up to the king and saved a magic worker's life. The contrast between you and the others is... hard to miss."

Warmth spreads through me, as insidious as it is unexpected. I am not accustomed to this kind of regard, to someone paying attention to the value I offer. We lock eyes and silence blooms, strangely heavy, between us.

A quiet knock shatters the tension. I hurry to the door and crack it open, peering into the dim hallway. Sybil's eyes widen at my hesitance to let her in. "Lady Annalise, you rang for me?"

"I'm sorry, Sybil. I'm not ready yet. I'll ring again later if I need you."

"Yes, Your Highness." She curtsies and heads back down the hall.

For a moment, I stand with my forehead against the closed door. Thinking. Thinking.

Breathe.

The Clearsee. The prince. The advisors. The Winterlands.

My magic strains at my skin, aching to burst out of me and smooth my way forward. But it lacks a target, and I lack a plan. So many barriers, so many threats. Where do I aim my arrows? How do I help myself and Tyne?

"So you're saying you're loyal to me," I clarify, rolling this problem around in my mind.

"You are the rightful heir," Burke replies. "I am loyal to you as I am loyal to the king and to Tyne."

I feel the air shift as he moves through the room. Inhale as his hand curls around mine. Slowly, he draws me away from the door, turns me to face him. Heat pools between our palms, and a spark. But not my kind of spark.

This is something new.

"Lady Annalise, I would see you become queen." He lowers himself to one knee, our clasped hands above his head. Supplication. Subordination. With the king still living, Burke is committing his own kind of treason.

"Advisor Burke," I begin, but my voice breaks. I can't stop staring at the top of his head, the soft chocolate curls of his hair. He is so big and broad; he uses his body to force the world to give him space, but here he is at my feet. Head bowed, his touch gentle. Electricity crackles along my bones, the kind that wants to erase hard hands and violent memories. The kind that leaves heat and wanting in its wake.

I cannot seem to move.

"Advisor Burke." I try again, but this time it comes out a question.

He doesn't raise his head. But his hands slide along my wrists to my waist, and he draws me closer as he stands, and then we are only a whisper apart, his bowed head and my raised chin so close that our breath mingles.

Our heartbeats pulse in time racing racing on the edge of the wild.

"This is treason," I murmur into the shrinking space. The word should be here. We should know what we are risking.

His lips meet mine as a promise, a secret, a sin. And, God forgive me, I lean in.

CHAPTER TWENTY

EVRA

*T*wilight cloaks the world in shadows. The field where I stand borders a forest, with a small gamekeeper's cottage tucked along its edge. It looks abandoned, with mossy thatch and broken windows. A musty, wild smell that reminds me of hunting with Tam hangs in the air. Perhaps it's the scent of the forest, pressing so close.

The door of the cottage creaks open. I wait and worry there will be blood.

But my Foundling emerges, dressed in purple velvet, as before. Only this time, his clothes are more than rags. They are finely sewn trousers and a soft, well-cut coat. A white shirt with a crisp, courtly collar. He looks around, hand on the hilt of the sword at his waist, his expression hidden by the dim light. I can tell when he catches sight of me. His whole body goes still, and then he's racing in my direction.

I hold my ground, even as my legs ache to flee. I don't

want to have to face the truth. But it's here, right before my eyes, in the fine clothes, the set of his golden eyes, so like his grandfather's.

"Evra," he says.

I take a deep breath. "Prince Kendrik," I reply.

It only takes a moment for recognition to spark in his eyes. He takes a step back.

"You're the prince. You're Prince Kendrik." I say it again to ground him, to ground myself, to make it real.

"How am I here?" he asks, shaking his sandy, overlong hair as if shaking off cobwebs. "Where *is* here?"

With a sinking in my gut, I ask, "Where do you think you are, Your Highness?"

He looks around, confusion tightening his soft features. "Nothing looks familiar. I don't—I don't remember anything. I don't *know* anything." It's what he always says. His gaze lights on me and something shifts. A hardness creeps into his face. "But you do. You know who I am. What else do you know?"

"King Alder told me that you abnegated, that you ran away from the castle. Do you remember that?" I don't want to believe he's dead, a ghost like my father. But what other explanation is there? My other visions—the past and future—don't speak back to me the way he does. They don't ask questions.

"I did...I did what?" This seems to draw all the air from him. He sits down on the grass, the sword at his side clanking. "Why would I? *How* could I?"

Slowly, I sink to the ground beside him. "No one in the castle seems surprised."

"Do you live there? In the castle?" he asks. "Is that how you know?"

"I am..." I pause. Swallow down my own grief. "I am visiting, at present. It is a Clearsee's duty to help her king."

"And there are rumors?" He doesn't need my answer. "There are always rumors about me. Grandfather is always telling me to be less sullen, to dance, to train with his captain of the guard. To *act the part*."

"Why is it an act?" I rub the back of my neck, under the twist of my hair. He is so reluctant, and yet we have all prayed he will be different from his grandfather, that we'll soon have less pain to bear. "Why do you not want to be king?"

He closes his eyes for a moment, tilting his head to the sky. "My grandfather can speak a word and command armies. He is blessed with conviction. In a king, this is more important than what is right. And I—I have never possessed anything close. I have never wished to be king, because I know I would be a poor one. And everyone around me knows it too."

Does he not know how his grandfather is despised?

"King Alder has terrorized the people ever since your father died. His conviction has cost lives." My voice trembles. "My father might be alive today, if not for your grandfather's *conviction*."

"I'm sorry for your loss, truly," Prince Kendrik says. He rips a blade of grass to shreds. "But you've proven my point.

My grandfather has done terrible things. But his conviction, his *commitment*, is what keeps Tyne together. Where are the rebellions? The coups?"

"Everyone is too afraid," I answer, anger rising to coat my words. Does he not see?

"Exactly," Prince Kendrik says. "The first unpopular law I attempted, the country would revolt. I do not scare anyone."

I try to understand why he says this so sadly. How can such a quality be a failing? How can he defend the cruelty of his grandfather?

"Perhaps you wouldn't pass unpopular laws," I counter. "Perhaps you'd be good to the people. You would help us." I don't want to believe that he's right, that doing good is a weakness. I don't want to believe King Alder is the best Tyne can hope for.

He shakes his head. "I've been told my whole life that good intentions do not make a good ruler. You must have strength."

"So that's why you ran away? Because you didn't feel strong?" Pressure builds in my chest. Before he can answer, I blurt out, "Do you know how many times I've felt weak? I am seventeen, and until three days ago, I had no magic. Every day that it didn't wake in me, every look and whisper, every uncouth suggestion...made me feel so powerless. So *useless*. But I didn't just give up. I took a step forward, and then another. I found other ways to be strong, to help my family and friends. Not trying is your weakness, Prince Kendrik. Your people were counting on you."

I'm ashamed to feel tears on my cheeks. With an angry swipe, I brush them away.

"I don't remember running away." He meets my gaze straight on, his own frustration clear. "I don't think I would. I am telling you why I have no wish to be king, but don't mistake my meaning. I had accepted my duty. I *was* going to try." Uncertainty tempers his outburst. "At least, I thought I was."

Slowly, my annoyance fades. If he didn't really abnegate, if he's here in the Clearsee ether with me...

"Do you think you might have died?" I whisper.

His face goes pale, a white blur. Something about the falling light, the darkness creeping, sinks into my bones. Makes the shadows more sinister. This night isn't natural. It isn't real.

"I'm dead?" His voice cracks.

"I don't know," I reply, desperate, as ever, to learn more about this magic that rides me. "Do you...do you truly not remember anything? Do you not remember how you got here?"

His gaze turns inward. The darkness reaches toward us. "No. No I don't," Prince Kendrik says, and grabs my arm. "What happened to me?"

The touch shocks me. How can I feel his hand? He is a ghost.

I open my mouth to respond, but our time is up. With a growl, the night swallows us whole.

I wake up curled on my side under a furred blanket. The prince's face, full of fear, fills my mind, but it has a distant quality to it, like a half-remembered dream. Sunshine streams through the cracks between the deep purple drapes, throwing bars of light across the floor. The dinner dishes have disappeared from the table, and a fire burns in the grate.

Slowly, stiffly, I sit up. A throat clearing catches my attention. Gianda is standing awkwardly by the door.

"Good morning," I mumble indistinctly. I don't have the parched feeling left by other visions, but my mind is hazy and my limbs heavy.

Gianda offers a shy smile. "Afternoon, you mean."

"It's already afternoon?" This news pierces the haze. I have to tell King Alder that I saw Prince Kendrik. But first…first I'll go to the library and read about the Clearsee magic. I'll look for another explanation. I don't want to have to tell the king his grandson is dead.

Dead. The word is a sledgehammer.

"Your brother said to let you sleep," Gianda replies.

I stand up with the speed and dexterity of Old Marnie. Aches in my legs and lower back remind me of the long journey. I look for my clothes. Guessing as much, Gianda hurries to a hulking armoire in the corner and collects a stack of fabric. "I had them cleaned," she says, handing me the worn leather riding pants and soft woolen shirt.

"Thank you." I dress quickly, despite my sore muscles.

Dread pounds sickly in my veins. And sadness too. Prince Kendrik seemed so lost, not at peace at all. *Please let there be another explanation.*

My hands clutch helplessly at the empty space at my hips, where my knife belt should be. When King Alder orders me to remain in the castle, I suppose I won't need my weapons anymore. There'll be no need to hunt for my supper, or to defend myself against thieves. The only thief here is the king.

I head for the door, but a plate on the table catches my eye. On it, a small, pillowy puff of bread rests beside a wedge of cheese. The food is gone in seconds. I don't even sit down. To her credit, Gianda doesn't eye me with disapproval. She just picks up the empty plate and follows me out the door. But when I pause to knock on Tamsin's, she says, "Your kin have gone to the stables to check on your horse."

My stomach sinks. "Oh."

They must have thought I needed the sleep, but I wish they'd woken me, taken me with them. I don't relish the thought of wandering the halls of the castle alone, and Tam will know how to broach the subject of Prince Kendrik to the king. I had hoped to have her help in planning out my strategy.

"Perhaps you'd like to stretch your legs in the gardens while you wait for their return?" Gianda asks, breaking into my thoughts.

"Has King Alder not asked for me?" It seems strange that no one is expecting me to be anywhere. At home I have duties. The day planned from sunup to sundown, each one an echo of the last. Farm chores, wood splitting and bowl carving and garden planting for Old Marnie and anyone else in the village who will accept my help. Here, I am unmoored, a ship drifting lost at sea.

Gianda shakes her head. "He has been indisposed all morning."

"I was told there were books about Clearsees in the royal library," I say. "Could you show me the way?"

Gianda curtsies. "Of course."

A cold draft caresses my cheek as we move down the hall. The chill dispels the last of the fog from my mind. I try to keep track of the route we take, but the corridors all look the same, gray stone and slits for windows.

At last, Gianda pauses by a heavy door at the bottom of a steep, twisted stair. "Here you are," she says. "When you're done, ask a footman to show you back. I'll help you get dressed for dinner."

She opens the door, gestures me through, and closes it before my thank-you finds voice. I turn, and my breath catches in my throat.

The royal library is unlike any room I've ever seen. Delicately carved wooden archways curve over a long galley lined with bookcases. Windows high in the wall let in the golden afternoon sunshine to play with the dust motes disturbed by my passing. Cushioned chairs and heavy tables parade down the center of the room, draped in rich burgundy. The stone floor hides beneath intricately patterned rugs. At the far end of the room, a fire burns in a massive hearth, and above it hangs a portrait of the former crown prince, Kendrik's father. I step cautiously inside, afraid to shatter the still, reverent quiet.

"The stable is out back," says a voice like the smoke from a blown-out candle.

I jump. A small, stooped woman glares from behind a desk piled high with books near the fire. Her white hair is as smoke-wispy as her voice. I approach cautiously. She sniffs.

"I need a book, not a horse," I say. At her derisive expression, I add, "King's orders. He said there were books here I would find useful."

The woman's suspicion sits in the grooves on either side of her mouth. My invocation of the king has had no effect. So, for the first time, I invoke myself. "As Clearsee, I demand that you help me find the books King Alder spoke of."

My words snuff the judgment from her face. Her paper skin slackens. She stands up, hands restless on the books strewn across her desk. "Books about Clearsees, yes."

She mutters to herself as she heads to the bookshelves, giving me a wide berth. For once, I appreciate my reputation as a harbinger of darkness. Perhaps Gianda is not the only one who's heard the rumor about me killing with my mind.

The stooped librarian returns with a single volume, a small, makeshift book, heavy vellum bound between two thin wooden rectangles. The cover is blank, save for a small, stylized eye burned into the wood.

"This is the last Clearsee's writings," she says. "It's about a hundred years old, so *be careful*."

I reach for the small book. When the wood touches my fingers, a current runs through me, so sharp and unexpected I cry out. A face explodes from the fire in the hearth: orange flame hair and two burning ember eyes. For a moment it hangs in the room, staring at me, and I bite back another scream. Just before the vision fades, the fiery face resolves itself into the colors of tan flesh and black hair and sky-blue eyes. I know without question that I am looking at the last Clearsee.

And, as the fire spits and blows smoke into the room, I hope with every frantic beat of my heart that the agony etched into his skin will not be mine to bear.

CHAPTER TWENTY-ONE

ANNALISE

 roll into wakefulness on a wave of terror. There's a heavy weight pinning me down. *Hot breath in my ear a body beside me I am in danger danger danger.* Magic lights me up, fingertips to toes. I am electricity and ire.

Fire.

"It's not yet dawn," a voice whispers. "Relax, love."

My frantic heart slowly calms. There is no danger here. I remember.

The hand that curves over my hip is not pinning me down. I am being embraced. The breath against my ear is warm and sleepy, a sigh. The voice a comfort, not a threat.

I remember.

I turn toward him as he burrows his face into my hair. His arm tightens around me and we are so close, skin to skin, all of us touching. Heat like magic everywhere.

"Burke," I breathe.

He kisses me.

"You have to go," I say against his mouth. "It's not safe to stay any longer."

He runs a gentle hand down my back, drawing me closer. His lips find my ear. "We have time."

He's wrong, and yet I can't seem to pull away. "The other advisors—"

"—are still asleep," he whispers against my throat, his beard tickling the sensitive skin.

"The Clearsee—"

"—will have answers for us, I'm certain." He presses the words against my collarbone. "But she is asleep too." He moves lower, kisses soft as butterfly wings. "My love...this is our moment. No one else's."

I melt slowly, snow in spring, heat blooming under the surface waiting to break free.

Vengeance for Mama, better for Tyne...I hadn't thought I might want something for me too.

But I do. God, I do.

Later, when dawn sips at the safety of our darkness, and Burke rises to dress, I think of all my waking threats. The advisors, the king, the Clearsee. And Burke's words suddenly come back to me, burrow beneath my skin.

The Clearsee will have answers.

"When does General Driscoll march for the Winterlands?"

Burke flings on his robe. "Soon. Days, perhaps. King Alder has taken to his bed and yet he still orders her to hurry. She cannot draw out preparations much longer."

"And is she part of the plot against me?" I pull the blanket to my chest and sit up. *If they can cast your claim as illegitimate, or suspect in any way . . . they can "hold" the throne for the prince, and rule in his stead.* His warning pounds in my head.

"I don't know," he replies. He leans against my door, his gaze drifting from my face to my bare shoulder. Warmth pools in my cheeks. "If she is, the situation is particularly dangerous. The troops will follow her commands."

"I need to ensure her support, then," I say. "I need her loyalty."

"It would help," Burke agrees. He moves toward me, close enough to kiss my forehead. "You will always have mine."

I give him a little push. "You must leave. Sybil will be here at any moment."

He steals a kiss and the friction of his beard against my skin sends ribbons of heat along my body. My hands go to his shoulders, his soft hair. And then he is gone, the door closing on his shadow.

I collapse back on my pillow, pulse dancing. But there is little time to linger with this new magic, this new gift. I must find General Driscoll and make certain of her loyalty. But first, I must speak with the Clearsee.

Sybil doesn't ask about my twisted sheets or my refusal to let her in the room last night. She helps me into my dress with a sweet smile and a small bit of gossip—the Clearsee is sleeping away the morning. Her maid has been stuck in her room for hours waiting for her to wake.

"I want to know where she goes when she does," I tell Sybil.

"Of course, Your Highness," she replies.

As she braids my hair, I stare at myself in the mirror. My chin and cheeks are red, razed by Burke's beard. My eyes burn a brighter green than usual. Overly bright. A bright to hide a lack of sleep, and the sin of treason. The crime is not new to me, but the company is.

Burke broke his vows for me. The thought sends a thrill through me.

The morning hours pass slowly. I ask for an update on the king's condition—still poor—and on the Clearsee's—still asleep. I sit by the window with my father's knife and watch the sun glance off the shining steel blade. The handle is polished cherry, with diamonds of ivory inlaid. I draw my finger along the smooth wood—my father's face, young and happy and soft-edged with time, in my mind. He stayed with us until I was seven. Mama said he was determined to provide a better life for us, that's why he left, but who's to say. He never came home. Maybe he's still alive, maybe he was hung for a thief long ago. I used to be angry. I used to think, if he'd stayed, he could have saved Mama. But I don't know. Maybe I would have watched him die too.

I tighten my grip on the knife.

Last night I planned to use this dagger to kill the prince. I'll have to find another chance. Soon.

I haven't fed him in a couple days. If he still lives, he'll be hungry. Weak. I'll do it quickly, before he—before I... my body shudders and my stomach roils. The dagger clanks against the window leading. I close my eyes, embrace the guilt, the pain. I've killed before. I can do this, I can. It's the only way to set us both free.

There's a knock on the door.

"Your Highness, the Clearsee is awake," Sybil reports. "She's gone to the library."

"Thank you, Sybil." I clasp her hand, reinforcing the threads of magic that bind her to me. Easing the headache I can sense through our connection. She leaves with her shoulders relaxed and a smile on her face.

I hurry to the library.

Evra is sitting in a chair by the fire. Crestin, the librarian, hides behind a stack of books, her expression even more pinched than usual. If she could bar everyone but the king from the library, she would. When I came to the castle, I sought books: manners, comportment, Tyne's history and peerage. Of all the minds I've controlled, Crestin's passionate safeguarding of these books made hers one of the most difficult to influence.

"Evra?" I say quietly.

She sits bolt upright in her chair and swivels to look at me. Her gray eyes are shadowed. Worried. Seeing me doesn't relax the tension that pulls her shoulders toward her ears.

"Are you well?" I ask solicitously.

She rubs a hand across her face. The other grips a book in her lap. "I'm—I'm sorry. You startled me."

I try not to loom over her. "That wasn't my intent. I had hoped to find you—I wanted to speak with you."

Her eyes dart to the book she's holding before finding my gaze again. I search her face for suspicion, anger, anything. All I find is fear. It's enough to make my own heart beat faster.

"I don't know if I—" she begins.

"Would you care to take a walk with me?" I interrupt, as politely as I can. Crestin might have her head bowed over a dusty tome, but her body bends toward us, her attention reaching.

Evra glances at her book again, looking reluctant. But she stands up, hands the book to Crestin, and follows me out of the room without protest.

"How are you finding the castle?" I ask as I guide her down the hall. Here, we are too open to being overheard for me to broach more serious subjects. She crosses her arms as if to ward against my question.

Her unease is starting to slip under my own skin.

My hand aches with the need to touch her, to slide my will into her veins and make her tell me what she's seen, but I know it won't work, not with the Clearsee magic protecting her. I don't want her to be a threat, I don't want to have to hurt her either.

At last, Evra shrugs. "It's very different from home. I—I find it hard to relax here."

"Have you had more visions?" I ask, striving to sound empathetic and not panicked out of my mind. Her mouth is drawn into a tight frown and it looks strange, unnatural, as if her face were built for a more joyful expression. Is it me? Is it my presence that's made her so uncomfortable? The familiar mantra *what does she know* pounds in my skull.

She stares down at her feet, nearly tripping on an uneven stone. "I—I—" And then something boils over—frustration, maybe—and she says, "There's so much I don't understand. I wish what I saw was *clear.*"

Ah. That's why she's scared. I breathe in my own panic and let it out. A soft, long exhale. I remember when my own magic came to me, how it frightened me. How I needed someone to help me make sense of it, and there was no one. Mama was gone, and I knew with great certainty that the world wanted to watch me bleed. My magic was a secret, a weapon. One I couldn't trust to anyone else. Perhaps Evra feels the same.

"It's overwhelming. I know." I carefully take Evra's arm, making sure that I don't touch her skin. I guide her down a staircase and out into the garden. A frigid blast of wind slices my cheeks, but once we get into the depths of greenery, where magic keeps the bitterest cold away, it is warm enough to stand comfortably.

Gradually, as we walk in silence, as I let her sit with her

thoughts and frustration, she relaxes a bit. She walks with a loose-hipped gait that suits her traveling clothes, but wouldn't be so comfortable—or possible—in a gown. She reminds me of the women in the village where I grew up, hardworking and strong. The ones who suffer when the king leaves them unprotected, their strongest magic workers pulled to the castle for his own selfish cause.

"Where do you come from?" I ask, when the high color in her cheeks has faded.

"Windhaven," she replies. "It's two days north of here. We had snow before we left. Nothing like the storms here, though." She glances up at the sky, but right now it's only cloudy, like a normal winter day. She must remember the thunder last night, the instability. I take a breath. Inhale. Exhale.

"We have unusual weather here," I explain. "Some say it's because of all the magic workers who live in the castle. That it creates a kind of disturbance, somehow attracts storms."

I watch her think about this, her brow furrowed. At last, she says, "I don't understand what the king needs with so many of us. Our best magic worker, Farin, just left Windhaven. She used to help Mama with the spells to keep pests off our corn. I don't know what we'll do in the spring. I wish...I wish the Clearsee magic worked differently. I can't help a crop grow or do anything, really, except let the visions come."

"It seems a heavy burden," I offer. Mine has been a boon more often than not, but it's still difficult, having a power so different from that of others.

The scent of honeysuckle wafts over us as we walk. The king's spring garden, even in winter, is one of the few magical indulgences I don't fault him for. Partly because it takes only a little coaxing to keep the flowers warm enough, to keep the green fresh and healthy. But mostly because this place gives me comfort. It has since I first arrived, when I was terrified of ruining everything with my grief and anger. This garden, these twisting paths, gave me freedom. Silence. Room to breathe.

I hope it's helping Evra. I want her to feel like she can trust me.

"I hate that I don't know more about my own power," she says, her gaze resolutely pinned to the ground.

I clasp her arm a little tighter and adopt a sisterly tone. "You said yourself that you're still learning. When I came into my magic, I nearly set my house on fire. You can't expect to be perfect at harnessing your gift before you even fully understand it. You're here now. I see you found a book to read. You can practice. Your magic will be just as useful as anyone else's, I promise."

"What will you do with *your* power?" she asks, and my pulse jumps so wildly it feels as if my heart will leap out of my chest. I wish I could grab her hand and use my power on *her.*

Before I have time to cobble together some sort of panicked answer, she adds, "You'll be queen soon. Will you change things at all, do you think?"

Oh. My power as queen.

I must have made some kind of noise because she pauses to

look at me, a strange expression on her face. "Are you well?" she asks. When I nod, she continues walking, pulling me along.

After a moment, I decide to answer her question properly. Honestly. "I want to change a lot," I say softly. "I don't want to be like King Alder. I don't want to only care about myself. He lost the crown prince to the Sickness. It was awful, and he mourned. We *all* did. But forcing the strongest magic workers to try to save Prince Josef's life—" My voice breaks. I can't seem to hold myself steady. "And continuing to force the strongest of us to come even after his death, to leave the rest of Tyne weak. To raise taxes year after year and do nothing as his people starve...Even the strongest magic cannot thwart death. His hoarding of power has done nothing but cause more pain."

Evra drifts to a halt, her gaze turned inward. I wonder if she's having a vision and brace myself should she swoon. But she blinks, and smiles a little, and says, "Whatever the wolf at your door means, I'll do my best to help you fight it."

"Thank you, Evra." Warmth radiates from the center of my chest. Like Burke, she is quick to trust. And whatever she knows or will know, it appears we want the same things. Perhaps we can be allies, after all. "I...I do need your help."

Raising a brow in question, she pulls her arm from my side and crosses both over her chest, as if she can't trust the artificial warmth in this bower, as if she expects any moment for winter to hunt her down.

"I am hoping you might ask the Clearsee magic for a specific vision, to help me avert a tragedy."

A new wariness seeps into her eyes. "What tragedy?"

"King Alder has ordered the murder of a group of refugees—he calls them rebels—in the Winterlands. They're people—families, with children—who've left their villages and banded together in an attempt to protect themselves from the king's whims. Some of them are strong magic workers who have been ordered to Ironwald and have refused to go. Others can't pay the taxes without starving. I have argued with the king, but it has not made a difference. I was hoping that perhaps, if you had a vision showing the folly of such a gambit, it might change his mind."

Her mouth tightens and the color drains from her face. "That's awful," she says in anguished tones. "Those poor people."

"Have you seen anything of this in your visions?" I ask. She shakes her head. "Can you help me?"

She tips her gaze to the ground, frowning deeply. "I wish I could. But I don't have that kind of control over my visions. I've only called one up willingly once before, and I had no power to influence what the magic chose for me to see. I'm so sorry."

She looks as if her inability to help is literally making her sick.

"Maybe we could try?" I ask gently. There's a bench not too far from where we're standing, protected by a graceful overhang of dogwood blossoms. "Perhaps if we sit down...I can help. Would you be willing? Is there any harm?"

She stares at the bench. "Right now?"

"No one will disturb us."

My heart leaps into my throat. What am I doing? She's just said she has no control over the visions. What if she sees the truth about me? We want the same thing, but that doesn't mean she won't tell someone what I've done. She is not loyal to me...not yet. I can hardly breathe and yet my hand still reaches for her arm, still draws her forward.

Because Tyne's refugees—they're more important. For them, this is a chance I'll risk my life to take.

CHAPTER TWENTY-TWO

EVRA

*A*s we sit beneath the flowers, I drop my head into my hands, trying to make sense of the snarl of thoughts and feelings cracking open my skull. I had just started reading the Clearsee's journal when Lady Annalise found me—I still don't know for certain if the prince is dead. But the Clearsee's words refuse to give me peace.

> *My dreams are now no more than nightmares. Awake, asleep, it matters not. I see their faces, always. The future, the past...they're all ghosts, haunting me. Day after day, and yet they never, never have anything useful to say.*

I didn't know what to say when she asked me about my visions. Should I tell her about the prince, when I am still unsure, when I am still looking for hope that he could be alive? Her whole world has been turned upside down by his abnegation—apparent abnegation—how can I turn it around again without proof? Without conviction?

And now, now she wants me to invite another vision in. I know it's possible—I proved that with Hagan and Tamsin. I wish they were here with me now—they'd be able to calm me down. Give me courage.

But I don't know how to focus the magic the way Lady Annalise wants me to. What if I see something completely different? What if I can't help those poor people in the Winterlands?

"I don't know if this will work," I say into my hands.

"But if it does, you could save lives." Annalise sits down beside me and stares into the rosebush across from us. The blooms are huge and heavy, a rich velvet red. They droop over shiny green foliage, hiding their thorns deep. "When you called up a vision before, did the magic take anything you were thinking with it?" she asks.

It's an interesting question, one I haven't thought to ask myself. I cast back to that night by the campfire, with Hagan and Tam beside me. Had I been thinking about anything specific? The previous visions and how frightening they were—the king's peeling face, and the wolf. But also Father. I'd been wishing he was there to guide me.

And then I heard his voice. What might have been his voice.

"I think I might have brought my father with me," I say quietly. I don't want to explain what I mean. It's too raw a memory.

Beside me, Lady Annalise shifts, clasping her hands together in the lap of her lavender gown. "That's good. So if you focus on the Winterlands, on the refugees, maybe you can bring them too."

I lean forward, watching a little breeze ruffle the bloodred roses. I take a deep breath and try to relax my shoulders, so tight they nearly touch my ears. My body feels strange in this garden, with its artificial spring. I should be shivering. I should be inside, huddled by a roaring fire. Is that where Hagan and Tam are? Waiting in their rooms for me, wondering and worrying where I went?

No. Stop.

I'm supposed to be thinking about the Winterlands. About the people risking murder to live free.

Annalise said there were families. Children. That the king had ordered them *all* dead.

Anger burns up through me, as searing as the firecane. I have to try. The Clearsee magic helped me protect myself, and Hagan, and Tam. Will its loyalties lie with the king, or the people of Tyne? Does magic *have* loyalties? I suddenly realize how often I catch myself thinking of the Clearsee magic as a living thing, and it bothers me.

I stare at the roses so hard my vision blurs. I hold what I've heard of the Winterlands—vast snowfield, jagged mountains—in my mind. I think of the people trying to carve out a life there, danger breathing down on them like fire. Is there anyone from Windhaven, from the villages that neighbor ours? Are they getting enough food? What about the bitter cold, the knife-sharp winds?

The roses dim, their vibrant red fading to an icy white. Just before the vision takes me, just before I lose myself, one last thought pushes through my mind: Will I see the prince?

I am blind. Blowing snow, a blizzard, a wall of white. There's nothing here, no sky, no way out. Just the snow and the whine of the wind and the blight. I stagger forward. What am I supposed to look for? What does the magic want me to see?

"Hello?" I scream.

The wind throws my voice back at me.

The cold feels like little flames licking at my skin. I blink, blink again, try to make sense of what I'm seeing. What I'm not seeing. And that's when something emerges from the swirl of snow.

In this wild, I expect it to be the wolf. But it's not. It's the female advisor, the one in uniform. She's walking toward me. Her unsteady gait, her slowness, strikes me as odd. When I step forward to meet her, she stops, her hands pressed over her stomach.

"Can I help you?" I ask.

But she stares through me, unblinking. Another step, and she crumples to her knees. With growing horror, I watch as she drops her hands. Red covers her belly, unfurling like a rose.

Blood. So much blood.

Her hands are covered in it, her uniform, the snow at her feet. Bright, vibrant red. She opens her mouth but instead of speaking she pitches forward, face-first into the bloody snow. She doesn't move.

I fight the urge to run to her. It's a vision. There's nothing I can do to save her. But even if it isn't real, I can't watch her die. Gasping for air that doesn't want to find a place in my chest, I turn around.

The wolf stands a yard away, staring at me. Its giant body tenses, and its mouth opens in an evil, toothy smile. It leaps, and I scream, and the snow eats me alive.

"Evra. Evra!"

I follow the voice back to my body, back to the garden, green and warm in the center of this bitter winter. My breath heaves in my lungs like I've run for miles. I feel as if I'm being chased.

Lady Annalise puts her hand on my arm. "It's okay. There is no danger here."

I don't believe her.

With shaking hands, I fumble for the firecane. The drought in my limbs eases slowly. I hate the taste of the spirits, the burn down my throat. It takes a few minutes before I'm able to sit back and regard the roses without gasping like a fish dying on dry land.

"You saw something," Annalise says, a little too eagerly. "Did it work? Did you see the Winterlands?"

I don't answer for another few moments, as I try to slow my erratic heart.

"I saw the wolf again," I say at last. "I wish I knew what it symbolizes."

In the Clearsee's diary, he recorded so many symbols—he saw them everywhere. Grims, ravens, storm clouds, ghosts.

They all meant darkness.

Death.

But they were always, always black.

Not big, golden beasts with terrifying yellow eyes.

"Is that all?" Lady Annalise says, sitting back. "I suppose we could tell King Alder we think it is a worrying omen, that the wolf trying to take his throne is also appearing in the Winterlands. Perhaps that would be enough...."

"I saw the woman advisor too," I say, breathing deeply.

"General Driscoll?"

I shrug. I don't know her name. "I was in the middle of a blizzard, maybe in the Winterlands. It was bleak and cold. The woman walked toward me and then fell to the ground. She was wounded. Bleeding. It was...it was horrifying. I think—I don't know, but I think if she goes to the Winterlands, she'll die."

Lady Annalise thinks this over. Softly, she says, "General Driscoll is one of King Alder's most trusted advisors. I think she's one of the few whose life he wouldn't risk. This is...well, not good, but this should help us."

There was so much blood. I can't get the image out of my

mind, and I feel the wolf's hot breath on my face even now. "What if it makes him angry?" I ask. "I don't want to make things worse."

She stands up, seemingly electric with a need to move, to act. "This may be enough to pressure him to stand down. His advisors will side with us."

With a last nervous look at the roses, red as General Driscoll's wound, I follow Lady Annalise out of the garden.

We meet the young advisor on our way to see the king.

"Advisor Burke," Lady Annalise says, curtsying. I make an attempt, but I lose my balance and bump into the wall. I really need Tam's help.

"I've been looking for you," Advisor Burke says, gazing seriously at Lady Annalise. "The advisors have called a meeting. They wish to discuss the"—he glances at me and then back at her—"the matter we spoke of last night."

Lady Annalise's face pales before suffusing with color. "I have information to share with them as well," she says stiffly, raising her chin. "And the king. The Clearsee has had a vision, one that shows a very clear threat."

He glances at me again. "Indeed. Unfortunately, the king is not presiding over the meeting. He is still feeling poorly."

I remember how frail King Alder seemed when I met him, his skull outlined by his thin, wrinkled skin. Something tells me this isn't a minor ailment, a single day abed.

My very first vision showed the king dying.

At their urging, I follow Advisor Burke and Lady Annalise

to a small, wood-paneled room that has a similar feel to the library, dusty and overflowing with books and maps. A room where work is done. But unlike the library, this room lets in little light, just a few bars through thin slits near the arched ceiling.

The rest of the advisors are already seated, already mid-conversation. It breaks off abruptly when we enter.

"What is the meaning of this?" asks one of the older advisors, the one with narrowed, angry eyes. He glares at Advisor Burke.

Mildly, Burke responds, "The heir has information to share with the council. She and the Clearsee." He turns to me, and I'm suddenly crushed by the weight of so many eyes.

"I've had another vision," I say hoarsely. My courage is caught somewhere in my throat, frozen in the act of fleeing. Instinctively, I seek out General Driscoll—yes, she is the same woman from my vision. The uniform, the tight black braids, the canny brown eyes. I swallow. There was so much blood.

"Well?" the old advisor speaks again, impatience and anger liberally coating the word.

"Advisor Veron, there's no need to shout at her," Lady Annalise interjects. "Her visions are traumatic, please give her a moment to collect her thoughts."

His face reddens. I have the uncomfortable feeling that Lady Annalise's defense has earned me an enemy.

Advisor Burke gestures to a chair, but I can't sit. I can't stand still. I feel like a snake, ready to shiver out of my skin. "I had a vision of the Winterlands."

Lady Annalise nods encouragingly.

"I saw General Driscoll with a deep and fatal wound." I say the words quickly, as if somehow that will dull their impact. "I believe if she leads her army to fight the rebels, the battle will go badly. Perhaps General Driscoll will die. Perhaps the image represents a failure of the campaign at large. I can't say for certain. Only that death is waiting in the north."

General Driscoll's expression doesn't change, but her body stiffens. The other advisors sit back in their chairs.

"Not all of us agreed with King Alder's order to murder the refugees living in the Winterlands," Lady Annalise says. She grips the back of a chair, her knuckles white. "This is proof that the plan is flawed. With the king indisposed, it is up to me to choose a safe way forward, and this is not it. We must wait, we must attempt less lethal contact. The tragedy the Clearsee saw can be avoided."

My tense shoulders relax a fraction. She sounds so controlled, so reasonable.

"But it is *not* up to you," Advisor Veron snaps. Any relief I felt shrivels. "There's been no ceremony. As far as I'm concerned, Prince Kendrik is still the rightful heir. My men are looking for him even as we speak. I feel confident he will be back soon to lead Tyne."

Lady Annalise's mouth thins. "King Alder has signed the decree."

"King Alder is dying," Veron returns. "He knows he has

run out of time. But we have not. We shall wait for Prince Kendrik. The council can shepherd Tyne through any hardship."

"Not all of us share that opinion, uncle," Advisor Burke growls.

"Not all of us are swayed by a pretty face," Veron claps back.

General Driscoll stands up. "There is no harm in taking the time to discuss, to weigh what would be best for the kingdom. With the king ailing and the Clearsee's vision to consider, I believe it is prudent for me to remain in the castle for a time. We cannot defend all fronts at once."

"I agree." The white-haired advisor sitting beside Veron speaks up. He doesn't hold the same viciousness in his face, but there's a wariness about him.

Panic is clawing up my throat. I don't fully understand what's going on, but I do know one thing...I don't have the luxury—the time—to go back to the library and finish reading the last Clearsee's writings. I have to share my suspicions. They can't deny Lady Annalise her role as heir, not when I know that what they're waiting for is likely never going to come.

"Excuse me." I try to tear a small hole in the argument building before me, but there are too many voices, it's too loud. I don't want to put myself in the middle, and yet I know I must. Lady Annalise has been so kind to me, and she wants so much for Tyne. I owe it to her, and I owe it to Prince Kendrik.

Perhaps, if they know, they can begin to figure out what happened and why.

"Excuse me," I say again, loudly enough that my ears ring.

Veron snaps his jaws shut and stares at me. The last advisor, the one in healer's robes, sits down. Lady Annalise reaches out, as if she thinks I need physical support. Maybe I do.

"I'm very sorry, and I didn't want to say anything until I was *sure*, but I feel you must know, in light of this...um... discussion," I try to keep my voice steady. "Last night, I spoke to the prince. In—in a vision. My magic...it allows me to speak to ghosts." My voice breaks. "To the—"

"Dead? Are you saying the prince is *dead*?" Lady Annalise asks, her face draining of color.

Miserably, I nod. "I believe he is."

CHAPTER TWENTY-THREE

ANNALISE

*L*anguage a true courtier would never learn rockets through my head. *She spoke to the prince all is lost all is lost.* A keening wail starts in my soul. She knows all my secrets. My *biggest* secret. Why did she not confront me before?

I stand, frozen, staring at this tall, square-jawed farmer, this *girl* who holds my life in her hands, and I want to cry, to scream, to let the wild sing. I cannot let her prophecies destroy me.

Outside, a storm builds.

"How did the prince die?" Burke asks, and *I* want to die because now he'll know. Everyone will know. I so desperately want to grab his hand, shield him from the truth somehow, but he's standing too far away—

Evra shrugs. "He has not said. He seemed...lost. He didn't know his own name until I recognized him, until I said it aloud. I don't believe he knows what happened."

He doesn't know.

Relief scorches through my body so powerfully I almost collapse. My hands are still clawing the back of the chair, holding me up. Shakily, I draw it out and sit down.

"So he might not really be dead," Veron says, agitated. "If he doesn't remember what happened, if he didn't *know*..."

Evra scuffs her foot. "I still have to finish reading the last Clearsee's writings—I've been trying to find another possible explanation. But I—I don't think there is one. I've had visions of the future, and they're nothing more than puzzles. Memories of the past, they are clear but move like plays—no one can see me. With the prince, we can talk. He *saw* me. I had a similar vision of my father, who's been dead these eight years."

My stomach twists. Perhaps Kendrik really is already dead. But I have to be sure. Would he visit Evra in her visions if he was at peace?

"I don't know the circumstances of his death," she continues, "not when it happened nor where to find his earthly remains. But it's possible I may be able to communicate with him further, and those details might come with time."

I want to applaud her. She doesn't back down from their shocked expressions and the sudden jumble of voices.

Advisor Halliday asks if the prince was murdered. "*Did* he abnegate? Or was it some sort of plot?" I swallow hard, but Evra shakes her head.

"I don't know."

Advisor Veron demands proof.

"I have none but what the Clearsee magic sends me."

Burke asks, "Did the prince suffer?"

Evra's face pales, and her voice hitches before she answers. "I don't know. I hope not."

For a while, the din of advisors shouting over one another and their thinly veiled panic rises in a miserable, invisible cloud over the room. Their grand plan to push me aside is in jeopardy and they know it. Evra has done me a great service, revealing this information now.

I slam a hand on the table. The room is silent as every person looks at me.

"We must move up the succession ceremony," I say calmly. "King Alder has signed the decree, but in this time of instability, the people need a visual display. They need to see how deliberate, how calm and informed, the king's decision was."

"King Alder is not well enough," Veron says gruffly. His eyes flick to Niall. Even now, they don't want this. They want to hold on to their power.

I can't let them take control. "No, he isn't. But his most trusted advisors and friends are. The castle is already rushing to prepare. The stewards from around Tyne will begin arriving tomorrow. We shall have the ceremony tomorrow evening, followed by the ball, to remove all suspicions of illegitimacy. And for now, we'll delay announcing the prince's death. Perhaps the Clearsee will glean further information in the coming days, so we'll have more to share with his subjects. We don't want panic or any whisper of doubt. Yes?" I stare them down, one by one. I feed them the most intimidating version of me—my magic, like their misery, seething invisibly through the room.

One by one, they fold, bowing awkwardly. Triumph bubbles up inside me. With Evra's help, I've called off the attack on the refugees *and* I've quashed the advisors' rebellion.

"Good," I say firmly. "Evra, please do all you can to learn more about what happened to the prince." When she nods, I turn my attention to Veron. "Advisor Veron, inform the kitchen staff of the change in plans." It's a low blow, sending him to the kitchen, but it's also important. These men want to usurp me. I must show them my strength.

His mouth twists as if he's tasted something revolting, but he nods.

I turn to Burke. "Advisor Burke, I wish to speak to King Alder. I know he's indisposed, but this may be my last chance."

Burke gives me a long look, feigning reluctance, before he agrees.

One last order. I focus on General Driscoll. "Please escort Evra back to her room, General. And have your soldiers stand down. You'll not be traveling to the Winterlands tomorrow."

She nods, and a hint of a smile graces her lips. I have gained another ally in my fight to save the kingdom.

With a final grateful nod to Evra, I lead Burke out of the room. We hurry down the hallway toward the king's chambers.

"What are you going to do?" he asks. "King Alder won't be able to speak to you."

"I know." Beneath my skin the lightning builds. "I just want to say goodbye. I don't want to miss my chance."

Burke lets the back of his hand brush against mine. I curl my fingers around his for an instant. By the time we reach the guards at either side of King Alder's door, we're yards apart. The guards hold fast until Burke orders them to let us enter.

Vast stone walls, warmed by faded tapestries, embrace us. A rattling cough echoes and lingers, taking on its own life among the sepulchral stone.

A massive bed, its headboard intricately carved with two giant hawks and a leaping deer, rests on a dais against the far wall. In the bed's center, King Alder's withered frame barely makes a hump in the layers of blanket that bury him. He coughs again, bringing bright red blood to his lips.

Around him, men and women in white robes hold vigil. I can taste their magic in the air.

"I'd like to say goodbye alone," I say softly, but with an edge of iron.

The magic workers look up at me, their faces gaunt with exhaustion. Burke ushers them out of the room. Before he leaves, I murmur, "Tell them their services won't be needed tonight or tomorrow. They've nothing left anyway. They need rest or they'll be no use to the king."

"Are you certain you don't want me to stay?" he asks.

"I'll only be a moment," I reply. "Please wait for me outside."

He catches my eye again, and a wholly inappropriate heat

kindles low in my belly. His thick beard is softer than it looks, his lips too. The heat climbs into my cheeks as his gaze lingers, drops to my mouth.

"You did well with the advisors, Your Highness," he says in his rough velvet voice. "You dismantled their plans at every turn."

I fight the urge to step closer, to breathe in his scent of old books and lemon, from the peels he keeps in his pocket to ward off unpleasant smells.

Behind us, King Alder coughs weakly again. Broken from the spell, I nearly push Burke out of the room. I don't have much time.

When I'm alone with the king, I kneel next to his bed and bow, my forehead touching the thick blankets. As if I am here to pray. But my power doesn't need prayers. All it needs is a way out.

Eyes closed, I slide my hands over King Alder's wrist, linking us. He doesn't flinch or make a noise, eyes closed, death waiting so close I can nearly see it in the air above him. The magic of the others leaves traces—they've held off the inevitable as long as they can.

Money and power have bought him time, but they cannot save him.

But I . . . well, I am my mother's daughter. And she was the strongest healer in Tyne.

Magic sparks to life beneath my skin and winds like heavy snakes along my veins. It fills me up ignites me. Slowly this

time slowly slowly I let it build I see Mama in my mind, her
soft hair soft hands. She touches me gently hands on my wrist
just like this. She feeds her magic along my limbs lifting me
up. Saving me.

I keep my eyes closed and Mama close as I feed my magic
to the king.

CHAPTER TWENTY-FOUR

EVRA

General Driscoll doesn't speak to me the entire walk back to my room. I don't know what to say either—all I see when I look at her is the blood, the wound, the red against the snow. It's not as if I can offer her a cheery, *I'm glad you won't die now.*

"Your room, Clearsee," she says when we arrive.

"Thank you." When I attempt an awkward curtsy, she purses her lips and departs without another word.

Knocking softly, I push open Hagan's door. A fire burns in the hearth, but he's not here. I try Tam's room next, and it's full of the same emptiness. Where are they? The hours since I last saw them suddenly seem far too long not to be ominous.

So much has happened today, and all I want is for them to be here, to reassure myself that they are well. That this one part of my life remains unchanged.

I lean against Tam's door and debate whether to head for the stables to look for them. But what if they've gone to get some food? Or they're taking a walk in the garden? Or—I cut off other, more dire possibilities. My mind seems intent on imagining the worst.

Perhaps Gianda will know where they are. I open my door, mind on the cord I'm supposed to pull if I need her. But the sight that greets me stops me in my tracks. Hagan and Tam are here, together, standing before the fire. Their arms are around each other, their bodies so close they only throw one shadow along the floor.

I might have assumed an innocent, friendly hug, or perhaps a comforting embrace in a moment of worry. But when they hear me, they spring apart as if they've been caught, and Tam's lips are flushed and swollen.

We stare at each other. I can't seem to dredge up a single emotion to cling to. There are too many. It is all too much.

"There you are!" Hagan says loudly, and too late. "Your maid said you went to the library, but we couldn't find you. We were starting to get worried."

"Yes," I say. "You looked very worried."

The furrows creasing Hagan's brow don't smooth now that he's found me. He looks as if he's waiting for an ax to fall.

Tam leaps forward and throws her arms around me, so tightly I can't breathe. I can't make my arms return the embrace. I am a statue. I am solid ice. She whispers, "I'm so sorry," into my ear. "I should have told you."

Hagan flops into one of the chairs by the fire. Shadows crawl slowly up the walls as the last of the daylight fades. It's disorienting, waking up as late as I did when I'm used to being up just as dawn breaks, and yet I'm tired already. Standing in front of the council, my heart hammering in my throat as I told them the prince was dead—it was enough to drain the life straight out of me.

I am done handling things today.

"Please leave." The words are unfamiliar, the opposite of what I expected to say to them.

Tamsin's mouth slackens. "But, Evra—"

"I'm tired. I need some time alone." I put a hand to my pounding head.

I don't want to be alone. I want things to stop changing all at once. I want my life to stop remaking itself, over and over, so fast, before I have time to adjust.

I want to sleep.

Hagan stands up. "Evra, truly, we're sorry. It's not, um—" His face goes scarlet and suddenly he is doing everything he can not to look at Tamsin. "Listen, please let us explain."

They're not going to leave.

"I had another vision," I say flatly. "Lady Annalise took me to speak to the king's advisors. No one was allowed to see King Alder. He must be very sick." I walk to the window and look out at the dregs of the sunset. Below, servants scurry to light torches in the courtyard.

"We heard rumors that he's dying," Hagan says.

I hate this time of day, when the world shrinks as night

descends. It's like heavy high walls pressing close. Like a well, featureless and dark.

"Evra, please let us—" Tamsin says, her voice a twist of anguish.

"Lady Annalise moved the ceremony to tomorrow night." I turn and put my back to the window. "I think she's hoping the king will be well enough to attend—she's worried about her claim to the throne. The advisors are not falling in line."

Tamsin's cheeks shine with tears.

"What did you see?" Hagan asks. He clears his throat. "I mean, your vision."

"It was useful, for once," I say, and a little of the triumph rises again. My vision saved lives. "I saw—"

But I don't get to finish because the dark takes me again, so fast.

I'm in a room as substantial as the one I left. There's no giant wolf, and no prince either. Just a small hearth, fire burning steadily, with a bed pushed near. A woman kneels beside it. She's praying or working a spell. By the tension in her shoulders, perhaps the spell *is* a prayer. A loud thudding interrupts the quiet scene. She turns her head toward the sound and I see her face—and recognize her. Dark brown hair, soft features. My vision with the child. The woman singing "My Lady Lost."

In the other vision she was happy, but this time loss tightens her face into a gaunt mask. She ignores the knocking. Her whispers over the bed become urgent. Desperate.

Behind me, a crash.

I whirl. A pair of soldiers have broken down the door. The woman doesn't look up.

"You've ignored a summons from the king," one of the soldiers says.

"I cannot do what he has asked," the woman responds, still bent over the bed by the fire.

"King Alder believes you can." The voice is implacable. I can't see the soldiers' faces—they never remove their helmets—but I can tell as easily as this woman can that they will not leave without her.

And still she doesn't move.

"My daughter has just died," she whispers. "I couldn't save her. What makes you think I can save the crown prince?"

"The king is desperate. He will have you killed." The soldiers hesitate. I know why—they don't want to get close to the body.

The woman turns to the soldiers at last. Tears stream down her cheeks, but her eyes are hard. "Let him. My daughter is waiting for me."

For another moment, the soldiers stand there. I wait for them to yank her up by her arms or perhaps argue more. But at last they leave and she falls sobbing against the bed. I step toward her, as if somehow I can soothe her agony. And that's when I see her daughter's face, still and pale. The girl is a child no longer, but a young woman, with fine brown hair, a pointed chin, and thin lips now purple in death.

How can the woman's daughter look exactly like Lady Annalise?

The world comes screaming back. I stagger forward into Tam's arms. Hagan tips the firecane to my lips. For a terrifying moment, the desert keeps reaching into my bones, even after I drain what's left in the bottle. Finally, my legs steady. My breath feels less like drowning.

"What did you see?" he asks.

I shake my head, confusion and unease tightening my stomach. It had the feeling of a memory, but how can that be? "Truly," I answer, "I don't know."

I sleep poorly, plagued by nightmares of Lady Annalise opening her dead eyes. The prince whispering words I can't hear. The giant wolf growling just out of view. And the king's face decomposing before me, again and again. It is all of my visions, all at once, haunting me.

I wake up shivering, soaked in sweat, chased by the fear that I'm succumbing to the last Clearsee's madness.

The sun has barely risen, and it is hours before I'm fed and clothed and ready to face Tamsin and Hagan again. We stroll about the king's garden, webbed in the scent of roses, because I need to keep moving. I don't want to sit with them in one of our rooms, with nothing to do but watch them try not to stare at each other.

"You're *sure* it was Lady Annalise? And that she was dead?" Hagan asks.

"I'm not sure of anything. It felt like a memory, but I know it couldn't have been." I want to hit something. I want to throw my knives. I want to chop wood until my arms are screaming and my mind is empty. "All I see is death. The king's, the prince's, the general's, and now this. It is *always* death."

Purple lips and dead-white skin.

"You could ask Lady Annalise herself," Tamsin suggests. "Perhaps she would know what it means?"

"I could." I should. This new vision *has* to show some kind of threat to her that I can help avert. I just don't understand how yet.

"Is it wrong to admit I am glad it's not me who has the Clearsee magic?" Hagan asks. Tamsin looks like she wants to elbow him, but she's feet away, leaving as much space between them as possible.

Ever since I joined them this morning, they've maintained this distance. They've barely spoken, and every time their eyes meet, they quickly look away.

I can't pretend I haven't considered the possibility of them being together. When we were young, Tamsin and I even made a game of it, imagining what her dress would look like, which flowers she'd choose for her hair at their wedding. The prospect of Tam becoming my sister has never troubled me. In fact, it's always been one of my fondest fantasies, and I the doting aunt for their adorably naughty children. If any couple were to raise hellions, it would be these two.

But now, with the Clearsee magic riding me, and the faces of the dead haunting my dreams, this new tension between them feels like a knife in the ribs. Why now? Why is *this* the moment things between them had to change?

Hurried footsteps find us at the base of the spelled fountain.

"Clearsee, it is time for you to prepare for the ceremony," the harried servant says, breaking our awkward silence.

"Of course." We follow him into the castle, and I try to swallow down my relief.

With a hug and a "We'll talk later," Tam disappears into her room, but Hagan lingers. Damn. He's going to make me face him now.

When we're alone, he says, "You weren't the only one surprised. I didn't, um, expect. I mean, I've thought about—" He cuts himself off. His cheeks are a too-close-to-the-fire shade of red.

"I know," I say wearily. "We've all known. You wear your heart in your eyes—you might not be able to see it, but the rest of us can."

He runs an embarrassed hand through his hair, making it stand up in spikes. "You seem upset. You know that nothing will change."

A bitter laugh escapes me. "Everything already has."

"Evra—" he begins, and the shame and regret in his face are too much for me.

I put a hand on his shoulder. "It's okay, Hagan. Really. We all know I won't be leaving the castle. It is good that you and Tam have each other." I mean it. Mostly. The tiny bite of jealousy, the sadness of change will be easier to ignore in time.

His face twists. "You don't know they'll make you stay."

I love that he's holding on so hard, that he keeps responding this way. But his false hope is just that—false.

Gianda opens the door. With a sad smile at Hagan, I slip inside. A steaming bath is waiting. Afterward, the maid offers me a silken dressing robe and goes to work on my hair. This time, she twists it into an intricate pattern along my forehead. When she's finished, she holds up a mirror to show me her handiwork. The crown of braids offsets the hardness of my chin, and my skin glows a freshly scrubbed pink. It will do. After all, this is about as presentable as I get.

"The dress I brought from home is not exactly, that is to say—" *The gown Tam lent me is a bit loose at the hips and chest, and a couple inches too short.*

Gianda shakes her head. "Lady Annalise has provided you a dress."

My stomach clenches, remembering the dead gray cast of her skin in the vision, but I force myself to focus on the kind gesture. The earnestness with which she asked for my help to save the people of the Winterlands.

Gianda flits to the armoire in the corner and returns with a massive heap of white and sparkling blue.

"How do we know it will fit?" I ask, with a wary eye on the tower of petticoats and yards of fabric.

"Her Highness made sure," Gianda says. "Now turn if you please, miss."

I could split all the wood in Windhaven in the time it takes Gianda to string me into the corset and petticoats, only to drop the gown over my head and begin fastening the endless row of tiny buttons at the back, which she attacks with an evil-looking hook. As each lavish layer is fitted and put in its place, she relaxes, humming softly to herself as she works, the motions obviously familiar to her. In contrast, as each stay is tightened and petticoat straightened, I feel more and more awkward. I have never worn a gown such as this.

It is a dress unlike anything I have even seen: an ice-blue silk sewn through with silver thread and seed pearls that shimmer in the firelight and weigh on my shoulders. The edges of my shoulders, to be fair. Most of my collarbone is exposed by the nearly indecent neckline and tiny cap sleeves. My sun-darkened skin glows against the pale silk and I feel desperately beautiful and horrified all at once.

Worse, I can't breathe.

Gasping a little, I ask, "Are you sure it's meant to be this tight?"

Gianda giggles. "Of course, miss. It looks perfect." She helps me step into a pair of soft, flat slippers and then directs me toward a long mirror beside the armoire. She angles it to give me the effect.

"I hardly know you anymore," she says in hushed tones.

I stare at the lovely, luminous stranger in the mirror. She doesn't smile.

"I don't know me either."

CHAPTER TWENTY-FIVE

ANNALISE

My gown is green as emeralds, with a high neck and tight sleeves. This is to accommodate the overlay—fine gold filigree shaped into chain mail that drapes along the tight bodice and belled skirt. Purely for decoration and yet it feels like armor. For once, my eyes sparkle. I spell the dress to ease its weight.

Sybil binds my fine hair up in golden netting. "You look beautiful, Your Highness," she murmurs at my reflection.

I smile at hers.

A knock sounds on the door.

"Thank you, Sybil. I'll ring when I return from the ball."

She curtsies and slips out of the room, just as Burke ushers himself inside.

"What did you—"

As I turn to him, he falls silent, his jaw slack. Most of the admiring glances I receive are false, for the king's benefit, not my own. But Burke looks truly stunned. I can't stop a smile from warming my face.

He has clipped his beard and is wearing a burgundy robe trimmed in gold. I take a step closer. He clears his throat and shakes his head, his face falling into more severe lines. "What did you do to the king?"

I pause, tilt my head, widen my eyes. "What do you mean?"

He can't quite hide the desire that still pulses beneath his concern. "King Alder was near death when you visited him last night."

"Has he died?" I ask tremulously, taking another step toward him.

"He has gotten *better*," he growls. Like an accusation. I almost laugh.

Instead, I freeze. Let my lips part in shock.

"Better?" I repeat, dumbly.

It's fascinating, how he almost looks angry. How his skin practically hums with indignation. Shouldn't he be pleased?

"He has gotten out of bed, where once he could barely breathe, let alone move. He has dressed. He has said he will attend the ceremony."

"Isn't that a good thing?" I ask. "You seem—"

"Suspicious?" he supplies. "I am. I saw King Alder last night. Death was sitting with him. I expected word of his passing by morning. And yet here he is."

I reach for his hand. Gently, I ask, "You are suspicious of me? What do you believe I've done?"

I can see him thinking about pulling away, but he doesn't. He shakes his head, his thick hair falling across his forehead. "Perhaps you healed him? But I don't know why—"

"I would think 'how' is the bigger mystery," I say. "All of Tyne's best magic workers have tried to stave off his death. And you think *I* can do the impossible?"

For a long moment, he stares at me without speaking. Eventually, his expression softens. "Can't you?"

My lips meet his with the taste of wanting on them. His fingers try to find purchase in my armor, grasping at the delicate gold. We are anxious and awkward and impatient, but the moment is an hourglass, the sand nearly run to ground. It's time for the ceremony, and the king will be there to make me his heir.

Yes, I think. *I can do the impossible.*

The Great Hall is silent as I step onto the dais with King Alder. Before us, the room is nearly full, courtiers and magic workers, servants and stewards all standing still as glass, staring at us. Four long tables run the length of the room, and the two massive hearths roar with flame. In a straw-strewn corner near the dais, musicians wait. Behind the king's throne, his advisors and honor guard stand tall. I am suddenly grateful for Burke and how many times he made me practice this. I hadn't imagined—I hadn't thought about the crowd, all watching me. There are too many people, too far away for my threads of persuasion to touch, but my magic sparks along my skin anyway, fed by the quickened beat of my heart and the tension in my shoulders. I force my fingers to lie quietly against my belled skirt, no balled fists or nervous drumming on my thighs.

Advisor Niall, as the oldest and longest-serving advisor, begins the ceremony by addressing the king. "Your Majesty, today marks a solemn and surprising day for Tyne. Our kingdom has been marred by tragedy, and unfortunately once again a change in the royal line must be announced."

With effort, King Alder stands.

"My people," he says, and it's clear a magic worker has amplified his voice, "it saddens me to announce that my grandson, Prince Kendrik, has chosen to abnegate the throne. The death of his parents was a burden under which he suffered greatly. I cannot know if this contributed to his decision, but I do know that our kingdom, our future, will be in good hands."

Here he shifts his attention to me. "My grandniece, Annalise, has my beloved sister's gift for speaking her mind, and respecting those who know more than she does. Lady Annalise will make a formidable ruler when it is her time." There's a challenge in his gaze, a subtle reprimand. He's reminding me—and everyone in the room—that my time has not come yet. It doesn't hurt to incline my head, a small nod of acknowledgment.

Niall steps forward again, this time with the royal chalice in one hand, and the succession decree in the other. King

Alder lowers himself carefully into his throne. The effort of his speech has given his skin a gray cast. As with the other magic workers, I have given him the smallest reprieve, a few days at most. But he is here, and with his own voice he said the words to give me this crown. Now, he signs the decree as I raise the gaudy golden chalice high above my head.

I speak the ceremonial words with conviction, daring Veron and the others to question my legitimacy. It is too late for plotting, too late to stop what the king and I have begun.

"I accept this responsibility with great humility," I finish, and turn toward King Alder.

His white hair falls in thin waves to the thick black-and-gold stole wrapping his frail shoulders. There's something like peace in his eyes as he watches me curtsy to him and drink from the cup. The wine burns my throat.

I kneel before him. His lips are dry on my forehead, his voice almost steady as he fulfills his final part of the ceremony.

"May you honor Tyne as you honor me."

And then it's over.

The musicians begin to play. Voices rise. Dishes clank in the hands of the swarm of servants who appear with the feast. Niall takes the cup from my hand, bowing with a reluctant, "Your Highness."

I murmur something about gratitude and honor. I search the swirl of people below us, my eyes lighting on the Clearsee. The dress I sent to her looks stunning. She notices me looking and meets my gaze. I expect a smile, a nod, but a strange urgency tightens her features. A small knot of ice forms at the base of my spine. She looks as if she wishes to speak with me. Even her lips part, as if somehow I could hear her from this far away.

I am about to move in her direction when Burke steps up next to me. "Would you like to be seated, Your Highness?"

From the corner of my eye, I note they've brought a second, smaller throne out and placed it beside King Alder's.

"No dancing?" I ask with a little smirk.

Burke's lip quirks in response. "No dancing, Your Highness."

As I arrange my skirts and golden armor to sit on my throne, I glance at the king once more. He is staring straight at me, eyes burning out of his wrinkled, rice paper skin. Quietly, dryly, so none but I can hear him, he says, "You've gotten everything you wanted, haven't you?"

And for the barest breath of terror, I can see him looking straight through to me. The real me. In the next instant, the fog descends once more, and he turns away.

But it's a reminder, a threat, a promise. I can never forget the knife's edge on which I balance, the razor point that could, should I fall, slice me end to end.

CHAPTER TWENTY-SIX

EVRA

I want to change a lot. I don't want to be like King Alder.

I hold these words in my mind as Lady Annalise raises the royal chalice above her head. I know she will be a good queen. But her dead face haunts me, and the Clearsee magic presses against my chest, pushing me to do ... something. I don't know what it wants. But it has me restless, breathless. This is worse than a vision. This feeling demands action, and yet there's nothing for me to do but stand here, next to Tamsin and Hagan, and watch. Soon I'll find a way to speak to her. Soon I'll tell her what I saw. But the magic doesn't seem satisfied.

"Are you all right?" Tam whispers, as the rustle of my dress betrays my shifting feet.

I nod. I don't trust my voice. But inside my mind, I scream, *What? What do you want me to do?*

I should know better. Because the Clearsee magic answers.

The room dips sickeningly and rights itself. Except the light has changed—the bright candlelight has become a wavering red glow. Music is playing, but it's faint and somewhat distorted, as if coming from another room. The king and Lady Annalise have disappeared. I look around for Tamsin and Hagan, but they're gone too. I'm standing in the center of the floor as faceless courtiers swirl in slow motion around me.

"Excuse me," a voice says over my shoulder.

I turn, head buzzing, breath caught in a cage of ribs and corset, and stare into Prince Kendrik's golden-brown eyes. He is holding out his hand, his expression uncertain. "Are we supposed to dance?"

"I don't know." But I take his hand, surprised at the relief that courses through me. Why should I be happy to see him? The thought trips me up, and I trip on my skirts, catching myself against his chest. He steadies me and suddenly we are far too close, so close that his warm hands touch my bare arms and his breath feathers my cheeks.

This doesn't feel like a vision. He doesn't feel like a ghost.

"I'm—I—" The words, the thoughts, won't come.

Prince Kendrik hesitates, hands still lightly touching my arms, as if preparing himself in case I stumble again.

"I don't understand how we are here," he says. The ball continues around us, and for a moment I wonder if there is no vision, if somehow the prince is really *here*. "I think you may have been right. I think I may be dead."

My chest tightens. I wish I'd found proof he couldn't have died. I wish I had the words to reassure him.

"King Alder is naming his new heir tonight," I say.

Kendrik's anguished laughter surprises me. "Do you know how many times I dreamed of walking away? Ever since my father died..." He pauses. "I thought he would live long enough, that I would never have to worry about being king. That my son or daughter would get the honor. Someday. But he died and my mother died and there was only me."

"And your cousin. Lady Annalise."

His hands tighten on my arms and he shakes his head, as if trying to shake off a dream. "I wish I remembered."

"And *I* wish I had the answers for you. For *me*. I need to know what happened to you." My dress is too tight, the magic is squeezing me, confusing me. And yet this is what it comes down to, the only thing that matters. Why did Kendrik abnegate? How did he die? Surely some foul mischief was involved. Surely this is the mystery the Clearsee magic is demanding I solve.

"Perhaps being here, in this room...does anything feel familiar?" I ask as we twirl awkwardly, the blank-faced courtiers insubstantial as a fog surrounding us. "Perhaps we're here to help you remember."

The music—faint and discordant—shifts into a slow,

haunting melody. Prince Kendrik pulls me closer still, into the steps of the next dance. As if we are compelled, as if the magic is making us. This is so strange, so unlike my other visions.

My hand tightens on the wine-red velvet of his jacket. I'm not so sure I need to be compelled.

"I do...I do remember a ball," he says, glancing around at the faceless dancers. "A ball like this one. I was lurking...I don't like to dance." Something changes in his face. "I remember there was an announcement. Lady Annalise...yes, Annalise's betrothal. The man...he was someone I barely knew of, someone from another kingdom, I think. And she was upset. Her face...she was horrified. She left the ball. Grandfather was angry."

As we sway in tandem, I'm acutely aware of his body, his presence, the *space* he occupies. Here, in this place of magic, the world is the ghost. *He* is real.

"And then...," I prod, quietly, afraid to break the spell.

"And then..." For a moment, there is nothing. The emptiness at the end of his memories, the well of darkness at the end of the rope. And then his eyes widen. "Evra, I—"

This time I can feel the magic holding on, as desperate as I am. But the veil drops, the prince disappears, and I'm left staring at Lady Annalise on her throne.

Lady Annalise.

It all, almost every vision, comes back to her. The dead face. The night of her betrothal. The wolf lunging for her. But why? Is it possible the same malevolence that did harm to the prince is targeting Annalise now? Is that the evil I'm meant to stop?

My knees threaten to buckle. A strong arm steadies me. I turn, instinctively expecting to see Prince Kendrik, but it's Tamsin wrapped in ivory lace, worry making her frown.

Before I can speak, another hand shoves a small bottle to my lips. Hagan. He practically drowns me. He's found more firecane somewhere. I take the bottle from him and swallow a few more sips. My legs steady. But my mind is still a whirl.

"You were gone longer than the last time." Tamsin tries to hide how unsettled she is, but I've known her for too long. The furrowed brow, the pinch of her lips, the tightening of her grip on my arm.

I look toward the two thrones. King Alder has slumped down; he looks better than I expected, but only just. Beside him, his grandniece glows. "I need to speak to Lady Annalise."

Before I can move toward the dais, servants swarm the room, encouraging everyone to be seated. A table is brought to the king and his heir. I'll have to wait. When the formal portion of the evening is complete, when the dancing begins, I'll request an audience with them both. Perhaps the king will know who threatens his heir. In the meantime, we head for the nearest table, and I notice belatedly the racket of competing voices has quieted to murmurs. Heads have turned my way. The king didn't announce my presence as Clearsee, but Tam did say there were rumors. I keep my head up and walk as I do when I'm hunting, with silent, deliberate steps. It's the only way I know how to be graceful. My gown, as confining as it is, floats around me like a pale blue cloud.

Hagan and Tamsin choose seats on either side of me. They form a sort of wall to block out the curious stares. Tam's parents are somewhere in the crowded room; they came for the ceremony like the other stewards of other towns.

In the lull before the food arrives, Tamsin tries again to speak to me about last night. "Evra," she says quietly, "I feel like I've betrayed you. Your brother and I . . . I think I've liked him for a long time. I was going to talk to you, I wanted to talk to you first, but . . . but you have so much on your mind, I worried it would be *too much*. And now, it is."

I turn to look at her and give her my full attention for the first time in what feels like days. Her blond hair is pulled off her face in soft whorls, her cheeks pink with agitation. There's a hollow dread in her eyes I've never seen before. She knows how difficult all of this is for me, and she feels she's made it worse. I can see everything in her face, in the tightness at the corners of her mahogany eyes, in the furrow between her brows.

And, for a time, she was right. But I can't be angry at her, nor Hagan either.

I take her hands and lean close, so no one else can hear. "You could never betray me. This is just . . . change. Everything changes, doesn't it? I'm happy, Tam. Truly. When I'm gone, while I'm here—" I pause so I can keep breathing without breaking into tears. "You'll need to take care of each other."

It's the same thing I said to Hagan, but Tam's response is different.

Her mouth turns up into a shaky, relieved smile, and then she rolls her eyes. "If you think we're going to leave you here alone with these wolves—"

A loud horn trills from behind the king's table, cutting her off. A line of servants enters the room, holding silver trays. They heap the tables with bowls of spiced apples, minted potatoes, and crisp roast goose legs.

I fight a quick and brutal internal war with my corset.

In the end, eating wins over breathing.

Dish after dish appears: curried snapdragon soup decorated with swirls of cream, fragrant baked pheasant with honey-tarragon sauce, dense cinnamon bread dotted with hazelnuts and golden raisins. I take a small spoonful of each selection and eat slowly, with tiny bites, until I feel like a swollen seed-pod about to burst.

Beside me, Hagan makes happy smacking noises. He doesn't bother talking. I envy him as he shovels huge bites of food into his mouth. When I glance at Tam, she's watching him with a mixture of amusement and horror. "Your brother is a glutton."

"After nearly a week without Mama's cooking, can you blame me?" Hagan mutters around a mouthful of wine-soaked beef and turnip stew.

"And this isn't even as good," Tamsin says. "Imagine what your mother could do with fancy gold-bird, or whatever this is." She gestures at the chunk of meat on her plate. It's probably just wild turkey, but her point rings true. The sugar alone in some of these dishes would cost more than our farm earns in a year.

After a final course of chocolate crème and hard cheese, the first lively strains of music skip through the hall. Soon courtiers are pairing up and filing into the open space between the tables.

"They're not *bad* dancers," Hagan says, holding out a hand to me, "but this is no country fair. Shall we show them how it's really done?"

I turn to Tamsin. We share a look of understanding. "I'm sure Tam would be delighted," I say.

Hagan's face goes red. They join the dancers, awkward at first, but they soon relax. For a while, I watch them spin around the floor, Tamsin's lace gown swirling. Her laughter, deep and loud, attracts a few looks.

I'm glad they're happy. I wish I could lose myself tonight with the same abandon. But I've put off my duty long enough. With a deep breath and a whispered prayer, I stand up. The walk to the front of the cavernous room feels long. I can't help but brace myself for crashing masonry and screams. I can't help but look for Prince Kendrik among the crowd. My visions have infected my waking life; I can't ever seem to fully escape them.

King Alder stares at me for longer than is comfortable

before recognition sparks in his eyes. "The Clearsee. Of course," he says at last.

Lady Annalise hovers next to him, his advisors ranged along his other side. You'd think I'd come to hurt him, the way they close ranks at my approach.

I wish I could speak to Annalise alone first. I could warn her she might be in danger. I could ask her what she thinks it all means. But, for now, I serve the king.

"I've had several visions, Your Majesty." He nods for me to go on.

I pray his advisors have already shared the news of Kendrik's death. I skirt it in my own recounting: "The prince can speak to me, which is unlike my other visions. We are trying to discover what happened to him, but so far all he remembers is the ball the night of Lady Annalise's betrothal."

The king nods. "The night he abnegated."

Something—maybe the prince's own doubt, makes me ask, "Forgive me, Your Majesty, but what makes you so certain he did?"

King Alder coughs, the sound scraping across his throat. "Prince Kendrik left a letter to me, written in his hand, with his signet ring. Indisputable, I would say."

A letter, written by him. His signet ring. What did he do afterward? Where did he go? What *happened* to him? I take a deep breath and try to focus. There's one more vision I must relay to the king.

"Your Majesty, I saw something else. Something I can't explain." I pause. My gaze flicks to Lady Annalise. She's bent solicitously toward King Alder, her hand on his. He raises a brow. As far as I can tell, he's ignoring his new heir. "I saw you dead," I say to her quickly, rushing now to get the words out. "It felt like a moment in the past, but surely it was a warning. I'm worried you're in danger."

"What exactly did you see?" King Alder asks, his rheumy gaze sharpening.

"Lady Annalise was younger, with a woman... perhaps her mother? There were soldiers. The vision didn't make sense to me, and I have no idea what it means. But it was unsettling."

As I speak, I can sense Lady Annalise stiffening. Her hand, resting gently on the king's, tenses, not quite a squeeze. I turn to her, beg her to help me understand. "How can it be a memory?"

"I was ill," Annalise says gravely. "I almost died. My mother was afraid I would. King Alder sent soldiers... he sent people to help. I lived, by the grace of God. That must be what you saw. I don't think—I hope it doesn't mean I'm in danger *now*."

Her voice is even, eyes wide with concern. The king relaxes. What she said is so reasonable, logical.

It is also a lie.

She's watching me closely. I can see when she realizes her mistake. The blood drains from her face, and her mouth opens a little, as if she silently gasps a breath. I can't hide that I know—whatever happened, it wasn't that.

Those soldiers had threatened her mother. They'd been cruel to her. They hadn't helped her. I am *certain*.

Why is Annalise lying?

King Alder nods and pats her hand. "I lost my son, my sister, and my niece. I couldn't lose you too."

This is wrong. I don't know the how or why, but I know that much. The wrongness pulses in the air, in my lungs, under my skin. It is everywhere. The Clearsee magic presses into my chest and unfurls. It says the word for me, over and over.

Wrong, wrong, wrong.

Lady Annalise holds my gaze like a drowning man holds a rope thrown from shore. She is begging me to pull her in. To line her lies so they look like truth.

Part of me wants to help. I promised to keep the wolves from her door. But the Clearsee magic tears at me, claws and teeth. In Father's voice, it orders me to *pay attention*.

The king so easily believes her lies. Why?

Why?

My voice strangled, my heart beating far too fast, I say, "Your Majesty, I'm very sorry, but that is not what the vision showed me."

Lady Annalise's face changes. Her open, anxious regard slips away. A new sharpness, a regretful conviction replaces it. She puts her hand on my back. "That's enough, Evra. The king is getting tired. You may speak with him tomorrow."

I don't want her to touch me. Something breaks apart in my chest and suddenly I'm certain I've failed my first test at court. I was too trusting. I didn't *see*. I step away. I push her hand away. *"No."*

I've been able to ignore the blasted corset for hours, but now, now when I'm panicked and desperate, now it fights me, squeezing until spots dance before my eyes. "Your Majesty, I think...I think there's something more here—"

I've gasped in all the air that will fit, and it is not nearly enough. My words trail into a blur of velvet-red darkness.

The serpent uncoils slowly from its place among the shadows of jars and dusty toys in the corner of my room. It slithers across the floor toward me with the sound of grain sliding into a metal pan, and I can't do anything but watch. I *want* to sit up, call for Mama, maybe even kick it down the ladder to Deward and Hagan's room so they can kill it, but I can't. I can't speak. I can't move. *Oh God, why can't I move?*

Panic tightens my throat and the muscles in my arms strain as I try to push myself up, to get out of here.

I lose sight of the snake. But before I can relax, the blanket at the bottom of my bed moves.

Oh God, oh God, oh God

I have never liked snakes; their shiny dead eyes and boneless undulations make my skin crawl. But the harmless black snakes that live in the dark, dank places around the farm can be easily avoided.

The sheet rustles again and when I feel the slick, dry weight of the serpent curl along my ankle, my entire body erupts in a tortured, silent wail.

The hell of paralysis seizes my every breath, every thought, until I am mad with terror.

And still, the snake slides inexorably along my skin, up my leg, across my thigh. Beneath the arch of my back, around my stomach.

Again, again, it wraps itself around me, until I am clothed in its coils, trapped within a corset of dusky red scales and slither and bone.

With a whisper of a hiss, it begins to squeeze.

And squeeze.

And squeeze.

There is no hope of screaming now.

I'm dying. I can't breathe.

Shadow skulls cling to the corners of my vision, chittering their horrible laughter. And, in what must be the last moment of my life, when the darkness hugs me close, the snake explodes in flame.

I am burning, I am burning, but finally I can breathe.

Without warning, Mama appears under the eaves, holding her hands out to me. Why won't she run? Can't she see the danger?

Snakes of flame slither from the bed, along the floor and up the walls, until she is embraced, engulfed. I am burning, melting into the bed and yet frozen still, unable to help her. The fire cracks and hisses, giggles with the voices of the shadow skulls, and above it all, as she burns, I hear my mother scream.

I heave myself up and into wakefulness like a swimmer bursting from water into sunlight. The fire is gone, Mama is gone, my room is gone. I'm sitting in an unfamiliar bed in a large chamber with velvet walls the color of a bruise. *The castle. I am in the king's castle.* Hagan and Tamsin are clutching my arms. Around me, my corset and fine gown are in pieces, as if they've been cut away, leaving me shivering in my chemise.

"Breathe, Evra. *Breathe*," Hagan says.

For a moment I can do nothing but suck air into my lungs, breath after breath until I'm dizzy with it. Tam stares into my eyes, deep lines framing her mouth. Her expression almost frantic. Hagan can't seem to stop patting my shoulder. "There, there," he keeps saying, over and over, his voice thick with fear. I pull the sheet to my throat and try to calm my chattering teeth.

My visions didn't disturb them so much before. Why do they look so scared? Then I realize it's because this time I'm shaking with terror.

"Mama's in danger," I whisper.

But Tamsin shakes her head. "No, Evra. *You* are."

CHAPTER TWENTY-SEVEN

ANNALISE

Evra knows. Her magic is growing and it's showing her everything. Mama, the soldiers, *me*...I don't remember the day she saw, when the soldiers came and Mama wept over my body. Because Evra was right. I *did* die that day.

It was the day after, the day they came back, that I'll never forget.

The prince will remember soon too. Every time Evra speaks with him, she gains more knowledge, gets closer to the truth. He'll remember, he'll tell her, he'll be my ruin.

No. No, it's too late. He cannot hurt me. And neither can the Clearsee.

The king will not receive another report from her, nor another reprieve from death, and the prince cannot return, whether I wish it or not. I am heir now, officially and before witnesses.

I am the heir.

Soon I will be queen.

What did King Alder say about the Clearsee? *It's your future she's here to protect.* At what point will the magic change loyalties? When I'm crowned? Or will it always seek to thwart me like it did today?

Maybe it's because of the prince.

I'll need to keep Evra close, even closer than I have. I'll need to keep her isolated, until I'm sure. Tightening the stays of her dress today was an impulse. A distraction. It was enough to stop her from talking, to keep her silent a little while longer. But I'll not hurt her, not more than that.

Not if I can help it.

I hurry out of my ballgown and into dark clothes. There's a certain level of relief, knowing my secrets are so close to the surface. There's no more waiting and wondering. Now I *must* act. The magic rises to meet me, spreading, filling, sparking. It is ready for what must happen, whether I am or not.

I hurry through empty hallways, the lingering music from the ball slipping around corners with me. There's an eerie symmetry to the night of the last ball, when all of this began. But I am calm this time. Full of regret, but calm. There is no other way out.

It is simple to slip out of the gate and into the forest behind the castle. The night is moonless and cold and smells of snow. I might have regretted leaving my cloak in the castle, except that the magic keeps me warm, millions of tiny fires sputtering to life along my veins. It doesn't take long to reach the abandoned cottage. I pause at the edge of the clearing, outside of the invisible boundary I created that terrifying first night. I'm blind in this darkness, but I can feel the magic's hum, steady and reassuring. Last time I was here, I threw meat into the enclosure and kept my distance. This time I will have to cross the line. And that means lowering my wards. Nothing living can get in or out right now, not even me.

I breathe. Pull the magic in, filling my hands, my mind, my mouth. I let it run along the dagger—my father's knife—I let it curve around my wrist, the muscles of my arm. I can do this. I *must* do this. I can put it off no longer.

I send a suggestion for sleep into the space before me, wait to give it time to take hold.

Then, with a snap of my fingers, I light my lantern. And with a spell that feels more like a prayer, I let down the boundary. Dagger raised, heart pounding, I enter the clearing. My lantern's glow only illuminates a few feet ahead of me, but my magic leads the way. It says *there, in there*. It coos to me. It knows its strength, as it knows mine. I pause a few yards from the cottage.

The door hangs open, shredded and dangling crookedly on its hinges. A heavy scent, like wild things and spoiled meat, fills the air, so thick it coats my tongue. The unladylike desire to spit overwhelms me. I take another slow step forward. The lantern throws long fingers of light into the small ruin of a cottage.

A table lies in splinters. Tin dishes are scattered across the floor, yellowed curtains in a heap by the single window. And there, on the mouse-eaten bed, lies the prince. The creature. Snarling in its sleep.

My heart seizes. Does it always sleep on the bed? Like it still remembers that much about being human? I need to believe that Kendrik is no longer in that vessel, that I'm not really killing *him*, but the thing that took him over.

And yet, no matter how I justify it, I'm the one to blame. This is my doing, and I must face it.

I stare down at the beast for a long moment. Its fur is matted and caked with blood; some of its nails are ripped out of its saucer-sized paws. *This is my doing.*

Oh God, I wish I knew how to turn him back. Seeing Kendrik like this, motionless—not trying to claw my throat out—makes it so much worse. I have been a liar since my mother died. But I'm a thief now too. I stole Prince Kendrik's throne, and his life.

Soon I'll be his murderer.

I raise the dagger over the beast's throat. My hand tenses and the magic jumps, ready to do what is necessary, and still I hesitate.

Until the creature opens its eyes.

Panicked, I slash downward, but it—he—is already moving. With a roar, he leaps, slamming into me. I try to keep my feet, try to hold on to the knife, but I'm so surprised, so off-balance that I tumble backward. My lantern shatters. The uncaged flame finds the dirty old curtains and *climbs climbs*

climbs. Too much light heat death. A growl echoes through the room, big enough to sound like it's coming from all sides, from everywhere. It surrounds me. Cold sweat pricks my temples. The fire licks higher. I throw up an imperfect, hasty magical shield and scramble on my hands and knees for the knife.

But there isn't time. The beast snarls into my face and then he's gone, his large, heavy body trampling me into the dirty floor as he leaps into the darkness beyond.

No. *No.* Prince Kendrik can't be gone.

I scream. Not an anguished internal scream. This one I let out. All of it.

I stagger to my feet, bruises blooming under my skin, and feed magic into my hands. I'll drop him where he stands.

Flames flicker across the ceiling. The old cottage wasn't more than kindling anyway, waiting for a spark. I run out into the open before it can consume me.

The clearing glows red and orange. I look everywhere, I send my magic searching.

There's no sign of the prince.

CHAPTER TWENTY-EIGHT

EVRA

$\mathcal{Y}$ou should go to your parents," I say firmly. But Tamsin isn't listening. She's too busy dressing me, as if I'm a small, reluctant child. *"Tam."*

"No. I'm traveling with you. We've been together this far, you think I'm going to leave you now?" She helps fasten my soft travel shirt and lays out my boots. I'm still shaky and out of breath, but urgency fuels me. Hagan has gone to the stables to see if he can retrieve Gobber. We're supposed to meet him there.

I grab Tamsin's hands and keep them still. "King Alder has not given me leave to depart. If you go with us, you could be in trouble. It's not worth the risk."

"Of course you're worth the risk." She flits around the room, grabbing a candle and flint, food that was laid out for a post-ball repast, stuffing it all in my bag. She's still in her gown. "You should have seen how pale you were when you swooned at the ball. The soldiers carried you all the way here and you didn't draw a breath. It took us too long to realize your dress was too tight, so tight you couldn't breathe. If Hagan hadn't cut you out of it, you would have *died*. You can't expect me to leave you now, Evra. I'm telling you, someone tried to hurt you. That gown was spelled."

And I know by whom.

"You'll draw every eye in *your* dress," I argue. It's not that I don't want her with me. I just don't want her to get hurt too.

"Come with me to my room," she snaps back. "I'm not leaving you alone, not for one moment."

I pull on my boots, checking the window again for any hint of the coming dawn. I wish for my knives, oh my knives. I feel so defenseless without them, even though I don't fully understand the threat I'm facing. Lady Annalise—

As soon as the name forms in my mind, a vision strikes with the speed and searing pain of an arrow. I'm in the woods—no, I'm in the castle—no, the woods. Lights explode and cascade in dizzying patterns, intertwining flashes of darkened forest and stone. Sickness, loss, my body is here in the castle, in the wood, in all places, when usually it is nowhere. I feel as if I'm being split apart.

And through it all, my ears ache under the onslaught of a single agonized howl.

I emerge from the vision gasping. Without Tam's fingers digging into my shoulders, holding me up, I would tumble into a heap.

"What did you see?" She sounds breathless herself.

All I can do is shake my head and try to catch my breath. After the clarity of my last vision, the frantic confusion of this one is an even greater shock.

But there is one element I feel no doubt about.

"We have to go," I groan, panic pulling me up on shaking legs. "We have to go *now*."

I don't know what I saw or what it means, but I know what I feel.

Horror. Grief. Fear.

The burning, parched sensation of the Clearsee magic tries to suck me dry. Hands shaking, I retrieve the flask of firecane and flick the cork stopper. I tip the liquid into my mouth and take a gulp. It burns a quick, comforting path to my stomach. Almost immediately, my legs strengthen and a rush of energy flows through me. But my mind is another story, a mess of symbols undeciphered and images half-formed. My heart beats too fast.

I grab my bag from Tamsin and we run to her room. Then it's down the empty halls toward the stables. Tam spells our shoes and clothes for silence as we run. I try to tamp down my panic.

I can't think about what will happen when we get back to Windhaven. What we'll have to do. Leave, flee, hide? Try to settle somewhere the soldiers won't find us, where no one knows us? Maybe the Winterlands, now that the refugees there are safe.

Will Lady Annalise look for me? If I disappear, will she let me go?

I know she was the one who sabotaged my dress. I know she tried to silence me. I know she lied. But I'm still not entirely sure why. Something to do with her childhood, perhaps. I think she thinks I know.

Somehow, we make it to the stables unchallenged. Magic flame burns in torches near the entrance, enough to show Hagan leading Gobber and the cart out into the forecourt. There's even a sleepy-eyed stable hand helping him. We climb up without speaking. I wait for the soldiers to raise the alarm, to surround us as Hagan leads us out behind the castle.

"We'll try the back gate," he whispers into my ear. My cheeks already burn with cold. "Perhaps they'll take us for the farmers we are. Hide your face as well as you can."

I hunch into my cloak and lean against Tamsin, try to make myself small and unremarkable. Tam, in contrast, sits up straight and leaves her head bare, so her thick blond hair, still coiled elaborately, will glow in the torchlight. As we approach the gate, I feel her heave a deep breath.

But, strangely, there is no one to stop us. No guard stands by the gate, no one shouts from the wall. The way is clear.

I should be relieved, but the easy escape only deepens my unease.

"Lucky," Hagan murmurs.

"It seems so" is all I can reply.

We travel as fast as we dare until the sun throws golden

fingers across the barren winter fields that stand between here and home. Hagan steers Gobber into a deep thicket well off the road and we climb down from the cart, aching and stiff. We risk a small, smokeless fire and eat the food Tam hastily packed.

"Evra." Hagan draws something from the cart.

I stand up unsteadily and hurry over to him, jaw slack. He's holding my knife belt, all of my knives tucked neatly inside. He hands it to me, and I breathe a sigh as I fasten it around my hips. They are a small part of me, perhaps, but a part all the same.

"How did you do it?" I ask.

"They were hanging in the stables, along with my dagger, Tam's bow, and some other weapons. There was someone guarding them, but he believed me when I said the king had ordered you to investigate one of your visions. He didn't strike me as particularly passionate about his job. Or, you know, smart." Hagan smirks.

Despite everything, I grin back. "Thank you."

It's full day now but still cold, with a sneaking wind that worries at our cloaks. The small fire does little to cut the chill.

"I want to try to bring about a vision," I say. "I need to know if the magic will show me Mama." The snake, the flames, Mama's screams... I can't forget the sight of her face, the feeling of strangulation.

"We will keep you safe," Tamsin says softly.

I pull out the firecane and hand it to her. Then I rest my hands in my lap and steady my breathing. In and out. Smooth, even, like the constant lap of water against the shore of Weeping River Lake.

My eyes find a small curl of flame. At first, I'm sure it won't work. For a long time, I listen to my breathing and the crackle of the fire. Dreading other sounds, like the scrape of scales against the ground. Dreading what the Clearsee magic might show me, even as I urge it to rise.

Our small campfire fades and, by degrees, the castle builds itself around me. A room, tapestried walls and a leaded window with a small seat below it. Lady Annalise sits in a streak of morning sunlight, in a silken dressing gown that practically floats around her, light as air. I've never seen cloth so fine. It's a pale, shimmering pink that draws delicate color into her cheeks and makes her green eyes glow.

Or perhaps...

Advisor Burke stands before her, still wearing his long burgundy robes. Something about the way she looks up at him, through her lashes, makes me wonder if he's the reason for the warmth in her eyes.

But that would be impossible. King's advisors remain celibate, unmarried. They make their vows to the king, as priests make their promises to God.

They do not visit ladies' bedchambers.

"You have news." She stands, slowly, the sunshine lingering like a lover's hand along her robe. If I had skin and bones and mass, my face would flush in embarrassment at the look in her eyes.

The advisor takes a step closer, until there is barely a breath between them. Before he can respond, she slides her hands around his waist and rests her head against his chest. There's no power or control in the gesture, nor the sense of her bestowing a reward. The way Lady Annalise sighs, her whole body relaxing into the embrace, speaks only of comfort. In that moment, she is a different person entirely from the dead girl on the bed, and the panicked heir who tried to silence me.

"I'm so tired," she murmurs, and the words go so deep, so far into her soul that I ache for her despite myself.

"I'm sorry to bear bad news," the advisor says softly. "But last night the Clearsee and her family left the castle. I'm assuming you didn't order her gone, Your Highness?"

Annalise's whole body stiffens and the color drains from her face. She pulls herself out of his arms. "The Clearsee is *gone*?"

I catch a hint of a nod from the advisor, and then Annalise is whirling about the room, a small, powerful hurricane. She knocks a short stack of books off a table, rips at her curtains, screams silently into her hands.

"What can I do?" the advisor asks.

The darkness swallows her answer.

My stomach clenches in my newly reclaimed body, my limbs shivering in the chill morning air. Tamsin hands me the firecane. Hagan pats my shoulder. For a long moment, I ignore them as I try to launch myself back into the vision.

What had Annalise replied? What did she want the advisor to do about me? A scream builds in my throat. Why did the magic not show me her response?

My visions are chasing me.

"We need to keep moving," I say.

"We need to rest," Hagan replies.

But I stand up and kick snow onto the fire. "They know I'm gone. Lady Annalise knows and she is angry. We have to go."

Somewhere in the distance, a wolf howls. Shivers scurry down my spine. The others don't acknowledge the sound. Is it only me who can hear it? Only me who sees the threat?

We travel through the day and night. Tam and Hagan hold me tight between them because the visions keep coming: the yellow wolf snarling from the edge of a snow-covered wood, Mama whispering for me to run as flaming serpents slither up her legs. I have only one vision of the king: fleshless, soulless, all white bones and white hair and gleaming red eyes that stare at me accusingly from the black holes of his skull.

I pray to see Prince Kendrik, but he never comes.

When we finally reach the southern edge of Weeping River Lake, the familiar shape of Windhaven spread along its banks brings me to tears. All the houses look the same; the dusting of snow makes the same hillocks and white tree limbs we passed when we left. I realize I was expecting something out of sorts, some wrongness I could see, taste on the wind.

Despite the apparent serenity, the Clearsee magic sits on my chest like an anvil, foretelling tragedy. I swallow back a sob.

"Another vision?" Tam asks.

I shake my head. "Everything looks the same. How can that be?"

"Let us hope we made it in time," she replies.

Please, I pray. *Please let us be in time.*

Hagan urges Gobber on, sweeping through the village and up the hill beyond. My heart echoes the rhythm of the cart, and I grip the seat so hard my hands ache. Another bend in the path, and the trees fall away, opening to reveal the wide, snow-dusted fields of our farm.

And there, at the end of the long, tree-lined lane, the house and barns are still standing. No smoke. No flame.

"Mama! Mama!" I scream as we thunder into the yard. From within the barn, Tansy bellows. Hagan yanks Gobber to a halt and I climb over him in my urgency to be on solid ground. To see her safe. "Mama!" I call again.

The house hasn't burned to the ground. Everything looks as it should. I want to feel comforted, but where is Mama?

Before I can call again, the kitchen door bursts open and she emerges, hands buried deep in her apron. "Deward, what—" She breaks off when she sees us. "Evra! You've come home!"

I break into a run and when I throw my arms around her, the force knocks her back a step, and then I sob against her shoulder like a child.

Mama is well now, but Lady Annalise knows I've left. She'll be coming.

CHAPTER TWENTY-NINE

ANNALISE

"Your Highness, if you don't sit down I'll not get your hair brushed and ready for bed." Sybil stands at my dressing table with her hands stretched toward me.

I pause. It's a wonder my constant pacing hasn't worn grooves into the floor. For the past two days I've done nothing but walk this same route, and worry at these same fears.

The prince has escaped. The Clearsee too.

And what bitter irony that they escaped the same night—and *my* spell cleared the way. Burke said the Clearsee and her companions left through the rear gate, that the soldiers there had fallen asleep. A dereliction of duty. I wouldn't let him punish them, but I didn't tell him why. Now Evra and her family are out there, and they know the truth about me.

"What can I do?" Burke asked when he came to me that morning. I'd just returned from my failed errand, mud and tear streaked, had just cleaned up with Sybil's help when he knocked on the door.

That morning, that moment, it had felt like the end of my world.

Resting my head against his chest so I couldn't see his face, I said, "Her visions...they haven't been kind in what they've shown of me. I don't know why. There are things in my past, things that could damage me, damage my future. *Tyne's* future. I'm afraid the Clearsee holds these secrets now."

I expected him to ask me what the secrets were. I might have told him.

"You need to stop her," he said instead.

"I need those secrets to be safe." I lifted my head, cupped his face in my hands. "*You* know that everything I do, everything I've done, is for the good of Tyne. She might not—she doesn't know me well enough yet. She might not understand. If she were here, if I could *explain* to her...I know she cares as much about this kingdom as I do. I know we could come to an agreement."

He brushed the hair off my forehead with gentle fingers. "I can do this for you, Annalise. I can ease this burden."

He'd left at once, and now I can do nothing but wait for his return. I've spent two days wondering if Evra went home to her small town, or if she fled farther afield. Perhaps she went to the Winterlands. I can't stop wondering when or if Burke will find her.

Storm clouds have settled above the castle. Sybil tells me

the constant, unrelentingly bad weather has become a source of discussion among the servants.

My magic seethes uselessly inside me, gnawing at my bones, thirsting for movement, for release. It doesn't wait easily. I don't either.

"You look tired, Your Highness," Sybil says. Our eyes meet in the mirror as she brushes my hair. Concern makes her frown.

She's right. My face, normally sharp, is downright gaunt, and my skin sickly pale. My eyes burn. I look more than tired. Sybil was being kind.

"I *am* worried," I say. "Advisor Burke has undertaken an important task for me, and every day he's gone is a day ill could befall him. I need him to find success in this. I need him to find his way back to me."

"He will do all he can to please you," Sybil says, her deft hands braiding my hair with gentle efficiency. "He will return quickly."

Something about what she says, *he will do all he can to please you*, sends a little twist of unease along my spine. I haven't hidden my relationship from her—I know she's loyal to me. But still, there's something...

"You think Advisor Burke wishes to please me?" I ask.

"Of course," Sybil replies. "Just as I do."

"Just as you do..." My voice fades.

But it isn't the same. Is it? I've never used my magic to will Burke's love or loyalty. Only his belief in me as the true heir.

I touch him, yes. I ache for him, for the feel of his hands down my bare back, the warmth of his breath on my face. The rough-soft friction of his beard as we kiss. I touch him. But I never used my magic to ensnare him. Not knowingly . . .

My chest tightens. I stare at my reflection, closely enough to see the doubt, the horror building. Sybil finishes my hair and pats my shoulders to let me know she's done. I reach back and grab her hands.

"Sybil, what do they say about Advisor Burke? Down in the kitchens?"

"They say he'll not lose his job once you're queen," she says, with a little smile. "They know he's loyal to you. The other advisors are frustrated, they're not as easily swayed. But Advisor Burke . . . everyone knows he's your man."

My hands tighten on hers without my conscious thought. No one questions his loyalty. This is good. This is what I need. But . . . but could I have forced that loyalty? Could his feelings, could they be the magic, the whispers, the wild?

That is not love.

What I feel . . . what I need from him . . .

Behind me, Sybil makes a noise.

I focus on her reflection, her face tight with pain. She's gasping soundlessly now, chest heaving uselessly. What is happening to her? What is wrong?

Then I feel it, the lightning springing to my hands, the conduits open and flowing. It's harder than it should be to loosen my grip. To stand up and step away.

Sybil drops to her knees.

My body shakes. "Sybil, darling, are you well?" I bend down beside her. I don't dare touch her, the magic still shivers through me *too strong too willful.*

She takes a shuddering breath. "I—I don't know what happened. I couldn't breathe."

"You're tired and worried too," I say soothingly. "You need not care for me in the morning. Please take some time to rest. I need you healthy."

Slowly, she climbs to her feet, her face ashen. "Perhaps a touch of fever. Just some sleep . . . all I need. I'm so sorry, Your Highness."

I risk a small, reassuring pat on the back. "Don't think of it."

She leaves, still small and shaking and disoriented. I pace and fret and stuff the magic down *deep deep deep.* I'm supposed to control it, but more and more it seems to control me.

Sybil doesn't deserve to bear the brunt of my fear.

Burke, please hurry. I need you.

Can I have him, can I be at peace, if it's the magic he's drinking in, not me?

I don't bother with the bed—I know sleep isn't coming tonight—so I'm up and still pacing when a knock sounds on the door. I run to it, relief like daylight breaking over me.

But it isn't Burke standing there.

"Your Highness." Veron bows, reluctantly.

"Advisor." I don't curtsy. "It's late. What news have you?"

His face is sharp as a blade when he says, "King Alder has died, God rest his soul."

I knew this moment was coming, and shock still courses through me. It is too soon, without Burke, without the Clearsee.

The king is dead.

Now it is only me and the wolves.

CHAPTER THIRTY

EVRA

We spend the afternoon preparing to leave Windhaven, but Mama insists on a family meal and a good night's sleep before we depart.

"We'll not get far with you as exhausted as you are," she says to me, brushing back my hair. I'm unwilling to linger, anxious enough that my skin crawls, but Hagan agrees with Mama.

"We have a long journey ahead. We need these extra hours to prepare."

And to say goodbye to Deward. He's decided to stay with his fiancée, Molly. "Whoever comes looking for you won't find me there," he says. "They don't know me anyway. And I can keep an eye on the homestead." He pats me on the back. "For when you return."

They're all pretending that will happen. But I'm saying silent, pained goodbyes at every turn. Goodbye to the little flower Tam and I carved into Daisy's stall door. Goodbye to the stand of trees just beyond the barn, where Deward first taught me how to throw knives. Goodbye to the bench Father built just outside the house, where Mama sits to shuck corn and I first saw Tamsin and Hagan blush at the sight of each other.

Tam has gone to her house. I tried, again, to convince her to stay there, but she insists on joining us, at least until we reach the refugees in the Winterlands and ensure they'll let us join them. "Otherwise how will you get word back to Deward?" she'd argued. But she has agreed to leave her parents a note. She'll return at dawn.

Supper is a somber affair. Deward tries to keep the tone light, but the conversation falters. Hagan looks as if each bite of Mama's dried fig and nut bread, his favorite, might choke him. Mama stands up every few minutes to stir the stew or plunk another dish on the table. She's made squash fritters with dried apricots, potato pancakes with a rich cheese sauce, warm cinnamon-scented goat's milk, and mulled wine. I am her shadow, helping with every step, carrying every heavy dish. This once, no one begs her to sit down or relax or stop cooking, even though much of the food will go to waste.

Everything that can survive our journey has already been packed in Gobber's cart.

My stomach churns and gurgles nervously but still I pile food into my mouth. I savor each familiar taste and smell. I eat until I can hold no more, until I worry I might be sick. At last

I push my plate away and get to work cleaning up the kitchen. I let the comforting warmth of the fire cushion me and the sounds of Mama whispering over her cooking and Deward showing Hagan a map flow around me.

I want to tell them all to stay. That I'll go alone, that this is my burden, my journey. But I don't know if that will keep them safe. I thought Lady Annalise was the answer to the problems in Tyne. But now, I don't know. I don't know what she's capable of, only that she hurt me. Only that the Clearsee magic says *run*.

"Forgive me," I say, my voice thick. "I wish...I wish we didn't have to leave."

Mama plants a fierce kiss on my cheek. "This is not your doing, Evra. The kingdom is full of darkness. *You* are the light."

I hug her so tightly she gasps. I don't let the tears come until I've made it to my room. Then I sink onto the bed and weep. I close my eyes and pray for a vision of hope. Some promise that my family will be well, that our plan to run and hide will be enough. I throw myself into the darkness, waiting for the magic to rise up and meet me.

But it doesn't.

The darkness is just darkness. Disheartened, I wipe at my face and try to pull myself together.

Without warning, a crash reverberates through the house. I stand and peer down the ladder to Deward and Hagan's room.

"Mama?" I call.

She doesn't answer. She screams.

For a sickening second, I'm sure I'm having a vision after all.

But the sound doesn't stop. There are no chattering shadow skulls or flaming serpents, and my body doesn't fall away.

"Mama!" I yell, just as other noises rise to engulf me: the clash of metal against metal, heavy thuds, grunts, yells, thundering footsteps that shake the house.

They've come.

Blood burns the word *danger* against the inside of my temples, pounding it into me with the strength of a hammer.

The edges of my vision go red.

I will *not* let them harm my family.

I draw one of my throwing knives and rush for the ladder. Below me, someone groans in agony.

"Where is she?" someone else growls.

Without pausing, I skate down the ladder on my heels, my empty hand gripping the side rail for balance. My feet hit the ground at the same time Mama and a soldier burst through the doorway. *A soldier, not a thief. A man in uniform.*

"Evra, run!" Mama ignores the man behind her as she rushes toward me.

Run? Run where?

She lands against me with a great thud, knocking the breath from my lungs. We fetch up against the ladder and start sliding to the ground.

The soldier stands over us, his hand on the hilt of his sword.

The sword that—that's sticking out of Mama's back.

Through Mama.

Into me.

All noise fades.

As I sink to the ground, Mama attached to me by burning steel, my knife leaves my hand. Buries itself in the soldier's neck.

Then he is sinking too.

"Mama," I whisper through the fire in my throat. My chest fills with ice.

Her head tips back just enough that she can meet my eyes. Her body lies heavy and inert on mine. We are on the floor now. Still joined to each other. Heart to heart.

Her hair wisps against my face. Her gray eyes hold mine. Her lips move. I don't hear the words. I am so cold.

The ice has moved from my chest to my belly, my arms, my thighs. My finger twitches—I want to hold her, assess the damage—but my hand won't move.

I am frozen.

Then the darkness comes. *No, no*, I want to yell, but the vision takes hold before the sound can leave my lips. Or maybe it's not a vision.

Maybe it is death.

"Evra, my love, you must listen to me."

Mama's voice wells up from the dark, bringing with it a warm, yellow light. I blink, disoriented. Before us stretches

Weeping River Lake. The sun is just rising, reaching golden fingers across the water, which is the gray-blue of Mama's eyes. The forest bends along the banks, lush with white dogwood blossoms and birdsong.

"Evra."

When I turn toward her, Mama smiles gently. A candlelight glow emanates from behind her, all around her, a luminous cocoon. Her faded hair is golden and shining now, her skin smooth and young. She is standing just where Father did when he appeared in my vision.

"You will survive this," she says.

"What, Mama? What has happened?" My body is numb inside and out. The only sensation I feel is warmth from her softly pulsing light—and from the tears winding down my cheeks.

"You won't be able to move for some time—I used the last of my power to ensure your safety. You must wait until they are gone before you try to get up. You are not injured, my girl, but they must not know that. Do you understand?" Her voice is urgent, but her face remains serene.

"No, I don't. I don't understand anything." And I don't want to. An awful truth lurks behind her words, but I won't examine it. I can't. If I do, it will break me.

Her face softens with love and sadness, and she drifts closer, tilting her head as she studies me, as if to memorize every detail. "Clearsee magic or no, child, you are a wonder. I have welcomed every challenge and joy that has come with being your mother. Even this. You must know . . . it will be difficult when you wake, so you must remember . . . we love you, Evra. Our sacrifices were gladly given, knowing that you will wake."

She blurs into a wash of light through my tears. "Mama, Mama," I whisper, over and over. I can feel the end of this moment approaching, and I'm not ready. I will never be ready.

My nose and throat burn. Panic wells in my chest. "Don't." *Don't leave me. Don't sacrifice anything. Don't go.* But the words stick in my mouth, ashy with agony.

Mama steps closer. Her breath is warm and familiar against my cheek when she says, "You will survive this. It's time for you to return now. I won't tell you to be strong; you have never been anything else."

Weeping, I close my eyes, and even as the vision pulls away, I bury my face against her neck, holding on as tightly as I can. I will not leave her. I will not let her go.

At some point, the light changes against my eyelids, the golden glow fading. Other things remain the same. Mama's hair resting softly against my cheek, her hands squeezing mine. They are wedged between us, her body weighing me into the floor.

My chest still burns, a bright hot point in the paralyzing cold that grips the rest of me. I try to shift my weight, try to pull my hands free, but nothing happens. I can't even open my eyes. Why doesn't she move? Is she frozen, like me? Why?

Did that soldier—

With a queasy jolt, I remember the soldier and the silver brilliance of his sword. I killed him. I watched my knife pierce his throat. Watched the life drain from his eyes. Why? Why did I do that?

The darkness becomes suffocating. My lungs try to heave in deeper breaths but Mama's weight acts as a corset, allowing only the smallest wisps of air. The snake from my vision returns to me. Those awful tightening coils, that terrifying vision of fire and pain.

The acrid smell of smoke reaches through the darkness of my memory; I can almost feel the tingle as it burns my nose.

The truth is just as insidious. I can't deny it any longer. The sword...the soldier's lunge. I hold my breath for what feels like a lifetime, straining to hear the slightest sound—a whisper of breath, the thud of her heartbeat. I embrace the stillness, praying I'll feel her hand twitch or the shift of her chest as she breathes.

I hold my breath until the darkness and silence are absolute. Until my whole body screams in protest. And then longer. Waiting. Waiting for some infinitesimal sign.

It never comes.

When, finally, I take a breath, the sharp taste of fire fills my nose, my mouth, my lungs. My body doesn't feel cold anymore. Just numb. Dead.

Like Mama.

"Evra?" A hoarse voice carries through the silence—only

it's not really silent anymore. The swoosh and crackle of the flames are getting closer. Louder.

For an instant, my body soars with hope, and I push against the frozen stillness as hard as I can.

This time, my eyes open. My head lifts, just slightly.

Sorrow slams into my gut as sharply as a blade. The voice wasn't Mama's. Her head hangs limp against my shoulder, her eyes half-open and still. The walls of Deward and Hagan's room are black and the air is thick with smoke.

The voice calls to me again. Filled with terror.

What did Mama say in my vision? When she was whole and healthy and glowing with life? *You won't be able to move for some time—I used the last of my power.... You must wait until they are gone.... You are not injured, my girl, but they must not know that.*

It was Mama—she's the reason I can't move. I'm supposed to stay still until they've gone. Lady Annalise's soldiers. She said she wanted to be different from King Alder, but she lied.

She is worse.

With a crack like thunder, part of the roof collapses. The room explodes with the wavy red light of flame. Stomping feet, and then Tam is falling to her knees beside me, weeping.

"Oh no, oh no, oh no," she cries, again and again as the house burns around us.

I struggle to blink, to move my head to the side. Anything to show her I'm alive. It's time for Mama's magic to release me, or I'll be another body burning to ash.

With all my strength, I blow air from my mouth. In my head, it's a scream, but it comes out barely audible. Still, Tam hears.

Her shoulders jerk and her fingers light upon my face, tilting my head back, smoothing my hair. "Evra? Evra, can you speak? Are you well?" I've never heard her voice so ragged.

I blink. Twitch my head a bit in her hands. It's not much, but it's getting a little easier to move.

Fresh tears pour down her face. "Oh God. I thought I'd lost you too."

My body moves again. The fire is slowly melting the ice in my limbs. Too slowly. Smoke fills my lungs. "Tam," I manage to whisper. It's so hot now, the air so thick I can barely breathe.

She whirls into action, gently disentangling Mama's body from mine. "We've got to get you out of here. Can you move?"

Another crash shakes the house. Smoke billows. Tamsin becomes a shadow in the red-tinged dark.

"Not well," I croak.

She grabs me under the arms and hauls me up. Just in time, my legs catch me, though they shake and tremble like a newborn foal's. I barely keep my feet as we stumble toward the hazy doorway. For an instant, I look back. At Mama's golden-gray hair. At her soft cheeks. At the still-shining sword buried in her back.

My eyes burn.

Tam shoves me toward a smoldering gap in the wall. The

wood is splintered and smoking, but it's a safer exit than the inferno to our right, where the kitchen used to be. With another heave and the scream of buckling timber, we burst through to the muddy ground outside.

Before I have time to take a full breath, Tam is pulling me up again and away, toward the frozen darkness of the woods. The heat of the burning house chases us to the line of trees. Ash and embers fall to the snow, hissing softly as they die.

Tansy bellows and the horses scream.

I try to change direction, but Tamsin won't release my arm. "The animals are free. They're safe. Just scared. They'll run to the village soon enough."

"Where are we going?" I pant.

She pulls me into the forest without answering. My legs are more or less working, but I stumble and trip, disoriented by the darkness and Tam's erratic route. At last she slows to a halt. I have no idea where we are, except that she's drawn us away from both the farm and the village, into a particularly wild stretch of forest. She slumps to her knees in the snow, a dark shadow against dull white. Her fox cap hangs askew and bedraggled, spotted and ratty where falling embers singed its fur. "We'll be safe here," she says. "For now."

And then she bursts into deep, ugly sobs, her face cradled in her hands.

I slide to the ground beside her. There are too many things I don't want to think about, but now that we're still and quiet, there is nothing else I can do but think. Wonder. Ask. Knowing

I don't want the answer, dreading what she'll say, I whisper, "Where are Hagan and Deward?"

She only cries harder, curling her body into itself as if to hold in the pain.

Her reaction is all the answer I need.

I don't cry. My grief seethes and plots, roiling like lava under the surface. Beneath the numbness, the blankness, it burns with hatred and anger and sorrow. It turns clear eyes to the events of the evening, trying to understand each action. Each reaction.

It begins to develop its plan for vengeance.

I should put my arms around Tam. Let her cry against my shoulder. I should let the grief come. But I hold myself straight-backed and rigid, scanning the woods for any sign that her noise has disturbed more than the birds. I will protect her from any threat.

As I couldn't protect my family.

CHAPTER THIRTY-ONE

ANNALISE

Even the golden candlelight can't mask the gray pall of King Alder's skin. His body, sunken and skeletal, rests quietly in the large bed. No cough. No breath. No need for the web of magic still caught around him. Even as I stand here, it fades in wisps that call to the power in my blood. I know much of the magic dissipating is mine.

Behind me, Veron clears his throat.

I ignore him, instead swallowing down my revulsion as I lean forward to kiss the king's papery forehead. Then, at last, when I've made a fine show of my grief, I turn to the advisors standing near the door.

"King Alder will lie in state for two days before the burning. We've only just sent his stewards home—it is too much hardship to call them back, but those from the far reaches that may still arrive can attend. The kingdom will mourn for six months."

My announcement is what they expect—Burke and I researched the protocols for a king's death. We were prepared.

"Have you made any headway in finding Prince Kendrik?" I ask, knowing the answer. Knowing I have to ask the question anyway.

Veron shakes his head. "It's as if he is smoke. We have found no hint of his presence or what's become of him." He and Niall are still clinging to hope that he's alive—Evra's vision was met with skepticism born out of their desire for his rule, not mine. A reluctant king is often an indifferent king, leaving most of the decisions to his advisors.

I am not reluctant nor indifferent, and they know it.

"It is late," I say softly, as if I do not want to disturb the dead. "But there is much to do. If you would, let us convene for a few moments before we rest." I ask King Alder's healers and personal servants to clean and prepare his body. They'll keep watch over him tonight. Tomorrow the priests will come.

With a last look at the king, I leave the room, the advisors behind me.

The king's study is cold and dark this late at night—I call for a servant to light a fire in the hearth. I'm sure the advisors would prefer to be sleeping, dreaming of ways to keep their claws deeply dug into my kingdom. But their machinations will have to wait. It's my turn.

When I've settled myself at the table, and all but Burke

have joined me, I steeple my fingers and draw my forehead into serious lines. "It is time we announce the prince's death," I say. "We've had no word of him, no sign that ill has not befallen him."

His abnegation should be enough. But I don't want whispers that he could return, I don't want Veron and Niall to attempt to thwart me in Kendrik's name. Best to make it clear that I am all Tyne has.

"I strongly disagree," Veron says. Of course he does. "We've more avenues to pursue. The king's greatest wish was to find his grandson."

"With all respect, the king is no longer here. And the prince's fate does not change his abnegation, nor his abandonment of his people. The Clearsee assured us he has died," I say. "Use those avenues to discover what happened to him, but let us not muddy the waters for the kingdom. The people need to put their full faith in their queen."

His face darkens. "Their full faith in *you*, a distant relative of the king, when the prince has disappeared? Your meteoric rise is bound to raise suspicions."

"As it has for you, quite obviously," I counter. "But prolonging the mystery of the prince's whereabouts will not assuage their fears. We must present a clear, firm front. The prince is gone. It is a heartbreaking mystery, one I fervently hope we solve, but it benefits no one to let questions linger. This is my decision."

I stare him into silence. General Driscoll says, "I can order more soldiers to the search, Your High—Your Majesty. Now that we are not invading the Winterlands."

"Thank you," I reply.

Advisor Halliday offers nothing. He's slumped back in his chair, exhaustion made flesh. He gave King Alder all he had. He deserves rest before I ask more of him.

I turn to Advisor Niall. "Draft announcements of King Alder's and Prince Kendrik's deaths and have them sent to me for approval."

He gives me a small nod.

"We'll do a small coronation ceremony on the morning of King Alder's burning," I continue. "And then I will travel to the Winterlands to negotiate personally with the refugees."

"You'll do no such thing!" Veron practically yells. "Of all the asinine—"

"It is *my* decision, not yours." I turn a sharp smile in his direction. "General Driscoll and I will discuss the particulars."

Glancing around the table at the others, I watch for derision, disapproval, for their ambitions to show too clearly on their faces. I thread my magic through the room, encouraging their loyalty. Veron is the only one whose expression never changes. Obstinate. My magic isn't as effective on the stubborn, the defiant. I'll have to influence him another way.

I decide on the straightforward approach. "Tyne is too important to risk ill-advised rebellion. Perhaps you would not try anything outright, Advisor Veron, but your wishes are plain on your face. You do not want me to be queen, and I suspect you're willing to act on that desire."

There's a pause before he shakes his head. "Of course not, Your...Majesty."

I can't help smiling a little. You'd think a revered advisor would be a better liar. "Thank you for your service, Advisor Veron. It's time for you to find your life's purpose elsewhere."

A storm breaks across his face. Before he lets loose the thunder building in his throat, I continue. "Your experience is too valuable to waste. While I am relieving you of your role as my advisor, I hope you will consider another opportunity, as Tyne's ambassador to Grinnauk."

He opens his mouth. Closes it. Burke told me once that his uncle loved Grinnauk, that he'd visited as a child and still talked about its warm beaches and white stone. It's a kingdom far to our south, farther than Maadenwelk. Far enough to keep him from poisoning the minds of those around me.

For the first time, he bows without sneering. "As you wish, Your Majesty," he says, and I know I've got him.

"Thank you," I reply demurely.

The energy in the room changes. I've surprised these men, so used to King Alder's erratic, selfish statesmanship. Niall sits back in his chair.

"Now," I say as I usher Veron from the room with a silent *good riddance*, "it's time to send home the magic workers compelled here by the king."

"All of them?" Halliday asks.

It is a small thing, Mama, but it is for you.

"All who wish to go," I confirm. "I will not be responsible for keeping families apart."

There is more to do, so much more. But the night wheels on and the advisors are restless for their beds. Perhaps some will mourn King Alder. More likely they will mourn their control over Tyne. Maybe I'm just being cynical.

Then again, *I* will not be mourning tonight.

CHAPTER THIRTY-TWO

EVRA

*Y*ou weren't due until dawn. Why did you come?" I ask Tamsin. The night presses winter's chill into our bones, taunting us with the distant, flickering fire. One we'd no more warm ourselves by than the devil's brimstone. I concentrate on Tam and let the cold keep me numb.

She sniffs and swipes at her eyes. "I couldn't sleep. I worried you might try to leave without me. I thought I'd come and stay until it was time to go." She shakes her head and clears her throat, which doesn't help the hoarseness of her voice.

I rub at a charred spot along the side of my boot. No, not my boot. It was Hagan's first. A slice of my heart shears away.

She breathes deeply, steadying herself. "I should have come sooner. If I'd only—"

"Don't talk like that. There was nothing you could have done." But if I'd been faster downstairs. If I'd known how to read my visions. If, if—

"You're wrong. Your family was outnumbered. I had my bow. I could have—" She cuts herself off with a groan, pounding a hand against her thigh. "By the time I arrived, the house and barn were burning and the animals were running. I thought that it was just a fire. But then I saw Deward, his throat..."

My stomach seizes. Images come easily enough, inspired by Mama with a blade in her back. Annalise's soldiers, for they must have been hers... they killed my entire family.

Hagan, Deward, my mother... how can they all be gone?

I scramble to my feet. I have to move. If I stay still for much longer, I'll have time to think about Hagan's dagger lessons, or Deward's stoic sense of responsibility, or Mama's gentle hands rubbing my back when I climbed into her bed on restless nights.

If I don't move, all of it will come crashing over me, and I may never move again.

"Evra." Tamsin stands up too, bow in hand. "You're bleeding."

I look down and see a dark slash of blood marring the white of my shirt. I pluck at the sticky fabric. "It's nothing."

She reaches for me. "How can you be sure? There's a lot of blood—"

"Leave it, Tam. We don't have time for fussing." I scan the forest, trying to orient myself. A crimson haze still permeates the darkness; the trees look as if they bleed. I shouldn't have waited this long.

Tamsin grabs my arm. "Where are you going? What will you do?"

The only thing I can do. "I'm going after them."

"You can't," she says firmly, surprising me. "They think you're dead. They think they've succeeded. If they discover you're still alive—"

I turn away, back toward the fire that was my home. "I have a reckoning for the men who did this, and Lady Annalise as well. I thought—I thought she was far better than the king. But I was wrong. And I'll not run and hide. She can't do more to me than she has already." My hand finds the knives I'm still wearing on my belt, though one of them is gone forever.

"Which way?" Tamsin steps up beside me as I slink through the trees.

I don't bother looking at her. "You're not coming. Your family needs you, Tam. This time you won't be able to come back."

She doesn't blink. "Hagan was supposed to be my family. He and I—" Her voice breaks. "I deserve justice too."

Another chunk of my heart falls away. I can't think of what was supposed to be. I can't think of them—not if I want to keep moving. Keep breathing.

"What about your parents?"

Tam narrows her eyes. "It won't kill them. I was never the daughter they hoped I'd be."

She has to understand. "This isn't really justice, you know. What we're seeking."

Her expression shifts. She holds my gaze. "I know."

The shadows are lightening. It's almost dawn. Hours since the soldiers attacked. Hours they've put between themselves and my knives. But they won't know they're being hunted. They think I'm dead.

I'll begin at the farm, find their trail. It won't be difficult, not with that many bodies moving through the snow.

We break into the clearing.

"I dropped my bag near the barn," Tamsin says, moving that way. I stare at her so I don't have to look at the flames eating my house. My family.

Another crack of pain shivers its way through my heart.

Our house is not what I would have wished for my family's funeral pyre, but I find small comfort in knowing I won't be leaving them to the bitter cold. I stand just out of reach of the firelight, watching the flames curl and smoke. Not much left now. Soon there will be nothing.

While Tam gathers her bag, I search the clearing for evidence of the soldiers' passage. The last of Mama's numbness drains from my limbs, but it isn't the exercise that warms me. Every step I take through virgin snow, every moment with no sign of Annalise's men, my anger flames hotter. I helped her, and she has done nothing but try to silence me. I thought we were on the same side. But she was using me, that's clear now. Whatever her secrets are, I *will* discover them.

I walk the boundary of our homestead twice and find

nothing. Perhaps they took the rough road back to the village, their tracks now hidden by Daisy and Gobber and Tansy fleeing.

But I must be sure.

This time, I don't waver. With feet planted and arms wrapped tight for strength and warmth, I close my eyes and fling myself into the darkness. There's no space for doubt; I *know* the Clear-see magic will come. And I know it will show me what I need.

"There are seven of them," I say. "Heading back toward Iron-wald on horseback. They're moving quickly."

"But they'll stop to rest. Today or tonight. They'll have to."

"We won't."

Tamsin and I jog steadily through the day. Whenever our legs start to drag, we pause for a bite of jerky or a little jolt of Tam's magic. We don't travel the main road, which slows us a little, but our path is more direct.

We stop once to eat a proper meal, because Tamsin forces the issue.

"I won't let you starve yourself. Or freeze yourself. Or," she adds more softly, "throw your life away to your vengeance. I'll not have Hagan slaying me when we meet again."

It's the first time she's said his name since the fire still burned. When I look at her, questioning, she shrugs and looks away. "I—I have hope we'll meet again, when my own life is over." She takes a deep breath. "And when that moment comes, I want to know in my soul I did everything I could to protect his sister. For her sake, yes, but for love of him too."

My heart splinters again, and this time it's too much. My tipping point has come.

"Tam—" Tears burn behind my eyes and my body begins to tremble.

Whatever she hears in my voice or sees in my face, it spurs her to reach over and wrap me tightly in her arms, comforting me as I couldn't comfort her.

With a shiver and a wail, I break apart.

In the distance, a wolf's lonely howl spins up into the frozen air.

I can't breathe, I can't move, I can't do anything but mourn Mama's smile and Deward's protectiveness, Hagan's loving acceptance. The older pain of Father's gentle encouragement buffets me too. At each tremor, Tam grasps me tighter, and because of her, the grief doesn't quite destroy me.

As I cry into her shoulder, she whispers, "You will never be who you were. Not without them. But you'll find your way to becoming someone new. Someone who honors them with every breath. I know you will, Evra. You'll be remade."

"I was content with my make," I sob. "Without my family I am only Clearsee. I am alone."

"No, you're not. You have me. And you always will."

Her words reach through the haze. With a savage swipe at my eyes, I sit back and stare her down. "Don't promise me always, Tamsin. You cannot promise me that."

She takes a deep breath; by her red eyes, I can see she's been crying too. "Okay. No promises. No always. But know that I'll be here with you, until my end." She shoves my shoulder. "Whether you wish it or not."

Another howl echoes in the distance. With a shiver, I finish the bread and cheese she forced on me. "Thank you," I murmur. It isn't just that she's here now. It's that she always has been.

We move on.

"How far?" she asks.

I do a quick inner search. "They're still traveling, but they've slowed. We're hours away." This version of the Clearsee magic doesn't speak in visions; I feel them like strings attached to my chest, pulling at the skin. I just follow the little points of pain and there they are.

When the soldiers make camp, I sigh with relief. We'll catch up with them before dark falls.

We smell their campfire long before its flicker reaches us through the trees. I used to love the scent of burning wood. It was the smell of home, of our small kitchen and Mama's cooking. Now, it's the scent of horror, pain, death. I'll never be free of it. Every fire, every torch will remind me that my family has been burned to ash.

By these men.

Tamsin and I hunt them as we would a deer. Downwind. Silent and deadly.

When we're in position, hiding behind a small abandoned shack near their campsite, we share a long look. Men are *not* deer. And this is murder. Just as my family was murdered. After a moment, Tamsin nods.

She fells two with her arrows before the men realize what's happening. I aim for the one in crimson, and I realize it's Advisor Burke—Annalise's paramour. If I had any doubt who was behind the attack, it's put to rest now. He moves just as I let my knife fly. *Damn.*

The soldiers catch on. They scramble. The stillness explodes into a blinding flurry of snow. Panic seizes me. I can't see them. Can they see us?

The hiss of a sword released from its scabbard echoes through the swirling white. Moving on instinct alone, I fling a knife. A shout fills the air a moment later. Was it the advisor? An angry buzz rockets past me; the snow clears in time to show Tam's arrow burying itself in a soldier's chest. Even as he dies, he lunges toward me, slashing with his sword as he falls.

I heave myself back just in time. But I can't escape the other black-clad figures. Three soldiers have fallen, but four more remain, including the one I nicked in the shoulder with my blade. The advisor brandishes his own wicked-looking knife.

What I wouldn't give for Hagan's dagger, and Hagan to wield it. Tamsin and I are ill-equipped for hand-to-hand combat.

One of the soldiers lunges. I let my third knife fly. He groans when it connects with his thigh but doesn't slow. His sword shoots off sparks of sunlight as he whips it into an arc above me. I take a step back, try to get another knife between us.

A hiss. An arrow. He goes down.

I glance back at Tamsin just as another soldier charges her, knocking away her bow. My knife sails through the air, straight for his throat. He stumbles backward, kicking up snow. A confusion of blinding white follows.

My heart pounds. Two knives left, and two enemies. Tam without her bow. For an instant the world seems to pause, encasing us in a muffling, comforting cloud of snow and sunlight.

The advisor's dark beard and piercing eyes materialize before me. He thrusts his curved blade at my gut. I have no choice but to use my throwing knife as I would a dagger, flinging my arm up to block the blow. The weapons meet with a ringing sound and a vibration that numbs my arm to the elbow. Before the man can recover, I shove my other elbow into his stomach. He tumbles backward into the snow. His burgundy robes tangle around him, but they aren't enough to slow him down. With merciless grace, he springs up and shoves the heel of his hand against my chin. My head snaps back. My eyes water.

I slash toward him with my knife, but he evades me. How can a stuffy advisor move with such speed?

His dagger flashes again. My blade dings against it, only slowing its path. A line of fire follows the weapon along my arm. I bite my lip to keep from crying out.

He will not win this easily. Not with my family's blood on his hands. I unleash a fury of kicks and punches, driving forward, looking for an opening. He deserves my knife in his heart. He *will* get his due.

Another slash burns my arm. But he is falling back, panting with the exertion. Another swift jab, another twist and kick, and—*there*. My chance.

I thrust the knife forward.

Behind me, Tamsin screams my name.

The world stops as several details coalesce in a corner of my mind. A hiss—that of a speeding arrow. A roar—menacing and wild, like an animal attacking. A violent pressure against my side. A flash of gold.

Nothing is clear and everything is clear.

My hand, covered in warm blood, a contrast to the icy air.

The advisor's knife, buried.

In me.

I twist as I stumble forward onto my knees. *Tam.* Where is she?

The last soldier lies on the ground beneath a heaving golden mass of fur and teeth. Tam's arrow bounces with the creature's movement, sticking straight out of its massive shoulder. And Tam—

She stands, open-mouthed, empty-handed, staring at the wolf. The wolf, *the wolf from my visions.* Not a metaphor, not a symbol for some looming evil. The wolf *is* the threat. And it is *here.*

And then, just as in my visions, the darkness swallows me whole.

CHAPTER THIRTY-THREE

ANNALISE

*L*ightning lashes the castle turrets. Snow sweeps across the city in blinding whorls and mini tornadoes. The fountain in the courtyard freezes, despite the spell to keep it flowing.

The wild is winning.

It's been nearly a week since Burke left and still there is no word. There have been no wolf sightings. My secrets are open wounds, bound to fester and rot. My magic is a mountain, taking up space I do not have to give it.

My coronation is tomorrow.

The dress King Alder commissioned for my wedding to Count Orlaith—before I was even informed of my betrothal— will serve as my gown for the ceremony. Perhaps my subjects will see the layers of frothy white as a sign of hope. They are to me. I could have been wearing this dress in Maadenwelk next to a wolf of a husband, knowing his jaws would close around me the second we were alone. The wrappings of a body to be claimed.

Now *I* am the one doing the claiming.

I sway a little, to test how the dress moves.

"Just a few small alterations left, Your Majesty." The seamstress speaks around a mouthful of pins. She tightens the bodice ever so slightly, and marks a new hem.

I stare at my reflection in the wavering candlelight. Tomorrow, I will be queen.

I will continue to undo the damage King Alder has wrought upon Tyne. I'll send soldiers to protect the smaller villages from thieves. I'll lower taxes so families aren't so burdened and desperate. I'll find advisors who care about the health of the kingdom and not their own wealth. Advisors like Burke.

Where is he? Did he find her?

I am removing the gown when there's a commotion at the door. The seamstress takes the heavy fabric from me. I throw a robe over my chemise just as Sybil hurries to my side.

"Down in the courtyard," she says breathlessly. "You must come."

I change quickly and hurry after her. She says nothing more; I'm not sure she knows what's happening, only that I am needed.

I have no difficulty imagining the possibilities: a mob that knows the truth, Veron with several generals bent on mutiny, a wealthy prince come to woo the new queen.

I pray it's Burke with the Clearsee, but I'm not prepared when I see him, slumped over his horse and covered in blood. Alone.

Where are his men? Where is Evra?

"Get him to his room. Call Advisor Halliday," I say quickly. As soon as Burke hears my voice, his swollen, blackened eyes find me.

"Your Highness—" he begins before falling senseless across his horse's blood-streaked mane.

"Get him down, get him down," I cry. There's a flurry of movement as the stable hands carefully remove him from his saddle. They make a sort of cradle for him with their arms and carry him into the castle. I follow, my heart pounding. Is he still breathing? Where is his wound? My magic springs to my fingertips, fiery and impatient. *I want to touch him I want to make whatever is wrong right.* I want to give him my mother's gift.

But there are too many people, the corridor is too tight, I'm too tight with fear. Still, for him—

We reach his chamber. The men lower him onto the bed. Already, Advisor Halliday is waiting with several other healers. They pull open his shirt. So much blood. Oh God, there's so much blood.

"What happened to him? How bad is it?" I ask. I push up next to the bed, reach for his hand but Halliday shifts, nudging me out of the way.

Burke doesn't wake.

"Knife wound," Halliday says. "Please, Your Majesty. You must give us room to work."

No, I want to scream. *I'll work on him. I'll save him. But I can't oh God I can't they'll know they can't know.*

I back up a step, two. But I can't stop looking at Burke's

ashen face, at the blood on his chest, at how quickly they work to stanch it. How had he even been riding his horse with a wound like that? My hands itch. I need to touch him, I need to heal him. I can't let him die—

"Your Majesty." Sybil is at my side. It's crowded here now, beside Burke's bed. Somehow, I've crept closer, just a few inches between our hands. I could—

"Your Majesty," Sybil says again, her voice a little louder, firmer.

"What is it?" I ask, but my mind is full of other words: *Don't die, Burke. Keep breathing. Don't die. I need you. Don't die.*

All the words I said to Mama.

"Your Majesty, you'll dirty your dress. Would you like to wait in your chamber?" Sybil has taken the liberty of touching my arm.

Her words pierce my fog. She's worried about my *dress*? What could she possibly be thinking? "Of course not, I must—" That's when I see the panic in her eyes. Her gaze keeps darting to the healers; she's not worried about my dress, she's worried about them.

Slowly, too slowly, I realize how I must look, panicked and desperate, hovering by Burke's bedside. No one knows what I sent him to do, and now he's back, bloody and wounded.

I straighten. Back away. Clench my fists to keep from reaching for him, even now.

"I must continue with my preparations," I pivot. To Advisor

Halliday, I say, "Please inform me at once when Advisor Burke wakes."

My legs unsteady, I leave the room.

I've just announced the prince is dead. The advisor most loyal to me has returned from a mysterious quest injured and alone. And I fuss over him like a lovestruck girl.

I am such a fool.

I move through the day in a haze. My body belongs to the tasks necessary of me, the preparations for my coronation, but my mind remains with Burke. Every time someone enters the room, my heart seizes. By late afternoon, I am mindless with magic and fear. Both need an outlet, both need my concentration, and I have so little left to give. I am full and empty and twisted and tired and testing every bond of my will.

I find Advisor Niall. The elderly man sits in the library studying a beautiful illuminated manuscript depicting Tyne's coronation of Queen Helania. She was our last queen, over a hundred years ago. Niall, as eldest statesman, will conduct the ceremony, just as he did the succession ceremony.

"Has Advisor Burke awoken?" I ask, using every faculty to rein in the agony I should absolutely not be feeling.

Niall looks up from the book, squinting a little as he focuses on me. All of these old men; I really must infuse the kingdom with younger blood.

"Not to my knowledge, Your Majesty. But Advisor Halliday keeps watch. He knows to inform you."

I bristle at the hint of reproach in his voice. I raise my chin. "Good. It is imperative that I speak with him. His mission—to retrieve the Clearsee after she left the castle—is of the utmost importance. I must know where she is and why he did not fulfill his duty."

Niall raises a thick white brow. "The Clearsee, you say? No one knew where Burke was off to. There were other conjectures."

My lips tighten to a line. "Advisor Burke acted on my orders as quickly as possible. Neither he, nor I, owed anyone an explanation."

He looks at me for a long moment, his eyes going shrewd and pointed. "Aye, lass, that's true. But as your *advisor*, I would have advised you to make Burke's task known. It was a simple thing, a good thing, to go after the Clearsee. No need to keep it a secret. If you start acting as if you've got secrets, people will start to look for them."

His words burrow under my skin. He's right. I was stupid not to make Burke's quest public. I was afraid of the Clearsee, and I acted it, trying to quietly bring her back. I didn't want to call attention to the fact that she'd left in the first place. Now I've given the castle a mystery, a secret.

Just as the Clearsee's whereabouts remain a mystery to me.

I give Advisor Niall the smallest of nods. "It was an oversight," I say. "I appreciate your . . . perspective."

But I can wait no longer. I hurry upward through the castle

to Burke's chamber, just as the last of the daylight fades from the sky. Icy wind sneaks along the corridor, making the torches flicker. Thunder rumbles, but it's soft and ominous now. A waiting sound.

I push into Burke's chamber without knocking. Veron is there, keeping watch over his nephew's bed. He looks up at the noise.

A healer, nodding off in a chair in the corner, snorts and sits up.

"How is he?" I ask brusquely, ignoring the anger reddening Veron's cheeks. No doubt he blames me for Burke's fate.

The healer rubs her face. It's not so late, just dusk, but she has great dark circles under her eyes and much of her hair has come free from its braid. "He is resting comfortably. I've cleaned and sewn his wounds, given him what I could of my magic, but I don't know if he'll wake. The damage is significant."

"I wish to have a moment with him," I say. "Leave us."

The healer yawns, curtsies, and takes her leave. Veron doesn't move.

"He's going to die," he says, his voice a low grumble.

I refuse to let my expression crack. "Then he'll die in service to his kingdom. Now, if you would." I gesture at the door.

"It is inappropriate," Veron says, but he stands up.

"It is my will." I am implacable. *Leave. Leave, damn you.*

At last, with a venomous look, he steps into the hall.

I collapse into the chair he vacated and reach for Burke's

hand. It's so limp and rubbery in mine. So cold. I bend over him and try to breathe.

I don't know if it's my magic, my will seeping into his clammy hands, or if he wakes on his own. But it's still a shock to hear his voice whisper my name.

"Annalise." A breath, only. No *lady* or *Your Highness*.

"Oh, Burke." I resist the urge to throw myself across him.

"I did…as you…asked," he whispers, swallowing thickly. "The Clearsee and her family will pose no threat to you or your secrets." The short speech exhausts him. His chest rises and falls in an awkward pattern, and I can barely make the words out.

"What *happened*? Where is Evra? Were there thieves? How can I help you?" Unconsciously, even as the questions tumble from my mouth, my magic slips from my skin to his, warming the place our hands are linked. He's wounded, yes, grievously so, but it's not so dire as I feared. His body is otherwise healthy and young, eager to heal.

"No thieves. It was Evra herself." Already his voice is stronger.

"She attacked you?" I ask, shock widening my eyes. Quiet, nervous Evra? The tall farm girl who could barely look me in the eye? What must she have seen, to fight my emissary? A heavy weight settles in my stomach.

"We thought we'd killed her in her home, with her family, but she followed us. We were not prepared. But I was able to deliver a mortal wound. The deed is done, my love. The deed is done."

My brain, my magic, comes to an abrupt halt. The blood drains from my face.

"You killed her? *You killed her family?*"

He nods.

Soldiers, swords drawn. Mama's single, anguished scream. The blood. My hands, deep in it, trying to close the wound, trying to put it back. Her life it's her life she needs it. Her lips moving soundlessly, the flash of light, the piercing pain. The filling overspilling of my cup her life her magic in my hands my veins her heartbeat silenced.

"Burke." I can barely form the words. "Are you telling me you killed Evra's family, and when she followed you, you killed her too?"

"You asked me to keep your secrets safe," he says, his bruised face tilting toward me. "I did, Annalise. They'll not haunt you now."

There's a pressure, a shattering, an ax taken to porcelain in my chest. I am, from one moment to the next, in pieces. Jagged, ragged, wretched pieces. So sharp they keep cutting. I am undone.

"Burke," I say softly, around the pointed edges of my broken heart, "I wanted you to bring her back. Not kill her. Not kill her *family*. I wanted to *talk* to her."

How did he misunderstand me so completely? *Did* he misunderstand me? What did I truly ask of him?

He blinks at me, slowly, his dark eyes soft and unfocused. "I kept you safe. You were worried. I felt it, every moment we were together. She was a threat to you. She and whoever she might have told. It had to be this way. You had to be protected."

Color has come back to his face. He shifts, pulls himself up carefully to a sitting position. He reaches for me, his hands cupping my cheeks. "I will do whatever I must to keep you safe."

I pull away. I—I can't. His hands have ended a girl's life. Her mother, no longer in this world. Did Evra watch, as I did? Was she forced to see her mother draw her final breath?

It is too much. Too much blood on my hands. This was never my intent. This I cannot bear. Burke, Burke...Oh God. I loved him. *I waited I prayed I wanted him here with me forever. He filled these holes these places of chaos he brought me quiet. And he's covered in blood now he's no better than the soldiers who slit my mother's throat. He has murdered in my name.*

I am no better than King Alder. I was *never* better. My vengeance, my magic...I have forced destruction everywhere I've gone.

The wild is with me, sifting through the shards of my heart, slithering up through my veins and nerves and breath and bone. It leaps to my hands as eager as a lover. It leaves me as quickly, as painfully as a broken promise. Thunder cracks above, rattling the stones of the castle. I grasp his face in my hands, kiss him at the last, shake as he pulls me close, as he breaks me, again and again.

I say the words out loud, even though I don't have to, even though the magic sears them into his brain, inescapable.

"You will walk to the Winterlands. Walk until you fall, until the snow covers you, until the white washes away the blood you've spilled. You will walk until you die."

I tighten my grip one last time. I regret. I ache. I cry.

I don't watch as he leaves, limping but whole, healed by the very magic that sends him to his fate. I don't hear the door thud closed behind me, don't wait or try to breathe. *I fall across the rumpled sheets still warm from his body, his breath, sheets still smelling of saddle leather and lemons and I weep I weep I weep as the center, the core, the heart of me dies.*

CHAPTER THIRTY-FOUR

EVRA

A light flickers, washing the backs of my eyelids with gold. I say a small but fervent prayer that Tamsin is safe. Hesitantly, I open my eyes.

My stomach tightens. Hundreds of candles cast tiny flames against my pale skin and the dingy gray walls of an otherwise empty room. The air is full of the scent of beeswax, and a honeyed warmth pools against my chilled cheeks. Where am I?

More importantly, where is Tam?

"Lady Evra?"

I know that voice. The emotions that surface jangle and fight for dominance. Sadness, fear, relief. Hope. I turn.

The prince returns my gaze.

"Where are we?"

"Am I dead?"

Our questions meet somewhere between us, amid the candlelight.

Kendrik slides through the shadows at the edge of the room, picking a path through the dancing flames. Toward me. His eyes never leave my face. "I can't answer your question."

"Nor I yours." If I am a ghost, my heart hasn't realized it yet. Its mad dancing makes me dizzy. Especially when Kendrik reaches for my hand.

"You are my anchor, Evra. I am drawn to you, I am nothing until you appear. I wanted to tell you that. The last time...we were pulled apart so abruptly." His fingers burn against my palm.

"Is this your memory?" I ask.

"I don't think so." His golden eyes glow in the warm light. "It feels more like a dream."

"A dream?" I don't have time for dreams. His hands are comforting, reassuring. But I know death and sorrow wait for me.

His fingers skim my cheek, light as a whisper. "I'm not sure you're real."

A small sigh escapes. "I'm not sure of anything."

"Why do you think you're dead too?" he asks.

It all comes rushing back. The soldiers, the sword, the fire, the fight in the snow. The vicious blade finding me.

"I have failed. In everything. I couldn't protect my family, I couldn't help you. I—I—" My voice breaks.

He moves closer. Flickering shadows play across his face. "So you're here. And I'm here. What do we do now?"

I use his favorite words. "I don't know."

I have lost everything, even my life.

"I'm happy you are here," I whisper. "I am happy I am not alone."

He slides his arms around me very, very gently. I lean into him, trying to quiet the memories, the grief. I lay my head against his shoulder. I rest. There is nothing I can do now, no reason not to let go. We have nothing but each other. Nothing but this moment, as long or as short as the magic wills.

"I wish we'd known each other before," he murmurs. "I want so much to know you."

I am not the person I was before. I don't know who I am now.

Gradually, our embrace shifts. The gentleness reveals a new tension. My hands are splayed on the waist of his velvet coat. His are tracing my spine in a comforting rhythm. They falter, slide upward.

He threads his hands in my hair.

I lift my head, so I can see his expression. His lips, so close.

Heat kindles in his eyes. "Evra—"

The room explodes in flames. My clothes ignite, burning through to my side, washing me in pain.

"What's happening?" I scream. A roar has begun, ebbing and flowing, as if the fire is a living, breathing thing.

Death is fire.

Kendrik doesn't answer. His face is ringed in smoke, his expression shifting to confusion. His arms tighten, but they feel like ropes of flame. I tear myself away.

I hear Mama's voice over the snap and crackle. "It's time to go, Evra. You must wake up now."

My gaze flies around the room in a panic. Mama? I cannot lose her to these flames again. "Mama!"

"Don't worry, love," Father says. "All will be well. Wake up now."

Hazy figures stand in the corners of the room.

Lost in the shadows, Deward says, "We love you. But you can't stay. It isn't time."

My family is *here*. But the flames are too high, too hot. I can't reach them. A sob rises in my throat.

"Wake up, Evra," Mama says. "You have to go now. Tamsin needs you."

My side screams. I scream. I cannot leave them. But Tam. *Tam needs me.* I can almost hear her begging me for help. I can't stand the fear in her voice.

With a horrible wrenching that tears my soul in two, I let go of Kendrik, the fire, my family. I let myself wake up.

Still the sound of the breathing flames pursues me. I push my heavy eyelids open as slowly as if they weighed a hundred pounds. Brace myself for the inevitable horrors they will reveal.

But it's nothing like I expect. There is no fire...no sign of Advisor Burke coming at me with his evil knife. Only Tamsin and that strange roaring noise. Her expression is strange as well, her eyes wide and staring, mouth open, shaking her head... her hands held before her as if she's afraid of something.

Afraid of me.

"What's wrong?" I move to sit up. "Are you—"

The roar intensifies and my fur-lined pillow jumps and bucks beneath me. Pain explodes through my side. I catch myself on one arm to keep from falling back.

"Wait, wait. No..." Tam sounds terrified.

That's when I realize it. The sound I'm hearing... it's not a fire. The rumble of breath deepens, sharpens... into a growl.

The wolf stalks forward, putting itself between Tamsin and me. Snarling. Automatically, my hand goes to my belt. Oh God. *No knives.*

"Tam, are you okay? What's happening?"

She's backed up against the wall, as far from the beast's gleaming jaws as she can get. I've never seen her this cowed before. *We* are meant to be the hunters. Not the hunted.

"Just, uh...," she mutters. "Let it know you're all right." Her focus shifts to the animal. "Easy, easy now."

It advances slowly, hackles raised. An arrow still sticks out of its shoulder, bobbing with each step.

Why doesn't she kill it?

Still groggy, I stare at the wolf. Its white teeth and thick fur are exactly as I saw in my visions, its menace clear. It seems even larger and more threatening in this small clapboard shack—

My brain rushes to catch up. We're inside. That explains the warmth and lack of howling wind. The dirty, cobwebbed room looks remarkably like the one from my dream. Only without my family and Prince Kendrik. Instead, Tamsin is here, being threatened by the very beast that threatens our kingdom.

"I don't have my knives, Tam," I say, urgency coating the words. "I can't help you. Where's your bow?"

She shakes her head, her eyes never leaving the animal.

Horror washes over me. This can't be happening. I heave myself into a sitting position, or at least try to. Pain explodes in my side so sharply I cry out and fall back onto the rough pallet.

Before I have time to try again, the wolf's snarl slides into a whine as it whirls and buries its nose under my arm. I freeze, like a rabbit that has caught the scent of a fox. But the animal never turns on me. It just nuzzles my armpit a few times and licks my face before curling up beside me, its eyes trained on Tam.

My mind goes blank. There is no way to explain this. The wolf has done nothing but threaten and destroy in my visions... it was *just* snarling at Tam. Now it's suddenly become my own personal lapdog? I must be feverish. Near death. Dreaming.

Or already dead, just as I thought.

"Please, Tam," I whisper, afraid to move. "Tell me what's happening."

She doesn't leave her place against the wall, but some of the tension bleeds from her shoulders. "I wish I knew. One of the soldiers got hold of my bow, and the wolf leapt in front of an arrow meant for your heart. It saved you."

"But—"

"But it's supposed to be evil. I know. I can't account for it."

It made so much more sense when I thought the wolf was a symbol of some larger threat. How can this animal bring Tyne to its knees?

"What about the soldiers?"

"All dead except the one dressed in red. I ran to you, and he ran away."

I swallow back a sob as my vision comes back to me—my family, telling me I had to return.

"He stabbed you," Tam continues. "You fell. I ran to you, but the wolf wouldn't let me near. It dragged you inside the shack near their campsite." She swallows. "I've never seen an animal do that."

Needles of ice pierce my spine. Nor have I. "Could it be spelled?"

Tamsin shakes her head miserably. "I have no idea. But, Evra, you're wounded. And by the trail of blood in the snow, I suspect quite seriously. I must tend you. I'm afraid..."

All of her bravado is gone. She sags against the wall. Her clothes are streaked with blood and pine sap, torn open in places, her hair stringy and tangled. *She* looks like the one in need of tending. As carefully as I can, I roll to my knees, then stagger to my feet. The wolf jumps up but doesn't growl. My steps are slow and jerky, my side aflame, but the room is small. As soon as I reach Tam, I wrap an arm around her, the other pressing against my wound. We lean into each other, neither of us quite strong enough to stand alone.

"You're okay. We're okay," I whisper into her dirty hair.

She shakes her head against my shoulder. "Those soldiers...killing them didn't bring Hagan back." Her sobs shake us both. "And there you were, pale and bleeding on the ground, and I couldn't even go to you."

I brush my hand along her hair, over and over, like Mama does—did—to me. "It's okay. All will be well," I murmur, wishing I could think of more to say. I can't examine my own feelings about the soldiers. I can't think of anything but helping her through this moment.

"I didn't know whether to kill the wolf...I didn't know what you'd want me to do. I thought...I thought you were dead at first...I thought I was alone."

My own tears threaten to spill. I don't want to imagine how I'd have felt in the same situation, with her lying on the ground. With a deep breath, I raise my head and put a small space between us.

"Why don't you look at my injuries now?"

A little light comes back into her eyes. "Let me see."

She pulls at the hand I've pressed against my side. I droop against her when I see the blood covering my palm. I'm still bleeding. That's not good.

"Oh no...no..." Tamsin's eyes widen at all the blood.

The pain is constant, a burning fire and soul-deep ache that tug at my consciousness. In the corner of my vision, I can almost see the warm glow of candlelight.

She puts her hand over my wound and whispers a spell. Knives of ice stab my side now, warring with the flames. My legs must be somewhere beneath me, but I can't feel them. The world tilts.

Behind me, the wolf whines.

I want to hold on to Tam. I want to thank her for being my friend. For going into this battle for me. I want to brush away the tears that are sneaking from her eyes, winding down her tight, pain-filled face, and tell her she is strong enough to survive, whatever happens to me. But my lips won't work. And this gray mess of a world is fading.

Praying a vision—not death—will catch me, I fall into the dark.

I land in a hell of wavering light and bitter darkness, of endless flames eating at my side, my arm. Kendrik calls my name through a vast, impenetrable fog, his voice competing with the sounds, far off, of Tam praying and weeping. Once, I think I feel his hand slip over mine, but a second later it's ripped away.

My family has forsaken me. No words of comfort from Mama, no entreaties to be strong from Father. Just an agony of pain and darkness.

Eventually, a face does coalesce before me, but not a

welcome one. The glittering blue eyes of the last Clearsee stare me down. A voice like the hissing of a hundred snakes fills my ears, but his mouth never moves. "You do not see clearly, even now."

"See *what* clearly?" My voice is a shrunken whisper.

"The Clearsee magic has shown you, but you do not see." The voice is so loud it rattles my bones, breaking me apart.

"Has shown me *what*? What is it that I do not see?" I scream.

Blood cannot lie. Are the words from him or my own memory?

The madness is overtaking me. I can feel it, slithering from the last Clearsee's too-bright eyes, flowing into my own gaping mouth. I will succumb, just as he did, the incomprehensible visions and helplessness too much to bear. The shadow skulls laughing, the embrace of a dead man…my family calling to me from a place I cannot reach. This life, this world of riddles and parched-desert dreams…the cold of the endless winter cleaving to my bones…it is too much.

I am done. I have failed. I will be unmade.

CHAPTER THIRTY-FIVE

ANNALISE

Niall speaks the necessary words in grave and sepulchral tones. I stare blankly at the courtiers and city dwellers who've come for the coronation, registering nothing but the weight of the crown on my head, the delicate but deadly strand of magic that stretches between me and Burke, who is slowly making his way north. I've no energy for more. I've no energy for anything.

I have already broken my promises to my mother, to my kingdom. I already know I don't deserve the crown Niall has placed on my head. But, because of me, there is no one else.

So I stand silently, a statue in my big white dress, and I wait for this moment to pass, for this burden to consume me.

"I present to you Annalise Elodie Renalta, queen of the kingdom of Tyne," Niall says at last.

I have stolen so much. Lives. A last name. A kingdom.

Mama, please forgive me.

The coronation ends with little fanfare. The country is in mourning for King Alder and Prince Kendrik—there will be no ball, no celebration.

The funereal atmosphere follows me back to my chambers. I must change and prepare for my meeting with General Driscoll. I must do this job, now that I've worked so hard to win it.

Sybil is helping me into a dark wool dress when the door flies open, crashing against the wall.

Sybil gasps. I pull at my magic reflexively, but there's little left. Most has gone to healing Burke and sending him away. I've not slept, nor eaten. I've not given myself time to rebuild my strength. I am a husk, and I'm not even sure I care.

Veron stands in the doorway, looking strange without his burgundy advisor robes. His gray hair spikes at his crown and his jowls pull downward, giving his face a haggard air.

"Where is he?" he asks. "What have you done?"

I have no answer. Just the invisible string tethered to my empty chest, pulling harder the farther Burke goes. It might kill me, that string, pull me right out of myself, unravel me.

Veron steps into my space and stares me down, hard-eyed and thin-lipped. "I see you," he says, voice low and dangerous. "I see your lies and manipulations. I don't know how you've done it, I know I can't stop you, but your theft of this kingdom is clear to me. You are a snake in a stolen crown."

Before he can move, I grab his hands. I dig my nails into his skin, I hold on tight. What little magic I have jumps and writhes and twists into him. "You will be happy in Grinnauk,

Veron. You will not think of Burke. You will do your job without complaint and you will prosper. Do not make this hard on yourself. *Please*."

He fights. I can see the wash of gold come and go in his eyes. I can see how valiantly he tries. But I will *not* let him force me to harm him. He can be happy, if he would just *go*. It takes some time, locked eye to eye with him, locked in a struggle of will and need. If I were at my full strength, I might have hurt him without meaning to, as I did with Prince Kendrik. I've so little control, especially now. Did I *ever* have control? Did I ever truly understand what I was doing? It takes some time, but Veron's hands relax in mine. His shoulders slump. He lets the lightning in.

"I want you to go and be happy," I say, and there are tears I will not let fall. Veron was one of King Alder's most ruthless architects. I could include him in my vengeance. I could make him pay. *He* deserves an accounting of his sins, but Evra and her family have paid the price—Kendrik has paid the price— and I've no currency left for bloodshed.

With a little shake of his head, Veron goes, his threats slipping into nothing. I hope they're nothing. The suggestion is merely that with him. He is too strong to command.

Sybil quietly closes the door behind him. For a moment, neither of us speak.

"I don't know what I'm doing," I whisper.

She finishes buttoning my dress. "Yes," she says. "You do."

"The stormseers see bitter weather coming," General Driscoll says. "If you wish to reach the Winterlands safely, it would be best to leave soon, tomorrow if possible. I've forty of my finest soldiers prepared. A larger contingent will take a bit longer, but I can muster up to a hundred men and still get us on our way before the storm."

"Forty is more than sufficient," I say. "We are not waging war."

A crease appears along General Driscoll's forehead.

"What?" I ask. I've tried to claim the king's study as my own—more candles, fewer books of wars past. No heavy carved wood. But I still feel like an interloper here.

Slowly, she says, "I know you thought King Alder was cruel in his orders to destroy the encampment in the Winterlands. And he was. But my men did perceive those rebels—refugees," she corrects at my look, "as a threat. My men were concerned about their capabilities, their eagerness to use violence. I believe we need to be prepared for the possibility, at least, that your efforts will not find the success you wish for."

"The last ten years have been difficult," I say.

General Driscoll nods. "And some have borne more than their share of hardship. They are spoiling to fight back."

I walk to the hearth and stare down into the fire. Orange flames lick at the wood, hungry. Wanting. A fine tremble runs down my legs. Don't I understand the impulse to fight back? Isn't that what I've done, why I'm here?

"Forty men will be enough," I say. "But we will engage carefully."

"And when do you wish to depart?"

The thread to Burke stretches ever thinner, pulls harder, tearing at my soul.

"Tomorrow morning, as you suggest."

In all the time I paced and worried for Burke, I didn't stop thinking about Tyne. I read books in the dusty library, I asked Sybil about her family, I made plans.

"In the meantime," I say, pushing to get through this moment, this day. "There is more to do. Thieves are preying on the weak and helpless in Tyne. We've done little to thwart them, and less to prevent our people from becoming thieves to begin with. Beginning now, there will be no fatal punishment for thieving. No man or woman shall be put to death or otherwise harmed."

General Driscoll makes a small, concerned noise, but she doesn't argue.

Still, I lay out my reasoning nonetheless. I want her to understand. "Why are people resorting to stealing? What are they stealing? Bread? Grain? Because crops are failing without magic workers to bless them? Because taxes are too high?" I turn away from the fire to regard her. "All of the magic workers King Alder compelled to the castle have been sent home. They've been paid the last of what King Alder owed them, and will no longer be paid extravagant sums as blood money for being separated from their families and communities." I speak increasingly quickly, forcing thoughts of Evra and her family from my mind. I *must* not think of that family. That separation. That horror. "Taxes will be lowered. But I need our soldiers to help ease the burden as well. We must send more men out, many more than are patrolling now. Any thieves deemed not violent will be conscripted. They'll be given jobs in the military, paid wages they can send home to their families. If they're violent or not suited for military life, they'll be jailed. We'll try this for six months, and we'll see."

General Driscoll nods. "Yes, Your Majesty."

I don't know whether I've convinced her fully, but her brow has smoothed and her body has tensed, as if she is eager to get to work.

"There is much to do before tomorrow," I say. "You are dismissed."

She stands up, and for a long moment, she looks at me, and I wonder what she sees.

"Until tomorrow, Your Majesty" is all she says.

By the time I return to my chambers, I am staggering. I've slept so little, eaten so little, and the wild is hungry, sucking at my bones. I send Sybil away. I lock my door.

I need sleep. I need to breathe.

Sometime in the night, the cold, cold night, my thread to Burke is severed.

In the darkness, in the pain, I grieve.

CHAPTER THIRTY-SIX

EVRA

$\mathcal{T}$he crackle of a log falling into a dying fire wakes me. Warmth presses gently along my side. My breath slides in and out of my lungs without pain, and the voice singing softly is one I recognize. With a tiny sigh, I open my eyes.

A healthy fire and two large, misshapen candles brighten the clapboard shack. I'm lying on a pallet in the corner, as I was before. Tamsin stirs something in a pot hanging over the fire, her quiet voice finding a melody I know well.

> *My lady, my love*
> *Where do you hide?*
> *Shall I find you in the garden*
> *Lost among the roses sweet?*
> *My lady, my love*
> *Where do you abide?*
> *Shall I find you in the meadow*
> *Lost among the grasses green?*

My love, my lady
Where have you gone?
My lady lost, my lady lost

The giant wolf is curled into my side, dozing with its enormous, heavy head on my chest. Its breath lifts the hair by my ear, almost as if it whispers its secrets so only I can hear. The thought sends a strange shiver through me, the tiny movement enough to wake it. The wolf huffs once, straight into my face, then raises its head.

"Evra!" Tam rushes to my side. I try to sit up, but she pushes me down with a gentle hand. "Don't bother. You're in no state. You've been in a fever for days. I've used every whisper of magic to speed your healing, but I was afraid you might not—I'm so glad you're awake." She's so close to the wolf her arm actually brushes its fur. No growl. No savage attack.

It seems they've made their peace.

Something about the song she was singing clings at the corners of my mind. *My lady lost.* That song—I had a vision. Young Annalise with her mother. Why? Slowly, I sift through all of my visions, beginning with the first. The wolf, a danger to the kingdom.

Or a danger to Annalise?

"What?" Tamsin asks, and I realize I've said the words aloud.

I sit up very slowly, but my thoughts are spinning. The wolf, growling as Annalise tried to sit on the throne. The vision in the king's receiving room, just as she touched me.

Why didn't I see it before?

I give the animal an awkward pat, as it whines and burrows under my arm.

"Tamsin, I don't think the wolf is a threat to Tyne. I think it's a threat to *Annalise*. In all my visions, it was growling at *her*, and I've only just realized it."

"How can a wolf, a real wolf, be a threat to her?"

Her magic has made my joints loose and my head fuzzy. "I don't know. But I think the Clearsee magic *knows* something...something about her." A new certainty rises. "I think it knows that she should not be queen. *That's* why she tried to silence me, why she tried to kill me. Because she knows it too."

Tamsin's eyes widen. "You're saying she's not the rightful heir?"

I nod slowly. "But I don't know how or why."

"And we have no proof," Tamsin adds. "King Alder is ill, the prince is dead. How does the Clearsee magic expect us to stop her?"

We stare at each other, wearing matching expressions of frustration. At last, Tamsin turns away to ladle whatever's in the pot into three wooden bowls.

She places one on the floor, and the wolf jumps up and trots over to it. It inhales the steaming food in what looks like one gulp, then returns to its place at my side. My hand brushes its fur accidentally; it's softer and thicker than the mangy pelts of the Windhaven dog pack.

"This is not a normal wolf," I murmur, eyeing it with

suspicion. "It must be spelled somehow. No wild animal acts like this."

"I know. It's so strange. It hunts for us too. While you were unconscious, it brought rabbits, squirrels...I can't account for it."

Neither can I.

"We have to get back to the castle," I say, the small sips of stew burning down my throat. "Surely there's someone who will listen. The king—he can appoint a new heir. If he still lives—"

"No. *No*, Evra. She'll finish the job if you go back."

"I have to, Tam. I have a responsibility to this kingdom. Lady Annalise m-murdered my family. She's no better than King Alder."

"But you don't know *why* she shouldn't be queen, beyond her trying to kill you. And King Alder has done that and worse himself. We need more information, and *you* need to heal."

"But—"

"All I've been able to do is stave off infection; it'll be weeks before you've healed enough to even *think* about such a journey. Perhaps that'll give you time to wrestle your magic into giving *real* answers."

I force down another bite of stew. "That's too long. The king will surely have died by then. There will be no one left to help us."

"I'm telling you, Evra, you need to eat and rest. Your recovery has barely begun. The journey itself would kill you."

A gust of wind rushes down the shack's flimsy chimney, sending a cloud of smoke exploding from the fire.

"Besides, a storm is coming." Tamsin readjusts the burning wood to better protect the flames from errant breezes.

"All the more reason to leave now, while we still can."

She doesn't bother responding.

I slam my good arm onto the table in frustration. "So that's it? We sit here and stare at one another for weeks? Pray that King Alder will keep breathing, that Annalise will not try to silence anyone else?"

"No." She meets my gaze squarely, unmoved by my outburst. "We gather our supplies and our strength. We leave our hot heads to Hagan's memory and try to be wise about this. We need to come up with a plan—it's not as if we can walk into the castle decrying the heir. We'd be hung for treason before the king or his advisors even had a chance to listen. Still worse, if the king has died. We have no idea who stands with her or who our allies might be. Evra, we must be sensible. You use your visions to glean as much knowledge—as many actual *answers*—as you can. We'll go, we'll confront Annalise. But we'll do it with as much strength and forethought as we can."

I am shamed to my core. "You sound like the leader of an army."

A little grin touches her lips. "I have ever been fond of organizing and executing conflict."

I can't help but laugh, though my mirth doesn't last long.

"So we sit. We wait, we plan, we scheme. But no action...no escape from this dingy, depressing shack."

"No escape *yet*."

I stare at the length of fabric that binds my arm, feeling a bolt of pain in my side as I shift positions. "When that man stabbed me, I saw my family." My voice breaks. "They told me I couldn't stay with them, that it wasn't time. Mama sent me back to you. She said you needed me."

Tamsin looks up from her bowl to meet my eyes. Tears make thin streaks through the grime on her cheeks, but her voice doesn't shake when she says, "She was right."

"You saved me, Tam. This time...and back at the house too. You're always saving my life."

She smiles, her dark eyes glowing in the firelight. "Well, it's a life worth saving. Now finish your stew before it gets cold. I've no magic left to keep it warm for you."

CHAPTER THIRTY-SEVEN

ANNALISE

*W*e are ready, Your Majesty," General Driscoll says. She is dressed in armor with an extra layer of sheep's wool beneath. Her breath makes a white cloud that obscures her face. In the forecourt of the castle, the horses stamp and whinny. Our entourage looks formidable—shining silver in their armor, tall astride their liveried warhorses. Several carts of supplies will bring up the rear of our company, stocked with food and the materials to make camp.

Sybil waits behind me, her face drawn.

I remove my hands from my silver fox mitt and reach out to grasp hers. "It will be all right. There's nothing to be afraid of."

She shakes her head a little. "I've never been on a long journey, Your Majesty. I've never been beyond the walls of Ironwald."

I feed a small amount of magic through our connected

hands, something to comfort and reassure her. "Then this will be a marvelous adventure. Don't fret, Sybil."

Gradually, the tension in her body eases. As we climb into the royal carriage, a small smile even graces her lips.

I have ridden in carriages before, but never one so fine as the king's personal conveyance. The walls are draped in red damask, the cushions deep and comfortable. Gold filigree frames the door, and the window is large enough that I can see General Driscoll mount her horse beside us.

Advisors Halliday and Niall stand beyond her, a tragic sort of send-off, their faces drawn into stern frowns. Neither offered to accompany us. I would not have permitted it anyway. *Wolves circling, seeking an opening.* I named Halliday my regent because I believe him the most unlikely to plot my murder.

With a jerk, the carriage moves forward, my advisors quickly disappearing from view. Sybil sits back against the cushions, her eyes half-open. I wish I could turn my magic on myself, let it feed into the tight muscles of my shoulders, use it to ease the knot in my stomach. But it only works to influence and affect others. At most, I can present the illusion of serenity. And that would be a waste here, with only Sybil to witness my agitated state.

Even so, I find that as we bounce along the cobblestones, drawing ever farther from the castle walls, my breath comes easier. My heartbeat slows. My magic settles into a low hum, instead of spikes driving into my chest.

This is what I needed: to move, to escape. To make space between myself and the memory of my sins. To seek out some kind of penance, to seek out the ways I can be worthy of Tyne. I've given up my soul for this kingdom.

I will not let it be another thing I destroy.

At midday, we stop to rest the horses. I stagger out of the carriage on liquid legs, my head pounding. Sybil climbs down after me, her face to the cold wind, gulping mouthfuls of air like water. I take her hand to steady her when she wobbles, and I can feel the woozy motion of the carriage still echoing in her bones. I transfer a whisper of magic between us, to calm her stomach and settle her mind.

An eerie, unnatural silence hangs over the company. There's no clanking of armor or jangling of horse tack, thanks to General Driscoll's silencing spell. But the forest still knows we're here. No birdsong fills the quiet, nor the rustling of small creatures burrowing in the icy undergrowth. Just the bitter sigh of the wind and the sound of my own pulse in my ears.

"Your Majesty," General Driscoll says, appearing at my elbow.

"Yes, General?"

"The storm is building more rapidly than the stormseers anticipated. I believe it may be prudent to camp here, within the protection of the forest, and wait it out." Driscoll's eyes flick to the sky. Above the trees, dark clouds play architect, building themselves into vast, ominous towers. They creep ever closer, pulled toward us by the frigid wind.

I know this storm. It's not one of mine, but I can feel it like a friend, all of its anger, its chaos, its taste for destruction. If we stay here and wait for it, it'll happily bury us.

"No. We must keep moving." Already, a creeping impatience is finding purchase in my legs. They ache to move, as if they wish to outrun the storm themselves.

"With respect, Your Majesty, I think it would be a mistake to underestimate this storm." She narrows her eyes at the roiling clouds.

"I agree," I say shortly. "That's why we must go *now* and pray it doesn't catch us."

Sybil and I are led to a protected grotto to relieve ourselves and then we are on our way again, the carriage bumping over the rutted road with renewed urgency.

Sybil naps fitfully on the cushioned seat across from me. I try to do the same, but sleep doesn't immediately come. Instead, the storm sings me a siren song of blinding snow and bitter winds. I lean my head back into the velvet cushion and close my eyes. I call back to the storm, my magic lighting the way.

I have never understood the thunder, the lightning, the imbalance in the air when my magic flares. I have never tried to rein it in, to call it back, or conversely, to call to other storms. I've never listened for another spark.

My magic curls through me, ribbons of electricity spiraling

along my veins. *It can heal it can hurt it is wild in a way I can never fully be. It speaks to the storm the snow the ice the clouds that fester and freeze.*

I send a message, a want. I send my will.

Let us pass let us pass.

I need to reach the Winterlands, I need to put this right.

Please.

Mama used to say that intent wasn't enough. Not with magic, not in life. "You can't just *want* to do the right thing," she would say. "You have to *choose* to do the right thing. Even if it means sacrifice. Wanting achieves nothing if you don't act."

"What if you make a bad choice? What if you think you're doing the right thing, but you're really not?" I asked, thinking of Papa and how he said he was leaving to seek his fortune, to put food on our table, and then never returned.

"Some choices will be clear and easy," she said. "Some won't. You'll do the best you can." She pulled me close and kissed my forehead. "I know you will. You're my heart, Anna. You're my heart."

I think she was wrong about me.

It starts with a murmur, a whisper, a familiar voice in the dark.

Mama singing, as she did when I was a child.

I am sitting under a tree and she is there. And Papa too, looking just as he did before he left. Young and healthy, chestnut hair ruffled by the wind.

We are sitting, we are singing, we are together.

Mama laughs. "Oh, you're covered in blackberries. What a messy child."

Papa reaches over to tap my cheek. "You are a greedy little one, aren't you? You'll eat yourself sick."

I laugh and laugh. Because of course I want more. The blackberries are delicious, so juicy and warm from waiting in the sun, waiting for us to pick them.

I look down, and my hands are running in the juices, except the color is wrong. It's too dark, it's too red. It's not blackberry juice—it's blood.

"Mama?" I ask in the voice of a child. Small and scared.

She doesn't answer. When I look up, she is gone. Papa too.

But I am not alone. The trees whisper angrily in the wind, and dark clouds crowd the sky, blocking out the sun. Burke, Kendrik, and Evra stalk toward me from the darkness of the forest at the edge of the storm. It is their blood I wear on my hands, their faces I can't forget. Their anger that beats at me with the strength of a hurricane.

Everything I wanted, everything I am is because of their pain. I wrap my bloody arms around myself. I don't know how to wash myself clean.

"Mama!" I scream. "Papa!"

The ghosts and the storm scream back.

CHAPTER THIRTY-EIGHT

EVRA

A storm rages. Its breath screams against the little cabin, piercing cold through the cracks in the splintered siding. I dream that I'm awake, shivering toward the giant wolf and trying to open my eyes. But I can't—I'm frozen in body even as my thoughts whirl and whir like broken toys. All the mysteries and questions and heartbreaks of the past weeks, every fragment of Clearsee vision...it all plagues me, demanding resolution. The maelstrom threatens to tear me apart.

Instead, eventually, it subsides. Reforms. Candlelight beckons.

A voice.

"Evra."

I turn around.

"Deward."

My brother smiles at me, his gray eyes, so like mine, clear and luminous. "Baby sister. I'd say you look well, but..."

I glance down. I'm wearing my stained, torn hunting

clothes, my shirt still dark with dried blood. No. I do not look well. But it doesn't matter. I reach for him, but my arms pass through his shoulders. There is no flesh, no body left to embrace.

My chest aches. "Why can't I touch you?"

Sadness touches Deward's smile. But only a touch; his expression remains peaceful. Steady. "You know why. We must be content with the miracle of this meeting. Just to speak, to see each other . . . it's a gift."

I want to wrap my arms around him, lay my head against his chest. But he is right. This moment *is* a gift.

Because I can't touch him, I study him instead. Note the soft glow that seems to emanate from behind him, just like Mama. There's a quietness in his eyes. It helps loosen the tightness in my chest. But I still can't bear that he's no longer in the world with me. That he has no future.

"I couldn't speak to Molly," I say, anguished. "I'm sorry, Deward."

"One day you will. You'll tell her how much I love her, and you'll help her find some peace. Once you've set things right."

Setting things right is a strange way to describe vengeance. I don't know what I'll do when we reach the castle. Tell the king of Annalise's treachery? And if Annalise is already queen—

Forlornly, I ask, "Deward, what am I supposed to do?"

He leans closer, and for one instant I feel a point of warmth against my cheek, like a breath or a kiss. "Evra, love," he says, "you're supposed to save the prince."

The storm blows me away. Wind rushes against my face, burning my cheeks with cold. Deward is lost to me. The world becomes an endless swirl of darkness and desolation. The shadow skulls scream in my ears, and I smell the hopelessness of burning ash and charred flesh.

Deward's words drive through the roiling storm and into my heart with the strength of a thunderclap.

Save the prince.

And there it is, lighting my way out of the black.... Hope.

With a loud crack, the chair breaks into pieces. Tamsin stomps on the wood again, demolishing it further. She grabs two legs from the pile and throws them into the guttering fire. Wind whines and claws at our shelter, desperate to seek us out. An icy draft sneaks along my neck and makes me shiver.

"So you really think the prince is alive?" Tam throws another piece of broken chair onto the fire and stacks the rest beside the hearth. "That's our missing piece?"

My hands itch to help, but I've been relegated to cleaning the last stringy squirrel the wolf was able to find before the storm.

"I believe so," I reply. A small, bright glow fills my heart.

Another gust of wind buffets the shack. We've been talking about my vision, about Deward and the prince, but we've said nothing about the storm. Not a word about the snow that has piled to the top of the door, trapping us inside. Or the freezing wind that keeps sneaking down the cracked chimney to threaten our fire. Nor have we catalogued what's left of the furniture and cupboards that could be used as firewood.

Tam prods the coals, her hand steady despite our dire circumstances. "But you said he's been in your visions. Like a ghost."

"He has. Only...I've been able to touch him. I thought it was a cruel trick of the Clearsee magic, letting me touch a dead man, but when I reached for Deward my hands passed straight through him. I think I could feel Mama, a little, because she was still physically beside me."

Tam glances back at me. "Touched? You've been *touching* the prince?"

I blush to the roots of my hair. "When I thought I was dead, he embraced me. It was nothing."

Except then we maybe almost kissed....

"Oh...," she says knowingly, "you *like* him."

I can't meet her gaze. Instead, I focus on the small, half-skinned squirrel on the table. "It doesn't matter. He's a prince."

Tam makes a dismissive noise. "So what? Whatever he is, you are fully worthy of his love. Or affection, or whatever has got your cheeks that lovely shade of red. The only real question is whether *he* is worthy of *yours*."

I want to laugh and cringe at the same time. She *must* be joking...and yet I can see she's not. I grab the skinned chunks of squirrel meat and lean over to toss them into the pot above the fire, letting one small chunk fall onto the floor for the wolf. It slurps up the morsel and returns to my side.

"I don't know what I feel," I say. "Or what he feels either. We've had bigger concerns." But some part of me, deep inside, considers the way his arms curled around me when we danced, the way he comforted me when I thought all was lost. I remember his fear that he lacks conviction, that he would be a poor king. And there was that moment, that instant when his fingers slid into my hair, when he looked at me as if ... as if ...

As if you're the sweetest berry on the vine.

My heart strikes a dangerous drumbeat.

The wolf whines again and bumps its head up under my arm. I finish cleaning my hands with an old rag and then, without really thinking about it, draw my fingers from the animal's soft, pricked ear along its neck to its shoulder, kneading the skin beneath its ruff, just as I know it likes.

Tamsin goes back to tending the fire, shuddering as another frigid gust blows down the chimney and anoints her with ash. She grins back at me. "Tyne could do worse than you for our queen."

I laugh outright. "He'll marry a princess or a wealthy courtier. *If* we can find him. *If* we can save him." Another howl of wind, this one bringing a swirl of snow from a corner under the eaves. I shiver. "*If* we can rescue ourselves."

Tamsin sits back on her heels. "As long as I can keep the

fire burning, we've enough wood for two more days. Maybe a third if my magic returns and you don't need it."

Reflexively, I touch my side. The wound no longer spits fire each time I move, but there remains a constant, endless ache. And my legs are weak and trembly. "When your magic returns, don't waste it on me. I'm healing fine on my own now."

Tam shoots me a skeptical look. "And when we *are* free of this storm, this hut, your wounds... where will we go? Where do we find Prince Kendrik?"

That is the question. Our plan had been to go to Ironwald, find a way to challenge Annalise. But we need to find Prince Kendrik first. "I'm not sure. I believe he may be trapped somewhere."

"Where does *he* think he is?"

"He doesn't know. He thought he was dead because that's what I told him. But he said when he wasn't with me, he wasn't really anywhere." I shrug helplessly. "I don't know what that means."

Tamsin shakes her head. "How can we save him if we don't know where he is?"

The spark of hope in my heart flickers. I can't stand the thought of solving the mystery too late... again. "Perhaps he's caught between worlds. Somehow. It must be Annalise's doing. I just don't know *how*."

Tam says, "So we'll go to the castle as we planned. We'll find a way to speak to her, to demand answers."

The giant wolf rests its head on my knee, gazing up at me. Its golden eyes catch the firelight and seem to glow.

"And what about you?" I ask, running my hand over its soft fur. "How do you fit into this mystery?"

It stares back at me, as if it understands. As if it wishes it could answer.

Then it whines, as if it *is* answering.

Something...happens. The puzzle pieces start to click into a strange, unimaginable pattern. The wolf's whine bites into my soul. I can't breathe. I can't look away from those strange, golden eyes. The firelight flickering...the animal's face so close.

The answer...*so close.*

Disbelief...a horrible, horrifying, *impossible* possibility...

Before I can say anything to Tam, a screeching howl rips through me, flinging me from the shack and spitting me out into a narrow stone corridor. There, just ahead, walking quickly...

"Prince Kendrik!" I call. But he turns the corner and disappears. I race after him.

I skid around the corner, but instead of another long, dark passageway I'm suddenly in Annalise's chambers. She is there, with him.

"Lady Annalise, you must come back to the Great Hall," Kendrik says.

"I can't, Your Highness. I need—I need a moment." Annalise paces. She looks upset. I watch her, unease coiling in my stomach. I don't know why, but I want Kendrik to run.

"I'm sorry, cousin. I know this news is a shock." Kendrik

closes the door and steps closer. *No, no*... Why does this room suddenly feel so unsafe?

"Surely you can talk to your grandfather on my behalf," Annalise pleads. "Please, Kendrik. I can't leave."

"I wish Grandfather would listen to me." His frown has a twist of anguish to it. "But I do believe he's doing what is best for Tyne. Count Orlaith is a powerful man."

Annalise rolls her eyes. "Of course he is. You are all powerful men, and my life is in your hands. But what if I don't *want* to live in Maadenwelk? What if I don't *want* to marry a stranger?"

Kendrik looks so sad, so uncomfortable. My heart aches for him. "It's not fair," he says. "And I will miss you. No one understands... listens to me the way you do. You're the only family I have aside from Grandfather. But we all have our roles to play. Our duties. It's what makes our kingdom strong."

"Our kingdom isn't strong," she replies angrily. "The king has drawn all of the strongest magic workers to the city, and what happens to the farmers and tradesmen, the mothers screaming their babies into life on dirt floors? Where's the magic to help and heal them? The king only uses his power for himself. The sacrifices he demands do *not* strengthen Tyne."

She looks as if she is about to be sick. My heart pounds. I want to stop whatever is about to happen because *surely* something is. I want to leave this room.

"You know the reason he does that," Kendrik says.

"That doesn't make it right," she replies. "It's been *ten years*, Kendrik, and still he orders them here."

I can't think or breathe or move. The air is so charged I can practically see sparks flying between them. Outside, thunder rumbles.

"Please come back to the ball," Kendrik says. "Count Orlaith expects to dance with you. Come, cousin. I'll escort you. We'll—we'll get through this together."

"Leave me alone. Please. I will not dance with that wolf. I will not leave with him in the morning. I *can't*, Kendrik."

Why doesn't he leave without her? Can't he see she is teetering on the edge? Her wide eyes, wild hair, the way she paces, her hands slicing through the air like blades . . .

Oh God. This is the moment. This is the answer to our mystery. I know it's just a vision and I can do nothing to save him, but I rush forward anyway, trying to put myself between them.

"What's going on?" Kendrik says, but not from there, near the door. To my left, by the bed—another Kendrik. This prince stares me straight in the eye. "What is this?"

"Kendrik!" I'm so happy to see him—*my* Prince Kendrik, the one who can see and speak to me—that I forget what's happening. I rush to his side, but before I can answer him, there's a flash of light.

Annalise's arms fling themselves up like they're bound on strings, controlled by a higher force. Lightning shoots from her fingers, making the room go bright as day. The air sizzles and crackles and spits and shakes. I fight to see what's happening, but the maelstrom makes it impossible.

Just as the present-day prince grabs my arm, the past one screams.

I crumple to the ground, Kendrik's arms around me. The cry that rends the air is full of anguish and hopelessness. It's the black places beyond the reaches of candlelight. The winter chill of a life suddenly, irrevocably changed.

The scream rips me apart.

When the sound and chaos pass, I finally lift my head. Kendrik and I are huddled together on the floor, our arms wrapped tightly around each other, our knees pressed into the plush carpet as if we're praying. And perhaps we are.

Annalise is gone. On the floor by the wall is a pile of clothing. And then...slowly...from beneath, a wolf lumbers to its feet.

The vision starts to pull apart in smoky wisps. I spin toward *my* Prince Kendrik, eyes wide. His shocked gaze matches mine. "You're..." I start. But I can't say the truth out loud.

He grabs me about the shoulders. "You have to find a way," he says, the words spilling out in an agonized rush. "Please, Evra. You have to find a way to free me."

The shadows morph into the flickering fingers of a fire. Kendrik's soft, golden eyes never leave mine. Now that I know the truth, it seems impossible that I never guessed, that I couldn't see.

The prince's eyes and the wolf's—they are just the same.

CHAPTER THIRTY-NINE

ANNALISE

The storm is an ocean, waves of snow breaking over us again and again. We cleave a path through the wind and white, my magic clearing the way. We don't stop until night has fully fallen, and even then I hold the worst at bay. I live in darkness, eyes closed, all that I am, flung to the sky. *The storm and magic and I, we dance, we do what is necessary what is possible I do what I can.*

We've nearly reached the edge of the Winterlands, the edge of the storm, when I feel the pull of my broken threads, the endpoint of my spell. Burke. His body, made marble by the cold, is here.

I feel the moment we pass him I look out from the window at the featureless hillocks of snow. He sleeps here sleeps alone and cold.

My heart shatters once again.

He killed an entire family. He killed the Clearsee. He thought he was doing it for me.

"Your Majesty, are you well?" Sybil asks.

I wipe at the silent tears that chill my cheeks like diamonds of ice. "Fine. Tired."

I close my eyes and return to the darkness.

CHAPTER FORTY

EVRA

*E*vra? Are you well?" Tamsin's voice cuts through the quiet of the cabin.

For an instant, I don't move or speak. I live on a knife's edge, teetering between heartbreak and happiness. The happiness: Prince Kendrik is alive and here with me. The cutting edge: He is trapped in the body of a wolf, with no voice to speak. We have no power to reverse the curse. No way to take back the life—and birthright—that have been stolen from him.

"Evra?" Tam gently squeezes my shoulder. "I know you had a vision. Please tell me what you saw."

I sit back, hissing when the movement jostles my side. My hands stay buried in the wolf's fur. I can't let go.

"I know where the prince is." I run my hand along his smooth, rounded head.

Tamsin lets out a breath. "You do? Where?"

For a moment, the happiness outweighs the heartache. "He's here, Tam. Right here."

"Here?" The excitement drains from her eyes, replaced with a sad and wary sympathy. "You know that cannot be. There is no one here but us, Evra."

I can't help but laugh. "Now, that's not exactly true, is it?" I gesture to our companion, who butts his head against my hand, baring his teeth in a wolfish smile.

Tam's eyes widen. "You can't be suggesting..."

I nod. "In my vision, I saw Annalise cast the spell that changed him."

Tamsin stands up, backing away from the prince, her face slack with shock. Outside, the storm still howls. "But that kind of magic...it's not possible. It can't be possible."

"I know. And yet, somehow..." I can *feel* the truth. No one has had this kind of power in generations, and yet Annalise does. The king couldn't have known. He would have used her for his own ends, as his own weapon.

And how did she use her weapons on him? His illness, his decision to make her the heir...suddenly I'm sure her hand was in all of it. That's why she tried to get rid of me. She was afraid the Clearsee magic would show me the truth.

Tam stares hard at the wolf. "You're *sure*. That's the...the prince."

"It is. I'm certain." With creaking knees, I stand up. The wolf leans against my legs.

Tamsin gives a surreptitious swipe at her limp hair and straightens her shoulders. We've washed up once or twice, dipping a rag in melted snow, but our clothes are dirt-covered and bloodstained, little more than tatters. Still, Tam's clear mahogany eyes and upright bearing are more suited to a ball at the castle than this teetering shack. She wears her rags and wounds as if they were silk and gold.

I can't help but glance down at my own wreckage. I have neither the bearing nor the confidence Tam has; my rags are just rags, hanging like empty sails from my newly bony frame. And everywhere dried blood, an unwelcome reminder of the advisor's knife.

Warmth swarms up my cheeks. I've no wish for Prince Kendrik to see me like this.

"Can he understand us?" she asks. "Does he know what happened to him?"

"Before the last vision, he didn't know where he was when we weren't together. He never spoke of the wolf nor gave any hint that he was aware of anything outside our interactions. Now...I don't know."

We both watch him. Waiting. Wondering. I don't know what to hope for; if he's aware, he'll have to live each moment knowing he may be trapped like this forever. But if he's *not* aware, his consciousness is imprisoned deeper, even further from salvation.

The moment only lasts a few seconds, but it feels an eternity. When the wolf moves, I start, my hands flying to meet each other at my waist, where they wring themselves into knots. I must convince Tam I'm well enough to carry my knives again, if only to give me something to hold on to.

Prince Kendrik backs away from me, slowly, and then, his large liquid eyes trained on Tamsin, he stretches out a paw and bends until his nose brushes the packed dirt floor.

Lord in heaven. He's bowing to us. Like a courtier. Or a prince.

He knows who he is.

CHAPTER FORTY-ONE

ANNALISE

"Your Majesty." A voice rouses me.

I rub at my eyes. "Yes?" I say, my own voice a hoarse echo of itself.

A bitter chill snakes through the open carriage door. General Driscoll's cheeks are chapped, her black eyes burning. "We have reached the Winterlands. The encampment lies ahead."

Immediately, I straighten up against the cushions and try to stretch the stiffness from my limbs. "Let us make camp here. Ensure the soldiers are fed and the horses rested. I require some time to prepare before we approach. Send a runner to inform the refugees that their new queen wishes to speak with them."

"And if they do not wish to speak?" she asks. "If they choose to attack?"

I peer out the open door, trying to catch a glimpse behind her. All I see is white.

"What do you suggest?"

She answers without hesitation. "We station archers around the encampment. My scouts found that the barrier that protects the refugees is strong but can be breached if attacked from many sides."

"Tell them to hide themselves well. I want it to be very clear to the refugees that I do not intend to threaten them." I glance over at Sybil, who sits slumped back against her seat. The journey was not easy on her. "Unpack my ivory gown and white wool cloak."

She nods and scurries out of the carriage to retrieve my trunk.

General Driscoll still hunches in the doorway.

"If you have more to say, come in and close the door. It is cold."

She does so, pulling the door firmly shut behind her.

"What is it?" I ask.

She sits on the seat across from me and clasps her hands together. "This is your first significant action as queen," she says. "You have the power to do as you wish. But it was customary for King Alder to discuss his major decisions with his advisors. And, as the only advisor present, I am offering you that chance, should you wish it."

She waits, quietly, for my response.

"Is there an opinion you wish to express?" I ask, searching her face for some hint at her thoughts. Is this truly a service she is providing for me, or is it for her?

"Do you know..." She pauses. Reframes her question. "You say you want to negotiate with the refugees, that you come in peace. Do you know what you wish to give them?"

"I wish them to feel safe returning to their homes," I say.

"Yes, but that is not a concession, nor a term. These people have threatened rebellion. It doesn't matter why, only that they have. What will you do if they claim this land again, and in the face of their queen? If they promise to defend their new settlement? Will you allow them to do so without condition? Will you force them back to their towns and villages, where they can spread their message of resistance freely and without fear? Do you have a *plan*, Your Majesty?"

I consider taking offense. She asks as if I am a child playing at being queen. And yet, am I not? Have I truly considered what *making it right* looks like? I stare at the tumble of furs in my lap, the whites and grays a swirl so much like storm clouds.

"I will offer them what they need," I say softly. "Assurances that no magic worker will be forced to the castle, the news that I have cut taxes and sent my soldiers to protect villages from thieves. I will tell them they may stay in the Winterlands, so long as they pay these new, lower taxes and swear fealty to me. Or they may return to their homes. The only term I require is their loyalty."

My heart gives a little stutter, thinking of Burke's loyalty. Of Sybil's. I pray this loyalty will be given freely, that I will not be forced to take it.

General Driscoll nods. "Very good, Your Majesty. While you are preparing to conduct this negotiation, remember... you must also decide what the consequences shall be if they choose to continue their rebellion."

She pauses halfway out of the door, another breath of winter slipping in around her. "Usually, the consequence is death."

With King Alder, it always was.

"Thank you, General," I say, dismissing her.

I stand before the encampment, just beyond the invisible barrier, with General Driscoll on my left, and her most trusted lieutenant, Avis, on my right. My white gown and cloak match the snowy world around us. I wear a thin, twisted circlet of gold on my head. It is heavier than its delicate design suggests.

Above us, the departed storm has left a jewel-blue sky.

The settlement boasts several wooden cabins, at least a dozen heavy canvas tents, and a large central cook fire, over which hangs a massive iron pot. The fire burns, whatever is in the pot steams, but there is not a single person within my view. The very air waits, tense as a bow string.

"Liam of the Winterlands," General Driscoll shouts. "The queen of Tyne wishes to speak to you."

Her announcement is met with silence. Moments pass.

I reach out and search for the barrier with my fingers. I touch it gently, feeling its thickness, its strength. Driscoll's scouts were right. This is indeed a powerful magic. The cage I built for Prince Kendrik was nothing like this. I test it, send a little spark, but the barrier swallows it. This spell I cannot break.

At last, several men emerge from a building near the cook fire. All but one of them are heavily armed with swords and bows. Dressed warmly in wolfskin, with a heavy blond beard and cutting blue eyes, the one without weapons stalks toward us until he's only a few feet away, still protected by the invisible shield. His entourage fans out behind him.

"Liam of the Winterlands, I presume," I say calmly, raising my chin.

"And you are?" he asks, with a small, crooked smile that doesn't reach his eyes.

I play along. "I am Queen Annalise of Tyne. Surely you are not so isolated here that you do not know of King Alder's death?"

"Oh, we heard," he says, and this time there's real joy in his face when he smiles. "Our celebration lasted three days."

"So you've found a way not to starve." I cock my head at him.

"Why do you care? Did you come to feed us?" Before I can answer, he flicks his gaze to his left. "Your archers would suggest otherwise." I don't look because I know he wishes me to. It appears our attempt at being covert was unsuccessful.

"I have come to offer you a way out. A way back to your villages and families." I can understand his bitterness. His distrust. Those very same feelings are why I wear this crown, why I am standing here. "I promise you, Tyne is no longer the kingdom of King Alder."

"No," he says, and his face turns to ice. "It is the kingdom of a woman who would kill her own Clearsee. Who would order the girl's entire family murdered. Tell me, how are you different from King Alder? *How?*"

His words are a blade that passes straight through to my heart. I was not prepared. I have no defense. Beside me, General Driscoll shifts, makes a small sound of horror or surprise. I can't look at her.

"She—she attacked my men," I blurt, scrambling.

"Liar," he snaps back. "Your men snuck into her house and killed her. She was defenseless, her own family laying down their lives in a futile attempt to protect her."

How does he know all this?

General Driscoll was right—I walked into this meeting naive. And my greatest fear, that my mistakes and sins would follow me, has come to pass. It won't help to tell this man I did not order Evra dead—Burke was my man. My hands will be forever stained.

But I must salvage this moment. For my queenship, and for Liam himself. For the families and children hiding within the encampment as he bargains with their lives.

"The fate of the Clearsee and the reasons for her death do not bear on your situation," I say. "I have done all I can to spare you—I reversed King Alder's order to kill you and everyone else in this settlement. I have come all this way *personally* to negotiate with you in good faith. I do not wish to continue the king's legacy. I am offering you safety. A future. Your loyalty is all I ask in return. I promise it is a worthy exchange."

For a long moment, he considers me. My magic sparks along my bones. It can sense how little I feel like a queen, how out of balance this moment really is, and it is doing all it can to keep Liam and his men from seeing the same. I let its heat warm me, prop me up. I am in control. The wild has not taken me.

"Your promises mean nothing," he says on a growl, at last. "This land is ours and we will defend it. We will not bow to you."

My stomach plummets to my feet.

"I cannot let you commit treason," I say, and to my surprise, it is not defeat but anger that bubbles up within me. They are forcing me, *forcing me*, to bring them harm.

"I am not King Alder, and so I will not kill you if you defy me." I stare Liam down, and I can feel myself gaining stature, gaining conviction. "But there shall be consequences. You believe your barrier will protect you, and it may . . . for a while. But eventually we will breach your defenses. All those who bear arms against the queen will be conscripted, and your wives and children sent home without you, to worry and wait, to pray you are not killed defending Tyne against another such uprising. Consider carefully before you give me your final answer."

A couple of the men behind Liam cut their eyes to him. Someone murmurs something too softly for me to hear, but Liam frowns deeply.

His support is cracking.

I am about to suggest that he and his men confer, that I'll wait for his decision, when another voice pierces the air with a single, chilling word.

"Die."

A flash of movement, a swirl of dark cloak, a shout.

General Driscoll shoves me into the white, white snow.

Chaos blooms.

Someone pulls Liam away from the barrier. Avis orders our men to attack. The hiss of arrows fills the air.

General Driscoll has landed at my feet. I struggle to my knees beside her. I am surprised she has not leapt up and started barking orders. Why does she wheeze so, her breath coming in short gasps?

That's when I see it.

The blood.

There's so much so much. It doesn't stain the snow it stains my white white dress.

The dagger twisted her chain mail it broke through it must have had magic behind it so much hate. It was meant for me it was mine to bear.

General Driscoll lies gasping as arrows hiss and men cry out. The barrier wobbles and weakens and blood, bright red blood, drowns my hands.

I thought I'd stopped the prophecy.

I was wrong.

CHAPTER FORTY-TWO

EVRA

*T*amsin and I clean up the cabin as best we can. The knowledge that we are trapped with a prince provides ample motivation. And there is nothing else to do—the storm still rages.

"We need to get out of here," I groan, when the walls press close and I can't fight them back. My breath catches again and again in my throat without fully filling my lungs.

Tamsin throws another broken chair leg on the fire, sending up sparks. "I think the wind is not so harsh as before. Tomorrow we can start digging out."

I brace my hands on the table and lean over, dark wells and tight, breathless walls pinning me in. "I don't think I can wait."

Tam must recognize something in my face because she moves quickly to the door. With her shoulder wedged against it, she heaves over and over. A good while later, she's made a small gap, which sends a tumble of snow across the threshold.

"I'm sorry, Evra, this is the best—"

Before she can finish, Kendrik trots over to the sliver of light. He wedges into the gap and digs in with his paws, sending an arc of white into the air behind him. As the little pile of snow on the floor of the cabin grows, and more and more sky becomes visible, the tension in my chest eases until I can almost breathe normally again. Tam collects the pile of snow on the floor and starts another pot to melt.

When the prince flops onto the floor next to the fire, steam rises from his fur. "Thank you," I say. He widens his jaw in a panting grin.

An hour of digging, and he's widened our world by a foot, maybe two. I pray the storm ends and warm weather chases the worst of the snow away. Our journey to the castle will be a difficult one either way.

"Time to look at your injuries," Tamsin says with mock enthusiasm.

I lean back in my chair with a grimace. This is the worst part of every day.

She removes the strips of cloth she's bound around my side, revealing dark purple bruising surrounding an ugly, puckered scab.

"Good. It's stopped draining." Tam puts her hands to the injury as lightly as butterfly wings. She closes her eyes and murmurs under her breath. Heat blooms beneath her fingers. When she's finished, the ache feels a little less than bone deep. She inspects the slash on my arm, which is nearly healed, and the divot where the sword that killed Mama pierced my skin. It's nothing but a scar now. I wouldn't let Tam make it disappear completely.

At night, when I miss the sound of Mama's even breathing beside me, when the memories of her comforting arms cut too deep, I touch that spot, that small gouge out of my chest, the missing piece of my heart. It makes me feel closer to her, like that little bit of me has gone with her.

"How do you know what to do?" I ask Tamsin, amazed at the depth of her ability to make me whole.

Most people can use magic for simple healing, but it takes practice and knowledge to do it well. There are as many accidents with healing spells gone wrong as there are with knives.

Tam shrugs. "I don't know. If I concentrate, I can sense where the body isn't right. It's more than asking a wound to heal. To do it properly, you have to guide the magic to the hurt places. It's easier the more you work with a specific body. If I hadn't been healing your cuts and bruises for years, I might not have been able to save you."

With that sobering thought, we sit for a while in front of the fire, watching the flames. Tam has more magic than my brothers ever had, but it still takes time for her to build up reserves.

"It's a wonder King Alder never demanded your healing services," I say, to make conversation. Farin, who did get ordered to the castle, never did anything so impressive as heal a knife wound.

"He did."

For a moment, the words don't make sense. "But you're still here," I say stupidly. "No one disobeys the king."

To my surprise, a deep red blush climbs Tamsin's cheeks. She looks down at her hands, fingers twisting together. "A few months ago, the king's soldiers came for me. My father—he... well, he paid them off, I suppose. I told him I would go, but Father spoke with the men privately and they went away without me. And then they took Farin."

She drops her head into hands. "I was—am—so ashamed. I couldn't tell you—I didn't tell *anyone*. But I haven't been able to look my father in the eye. He won't let me work in the village, hasn't let me heal anyone since, afraid I'll attract attention again. When Farin's mother got sick just after the harvest... I snuck out after he went to bed. She almost *died* because of my father's selfishness. Because he had money when Farin's family did not."

I hate the miserable twist to her mouth, the self-loathing in her eyes, but I understand it. How would I feel, knowing the privilege of my parents meant someone else suffered in my place? "It was not your doing, Tam. You were willing to go."

"I *should* have gone anyway."

"Maybe," I say, with a small, painful shrug. "But then who would be here to patch up my wounds?" I am ashamed too, because I am happy to have had Tam these past few months. I am happy she wasn't sent away.

I think of Lady Annalise, how she said she'd send the healers home. How she'd change the king's rules to help the people.

But they're empty promises, with my family's lives at her feet.

When I lie down, the wolf doesn't immediately curl up beside me. Instead, he sits a few feet away, his head cocked, and stares at me. As if he's asking permission.

I nod, and my blush flares as he curls into the curve of my body. He settles his head on my thigh. It's a position we've slept in frequently since I awoke in this cabin, and yet I can't get my limbs to relax or my eyes to close. Knowing the wolf is the prince—knowing he *knows* he's the prince—the intimacy of our shared bed takes on new life. His head on my thigh, my hand resting on his hip . . . it's all I can do to keep from jumping up and crossing the room to put more space between us. And, as my eyes drift closed at last, it's all I can do to keep from remembering him as he was in my visions, imagining him this close . . . limbs touching limbs, breath sharing breath . . .

Half asleep, I hope we'll meet in our dreams.

"What were you before you became the Clearsee?" Prince Kendrik asks. We are sitting beside each other in the grass. The sky is a watercolor wash of sunset. The world around us is a blur, insubstantial and unimportant.

"My family are—were—" I swallow. *Were.* Past. Gone, forever. "Farmers."

"Did you enjoy it? Do you wish you could have stayed a farmer, instead of a Clearsee?"

I glance at his profile; his hair, his eyes, his skin are touched with gold. We've lost the urgency of not knowing. The magic doesn't press. It sits, and waits, and lets us breathe.

"I loved my life. My family. But it was starting to become more difficult....I had no magic, and the people of my village were..." I think of Ronan. "They were starting to notice. Some of them were afraid of me."

"Are you sure they weren't intimidated?" Kendrik smiles a little. "You have a very capable air about you. And you carry knives."

I look down—my knife belt hugs my hips. I remember when Deward decided to teach me to throw. He said the knives would be good for the small, important things—distracting a thief, taking down smaller creatures, like hares and pheasant. Helping me feel safe. At the time, shortly after Father had died and the Sickness had abated, the whole world felt dangerous. Deward knew I didn't need him to protect me—I needed to feel like I could protect myself.

"That was my goal. To be capable, even without magic," I say. "To be so useful no one would notice. I chopped so much wood I'd hear the thud of the ax in my dreams. I brought Mama's cooking to the elders, ran messages. I tried to pretend it didn't bother me, but I hated the way people looked at me, like I was something unnatural. Before it was clear I had no magic, everyone seemed to like me. It was sobering to realize how quickly they could change their minds." I stare down at my hands, calloused, knobby knuckles, browned by the sun.

"I don't know how they'd treat me now. Probably the same. The Clearsee magic is unnatural too."

Prince Kendrik reaches for my hand and threads his fingers through mine. His palm is warm. "But I am grateful for it. I am grateful it led me to you."

"Do you miss your parents?" I feel as if shards of my soul have been torn away.

"I miss what I might have known of them, had they lived as I grew up," he says. "I was a child, royalty, in a castle. I had nannies. But I remember Mother visiting me in the night sometimes. She would brush my hair off my forehead and kiss my temple. She'd whisper, 'My sweet boy,' and sigh. I remember how warm her breath was." He pauses. His voice a little rougher, he says, "When I caught the Sickness, she nursed me. They told her to stay away, but she didn't. And she died."

"It wasn't your fault." Is it my fault that my family is dead? Tam would say no, as I am saying no to Kendrik.

"I know it isn't," he says slowly. "But the heart sometimes believes its own lies, doesn't it?"

"Yes," I say, feeling his words deep in my soul. "It does."

We are quiet for a time. My head fogs a little, as if this is not a vision so much as a dream. Weariness seeps along my spine. I let my body slump back until I'm lying in the grass. I pull the prince down with me. We lie beside each other, hands linked, staring at the watercolor sky.

"You don't want to be king," I say. "What would you do instead, if you could be anyone? If you were not tied by birth to the kingdom?"

"We are all tied to our kingdom," he replies. I don't expect him to say more. But he continues, after a pause, "I think I would...I don't know. I would find other ways to help. I love Tyne."

"You'll be a good king, Prince Kendrik."

He makes a noise in his throat. "I want to feel confident that I am helping, not making things worse."

I squeeze his hand. He glances over at me, and suddenly I realize how little space lies between us.

Flustered, I ask, "Is it strange, living in the body of a wolf?" and then feel ridiculous. "I'm sorry, what a silly question. Of course it is." Even as a blush climbs my cheeks, an invisible weight drags my eyelids down.

"It is not a silly question. And it *is* strange, but also...also, it is a strange relief. Before, I was not...conscious...in that form, the way I am now. But there are pieces I remember. My body stretching, striving forward, a wind that told stories, a... freedom."

I sigh. It's too hard to keep my eyes open. His voice is soothing, like a soft spring breeze.

"I was always seeking you," he adds.

Warmth blooms in my chest.

"You don't feel trapped?" I murmur.

"I do." A longer pause, a softening of his voice, like he's getting tired too. "But I have always felt trapped."

"I'm going to save you," I tell him as I dream.

"I know, Evra. I know you will," my dream answers.

When I wake, a chill silence hangs in the air. Sunlight filters through the one tiny, dirty window, catching on dust motes and making them sparkle. I feel more rested than I have in weeks, since before Ronan asked me to meet him in the chapel. Prince Kendrik stirs and resettles. My hand smooths the fur along his side. Warmth has collected between us, an effective weapon against the cold that seeps through the walls and down the chimney, its fingers tickling my nose.

Across the room, Tam sighs and stretches. "Storm's over," she mumbles as she stokes the banked fire. Orange coals glow.

We spend the morning clearing a path from the shack toward the road. We've nothing to dig out with, so instead we use our cloaks, spreading them out and then falling into them so our weight will pack the snow. The road is strangely clear, as if the storm raged more gently there. We plan to leave tomorrow.

In the afternoon, I take up my knives for the first time since Advisor Burke's blade did its damage. Their familiar weight fills my hands, and my heart fills with something like joy. I think of what the prince said, about me being intimidating.

I think of Deward and the gift he gave me in teaching me to protect myself.

The motion of throwing a knife hurts my side, and my aim is off. Still, the sound of my knives thudding as they bury themselves in a silver birch—even if they're landing well away from the strip of peeling bark I'm aiming for—is comforting. This is a piece of my life that has been the same—aim notwithstanding—since before the Clearsee magic came. These knives, the fluid motion of launching them through the air... it's a routine that feels familiar and safe. Even my side twinges less than it did yesterday.

I can almost hear Hagan teasing me for my bad aim. Almost smell Mama's roast pork with spiced walnuts wafting from the half-open kitchen door. How many hours, days, did I spend throwing knives at crooked logs or marks Deward made on the barn door?

Memories hammer at my soul, and I welcome them, smiling through the pain.

Afterward, Tamsin inspects my wounds without a word. Prince Kendrik appears with the day's hunt, a rabbit and two squirrels. We eat until our stomachs bulge; the time for conserving our food has passed.

Tam and I sit at the table until long after sunset. We should be planning, reviewing what we'll do if the king still lives, what we'll do if he doesn't—but instead we speak of Hagan and Deward. Our parents. Dreams lost. Childhood victories.

Prince Kendrik sits beside me with his head on my knee,

listening to our stories. I wish he could share his own—his are no doubt full of fine things and daring escapades. If he could, would he speak of his parents, also lost to him? Tell more stories of his mother comforting him in the night?

If we succeed in reversing the spell, he will be king. Surely, he will be in need of the Clearsee. I tell myself there will be cause to speak to each other, that we won't leave each other's lives completely. But the truth is I don't know what the world—my future—will look like, once this is finished. The prince a king. My family gone. My purpose fulfilled.

It is far easier to imagine my death than a life beyond this journey.

CHAPTER FORTY-THREE

ANNALISE

*D*o not kill any women or children! Avis—" I yank on his arm, shouting to be heard over the sounds of battle. "Contain this. When you get through the barrier, be as merciful as you can. *I am not King Alder*, do you hear me?" My scream cracks my throat with its force. I grip his arm until he meets my eyes and nods.

Bright flashes spark. The barrier is close to falling. Horses rear as some of the soldiers try to drive them through. Soon, soon we will breach their defenses. I can't see Liam in the haze.

In my lap, General Driscoll groans. "Someone!" I shout again. "Help me!"

Avis himself helps me drag the general away from the encampment. Together, we haul her into the carriage, where a white-faced Sybil waits.

"Remember, Avis," I say as he moves to return to the battle. "Remember what I said!"

"What's—what's happening?" Sybil whispers.

I don't have time to answer. General Driscoll lies on the carriage's cushioned bench, her eyes closed. Her breath has slowed. I put my hands on her abdomen and connect us, skin to blood to skin.

My magic swarms from my veins to hers. I pour as much of myself, as much as I have, into her. It would be easier if I knew her body like I knew Burke's, but I find the right paths anyway. Golden light skims along her skin before sinking deep within.

I *will* save her life.

It takes a few minutes, but soon I am the one prone on the bench and General Driscoll the one sitting up. Her wound was deep, and I have not cared for myself well these past few days. I lay with my head back, eyes closed, and wait for the battle to end so that I may eat and sleep and regain my strength.

"What you did to me...," General Driscoll says. "That should not have been possible."

I don't open my eyes. I don't have the strength to influence her mind anyway. "The king never knew the weapon he had, right under his nose."

"Could you have healed him?" she asks.

"Even I cannot stop time." I am so very, very tired.

Suddenly, the door of the carriage flies open, banging against Sybil's knees. She squeals and burrows against me, as if I offer some protection.

Avis stops dead when he sees General Driscoll, whatever he came to say frozen on his tongue.

"What news?" I ask.

"Your Majesty," he says, still staring at General Driscoll. "The boundary is not breaking. We've lost at least ten men to arrows and thrown daggers. Every time we think we've breached it, the damned thing glows like the sun and thickens again. I think, Your Majesty, I think..."

"It is time to retreat," General Driscoll finishes for him, her voice hoarse. "We've suffered a blow today. We must regroup and return with more men."

"Yes," I say faintly, a weight settling on my chest. "We must regroup."

My first act of diplomacy, my first battle, and I have failed.

"We shall return to Ironwald," General Driscoll says, but I find myself raising a quelling hand.

"No," I say softly. "We will go to Nell." My heart curls around the word. Phantom hands reach for me, the quiet arms of the tree rustle in a soothing breeze, soft as a kiss. *She calls to me she knows I cannot last like this she knows I need her.*

"Nell?" General Driscoll looks at me strangely. "But we've no barracks there, no soldiers."

I grasp for a logical explanation. "You need a place close by to recover. It is a day's journey from here, perhaps less. It is a good place to rest." I have little strength left to assert myself, but I don't need it. The band of gold encircling my head speaks loudly enough.

Avis bows and disappears to organize our retreat.

"You are more in need of recovery than I am," General Driscoll says, with an expression I can't read. She isn't wrong.

The dark is pulling me close. I am but a vessel that has been emptied, emptied, emptied. I have nothing left.

"Sybil, when I wake, I'll need some food," I murmur, fading. I fall asleep just as the carriage jerks forward.

Mama, I am coming home.

CHAPTER FORTY-FOUR

EVRA

The morning dawns clear and bright and cold. Overnight the winds slept, a stroke of luck that has kept our narrow path to the roadway clear. Tamsin studies the sky. "If the weather holds, and you don't overdo it, we should make it to Ironwald by tomorrow evening."

"I—" The moment my foot touches the road, a wave of darkness pulls me under.

Bump, bump, bump.

The world rocks with a steady, sickening lurch. Across from me on a thick, golden cushion, Lady Annalise sits stiffly with her gaze pinned to a small window. Dark circles shadow her eyes, and a thin golden crown circles her brow.

I lunge for her. But there's nothing of me here. No form or

mass or muscle. If I had a body, I would pummel her senseless. I would kill her for what she's done.

"Nell is not so far now," she says, speaking to the girl beside her, who's looking decidedly unwell. "The river, here, leads straight into the village."

The girl, in a gray maid's uniform, swallows audibly. "Have you been to Nell before, Your Majesty?"

There's a long pause. A muscle in Lady Annalise's jaw jumps. Her expression is a wound, raw and open. "It is where I am from."

"But I thought—"

Annalise grips the maid's hand. "You thought I was from Barstock, where my grandmother, Princess Renalta, settled. And you're absolutely right. For anyone who cares to ask, that's what you say. Barstock. Not Nell."

"Yes, Your Majesty."

"Now, dear, let's ask General Driscoll to stop for a bit to let your stomach settle." Her gaze turns back to the window, worry tightening her mouth. "And I'll ask about our defenses. I thought I saw—I'm sure it's nothing." Lady Annalise raps twice on the roof of the carriage, and I'm thrown out, landing on shaking legs beside Tam.

She wraps an arm around me.

"What did you see?" she asks.

First, I breathe. The Clearsee magic was kind this time— the vision was clear, and my body doesn't thirst beyond what a few drops of my dwindling firecane can quench. Still, seeing Annalise was a blow. Prince Kendrik pushes his soft head under my hand. His presence is both a comfort and a curse, every moment a reminder that she's destroyed his life as well. And so far, I've been able to do nothing to help him.

"Lady Annalise isn't in Ironwald," I say. "She's traveling to Nell."

"Nell? That's not so far from here."

"And not in the direction of the castle."

As one, we turn and stride the opposite way down the road. Nell is northeast of us, a small village, smaller even than Windhaven, along a narrow river.

Every now and then, Tam glances over her shoulder to check on me. "How are you holding up?"

"Fine." I swallow back my panting breath. I won't tell her that my legs burn, my side aches, and my head feels heavy as lead. It won't make a difference; I refuse to let these annoyances slow our journey. Beside me, Prince Kendrik whuffles through the snow, his ears pricked. Sometimes he snakes ahead of us, using his canine intuition to help us avoid the most dangerous footing.

By midday, my breath is coming in short gasps and I'm staggering. When Tam stops to rest, I don't even bother to argue. Until she says, "That's enough for today."

"For today?" I stare at her in shock. "Surely you don't mean to camp here. We'll take a rest, eat, and then carry on."

She shakes her head. "You're not up for it, and I'll not have you die for your impatience. We'll rest here, hunt for our dinner, build a decent windbreak. Tomorrow, if we push a little, we might reach Nell by nightfall."

"But—"

"Don't bother." She flashes me a look as implacable as stone. "Think of it this way. You'll have a chance to practice with your knives by catching our dinner."

A part of me wants to insist we keep moving. But a smarter part acquiesces. I *do* need to work on my aim. I *do* need to sit down before I fall.

Silence surrounds us. The only noises are those we make ourselves: Snow crunching under our feet as we clear a place between two massive spruces. The snap of branches as we assemble our shelter, a combination of living tree limbs and dead wood. As she works, Tamsin laughs a little to herself.

"What?" I ask.

Shaking her head, she gestures vaguely toward her body, toward the bow strapped to her back. "I knew, somehow I knew, that one day I'd have to choose. But I never thought it'd be like this."

"What do you mean? Choose what?"

Despite her laughter, sadness fills her eyes. "Choose between Tamsin the steward's daughter, and Tam the...well, the archer, I suppose. All my life I've been torn. One day I'm dancing among the courtiers at the king's castle as if I belong there, and the next I'm in the woods with you and Hagan, bringing down deer and mussing my hair." She sits next to our small campsite and stares into the newly born flames. "My parents—they only wanted to see the pretty side. They wanted to marry me off to some boring noble and forget that most of the meat on their table came from me. Father didn't pay off the king's soldiers out of love. He did it because he thought he could get a better deal."

The words burrow into my chest, making it ache.

It's hard to see the "pretty" side of Tamsin now. Her fox hat lists precariously over a tangle of blond hair and the occasional stick and dead leaf. There's a scratch on her cheek, a smudge of dirt on her neck, and an angry red spider bite by her ear. Her sheepskin coat, which started out a buttery yellow, is now soot-gray and singed in places, its arms dark red with dried blood.

"I'm sorry, Tam." It would be strange to tell her that this is how I always picture her, with a bow and quiver strapped to her back and that silly hat on her head.

"I'm not sorry to be an archer. To be this and this alone," she says, glancing at me. "I'm only sorry it happened this way. This Tam would have found her home in Windhaven, with Hagan. This is who I would have chosen. I just never thought—"

"You never thought you'd be seeking vengeance with the Clearsee."

She rolls her eyes. "I *always* thought I'd be at your back, Evra. We fight our battles together; we always have."

Chastised, I consider her words. "I never thought either," I say softly, staring at the snowy ground beneath my feet. "That it'd be us, alone. That your choice would be so absolute."

"Yes," she replies. " 'Absolute.' Exactly."

I look up at the barren land we travel, silent except for the thud and shush of our boots through the snow.

The harshness of our surroundings, my hatred for Annalise: It is a time and place of absolutes.

When we pass Windhaven, I don't bother begging Tam to visit her parents, as I might once have done. They'll assume she has died, and her father will have to accept she's no longer something for him to bargain with.

We avoid my family's holding, too; I've no wish to see the ashes. Neither of us speak as we trudge through the forest around the outskirts of town. Thinking, remembering... trying not to think and remember. Even the familiarity of the forest fills my eyes with tears and my heart with agony. The skittering path of Weeping River, the blue eye of Weeping River Lake... I should have prepared myself for the memories that swarm me. The sense that Mama, Father, Deward, and Hagan are walking with us through this forest, their spirits accompanying us along these familiar trails. Even though Father's been dead for years, my grief for him is as fierce and cutting as my grief for the rest of my family. It has lost its soft edges. Now, it all hurts.

We don't reach Nell until the morning of the third day.

Even moving slowly, the travel has drained me. Tamsin wants to wait a day, rest before we stage our confrontation, and she's absolutely right that it would give us both new strength. But I can feel Lady Annalise now, feel her presence like a black well in the back of my mind. She waits for us at the far side of the village, near the river.

Prince Kendrik and I have spoken each night of this journey, in our dreams. He is impatient too, anxious for his old self back, if not his old life. The freedom of the wind and a good long run only go so far.

"Why is she here, do you know?" Tam asks, as we walk slowly down Nell's main street.

"I don't know what the official reason is, but she told her maid she grew up here." Here, there's no snow on the ground, but it's still bitterly cold; my cloak is little defense. "Which is strange—she said Princess Renalta, the king's sister, was known to have settled in Barstock. She's lying about something. Hiding something, maybe."

I'd asked Kendrik, but he didn't know. His memories of Annalise are strangely hazy; he doesn't remember her as a child at all.

I keep my hands on the knives at my hips. Prince Kendrik stalks forward, hackles raised, looking particularly feral. The few people we see give us a wide berth, but I catch snatches of conversation as we pass a place called the Crooked Feather, just as a group of men spill out into the sunlight.

"—heard the queen offered the steward grain from the castle's own stores, enough for every family in town."

"She's traveling all around the kingdom. Wants the people to know her. That's a good move, I say. Don't think the king ever bothered. Certainly didn't care none when he was having his soldiers drag our best healers away."

The two men nod to each other as their companions add their own opinions.

"She's queen now, it seems," Tam says under her breath.

She was wearing a golden circlet in my vision. Of course. *Your Majesty*, the maid called her.

"And on a tour to see her kingdom. Interesting." I wonder if she's looking for me, if she knows I survived. Nell is not so far from Windhaven. Perhaps she's determined to finish the job.

"How will we get close to her?" Tamsin asks. "She'll have guards, lots of them."

Suddenly, Prince Kendrik's head goes up, his nose pointed into the wind. The group of men notice him and stop abruptly, their conversation grinding to a halt. With a quick, knowing glance at me, he takes off, darting between houses and down toward the river. He's moving in the direction of that dark, oily hole that fills my mind, the Clearsee way of telling me where Annalise is. Tamsin and I hurry to follow, ignoring the shouts of the men.

Does Kendrik understand that she'll be guarded? She's probably inside the steward's house even now. We'll never make it to her rushing headlong this way. And yet, I can't stop. The same urgency that has struck Prince Kendrik has infected me too. I slip a knife into my hand.

We soon leave the village behind, pacing the river on our right as we jog upstream. Houses dot the landscape in an irregular pattern. One stands quite close to the river, with a large maple overhanging the water. I see Annalise in my mind before the small, curved form of her becomes clear. She is sitting at the base of the tree, legs curled to her chest, staring out at the cold, gray water. Her back is to us.

Prince Kendrik slows abruptly, hackles rising once more. I tighten my hand on my knife and stalk forward. She will hear us soon. She will turn. I want to see her face when my knife finds its mark. A flesh wound, so she knows I'm serious. Then I'll make her change Prince Kendrik back.

"Evra, *Evra*." An urgent whisper makes me pause. For a second, I think it's Kendrik somehow speaking to me. But he's turned his nose toward the woods.

Beside me, Tamsin gasps.

I follow Kendrik's gaze, follow the voice that's whispering my name over and over. There's something—some magic—that suddenly feels just within my grasp.

A figure stands shadowed within a stand of trees.

It lifts its hand, tips back its hood.

And I am staring at a ghost.

CHAPTER FORTY-FIVE

ANNALISE

At the base of the tree that shelters Mama's grave, a small stone marker is carved with her name. It's nearly invisible, tucked in among the roots—soon the tree and the earth and the river will take it and make it their own.

I rub a corner of my black wool cloak across it, cleaning off the dirt. I trace the letters with my fingertip.

Mama, are you at peace?

At my order, General Driscoll, Avis, and Sybil are tending the wounded in the small house where I grew up. We found it uninhabited, moth eaten and musty. Empty except for memories. The rest of our men are camped in the forest on the far side of the building. Twelve soldiers we carry wrapped in canvas, so their families may attend their burnings when we arrive back in Ironwald. Right now, for this moment, I am alone. Well, not entirely. Mama is here with me. I close my eyes and spread my hands on the cold earth, scraping my fingers as I dig in. Trying to get a little closer.

Mama, I've made so many mistakes. I've hurt so many people. I've hurt myself.

Burke's face appears in my mind, and I remember the way he held me so gently, as if he knew I was glass inside. *I have shattered into too many pieces. Mama, even you could not heal me this time.*

Behind me, the frozen ground crunches. Once. Someone who knows to walk silently, someone who took a wrong step. I turn and stand in one smooth motion, hand held before me, magic springing to my palm.

The only people who creep up on you are those who want you dead.

Or ghosts.

Evra stands before me, a giant wolf—Prince Kendrik—by her side.

My knees threaten to give. Bile rises in the back of my throat. How does the Clearsee still live?

She holds knives in her hands. Kendrik growls, baring his teeth.

It is clear in every line of Evra's face, in the tension of her body, that she does indeed want me dead.

But she—she is very much alive.

And Kendrik is with her. He is safe too.

"I—I—" I burst into tears.

I can't help it. I know they mean to kill me, that I can't

afford to lower my defenses, but I cradle my face in my hands and sob anyway.

The Clearsee is alive. Prince Kendrik is alive. Somehow they found each other, and then they found me, in the very place I buried Mama years ago. With a deep breath and a swipe at my eyes, I collect myself. Evra and Kendrik stand frozen before me; no doubt my reaction surprised them.

"You are here to kill me," I say, and my voice only shakes a little.

Evra's lip quirks in the smallest, angriest smile. "I'm here for Prince Kendrik, not for myself." Her eyes cut to the cabin, to the forest beyond, where my soldiers wait. She is trying to gauge how long she has before I order them to take her down. All I need to do is shout.

"You killed my family. You tried to kill me." Evra's voice is a blade. I feel the bite of it from my throat to my feet. Beside her, Prince Kendrik growls. I study him, strangely fascinated. He is no longer the mindless beast that I tried to contain. He is hostile, yes, but in control. Interesting.

"So this *is* about vengeance," I say.

Evra's face reddens, and she clenches her hands into fists. Maybe she *would* try to kill me, if she didn't know I could fell her with my magic before she raised her knife. Evra, more than a single other soul, knows what I'm capable of.

"Do you know I can still hear my mother's scream in my nightmares?" she asks. "My family did nothing to you. They were not a threat. But they were *everything* to me. You had no right to take them away." Her words, the tears falling unchecked down her cheeks, rip me open inside. Her horror and pain are mine.

I know it is worth nothing, but still I try to explain. "I told Advisor Burke that I wanted to speak to you, that your leaving the castle was a problem. He interpreted my orders in a way I would never have endorsed. His loyalty to me was deeper, more dangerous than I knew. He went too far. I am sorry, Evra. You don't know how deeply sorry. Truly, I did not intend harm to come to you or your family."

"They are still dead because of you," she snaps back.

And she is right.

Softly, I say, "I know what you are feeling right now, and if I could change the past, I would."

Her face goes quiet. "Don't tell me you know how I feel. Don't offer me empty words."

With a sigh, I sit down again. I am weary, so weary. I have been weary since the day I buried my mother here. I was never the right vessel for this fearsome magic, this vengeance, this life.

"Queen Annalise—" Evra continues, probably with her demands for retribution, but I stop her there.

"It's Anna," I say, and I feel suddenly lighter and heavier all at once. "My name is Anna. And this is my home."

Evra glances at the tiny cabin, at the briars that crowd its small windows, her skepticism clear.

And I know, I know the name is just the beginning. I owe this girl, who I've taken everything from. I owe her the truth.

"When I was seven, my father left to find his fortune and never returned. When I was twelve, I caught the Sickness." The words come fast, painful and hard and easy and freeing and wild. "I died, though it was just for a few moments. Your vision showed you the truth. The king's soldiers came just after it happened—they ordered my mother to Ironwald. But she wouldn't go. She knew she could bring me back, she could heal me. She was the strongest healer in all of Tyne. The next day, the soldiers returned. They slit her throat when she still wouldn't come. I tried to stop them, but I was weak. I hadn't come into my magic yet, and I was still recovering. I was just a girl."

I pause. Breathe. The memories push through my mind, unwelcome, agonizing. I can't hold them back, I was never able to hold them back. I do what I always do. I breathe and invite them in. I breathe and try to remember how they gave me strength. But they broke me too, in ways I'll never be able to fix. Embracing the pain doesn't make it go away, any more than it can bring Mama back.

"The soldiers took it into their heads to hurt me, too," I continue, my voice shaking. "While my mother drew her last, choked breath, she—did something, I don't know what. Somehow, she gave me her power. My magic awakened at the same time. One soldier's hands were around my throat, the black was dragging me down, and suddenly I could feel magic coursing through me. A strength, a *force*...With a mere thought, I threw the one who was hurting me across the room so hard he broke his neck when he hit the wall. I don't remember what I did to the other soldier."

I don't look at Evra or Kendrik. I pat the frozen ground gently as I say, "I buried my mother right here, under this tree. I spent three years learning to control this gift she gave me. I traveled to the castle, used the power to make simple suggestions, to control. I wove a web of influence that should have been impossible, and yet, for me, it wasn't. I worked my way from servant to courtier to Lady Annalise, the king's grand-niece. It wasn't difficult to convince those around me...every day I've gotten stronger. I wanted what you want, so badly. I wanted vengeance against the king who sent those soldiers."

"You can control people's minds?" Evra asks, sounding rightly horrified.

"I can."

"Have you controlled mine?" She looks as if she's about to be sick.

"No," I say. "You, I cannot control. The Clearsee magic protects you, I think."

"And you're not related to the king." Evra sinks to the ground beside me, her hands clenched around her knives. Her face is frozen in a mask of disbelief.

"I am not," I confirm. "I am an imposter in every sense of the word."

"Why are you telling me this?" She thinks I'm going to kill her, I can see it in her eyes.

But that's not what I have in mind. That's not what Mama would want. I've been so lost, but I've found my way back to her again.

"Because I don't want to carry these secrets anymore. The Clearsee magic knows—it's shown you all along. *I* am the threat to the kingdom. *I* am the darkness."

Evra brings her knees to her chest. I'm surprised that she's not yelling, or railing, or attacking me. She looks at the beast, sitting there, panting.

"Did you mean to hurt the prince? Was it all part of your plan? I saw the moment it happened, in a vision. You seemed... desperate. Did you do it on purpose?"

"No, I didn't," I say. There is so much freedom in this, in the truth. "But when I realized what it meant...I...I was glad. I could be the heir. It meant I could keep King Alder from destroying Tyne. It meant I didn't have to marry a man from Maadenwelk and leave my kingdom. I know it's difficult to believe, given everything I've done, but I've only ever wanted to help Tyne."

"You don't think Prince Kendrik wanted to help?" Evra asks, defensive on his behalf.

"I don't know what he wanted, but it wasn't the throne. I didn't have to force King Alder to believe Kendrik abnegated. He'd talked about not wanting to be king for years."

Evra shifts uncomfortably. "But that doesn't make it all

right. You turned him into a *wolf*. You stole his life. Queen Annalise—Anna, whatever your name is...you *must* turn him back."

I stare at my hands, feel the magic coursing beneath my skin, electrifying my fingertips.

"I tried, not long after. It almost killed him. *I* can't return him to his true form," I say, sadness following the path of the magic, tingling down my arms. I'm sorry that it's come to this, sorry I made so many poor choices, sorry I couldn't make my mother proud. "But *you* can, Evra."

"The Clearsee magic doesn't work that way." Her face is caught between relief and confusion, hope and despair. She doesn't understand what I'm saying, she doesn't know how she can help. That *she* will be the one to make everything right.

"I believe the only way to end the spell is to end the one who worked it." I stand up, dust off my skirts. Breathe my last breaths with Mama at my feet. This is right, I know it is. The last few days, the last few weeks, it's all been leading to this. I can't have sent Burke to the Winterlands to die if I'm not willing to reckon with my own sins.

"Evra, to set the prince—and Tyne—free, you must kill me."

CHAPTER FORTY-SIX

EVRA

The Clearsee magic leaps and lifts my hands to brandish my knives before my brain can catch up. The speed, the surety, the sudden sense of displacement frighten me. I force my fingers to put the weapons away, force them to push me to my feet. I back away from Annalise, my heart pounding. "This is a trick. You're trying to trick me."

The Clearsee magic doesn't care. It has risen to fill me, fire through my veins. This is what it wants. Annalise dead, Kendrik restored. The royal bloodline restored.

Blood cannot lie.

At last, Father's words make sense. Annalise is not of royal blood.

The magic beats against my brain, my bones. I can't clear my mind, whirling with her words, her memories. I want to take a moment, think about what she said, but the Clearsee part of me is *screaming*. The shadow skulls are *screaming*. This is not a vision, it's an assault.

If I don't kill her, the Clearsee magic might kill *me*.

"You're using your magic to influence me, to make me feel sympathy for you." The words are shaky, I don't know if they make sense. I don't know if anything makes sense. The magic won't stop flaying my mind.

I think I'm going to be ill. I turn, panicked, and search the woods. They've hidden themselves well; even knowing to look, I cannot find them. Will they see my distress? Will they have heard what Annalise said?

Will Hagan finish what he started?

I still cannot fully believe that he is alive.

When I saw him standing in the woods, surrounded by the darkness of shadow and the black of his hooded cloak, I thought he was a ghost. Or a devil, maybe, who'd stolen my brother's face. But the shock and love and pain in his eyes were real. He staggered toward us, the hand holding a dagger falling to his side. My arms had only just encircled his shoulders when Tam rammed into us like a thunderclap. Our three-pronged embrace had lasted long enough, with enough tears and whispered *how*s that Prince Kendrik had whined.

We hid deeper in the forest, and I cupped my hands around Hagan's face and stared.

"How are you here?" I asked, voice thick. "You died."

He shook his head. His eyes were shadowed, his face chapped and ruddy from the cold wind. "*You* died. I was in the barn when they came, I let the animals loose. I got a pitchfork, I went to help, but they lit the barn on fire. The way was blocked. I climbed up to the loft, used Father's ax to chop a hole in the roof. It took some time to sort out how to get down, and I had to hide when the men left. I thought my eyes would burn out of my head. I tried to find you, but the flames were too hot."

"We escaped out the wall of your room," I said. "We hid in the woods. We should have looked for you. We thought...we assumed..."

"*I* assumed," Tamsin said. She was gripping his hand so tightly her knuckles were white. "I didn't know you were in the barn. I saw bodies on the floor in the house, Deward and another in a dark cloak just like yours. His face was covered, and I couldn't bring myself to look. I didn't want to remember you...I saw Evra and your mother...Oh God, I should have made *sure*."

"I went to your house, but you weren't there," he said. "I thought maybe you'd seen the fire, maybe gone to the Winterlands like we planned. I didn't know. I hoped. So I went north. I spoke to Liam. He's their leader. He hadn't seen you."

"We went south," I said. The words sounded so normal, the conversation so matter-of-fact. But my whole body buzzed, my brain filled with bees. This couldn't be happening. Hagan, alive. "We followed the soldiers. We...we sought vengeance."

"So did I." Hagan held us both at arm's length. Looking as if he too was scared to believe. Prince Kendrik stood with his back to us, his ears perked. Guarding our reunion.

"I told Liam what Annalise had done, how she'd killed you, the Clearsee, and our entire family. I told him she was not to be trusted. And then she appeared."

"She went to the Winterlands herself?" Tam asked.

Hagan nodded. "She wanted them to swear fealty to her, to go home to their families. She told them the king had ordered them killed for treason, but she had different ideas. Liam laughed in her face. He called her a liar. And then…then I tried to kill her."

"We can't kill her yet," I said, my gaze darting to Prince Kendrik. "First, we must get her to change Prince Kendrik back. If she dies, he'll be a wolf forever, when he should be king."

For the first time, Hagan noticed our wolf companion. His sky-blue eyes widened. "You mean—"

Tamsin nodded. "It's mad, but it's true. Your sister's been romancing him in her dreams."

I rolled my eyes at her. "How did you end up here, Hagan?"

"I followed Annalise's entourage. I've been waiting for my chance, and she just walked right out of that cabin over there, alone. She sat down, utterly defenseless. I've been waiting, watching, to see if it's a trap. And then you went strolling down the path and I thought I was having my own Clearsee vision or something. I never thought—" His voice cracked and he closed his eyes. "I never thought I'd see you two again."

With a quick, questioning glance at me, Tamsin pulled him to her for a fast, fierce kiss. "We thought the same of you. I'm happy we were all wrong."

I glanced down at Prince Kendrik, his thick fur ruffled by the wind. "It's time to make things right. Annalise is alone. This is our best chance. We'll demand she change Kendrik back. And then...and then he can decide what her punishment must be."

"Hagan and I will stay out of sight," Tam said. "Kendrik or no, I will not let her hurt you."

"Nor I." Hagan gripped his dagger more tightly.

"Hide well. Your lives are no less valuable to me." I gave them both tight hugs before turning to Kendrik. "Are you ready?"

He opened his mouth to show his teeth and nodded. Communicating with him this way, in this form, was still deeply unnerving. I said a prayer that Annalise would be scared enough of us, that somehow we could convince her to turn him back.

I was not expecting this. An invitation to kill. A subtle flash of light alerts me to Hagan's presence—he's let the sunshine catch against his dagger for an instant. I take a deep breath, I push back against the magic making havoc in my head. Hagan is here. Tamsin is here. Kendrik leans his warm, furry body against my leg and growls at Annalise. They pull a tiny bit of me, of *Evra*, back from the angry, elated Clearsee storm.

"I am not asking for sympathy," Annalise says. "I'm asking for forgiveness. This is not a trick. It's a confession."

It's a death wish. And the Clearsee magic wants it. *Oh, it wants it. So much it's tearing me apart.* I close my eyes, force my hands to stay at my sides. Why am I fighting? Why, when this is what Tyne, what Kendrik, needs? When she is the reason my family is dead?

No. I'm not fighting, I'm just trying to *think*.

Through the haze, the push, the righteous fury of the magic, I try to clear a space for *me*. I stare at Annalise, bleary-eyed, brain blistering from the internal war. "You want me to kill you. You want to die."

Something in her face cracks. For a second, she looks scared and small. "No, I don't want to die. But this is what I deserve. And it's the only way to bring Kendrik back." She straightens her spine and lifts her pointed chin. "Why are you delaying? I am responsible for killing your whole family, Evra. I have misled an entire kingdom. Can't you feel the Clearsee magic? Surely it's telling you."

Yes, yes. Do it. Now.

The skulls speak in a snake's slithering voice. The magic pulls my hands, pulls them to my waist.

Why? Why do I resist?

"Your—your soldiers," I grind out. "They'll kill us."

Annalise nods to Prince Kendrik. "The prince will order them not to."

Oh God, she's begging me. The Clearsee magic is begging me. My own heart wants her to suffer as I have.

But she already did.

She already did.

The whisper sounds like my mother's voice.

Kendrik told me to save him. He told me. He pushes up against me, voiceless, now.

I wish Tam and Hagan were here beside me. What would they want me to do? Perhaps a trial, an—an execution...

The Clearsee magic screams, *Now.*

It's too much, too much.

I back away farther, I want to run. I don't know what I expected—No, I do. I expected her to kill me. And I—I—

It's like the magic knows my thoughts. It twists and shrieks and demands.

I can't.

I can't.

Not even for my family.

Not even for Kendrik.

Not like this.

Annalise takes a step toward me. "Evra, you must," she says.

I say, "I can't," and the Clearsee magic screams again.

She stops. Studies me. Then something in her face changes. Her eyes harden. Her fists clench. Her cheeks flush. Above us, clouds roil across the sky. The beautifully cold, sunny day disappears.

This. This is what I expected.

Fog and lightning fill the space between Annalise's hands. "I tried," she says between gritted teeth. "I really did. I wanted to fix this."

"No," I blurt, backing away. "You wanted *me* to." Kendrik stalks toward her, a growl like thunder building in his throat.

"Either way, it *must* end." She raises her hands.

Prince Kendrik howls as he leaps toward her, teeth bared. I reach for my knives, letting the Clearsee magic guide me this time, but I know I will not be fast enough.

Annalise's eyes gleam like liquid gold as she shoves her hands toward me ... just as, with a soft, deadly hiss, Tamsin's arrow speeds through the air and buries itself in Queen Annalise's throat.

Tam has always had perfect, deadly aim.

CHAPTER FORTY-SEVEN

ANNALISE

I am afraid I am not afraid. I am pain I am the wind rustling Mama's tree. I am sunshine clearing and candlelight. I am free.

It worked I think it worked. The wild is quiet the world is quiet—

"Annalise?"

It's not that I open my eyes so much as the glow brightens and defines itself. I am standing in a field far from Nell. It's spring, and there are long grasses whispering against my legs.

Evra is here. Kendrik is here.

"I am dead?" I ask, and the warm, soft air parts to let my voice through.

Evra tries to take my hand, but she can't touch me. *I am air and light.* I am peace. "Yes," she says. "Yes."

"Why did you do it?" Kendrik asks, his puppy dog eyes liquid with betrayal.

"I told you, it was an accident. I never meant to hurt you. I am sorry. Sorry for everything." I was sorry. Now I am calm. Nothing can hurt me, no one can hurt me, and Mama... maybe Mama is here too. I glance around, but there's no sign of her in this field, in this place of change. Of waiting. I feel it, the waiting. This is not... this is not where it ends. Not where I end. Not yet. Mama is waiting. I am waiting.

"No, not what you did to me," Kendrik says. "What you did to Evra."

What did I do to Evra? I cast back, my thoughts hazy. Not her family, no, I explained that—oh. I remember. "What do you think I did?"

"Did you kill me?" She looks around too.

I smile. "I wanted you to think I would so you'd do what needed to be done. But no, I didn't kill you. I gave you a gift."

Evra's brows draw together. "There is nothing I want from you."

"You want him back," I say, pointing at Kendrik. He looks older, more grave. Is it this place, or has he changed?

"When we leave this vision, I'll be a person again. I'll be like this?" He looks afraid to hope.

I shrug. "That is what I think."

When Burke died, the thread snapped. Surely it works the same in reverse. Because most spells are small, they burn themselves out quickly. But mine don't. Mine last with me. And now I'm gone. All the webs I've woven have broken now.

"Annalise—Anna... do you have regrets?" Evra asks. She

looks sad, confused, conflicted. I am happy to be free of all that.

"I regret everything except my actions as queen," I say. "Tyne deserved better than King Alder, and—" I eye Kendrik with reproach. "And you, Kendrik. You didn't care, you didn't want the job. You would have let Alder's advisors run roughshod over you, over this kingdom. You would have done nothing useful."

His cheeks redden, and he looks down. "I know."

"Maybe now you'll do it differently. Maybe the Clearsee will help you." The field grasses are brightening, their feather-light touch fading. Evra looks less distinct. The waiting, it's nearly over. There, in the distance, where the light is brightest, a figure appears.

I know who is waiting for me she is waiting for me.

I give Evra one last look. "Do better than I did with this gift. It doesn't have to be a curse."

I don't wait for her reply. It doesn't matter. Nothing does, except that figure there at the end and beginning of this place, at the end and beginning of me. The weariness, the regret, the pain of the past, and the magic lancing through my veins—I leave all of it behind.

I've been granted grace, I've been granted the one thing I wanted the one thing I ached for the one thing I fought for sought vengeance for.

Mama is here again. With me.

CHAPTER FORTY-EIGHT

EVRA

*F*ire burns along my skin. The vision releases me, but the flames do not. I don't know what this is, but I think it may kill me.

"Evra, Evra, are you all right?" Tamsin is calling me. I can see her, I can hear her, but I can't quite put words into my mouth and spit them out.

I am lying on the icy ground, my eyes to a heavy gray sky. It was sunny this morning. Sunny and cold as a knife.

"Evra. You sit up and speak to me this moment or I will cry. Do you hear me?" Tam's head appears above me again, blocking out the clouds.

Beside her, Hagan's face appears too. His brows are drawn together with worry. "Evra, don't you dare die on me again."

With a groan, I start to push myself up. He helps me, hissing when a stray spark of static jumps between us.

"Oh, thank God," Tam says. She rocks back on her heels.

"I thought she'd killed you. Your brain still works, right? Say something. Are you still you? There was a flash, like a lightning strike—I couldn't think."

"I'm—I'm well," I say around the buzz of lightning in my throat. "But I think she did something to me...."

I gave you a gift.

"Where is she?" I ask suddenly. "Where is Annalise?"

And Prince Kendrik. But I'm scared to look for him. What if the vision was wrong? What if Annalise was wrong?

Tamsin points to a still body on the ground.

"I killed the queen." Her eyes find mine. They ask a question for which I have no answer.

"Tam—" I begin, willing my head to clear. She sent an arrow through Annalise's throat. She did it to save me. Was I saved?

"It doesn't matter that she was dangerous, or that she was about to kill you. As queen, she can murder whoever she chooses." A hardened resignation enters her voice. "I'll be put to death."

Hagan puts his hands on her shoulders. "We won't let that happen. We'll run."

Panic rises in my throat. Annalise's soldiers don't know she asked me to do it. They are going to come soon and see the carnage. Tamsin is right.

"No one will lay a hand on you. There is no need to run." The voice is coarse and quiet, but still I recognize it. He's hunched near the tree, trying to hide his nakedness.

Oh my God. Kendrik. *It worked.* For a moment, I can't

think for joy. But his discomfort, *his nakedness*, bring me quickly back to myself.

I unpin my cloak and shove it into Hagan's hands. "Take that to the prince."

As he hurries over, I struggle to my feet. The burning sensation is subsiding, but I still feel strange, like I don't quite fit the same way inside my skin. There's a . . . a *something* in here with me.

I search for some kind of signal from the Clearsee magic, some sense that we've done as we ought, that things will be right now, but it's not pressing against my chest, it's not screaming anymore. I suppose that's my answer. I should take the silence as peace. Why do my doubts and fears linger?

I approach Annalise slowly. The arrow still protrudes grotesquely from her throat. It's hard not to feel sympathy for her now, in death. Now that I know about her mother, about the vengeance she sought. Now that I know she didn't intend to kill my family, now that I have the miracle of Hagan back with me. But I am angry too. She was at peace in my dream, calm as my mother was calm in death. Annalise won't have to live with the consequences of her actions, she won't have to make amends. She won't have to look into Kendrik's eyes, in the harsh light of real life, and face what she did to him.

As if he feels my thoughts, Prince Kendrik steps over to my side. He's shivering, my cloak doing little more than hiding his bare skin. I can see the wolf in his golden eyes, in the way he hunches, unused to his human body. He meets my gaze, and memories of our conversations, our hands entwined, wash over me.

"Your Majesty," I say.

He makes a strange noise in the back of his throat, almost a growl. "You know I don't deserve that honor."

"You do deserve your life back. I'm happy you have it."

He looks down at Annalise's pale, purplish cheeks. "I'm not entirely sure this is what she deserved."

I don't know if he means death is too harsh a punishment, or too easy.

I don't know either.

But as I gaze at Annalise, a strange feeling steals through me. A charge, an awakening. My skin tingles, my breath catches at the back of my throat. I drop to my knees.

"What is it, Evra?" Hagan asks. "Another vision?"

I can't speak. There's something I think I can do, but do I want to? The *something* inside me, the buzz in my fingertips and the pulse of electricity through my veins, wants me to. It knows it has the strength.

As I cup my hands around Annalise's throat, I understand, at last, the gift she gave me.

I can taste her mother's love, I can taste her own regret, I can taste myself, thirsting all my life.

"Prince Kendrik," I say, and my voice shakes. "I don't think Annalise has paid the right price for her crimes."

"What do you mean?" he asks.

But I'm beyond speaking. I cannot tell him, I can only show.

It fights me, the Clearsee magic. It cracks my skull, it rips me open. I can't breathe, but I don't need to. I have a new strength now, this borrowed strength, it fills me up, it fights back.

You will not stop me. This is what is best for Tyne.

Kendrik said his grandfather was a good king because of his conviction. That his commitment was more important than his ideas. His ideals.

There is no room in my mind or my heart for anything less.

I know this is the right thing to do.

The Clearsee legacy disagrees. It throws vision after vision at me. A castle crumbles at my feet, the earth shakes, the king's skeleton screams in my face.

Tyne is not yours to use anymore! I scream back.

The last Clearsee appears, eyes burning. "You do not see."

But I do.

Tyne must be about more than a bloodline.

Just as I am more than a vessel. I refuse to be a conduit alone. This is *my* body, *my* mind, *my* soul. Mama said I was strong enough. I know with every fiber of myself that she was right.

I have lived my whole life without magic. I refuse to believe I've been given too much.

I imagine the Clearsee magic as an ax—a tool to be wielded. It is useful, dangerous, but it is also at the mercy of the one wielding it. It is *my* hand on the handle, my strength that drives the blade. I hold the image in my mind and ignore the ripping and splitting and pounding in my head. I ignore the dire warnings and the stormy skies.

I am not the ax. I hold the power, it does not hold me.

Eventually, the winds calm and the pain eases. I've claimed a space in my head to think. I can focus on this other, newer power now. The one that flows from me to Annalise.

The one that will bring her back to life.

CHAPTER FORTY-NINE

ANNALISE

I wake slowly with Mama in my heart. I was dreaming, dreaming I had found her, that we were together. The peace follows me, cradles me, until I open my eyes.

I recognize the rough wooden beams above my head and the faces staring down at me.

Prince. General. Clearsee. Maid.

"You see," Kendrik says. "She merely swooned at the sight of me. I didn't mean to shock her."

"I'm sure it will not take her long to recover," Evra adds. Her face has a gray cast, her body trembles. What is wrong with her?

What is wrong with me?

I don't feel as if I've swooned. I feel as if I've died.

I did die.

"What did you do?" I try to scream at Evra, but my voice comes out a faint whisper. My throat hurts, God it hurts.

The arrow.

I should be dead. I *was* dead. I was with Mama. My heart shatters awake. *I was with Mama.*

"Your Majesty, you've had a shock," Evra says. "We'll speak when you've rested."

"No," I say, the words scratching along my burning throat. "We'll speak now. General Driscoll, leave us. Send your men away. You too, Sybil dear."

I speak as if I am still the queen, and they listen as if it is so. The prince stands right beside me, the proper ruler. And yet, even now, General Driscoll does as I say. Her face disappears from view, I hear the thud of footsteps fading away. Sybil lingers a moment longer. She's lost the innocent fawning regard my magic instilled in her, and I can't tell what it's been replaced with. Hatred? Suspicion? She leaves with the injured and the healers, and I wonder what I'll say to her the next time we're alone. Perhaps, *I'm sorry.*

Anger and anguish war in my chest. I shift my gaze back to Evra. "You were supposed to leave me dead. I was content. You had what you needed. Why couldn't you let me go?"

Evra glances at the prince. "This is your penance," she says simply. I know why she looks so sick now. I know how I'm here. She used my magic, my mother's magic. She used it to heal me.

"You were right, Annalise," Kendrik says. "I wouldn't have made a proper king. And I would have abnegated myself, if I'd been brave enough, if there'd been a viable heir. You were a good queen and Tyne needs you."

I want to laugh. "A good queen? Have the rebels of the Winterlands heard the news?"

Evra clears her throat. "The situation in the Winterlands would likely have gone differently were not my brother involved. Your advisor didn't quite manage to kill my whole family after all. My brother went to the Winterlands in the hopes I'd escaped, only to find men eager to distrust you."

I stare at her. I can't—I don't know what to say.

"But things will be different now," Evra warns, her brows drawing together. "You will not be queen as you were. You've no magic now. You'll have to rule with diplomacy and compromise, not manipulation and unfair influence. And you'll name Prince Kendrik and me, your Clearsee, as advisors. This is not a gift. This is your chance to prove your intentions were indeed good. You made yourself queen. You said it was to help Tyne. You don't get to rest until that duty is done."

She is right. This is not a gift.

And yet it is also far more than I deserve.

"How will you explain the prince?" My eyes close, weariness overtaking me. My body is heavy and slow, sore and strangely empty. I feel lost without my magic, for Evra is right...it's all gone. Mama is in my mind, but my time with her is hazy, soft and light as a dream. Maybe it *was* only a dream.

"I abnegated already, thanks to you," Kendrik says. "I've only to explain that I wasn't really dead but hiding in this village to get my bearings. You came here to speak to me, to tell me my grandfather was dead. You convinced me to return to Ironwald as your advisor."

They have a plan. It's clear I have no say in it, that my role has been chosen for me. And yet, as the dream of Mama slides deeper into the corners of my memory, as I wake up, breathe, live more fully, I find a certain hope in the idea of making amends.

"The rebels in the Winterlands...," I say. "I must speak to them again. I cannot let them poison the minds of others, not while I'm just beginning to set things right."

Evra and Kendrik share a look.

"I think perhaps my brother should go," Evra says at last. "With some of your men, of course. He's the one who told the leader of the rebels what you did. Perhaps he can help change their minds. It would be best for you to take some time to recover."

Recover.

It is a strange word. I know she means *recover* from my death, from the arrow through my throat, but it resonates deeper. These rough-hewn beams of my mother's cottage, my childhood, my earliest agonies...perhaps, here, I can begin to recover from other wounds. I've been brought back to life twice. There must be a reason. There must be more for me to do.

"I defer to you, my advisors," I say as the world goes soft around me.

Recover.

Now I know Mama is there. Now I know she is waiting.

Something like magic sparks in me.

CHAPTER FIFTY

EVRA

If the Clearsee magic is an ax, Annalise's gift is a wave. Harder to control, a building power searching for release. But just as I am the hand that holds the ax, I am also the moon that moves the tide.

Tamsin and I sit cross-legged facing each other and holding hands. She is helping me practice my control.

"Breathe," she says. "One, two, three, four...in. And now exhale...one, two, three, four."

I breathe.

I breathe.

I breathe.

I breathe.

"Mine felt like a storm at first," Tam says. "But it became manageable. Rain and a bit of wind. You can manage rain and a bit of wind."

I breathe so the rain doesn't drown me, so the wind doesn't blow me away.

"Find the quiet, the woods, the deer sniffing the air. The stillness before you let your knives fly." Her voice flows as surely as Weeping River.

I close my eyes. Imagine standing at the banks of the lake, the first dogwood buds waving above me, the water gently lapping, the breeze smelling of woodsmoke and new blooms.

Along my veins, the fire slowly subsides. My breath comes easier.

One, two, three, four.

"Thank you for your help, Tam," I whisper, eyes still closed. Somewhere inside me the Clearsee magic is there too, but I can't feel it. It has stopped its screaming, for now.

Hagan is outside with General Driscoll and her troops. They will leave in the morning for the Winterlands. The injury he gave her when she leapt in front of Annalise has healed as if it never happened.

Annalise told me how she felt when my vision came true after all. I don't know what to think, exactly, except that I'm happy she was able to save General Driscoll. Not as much for her sake, as for Hagan's. I don't think he regrets trying to kill Annalise, or what he said to the leader of the rebels. I don't think he should. But the situation has changed. Because of what I did, we all must put our faith in Annalise's desire to make amends. No, not our faith in her. Our faith that Mama and Deward would not have wanted us to live with revenge in our hearts, would not have wanted us to become murderers when there was another way. It helps, knowing Annalise didn't explicitly order me dead, that she and Burke both paid dearly for the crime. It helps, knowing what she did to Kendrik was an accident.

It helps, knowing she'll have to learn to live in the world without her magic. That she won't be able to control anyone else's mind.

In the morning, Tamsin and I will return to the castle with Kendrik and Annalise.

"I think I'll visit my parents when we pass through Windhaven," Tamsin says, as I open my eyes. "They think me dead. Word that I've become a queen's advisor will travel."

"Your father will be pleased," I say.

Annalise said she wanted Tamsin and Hagan as advisors as well. With General Driscoll that makes five—she plans to remove Advisors Niall and Halliday when we return. We'll also have to manage the broken threads of Annalise's deception. There are those in the castle who will remember her as a servant, as a nameless courtier. We'll have to convince everyone all over again that her claim to the throne is legitimate. With Prince Kendrik's backing, and the support of General Driscoll and her troops, it should not be too difficult, but it may take time.

A single candle lights the small room in the eaves of Annalise's childhood home. Hagan and Driscoll's men are asleep in the forest, and Kendrik is downstairs with Annalise and her maid, Sybil, in what had been the makeshift infirmary until General Driscoll ordered her healers to move the injured to tents outside. Kendrik is acting as a sort of guard for Annalise. To protect her from herself— and us from her. She was not thrilled we brought her back.

But I saw Kendrik's face at the thought of being king. I didn't want him to be trapped again. I wanted him to have a choice.

"My father will try to leverage me," Tamsin says. The candle-light casts dark circles under her eyes.

"He does not deserve you," I say. "Tam, *we* are family. If your father brings you pain, let him go. You will always have me. And Hagan." There I go, using *always*.

She leans into me. "I'm so tired."

I am as well. Not just of this day, or this journey. The grief, the worry, the pain has drained me, as surely as the Clearsee magic after a vision. But there's no spirit to ease this desert, no firecane that'll heal my parched soul.

"I know," I say.

We curl up on the bed, our hands clasped and foreheads touching, like we did as children. Annalise's magic sparks under my skin. I wonder how long it will take before I think of it as mine.

"You're hurt," I whisper.

Sleepily, Tam shifts. "Not really. Just a headache."

I can see the sore places in my mind. I let the smallest rivulet of magic flow from me to her. She sighs. "Well done. I feel much better."

I smile into the darkness. Rest, love, time. That's all we need. *Breathe.*

Too soon, I wake. My mind fuzzes around the edges, the darkness blankets me. But I can't fall back asleep. This room, up in the eaves, is too much like my bedroom at home. There are too many memories crowding close.

I leave Tamsin and climb downstairs. Annalise rests on a cot by the fire, flanked by Sybil and Kendrik. Her eyes are closed, her breathing even. I look at her tucked into an old wool blanket by the coals of the fire, and wonder at the magic of her life. I wish I could have saved Mama and Deward the way I saved her. Drawing the arrow out with magic alone, stitching together sinew and bone. Her mother's magic knew her body, just as Tamsin's knows mine. It knew where to sew, where to curb the flow of blood. I was a conduit for a mother's love.

I slip out of the cottage and into the glass-sharp night. The horizon is graying at the edges, the sun sneaking closer to rising. Cold, still air embraces me. The quiet, I store inside, I breathe it in. I'll keep it for when my warring magics are fighting me.

"Can't sleep?" Prince Kendrik's voice cracks the silence like a pail tossed into an ice-crusted well. He has followed me outside.

We lean against the house and watch for the sun.

"Did I do the right thing?" I ask. It feels right for us to speak this way, as we've done in our dreams the past few nights. Maybe that's why I woke. I missed him.

He hunches into his borrowed soldier's uniform, his sandy hair a messy whorl. "I don't know," he replies. "But I am happy Annalise will not pay for my grandfather's legacy with her life. I wish my parents could have been saved. I think about them a lot—I dream of them. But their lives should not have weighed more than others. My grandfather let *many* mothers and fathers die to try to save mine, and to give himself more time. It wasn't right."

I think of my own family, and how Annalise's advisor went too far. How much life and love he destroyed in his efforts to please her. "Maybe we can build something good from all of this," I say. "A new legacy. One our parents would be proud of."

Something in Kendrik's face shatters. Suddenly, our arms are around each other, so tightly we can barely breathe. I bury my face in his shoulder, and he holds me, and we both cry. It is like my visions and not. I can smell him, I can feel his heart beat. We've been through so much together.

Eventually, we pull apart. I've wet his shirt with my tears. I brush at the rough fabric, a small laugh escaping. "No more shedding."

He grins. "I'm still fighting the urge to lick your hand."

"I suppose a wolf wasn't *so* bad. She could have turned you into a toad." I glance up at the glow along the horizon. Not long until the day begins.

"Evra."

I turn back to him. He no longer sounds like he's joking.

"I wouldn't have survived without you." The intensity in his eyes sends heat through me. "When we weren't together, I was nowhere. I had nothing. You were my light in the darkness."

"The Clearsee magic connected us, in service to the kingdom," I say, brushing off his words. I can't let myself lend them more meaning.

He shakes his head. "I searched for you, I could feel you waiting for me. It wasn't the magic." He puts his hand to his chest, over his heart. "Unless this is magic."

My breath freezes in my throat.

He swallows, as if getting up his nerve. Then he cups my face in his hands, his fingers cool against my blazing cheeks. He tips his head toward mine, hesitating just before our lips meet. "May I?" he whispers, his breath warm against my face.

I want to say *yes* so badly. Instead, I let out a strangled laugh. "But you're a prince."

"I'm not, not anymore. We are both advisors to the queen, remember?" He brushes my hair off my temples. "Evra, if I *were* a prince, even a king, I would still wish to be with you."

My heart pounds.

The cold can't touch us, nor the past. But the future, the future still pains me.

Because it is a future without Mama, without Deward. Without Father.

A few tears slip down my cheeks.

Seeing my expression, Kendrik's face falls. And then I fall away.

Sunlight rises to meet me.

I see my family standing outside our worn, clapboard home, a whisper of smoke rising from its chimney. The air smells of pine sap and Mama's roast potatoes.

Mama's arms are wrapped around a basket of bread. Father holds his ax, his back straight, his favorite hat flopped forward on his head. Deward looks at me and smiles.

Suddenly, warmth blooms around my left hand. Hagan appears at my side. His grip tightens. "My God," he murmurs. "Is this a dream?"

"No," I whisper back. "This is magic."

"Evra," Hagan says. "You are a miracle."

But I'm not the miracle—this is. Our family—our home—is here.

It is whole. Waiting, still.

"You saved the prince, and Tyne too," Deward says. "Annalise will be a good queen. And if she isn't, you two will be there to keep her in check, won't you? You won't let the darkness come again." His familiar voice falls against my face like rain. The good, nourishing kind that keeps our crops thriving.

Hagan's hand keeps me steady and strong.

Mama glows. "We are here."

Father tips his hat. "We are with you."

Deward smiles. "Always."

Their voices fade, but their love carries me.

Back to Kendrik. Back to myself.

"Evra, are you well?" Kendrik's embrace keeps me on my feet. The rising sun glows against his skin.

"Yes." I smile, soul unfurling. "Yes."

I find I've no need for firecane; the Clearsee desert never comes for me. My limbs stay loose and strong, warm and willing in Kendrik's arms. His frown eases at the light in my eyes. I kiss him, curling my hands into the golden curls of his hair. Our lips sigh and slip together, drawing heat from the memories of our watercolor dreams.

This spark between us...it is *more* than magic.

And so am I.

ACKNOWLEDGMENTS

In the summer of 2011, I was vacationing at my parents' cabin in northern Ontario. I was grieving a writing career I thought was over before it began. I was at a loss. My husband and my dog were there, doing their best to comfort me. I remember the exact moment I decided to stop trying to write what I thought would sell and just write for myself. I had an idea for a fantasy inspired by my dog, Scrabble (he's quite the muse). I wrote it to rediscover what I loved about writing, to process my grief, and to give myself hope.

A Season of Sinister Dreams is very different from the words I began putting to paper *ten years ago*. (You think publishing is slow—sometimes writing can take its own leisurely, circuitous route!) I'm thrilled and grateful that the last ten years led to this moment, and to this book becoming real. It couldn't have happened without Pam Gruber, and the faith she had that I could realize Evra's and Annalise's potential. It couldn't have happened without Linda Epstein, my agent, guiding my way. And it couldn't have happened without Deirdre Jones taking the reins and loving the project as her own. I am so grateful for these amazing women. Big thanks, as well, to Megan Tingley, Jackie Engel, Alvina Ling, Hallic Tibbetts,

Katharine McAnarney, Karina Granda, Patricia Alvarado, Marisa Finkelstein, Kelley Frodel, Bill Grace, Savannah Kennelly, and Christie Michel, who've all had a hand in making this project shine. It means so much to know that many talented people are championing my book baby.

As I said, iterations of this book have been around a long time, and that means I've gotten feedback and encouragement from *lots* of people. Thank you to the Critters of Winston-Salem, who were among the first to read and cheerlead for Evra, to Jessica Spotswood and Victoria Rae Schmitz, who offered valuable insight, and to Jennifer Walkup, who graciously read some *very* early drafts. To Kyra Whitton, Rachel Hamm, and Ellen Goodlett, who reassured me that the new direction was working and who continue to be the most supportive and kindest of friends.

Thank you so much to other friends who helped me make it through: Michelle Nebiolo, Dr. Jody Escaravage, Jax Abbey, Paige Nguyen, J.D. Robinson, Crystal Watanabe, Morgan Michael, Kaitlyn Sage Patterson, and Natalie C. Parker.

To Danielle, Kwame, Payton, and Paige Boateng, who cheered me on, who willingly (?) listened to me talk endlessly about writing and publishing, and who entertained my kids so I could finish this book, thank you from the bottom of my heart. You were the best #quaranteam anyone could ask for and are still the best of friends. We miss y'all so much!

To my parents, thank you for making Temagami a part of my life. You introduced me, in a real, tangible way, to magic.

To Oliver and Mena Michelle, you are my world. I am the luckiest person on the planet to have two such amazing kids.

Andy, I know you remember how I was feeling when I began this story; I'm so happy I can share the joy of seeing it out in the world with you now. I can't imagine experiencing this wild adventure of life with anyone but you. Also, thanks for thinking my writer brain is cool. That's true magic right there.

And finally, thank you to my readers. You're magical, each and every one of you.